THE FAMILY BUSINESS

TK CHERRY

Cover Design By: Shannon Passmore, Shanoff Designs
Editing By: Christi Whitson, Essential Edits
Interior Formatting By: Stacey Blake, Champagne Book Design
Proofreading By: Dawn Lucous, Yours Truly Book Services

Love or Family

Prologue

Ford
Age 16

Even though it was a typical sunny afternoon in Central Coast California, I couldn't begin to describe the beauty and vibrancy of my surroundings. I lay prone in the grassy meadow on my family's enormous estate in Arcadia's Crest, an affluent seaside town located fifteen miles northwest of Los Derivas in Santa Barbara County.

My current setting provided the perfect recipe where I could inhale the fresh scent of crisp green grass and take in the salty, cool mist, courtesy of Arcadia Beach, which was literally our entire back yard. At first, I heard nothing but the humming, buzzing, and chirping of *sweet, sweet* serenity. Just when I thought things couldn't get any better, I heard a sound even sweeter.

The sweetest.

"Puffin?!"

My heart skipped a beat at the sound of her angelic voice. I emerged from the grass like a meerkat and twisted in the direction of the sweet melody. I spied a blonde. The beautiful blue-eyed goddess in a yellow summer dress beamed brighter than the sun above her. Eventually, she located me way in the field and darted in my direction. On her way, she stumbled. I stifled a laugh. I could tell she was frustrated by her own lack of speed long before she decided to kick off her sandals. She left them behind, buried in the lush green grass before resuming toward me even faster than before. Grinning like a lunatic, I jogged to meet her.

This. Is. Home.

She and I have been running to each other on this very property ever since I was old enough to walk. Back when we were little kids, we'd played a lot together here. Lately, we'd been running to each other for an entirely different reason.

We were in love.

When we were finally face to face, I stretched my arms wide, letting her fall on my neck. Breathing heavily, she littered my exposed skin with kisses. I wanted to claim her mouth so badly, but we had to be careful—no telling who could've been watching us.

I gasped with relief. *And* want. *And* need. "Harper..." She pressed her index finger to my lips and silenced me.

"I'm here. I'm not going anywhere," she panted deep, still catching her breath.

I don't know why she felt the need to say it out loud. There was no corner in my imagination that ever envisioned her leaving me. She'd always been there, so it only seemed natural that she'd continue to be by my side.

"I have a feeling your dad might suspect there's something going on between us."

She spoke quietly, as if the one in question had the ability to teleport. It wasn't a farfetched sentiment since the man was beyond powerful. I took each of her hands in mine.

"Why do you say that?" I asked, puzzled.

"I don't know. I just have a hunch. I don't feel the warmth like I used to. He never smiles when I'm around."

Although my father was a certified asshole with a far smaller emotional capacity than a guard at Buckingham Palace, I hadn't seen him treating Harper any differently than he had in the past. He'd nod whenever she said hi and never questioned why she was always around. She practically grew up with me, so she had free rein to come to the main house as often as she pleased. Her father and stepmother had worked for my family since before I was born and resided in the guesthouse on our property.

It's true, my father never smiled at Harper, but that shouldn't have been cause for alarm. He rarely smiled at anyone. He stopped throwing awkward smiles my way years ago. In his eyes, I was already a man, so he began treating me as such. The only genuine smile you'd see out of him was for my mother and my three little sisters.

I think most of Harper's paranoia is misplaced, yet seeing that look of uncertainty on her angelic face does something to me. In that moment, I didn't want to do anything but protect this girl, even if it meant being shunned by my own family. I needed to reassure her that *we* were the end game.

"Look, I'm sixteen now. I'll be graduating early from high school next year at seventeen. After that, I'll enroll at UC Los Derivas with you," I tell her. Her reluctant expression told me she wasn't all that confident with my plan.

Harper squeezed my hands to get my full attention. She looked earnest, which unnerved me. "You know good and well that nothing other than the Ivy Leagues will ever be good enough for a mind as sharp as yours. You're destined for great things. You have a 4.8 GPA right now, for crying out loud. A *freaking* 4.8 on a 4.0 scale. Who the hell gets that?!" she chuckled.

"It's all because of AP classes," I grinned.

"That's just it, Ford. You're not even in college yet, and you already have university credits on your transcript. You'll be even further along than I will by the time you get into college, and I'll have had a three-year head start on you."

"So, when we're both done with college around the same time, we can finally be together," I declared. Her answering gaze was one of uncertainty, and it pricked me.

"I hope you're right," she exhaled after a beat.

"I am." I wrapped her in my arms and placed feather-light kisses across her rosy cheek. In a safe amount of time, we mutually pulled away. Up to that point, we'd been extremely careful in remaining secret lovers.

"You have the entire world at your fingertips—even now. And the most popular girl in the entire school wanted no one but you to take her to senior prom," Harper bitterly recalled. The explosion from two months ago was still fresh in her mind.

The most attractive girl at school had an unrelenting will to snag me. This so-called *will* had resulted in her showing up to my house unannounced. My father had been stunned when I'd sent her away in tears. As she'd left, Harper had shown up at the main house to babysit my little sisters. The sight of a pretty girl bawling on the front steps because of me had spooked Harper.

Taking Harper's hands once more, I gently swung her arms with mine. "Only one girl has my heart, and I'm holding hands with her right now. I could never be with another. You're the only girl I'll ever give my heart to."

Her answering smile made me melt as her eyes shimmered like the bluest of waters. Yet, something in me still cried out to her, begging her to show me that we were on the same page. I looked deeper into her gaze, still seeing traces of doubt lingering within. My scrutiny prompted her to speak.

"I know what I feel in my heart," she declared, pointing to said organ. "But is it wrong?"

I released her hands and used mine to cup her face, forcing her to look directly at me without turning away. "No, it's not. Follow your heart, Harper. I can't help but follow mine. Promise me we'll be together—always."

"Yes," she uttered with tear-filled eyes. "Always."

She leaned in, and I met her in the middle to seal our promise with a kiss. My entire being ignited like a fuse ready to paint the sky with so many colors.

If only I could live in this moment for the rest of my life.

When you're young, you assume your grand plans will come to fruition. You forget all about the manipulative billionaire mogul father who's dead set on his only son taking over the family business. The last thing he wanted was for his son to give up his birthright for *the help's* daughter, who happened to be four years older than said son. Rarely do you ever make plans for heartbreak, disappointment, or betrayal.

But all three would happen to me. Not only would I experience those devastating things at the hands of my family, but I'd receive much worse from the one girl I loved more than life itself.

One

Ford
Age 18

He's lame; she's lame...

It was my first day back after summer. I sized up the other ten students at the round table, wondering who among us would be crowned king in here by the end of the semester. The setup and class size weren't typical of Stanford University. Our Project Management group was small because we were a select group of elite individuals. We were the so-called *brightest and best* of the *bright and best.*

"How about we go around and introduce ourselves," the middle-aged male professor pacing the floor announced. "State your name, where you're from. Then, tell us where you see yourself five years from now."

I rolled my eyes super hard. The company wasn't the only lame thing happening here. Introductory icebreaker exercises are trés lame. I'd rather be doing anything *but* this.

Kicking off the introduction was a junior hailing from Iowa. He spoke of his hope of eventually landing a tech job in Silicon Valley. *What an idiot. He has no clue robots will be doing all of the programming by the time he pulls his thumb out of his ass.* As each student gave their introduction, I mentally mocked them in a similar fashion. Soon, it was my turn for an introduction.

"And you?" the professor prompted me.

"Ford Pope from Arcadia's Crest."

I didn't know what part of my statement caused jaws in the room to drop while other's eyes rolled. It may have been due to the fact that I came from the richest town in California. Orange County is the hood compared to where I grew up. If it wasn't my hometown that turned heads, it was most definitely my last name.

The Pope name was revered in this part of the world. My family pretty much owned the Pacific coast. But anyone in the room originally from the east coast or abroad whose parents were rich enough to foot their entire tuition, they knew good and goddamn well who my father was. Either Dad had made them a lot of money, or they'd personally helped him beef up my trust fund like a wrestler on steroids.

Mason Charles Pope was the head of a multi-billion-dollar empire. I'm talking in the high eleven-figures. A popular financial magazine had a dedicated page on their website showing a countdown to when Mason Pope would finally leapfrog over the second richest man in the world. Lyndon Reginald Pope Sr., my great-great grandfather, founded the multi-national conglomerate, Lyndon Reginald Pope Industries, or LRPI. Specializing in booze and luxury goods, the Pope name had been in corporate existence for over a century.

Mason, my father, may have been born with a silver spoon in his mouth, but he was no slacker by any stretch of the imagination. With my mother as his right hand, he had taken LRPI to the next level. He was the reason the next ten generations of Popes would never have to work a day in their lives. *Well*—except for me and my future heir. Someone has to operate the Pope machine.

I answered the second part of the professor's question.

"Five years from now, I'm going to take over the world."

Everyone in the room laughed but me. I was dead-ass serious.

"Take over the world doing what?" the professor challenged.

A shocked expression replaced some of the earlier looks of

skepticism around the table. It had obviously registered to some of them who I was. But what they didn't know was that Professor Ship and I went back since freshman year. He was giving me crap, so I decided to dish it right back.

"Everything under the sun. It's difficult to pinpoint just one thing in particular."

"Oh, it's the *Pope kid*. He doesn't even have to work for a living," one student whispered.

"His parents are *gazillionaires*," another scoffed quietly in the background.

Ship hadn't heard what they'd said, but I did.

Haters gonna hate.

"Fair enough," I said, nodding smugly.

I decided to address my *fans* in the room, turning my head to give each of them direct eye contact. "I'm in college because I *want* to be. You're all here because you *have* to be. So, who among us here has the most heart?" My statement was met with a few chuckles, scoffs, and eye rolls. I expected as much.

Now, ask me if I gave a fuck.

"Mr. Pope, not only do you have heart, but you apparently have great balls to match. We'll find out by the end of the semester if your heart also matches that big mouth of yours," the professor quipped.

The classroom burst out into laughter while a shit-eating grin formed across my face. My smug demeanor was my shield. No one in the room had a clue that on the inside, I was the polar opposite of the asshole I portrayed to the world. My outward personality was nothing like the fragile heart encased in a thick, tough shell that I constructed.

Hidden inside the charade was a young boy who desperately wanted to please his father. A young boy with big, impossible shoes to fill.

Right about now, my family was probably gathered around the dinner table enjoying a wonderful meal prepared by Mrs. Benton. I can see my three little sisters laughing it up and having a good time with our parents.

I'd be lying if I said I didn't miss that.

On the flip side, I was sitting alone in my dormitory, eating a bowl of skanky *just add water* noodles. Yeah, it's pretty hilarious if you ask me... Being that my folks were billionaires and all.

My father had refused to pay for me to get an apartment. He told me living the dorm life would keep me humble. Quite frankly, I think it's the institution of quiet hours at the residence hall that was the most appealing for him.

If I lived in an apartment, there would be no rules. Yet, I was just as sure he'd pay a pretty penny for some henchman to monitor me around the clock. Hell, who's to say my father—*The* Mason Pope, one of the world's most powerful businessmen—doesn't already have one of his goons hot on my tail right this second? The feeling of being watched was second nature for me. I was even convinced that he may have personally hired the RA here. I wouldn't have put anything past good ol' Dad.

I had no doubt I was living in this shoebox as punishment. Deciding to attend Stanford instead of Yale had seemed like the ultimate 'fuck you' to my father. In reality, it was a big joke because there was no love lost with Yale. The trust fund billionaire never even finished college.

Underneath all his bullshit disappointment over where I decided to go to school, I knew the truth. My father wanted to keep me as far away from Arcadia's Crest as possible. Ever since the day my mom caught me alone with Harper Benton, things had never been the same between my family and me.

Liza, Ford's Mother

Staring *forty-two* straight in the mouth, I was just a breath away from its sharp clutches. It was going to chomp me to bits like chum and gobble me up. As difficult as it had been adjusting to turning forty the year before last, it was nothing like this. I was clearly on my way *deep* into the dreaded *over-forty* category. The only upside was that many often complimented how I didn't look my age, especially my children and their friends. That sort of helped soften the blow.

My four kids were my entire world. The youngest two, identical twins, were turning thirteen the following month. Beth and Brie were difficult to tell apart, but I was their mother and the only person they couldn't dupe. They were inseparable and absolutely adored their older sister.

Next up was Eva. She reminded me a lot of myself at her age. She was sixteen and had just entered her junior year in high school. At first, Eva had tried keeping to herself by sticking her nose in books without coming up for air, but people still gravitated to her like a magnet. Her beauty and natural radiance were things she tried but failed to hide. Her aura was loud, even when she remained silent. Not only was she very close to her younger sisters, but she had quite the bond with her big brother, who was away at college.

That left my oldest and only son, Ford. The stellar student had just begun his second year at Stanford. At only eighteen, he was not only strong academically, but he had the gift of gab. Well, it was both a gift and a curse. Bradford Cooper Pope could negotiate himself out of one jam while talking himself into another all in the same breath.

For some reason, members on the Pope side of the family took issue with Ford choosing Stanford over Harvard and Yale. All three universities extended an offer to my bright boy. I had a hunch as to why Ford had chosen to stay in California. Not only had he wanted to remain close to family and friends, but there had been someone else keeping him here.

He'd never fessed up to it, though.

Mason, my husband and Ford's father, had the same suspicion. It was why Mason had tried strong-arming Ford into selecting an Ivy League institution far away from Arcadia's Crest. Instead, Ford had ended up doing the exact opposite of what his father wanted. Mason often said our son got his stubbornness from me. He was probably right.

I arrived home from work just as our longtime housekeeper, Trisha Benton, and the girls were preparing the table for dinner. As a rule, we Popes always ate dinner as a family.

"Mom—after dinner, can me and the twins go to the mall real quick? There's this *really* cute skirt I want," Eva pleaded.

Before I could respond, Mason breezed in while tugging off his expensive necktie. It was one of my creations from when I worked as a designer at our premium fashion subsidiary, Isla Cole Fashions, or ICF. He swiftly kissed me on the cheek before turning to face our eldest daughter.

"Not tonight, Eva. You girls can wait until Saturday. It's late and a school night," Mason said authoritatively. Eva gaped at her father before shifting her focus to me.

"Mom..."

"You heard your father. *Saturday,*" I said sternly.

Eva and her siblings knew better than to pit their father and me against each other. When it came to our crafty children, Mason and I remained a united front. Eva pouted, but her loving dad kissed her forehead anyway. Our daughter's lip jutted out just a tad bit more, but I knew it was her forcing the emotion. Although she and her father weren't seeing eye to eye at the moment, she was still daddy's little girl.

"Bethany, Brianna..." Mason summoned the twins by their proper names from across the room. They both approached their dad for a hug before embracing me in turn. "Let's eat," he ordered, rubbing his hands together in grand anticipation.

Finally—it was quiet in the house.

I sat alone in the dimly lit kitchen at the breakfast nook, sipping my tea in my nightgown and robe. The girls were asleep in their rooms, and Mason was hard at work in his study. Meanwhile, I couldn't sleep. I lay awake, mindlessly staring at the ceiling while wondering how classes were going so far for Ford. I wanted to call him, but he'd tell me to stop babying him. It was his second year at Stanford and all, but I couldn't help it. No matter his age, Ford would always be my baby.

Silence in the kitchen was more tolerable than silence in the bedroom. Maybe it was the comforting hum of the appliances. Here, I was able to sit back and count my blessings. Most of the time, life just… *happened*. But it was in the still and quiet of the night that I could finally sit and reflect on my life so far.

Business at Lyndon Reginald Pope Industries was going exceptionally well. Who would've thought that twenty years ago I'd be co-CEO of a multi-billion-dollar conglomerate alongside my husband? Running the company my husband's great-grandfather had founded was something I'd fought against for a very long time. But now, I couldn't see myself doing anything else. Like my husband, I ate, slept, and breathed the business.

Despite that, LRPI came in a distant second to my family. I no longer travelled for work unless it was absolutely necessary. My priority had always been and would continue to be my children. I refused to abandon them, leaving them at home to be raised by a team of nannies while I jetted across the world. I knew how it felt like to be on the receiving end of that. Unlike my parents, I wanted to be there when my kids scraped a knee or had a recital at the school's winter concert. I wanted to hug them the moment they experienced their first heartbreak.

One day a few years ago, when I was bored at the house, I decided to tidy up on Trisha's rare day off. While tackling Eva's room, I came across a recently graded paper for her English class. Eva pretty much gets nothing but A's, so the high marking on the paper didn't surprise me. However, when I glanced at the subject matter, I was intrigued and decided to read on. The assignment was for her to write about her best friend. I couldn't help but smile as I took in Eva's touching words about her best pal, all while trying to guess who the person was.

Which siblings was it?

Or maybe it was one of her many close friends at school.

I wracked my brain trying to figure out who my daughter was heaping such high praise upon. When my eyes approached the final paragraph, my heart had expanded to twice its original size. Eva was such an old soul, wise beyond her years with a solid head on her shoulders. And with this special best friend by her side, she was definitely in the position to continue making smart decisions moving forward.

Finally, my eyes encountered the very last sentence of her paper.

"My best friend is none other than my mother, Mrs. Eliza Cooper-Pope."

As I recalled how I felt reading that, tears brimmed in my eyes, threatening to spill over as they did back then. It was as though I'd eavesdropped on Eva's paper a second ago. There's nothing like taking in the high praise of your children. It goes to show the choice I made years ago to always be there for my children was indeed the right one.

Their upbringing had been a stark contrast to how my sister and I were raised. Jessie and I had the proverbial staff-of-nannies who saw to us for most of our youth while our father worked his ass off and our mother… God only knows what she did.

I'd gotten my associates degree in fashion three months after turning twenty. The original plan was to transfer schools in Texas and work toward my bachelors. Instead, Jessie and I left Texas and moved to California, against our mother's wishes.

Julia Hunter came from old oil money. Her maiden name was Battle, which garnered as much respect and fear as the name

Pope. My mother was a Battle through and through, so it was expected that her daughters either marry or work for Battle-Wooten Industries after college. Every Battle offspring's inheritance was contingent on that person either working to ensure the strong ongoing legacy of the company or joining with someone who had the means to donate lots of money toward the family's charitable foundation.

Mom had made her choice long ago, opting to be arm candy instead of an active, contributing member of the family. When she was eighteen, she'd married my father, an investment banker with a gentle soul and the personality of a damp sheet of paper. She immediately got pregnant with my sister, then I came along thirteen months after her.

My parents' marriage lasted eight years before my mother decided she was bored. The woman chased love like an addict searching to recapture her first high. She burned through two other marriages before Jessie and I finished high school. My sister and I often joked about how Julia Battle Cooper Thompson Richards Hunter had been aiming to give Elizabeth Taylor a run for her money.

Our mother never forced us to marry. In fact, she forbade us to get hitched for any reason other than love. Still, she wanted us to be financially stable, which meant we were expected to work for her family's company. The problem was I had dreams of working in fashion, while my sister aspired to be a news anchor. Mom couldn't have cared less because what we wanted never mattered. Ironic how she managed to live her life exactly how she wanted.

Instead of fighting back, my sister did her time for one year at Battle-Wooten and absolutely hated it. Jessie was not only my sister but my very best friend, and because of that, I let her in on my plan to ghost Texas and pursue my dream of fashion. I was either going to New York or LA—and because I despised the cold, California it was. Jessie desperately wanted to leave Texas as well, so she came along.

It was a rough first two months in Cali. Mom had frozen our assets in order to force our hand to return home. We stuck it out anyway to spite her. Since we had no money and no decent paying jobs lined up, we had to take what we could get. My sister began waitressing during the day while interning at a local news station for free at night. Meanwhile, when I wasn't actively seeking a break in the fashion biz, I moonlighted at an office cleaning company.

One of the office buildings we contracted for housed LRPI's brand-new satellite office. I met my future husband one night after tiptoeing into his office to collect his trash. He was on a call at the time, screaming at someone over speakerphone. Being Mason Pope. As soon as our eyes met, he mindlessly hung up on whomever he was ripping into.

It was literally love at first sight.

Days went by before I'd put two and two together. The devastatingly gorgeous man who'd swept me off my feet and hooked me up with a job at the company's fashion arm was more than powerful. He was the owner and CEO of the mega global conglomerate, which was headquartered in Los Derivas. He'd been much too young to be so darn successful, running a business with over forty thousand employees at the time. Twenty years and eighty thousand employees later, his sultry good looks remained intact. These days, Mason was fifty-two and looked just as gorgeous as he did when I first laid eyes on him. His once brown hair had turned mostly gray, making him the ultimate silver fox.

People often asked his secret to looking so young. Mason said it was due to me and the kids. I begged to differ. It had to be his great genetics. His parents, Lyndon III and Diane, were senior citizens, yet they still looked magnificent. Regardless of what Mason said, I was certain the kids and I were the ones who contributed to his gray hair. He often scolded me about worrying all the time, but he was way worse than me.

Through our many ups and downs, Mason Pope and I were still going strong. We made an exceptional team, both in the boardroom and at home. And well, let's just say his sexual appetite was keener than ever. They—whoever *they* were—said that a man's sexual prime was in his twenties. Whoever said that had never met my husband. Either that, or Mason hadn't gotten the memo. He had the libido of a man more than half his age, and I had so much fun keeping up with him.

I wasn't too shabby, either. All those rumors about forty being a woman's sexual prime were panning out to be true. I'd always been eager when it came to intimacy with my husband. But as of late, much to Mason's amusement, I'd been rather, um—*insatiable*. In fact, it seemed even more so than normal.

I wanted Mason everywhere and at all times. In the bedroom, in the shower, on the floor, in the garage. Yes, we were adventurous like two horny teenagers. But with our own teenager and two preteens still at home, Mason and I had to be on high alert, remaining careful at all times.

There is nothing more traumatizing than catching your parents in the act.

I shuddered at the thought.

I'd obviously had *the talk* with the girls. I laughed each time I thought back on the horror Mason had to endure when he'd become the first of us to have the talk with our son years ago. It had been like pulling teeth to finally get Mason to have the required discussion with Ford.

Mason and Ford.

The thought of a rift existing between the two most important men in my life brought a lump to my throat. I sipped my now lukewarm tea with a heavy heart before hearing footsteps approaching. I looked to see my husband entering the kitchen.

"Mrs. Pope, I thought you'd be in bed by now," he said, looking puzzled. I sighed.

"Me, too. I was thinking about Ford. Couldn't sleep, so I decided to make chamomile tea."

"Ford is fine, Eliza. Quit your worrying," he scolded, brows furrowed.

"I'm his mother, so of course, I'm always going to worry."

"You're wasting your time, baby. He is safe—I assure you," Mason murmured gently while smoothing down loose tendrils of my pulled-back hair.

How does he know he's safe?

I quickly thought better than to ask the question out loud. After over twenty years of marriage, I'd learned never to ask if I really didn't want to know the answer to the question. Whatever the answer was, I probably wouldn't like it. I was dealing with the same person who had his righthand man, Russ, stalk me on a regular basis before we started dating. And during. And after we got engaged.

If Mason Charles Pope were Bruce Wayne, Russell Benton was Alfred Pennyworth. No—more like Charles Bronson playing the role of Alfred. You didn't mess with Russ. He was a tad bit scarier than my husband, and Mason could be quite intimidating.

Once Mason and I married and had kids, Russ' eyes couldn't be everywhere. Mason and Russ thoroughly vetted then hired Greg Donner to *keep the children safe*. That's Mason-Pope-speak for, *"Make sure they don't cough without me knowing."*

With Russ and Greg being here in Arcadia's Crest, God only knew who Mason had on hand at Stanford to keep watch over our son. Ever since Ford's senior year in high school, things hadn't been the same between him and his father. My oldest had been a little standoffish with everyone in the family as of late. My once carefree Ford had been keeping way too much to himself these days. It was heartbreaking to see.

They say a mother's intuition is everything. I only wish I'd taken heed to that little nudge in my heart when I first laid eyes on that little angel. Not my son, because he's no angel. I'm talking about Harper Benton, Russ' daughter and only child. If I'd paid attention to my intuition, I would've saved my first born a lot of time and heartbreak.

"Come to bed with me."

My husband's voice was low and husky. He carefully lifted the teacup out of my hands. His hooded gaze revealed that what he had planned for me would help me rest much better than that tea.

Two

Ford

Cheerleader Rebecca, an attractive blonde with perky tits and a nice ass, was usually the first person to roll her eyes at me in the crowd. But behind closed doors, she was quick to drop to her knees before me. Literally.

I got a surge in my belly and took a sharp gasp of air. *That Rebecca has the jaws of a beast,* I thought. No wonder the football team kept her around.

After I exploded, she wiped the excess from her mouth before standing to her feet. We faced off in the center of my dorm room, which was smaller than my closet back home. I bent to retrieve my pants from my ankles.

"Whatcha got here to eat, Pope?" she asked—all bubbly and casual as if she hadn't just had my dick in her mouth.

"Nothing." I narrowed my eyes, hoping she caught the hint to climb her ass back out of the window she crawled into.

I'm finished with you. You can go now.

"You're the richest kid here, but no one would know it by this place." She frowned, panning her surroundings with an expression of pity.

"My folks believe in keeping me humble," I said, tongue in cheek.

"I'd say. Hey…" she started, closing the gap between us once again. I winced.

What's her angle?

"Why don't you ever end up having sex with me? Since freshman year, I've come here only to blow you. I mean, I enjoy doing it—don't get me wrong. You have a great big cock, and I'm sure you're killer in bed," she purred.

And there she goes.

"Rebecca, I enjoy what we've got going here, don't you? I'm not like those other guys just wanting to pound you and leave you out to dry. You know, like Chase and all of those other meatheads on the football squad."

Honestly Pope, what makes you think having this girl sneaking over here just to blow you is any more honorable than fucking her?

"I *do* like what we have. But one day, I might want you to be my boyfriend, Pope," she said sweetly.

I laughed, which took her by surprise. "Really, Rebecca? I heard about you telling your sorority friends that I'm an asshole."

"And you are, but I think it's sexy. *You're* sexy," she murmured before inching her head toward me. Her lips puckered outward for a kiss, but I placed my palm flat over my mouth to block her before stepping back.

"Rebecca… This isn't working for me."

Panic shot in her eyes. "What do you mean?"

"*This.* This isn't working for me anymore."

She looked appalled. "Who are you fucking?"

"Excuse me?" I frowned.

Rebecca raised her voice. "You're obviously fucking someone if it's not me!"

"*Quiet,*" I shushed her. It was well past quiet time at the residence hall. Thankfully, she remembered herself and brought her voice way down while her jealous rage remained intact.

"Who is she?"

"There's no one. But if there was, don't you dare claim I'm the only guy on campus you're doing this with," I chastised.

I was certain that bit of news about her being the only one giving me blowies put that new glint in her eye. She thought she had the upper hand. I knew it even before the words spilled out of her. "If you're honestly committed to me, I will be committed to you and *only* you, Ford. All you have to do is say the word, and I'm a one-man woman."

Yeah, Becky—it's time for you to go. It's been fun. Peace out.

By now, I was in by-any-means-necessary mode. Whatever would get this toxic chick out of my room and off my back for good was ideal. I'd had this one in the coffers for a while. It was time to test it out to see if it would yield the desired result.

"Rebecca, I'm gay," I said dramatically.

It had the desired effect. Her eyes nearly popped out of their sockets. "I don't believe it!"

"Believe it. It's why I wouldn't have sex with you. Haven't you put two and two together yet? I mean, we've been doing this *arrangement* for a year now."

As she stood there, stunned, I could see the hamsters churning on that wheel in her little brain. *How did she get into Stanford?* Then, I quickly recalled what had just happened here moments ago. I knew exactly how she'd gotten in.

"Oh, my God. Ford..." She caressed me on the shoulder and gazed at me with compassion. "I know it's gotta be extremely hard keeping such a secret, but you can trust me. I won't tell anyone. You're so brave."

Hey, whatever it takes to get her out of here.

"Does your family know?" she asked.

"No—they don't."

"Wow. I feel so honored you'd share something *so*... so sacred with me. I feel way closer to you now."

And you didn't feel close enough to me when you were swallowing my semen?

Yeah, I was so done with this girl. She needed to find another boy toy to play with.

"I need to get ready for bed. I have an early class tomorrow. We'll talk later."

Or not. Preferably *not*.

"Oh—of course. I'll call you. Maybe we can do lunch tomorrow or something?"

"Sure." For fuck's sake, I needed to lose her.

"I'm here for you whenever you need me. I'll be your shoulder to cry on. You can trust me with anything."

Give me a fucking break.

"I know, Rebecca. Thank you," I say, pretending to be sincere.

She hugged me tight, damn near strangling me before she walked backwards toward the window. She didn't take her sad eyes off me.

"Damn, I can't believe you're actually gay. I didn't want to believe it. The boys would always joke about it, but I didn't see it. They claimed you were such a prick because you were hiding your true identity."

She wasn't making this any better with her filter-less babbling. I was pretty sure her jock pals didn't want her narcing all their bad-mouthing about me *to* me.

"Goodnight, Rebecca," I said with zero emotion.

"Until tomorrow. Call me if you need anything. Okay?"

I didn't acknowledge her pity with a response. Finally, she climbed out the window, and I breathed a sigh of relief. When I approached the window to lock it, I saw her performing the walk of shame across the expanse of green grass. A beam of light caught her back and bounced off her blonde hair, and I did a double take. For a fraction of a second, I saw *her*. No, not Rebecca the BJ Queen. *Her*. She was the only girl who had and would always have my heart.

A year and a half ago, around late spring/early summer, I was in high school and ditched after lunch period to see *her*—Harper. She was twenty-one, I was seventeen. She'd lived on campus at UC Los Derivas, but she was done for the semester. Her dad and step-mom were out of town on a well-deserved vacation, so she hung out at their place, located on my family's oceanfront property.

Her dad's place was beyond upper-middle class to the average guy. The architecture of the just under three thousand square-foot residence was a cross between mid-century modern and Mediterranean. With an uninterrupted view of the ocean, it was any man's dream home. However, the main house, where I lived, was a Nantucket-style beach home, three times as large, and a closer proximity to the ocean.

At the appointed time, Harper walked the point-four miles to the main house to meet me. She'd taken the journey for many years, so it was second nature for her. We'd literally grown up together. The only time I didn't see her around was when she spent weekends, summers, and certain holidays with her mother in Los Derivas.

Prior to college, she'd lived with her father and stepmom full-time. The private schools in Arcadia's Crest were top-notch, even better than those in Los Derivas. As part of the Benton's contract, my family covered Harper's tuition from kindergarten through twelfth grade.

As soon as she stepped into the foyer, I pulled her in my arms and kissed her hard. I felt the vibration of her laugh as I explored her sweet, warm mouth. My urgency for her took her by surprise. I remember everything going great after that. We'd eventually made our way over to the theater room to watch an obscure classic science fiction movie. I couldn't have even told you the name of it, and neither could she. We'd kissed nonstop. Being with her was a dream come true. I'm convinced I've always loved her. In fact, I believe the first word I ever spoke was *"Hah-pah,"* my poor attempt at pronouncing her sweet name.

"Ford?"

I could still remember the traumatic tone of my mother's voice and my heart dropping in my chest like a barbell. She'd come home way early from work and walked in on Harper and me making out.

"You understand that I have to tell your father about this, right?"

No, Mom, you didn't have *to tell him*. It could've remained our little secret if she'd wanted it to be. But *noooo*. The moment *The* Mason Pope had heard that his only son skipped school to make out with his estate manager's daughter, he'd completely lost his shit. From there on out, my father had been set on keeping Harper and me apart.

What loving parents I had.

Growing up, I'd always had to contend with the Pope name. Not only that, but I'd had to deal with the fact that my parents were very attractive. To this day, my friends and friends of my sisters regularly referred to Mason and Eliza Pope as *DILF* and *MILF*.

Although it was extremely annoying, I could only hope to look as good as my dad once I reached his age. My sisters could only dream of looking remotely as hot as our mother in their early forties. No wonder Dad put four babies in her. I was shocked they didn't have more kids after the twins were born.

People often told me I was the best of my parents.

"You have your father's dreamy green eyes and your mother's gorgeous hair. I'm sure the girls are lined out the door just for you!"

"Ford, you think on your feet like your father with the creativity and book smarts of your mother."

When I was a kid, my dad had been my best friend. We did everything together. *Everything*. Hockey games, fishing, mountain biking. He taught me how to play the guitar. He read to me every night until I was able to start reading to him.

It wasn't until he started riding my ass that our dynamic had changed. For some reason, my dad remained sweet and gentle with my sisters. Once I turned fifteen, he became a lot stricter with me. That's when I became a bonafide mama's boy. Liza Pope was the peacekeeper of the house.

"Mason, you're blowing things way out of proportion. Ford made a simple mistake. Go easy on him."

I shook off the bittersweet memory as I made my way over to the showers outside of my room. When I returned fifteen minutes later, damp and donning my robe, my cell phone buzzed wildly against my wooden desk, startling me.

Who the hell's calling me at one-thirty in the morning?

I was pretty sure it was my mom. She was probably restless and worried sick about me, as usual. I didn't bother calling her the day before, so it was pretty plausible it was her. But when I retrieved the phone from my desk and viewed the screen, my stomach turned. It wasn't Mom. It was Dad. That man never sleeps.

Shit—what does he want? Did Mom make him call me?

I picked up just before the call rolled into voicemail.

"Dad?"

"I'll keep this brief. I know what you've been up to. Stop it. Stop it now," he said angrily.

What in the hell is he talking about?

My stomach roiled as my eyes panned the entire room in search of hidden cameras. I was extremely paranoid.

"Ford, you're not in college to fuck around with cheerleaders. You're there because you're next in line to take over the family business. You need to take this thing more seriously. There's way too much at stake here."

Fuck, how does he know about Rebecca?!

"Yeah, Dad… I got it."

"'Night, son."

He hung up before I could answer back. I stood in place with the phone still to my ear, stunned. My mouth was agape. Had he put fucking cameras in my dorm room? Were he or his henchmen watching me receive oral? The man knew *everything,* and it was beyond disturbing.

I wondered if Mom and my sisters ever had to deal with Dad stalking them.

Three

Liza

I sat at the head of the table in a conference room. A young woman from the IT team took the floor and discussed some of the patents that LRPI had pending. Listening intently, I gently smoothed out the creases in the lap of my gray wool skirt-suit ensemble. My phone buzzed on the table, and I quickly picked it up to view the screen. It was my eldest daughter.

Eva: When will you be home?

Uh oh. The tone of her text alarmed me.

Me: I can head home as soon as I'm done with this meeting. Is everything okay?

Eva: It's fine. I just need to talk to you about something.

Me: Sure, I can call you the second I get back to my office.

Eva: I want to talk in person. Can you get home before Dad?

My eyes were wide. That didn't sound good. Not one bit.

Me: Yes, I'll leave soon. You sure everything's fine?

Eva: Yes, Mom, I swear. I just need to talk to you.

That was very un-Eva like. Normally, she just came out and said whatever was bothering her.

Me: Ok, sweetie. I'll see you shortly.

I wondered what was going on. Eva had just begun her junior year at high school that week. She was in the process of narrowing down her college choices from a list of six. With stellar grades like hers, the world was truly her oyster. I figured she wanted me home early in order to help her decide which college to pick without her father's influence.

Her brother was her role model, and since he'd gone to Stanford, I'd assumed she'd follow suit. But at the rate Ford was going, he'd be long gone by the time Eva got there the year after next. This semester, Ford was taking over twenty credit hours and planned on enrolling in summer courses in order to accelerate his degree.

It was great that my son was so driven and focused on doing well and finishing his degree so far ahead of schedule, but I was afraid he'd burn out. I'd rather he took his time and graduated in four years along with his peers. Then, he could return home during summers and intern at Pope Tower, LRPI's global headquarters in Los Derivas. Of course, Mason thought Ford's accelerated strategy was a great idea. It would have our son training to take the mantle sooner rather than later.

Two minutes after sending the last text to Eva, I kindly adjourned the meeting and headed up the elevator to the thirtieth floor to the CEO suite. When the silver doors parted, a warm, familiar face that had made me feel at home for the past twenty years greeted me from behind the marble-crafted reception station.

Sherry Anderson, Mason's executive assistant, was surrounded by tempered glass and shiny wood trim to the right and left of her. The look of the massive glass-encased, man-made waterfall behind her was a mind bender. Anyone seeing it would think the aggressiveness of the cascading water warranted a crashing sound to go with it. Lately, Sherry had to explain to guests that the waterfall was encased in soundproof glass, and she had the ability to mute it with the touch of a button. The recent CEO reception area re-design wasn't my idea or Sherry's. It was courtesy of my husband's long-time interior designer, who often came up with creative new ways to get Mason to write her a blank check. Sherry, a kind middle-aged blonde dressed in a navy-blue pants suit, illuminated the lobby without the help of her flashy surroundings.

"Liza!"

"Hi, Sherry. I'm here to grab my things and head home a bit early today. Where's Lola?" Lola Gibson was my new executive assistant, who had taken over two months ago after my last one had retired.

"She's meeting with the auditors on the twenty-third floor to gather the data you needed."

"Awesome. Please thank her for me when she gets back," I implored. "She's been working so hard. I'll thank her in person tomorrow. I have a gift basket and a two-hour massage with her name on it."

"She will love that," Sherry beamed. "Lola's kicking butt. I appreciate her sharp mind and drive. I only hope she doesn't have a desire to branch out into other areas of the company anytime soon. I need her drive up here—at least until I retire. I'm the only EA who has remained since you got here." She chuckled, and I laughed right along with her.

"Well Sherry, you know, Mr. Pope and I have always encouraged you to explore new horizons if you wanted to."

"I know, I know. But I absolutely love my job here and can't see myself doing anything else. It's awesome to see how this company has grown since I've first started. I've also witnessed how you and Mr. Pope have evolved together and raised such wonderful children."

Sherry's expression of pride wasn't lost on me. I blushed at her kind words. It was both embarrassing and heartwarming. Parents want to know if they are doing a good job raising their kids, so it's wonderful having validation, especially from those who aren't related.

"I'm sure I'll be seeing plenty of Ford walking the halls soon. Will he be interning next summer?" she asks.

My smile faded, and I shrugged in response. I used to know my son very well. Lately, getting a straight answer out of him was like pulling teeth. It broke my heart that my son and I weren't as close as we used to be. There had been a time when he'd told me everything.

Thankfully, Sherry shifted the topic away from Ford. "Will and I very much enjoyed the last time you had us over to your home for dinner. It's always wonderful visiting you two outside of work. Oh, by the way, I was thinking about Lacy. Have you heard from her lately?"

I missed Lacy Stevens-Lund. She was a really good friend and a former LRPI employee who had Lola's job at one point. Lacy and her family moved east a few years back. "She's doing great in Chicago," I told Sherry. "I keep up with her on social media. Her kids are growing up so fast. My, how time has gone."

"Tell me about it," Sherry sighed. "Well, I won't keep you, Liza. I know you need to head home," she smiled warmly.

I assured her I'd catch her on my way out before I headed over to my office to pack up my leather satchel. It was a quarter before four when I knocked on the adjoining office door. Not waiting for a response, I opened it, revealing an office identical to mine in size. Mason was in his office meeting with Michael 'Mick' Riordon, our executive vice president, and two other male executives. My husband was seated behind his grand mahogany oak desk. The sunny backdrop of downtown Los Derivas shone through the floor-to-ceiling windows. Everyone in the room faced me and immediately rose to their feet like perfect gentlemen as I walked in. I silently shook my head and motioned with my hand for them to take a seat. All but Mason remained standing. I approached him as a spark of concern flashed in his eye.

"Sweetheart. What's up?" he crooned, placing his hand on the small of my back.

"I'm heading home to get the girls situated with homework while Trisha finishes dinner. Call if you need anything," I announced to my husband in front of company.

"Sure thing. I'll be home in time for dinner," he answered lovingly. We embraced, and he planted a sweet kiss to my cheek. I tightened my lips, disguising a grin, and gently patted him on his back before walking away. Even after all these years, PDA in the office would never cease to feel awkward. Still, I adored it when Mason did it.

"See you then," I murmured.

"Have a good night, Liza," Mick chimed, with the other two execs echoing him.

As I entered my office to grab my things on the way out, I reminisced to a time when Mason would constantly work late nights at Pope Tower. As our household grew over the years, he remained focused on the business while making sure he came home every night in time for us to have dinner as a family.

I arrived home an hour after leaving the office and could barely remove my thin trench coat when the girls all bum-rushed me in the main room.

"Mommy! Mommy!" the twins echoed each other, throwing their arms around me. I embraced them in return, laughing at their twin-unified voices and their child-like enthusiasm. I hoped they never grew out of it. Brie wore a knee-length skirt with an Isla Cole baby tee and jean jacket. Beth had on over-washed jeans and a colorful t-shirt touting some obscure band. Eva followed in afterward, compounding the ball-of-Pope-girls embrace. Her style today was more Beth than Bree as she wore an unbuttoned gray long-sleeved shirt over a white tank top and faded black jeans.

"Girls... Hey!" I giggled, overwhelmed by all the extra love I received from the three of them at once.

"Mom—quickly. Let's go talk privately in your study," Eva said, taking control.

I flinched in surprise when the twins eyed each other with a discreet smirk.

What's this all about?

Before I could call them out on it, Eva took my coat and

handed it over to Brie. Eva then took my hand and led me all the way to my study. I side-eyed her the entire journey, stopping only when the two of us were behind closed doors. We sat side by side on the black leather sofa, facing the blank wall where my overhead projector normally shone when it was powered on.

"So… I wanted to talk to you about something," she started nervously.

Her nervousness somehow transferred over to me. "Sure, what is it?"

"You remember Knight Thibodeau?"

Of course, I knew who Knight was. Not only was he one of my son's best friends, but his mother was an insane NKOTB fan who'd followed them everywhere on tour. She'd even gone as far as to name her son after Jordan and Jonathan Knight from the group. I chuckled at the absurdity.

"Knight played on the high school baseball team with Ford. They're very close," I mentioned to Eva. When Ford was in high school, he often had Knight and some of the other boys from the team hang out at the house and play video games.

"Knight received a full scholarship to play ball at UC Los Derivas, where he's a freshman," she says with a proud smile.

"Oh, wow. I didn't know. That's great." I lacked in enthusiasm because my brain was still running. My daughter seemingly dropped Knight's name out from left field, no pun intended. I was pretty sure the news about him playing for UCLD wasn't why she'd asked me to get home before her father did. My expression must have spoken for me because Eva came clean.

"Well, I've been keeping in touch with Knight over social media. He told me over the summer that he had a crush on me back in high school. He always wanted to ask me out, but *um…*"

My eyes went wide at my beautiful teenage daughter. There was no that doubt boys wanted to ask her out. She was gorgeous, brilliant, and popular. Who wouldn't have wanted to take her out?

"Dad sort of freaks him out," Eva continued, biting her bottom lip. "Knight has heard stories about Dad being crazy strict. I'm sure Ford put that in his head. Anyway... Knight asked me out on a date this Saturday. He wants to do pizza and a movie, and I'd really like to go."

I didn't even fight it. I smiled like a loon. "How sweet! I really like Knight. He's a nice young man."

"He is." The stars in my baby girl's eyes were hard to ignore.

"You like him," I grinned. It's wasn't a question at that point. Her feelings toward him were obvious.

"Yes, I do." Her sincerity practically melted my heart.

"Since I know Knight's family, I'm good with the two of you going out on Saturday night. You'll just need the okay from your father," I said confidently. But with a flick of the switch, Eva's spirit plummeted. It was jarring.

"I just figured you'd say *yes* and keep it between us. If it makes you feel any better, you can drop me off at the mall, and I could meet Knight there—"

"Eva—*honey*," I cut her off. "You know it doesn't work that way. We can't keep your father in the dark. I mean, why would you want to?" I said, perplexed.

"Mom." Her wide eyes became narrow slits as if the answer were as clear as day. I was genuinely confused by her reaction.

"What?"

"You know Dad's going to want to take Knight into his study, sit him down and ask him a *million* questions before he lets me go out with him," she sighed in exasperation.

"You're overreacting, sweetie. Your father might ask Knight a couple of questions, but that's it. He only wants to make certain your date keeps you safe."

I saw the fire rise in my daughter's blue eyes that she inherited from me. "Me and the twins have freaking bodyguards following us everywhere, Mom! I mean, how much more safe can we be?! Look—if you tell Dad about this, he won't let me go."

"Calm down," I rumbled in warning. "Look, I know Knight's

parents from fundraisers and the like. Your father has met them. I can't imagine him saying *no*."

I sat up in bed with an open book in my lap, not reading it. I was somewhere in la-la land. I shook out of it once Mason crawled into bed beside me.

"Does reading by osmosis actually work?" he quipped.

"I wished it did."

I closed the book, placing it on the bedside table.

"You know, they have this neat little thing that actually reads to you. It's called an audiobook."

"Mason, you know I'm old fashioned when it comes to my books," I shot back, rolling my eyes.

He leaned over to me and wrapped his arms around me before pressing his lips to mine. "I've always loved that about you, Mrs. Pope. I hope that you never change."

"That's one thing you can count on," I said, flirty. He kissed me again, and our exchange heated up quickly. His lips soon slid down to my neck, and I knew exactly what he was up to.

I had to pump the brakes, or I wouldn't be able to get what I had off my chest. "Hey... I need to talk to you about something first." He hummed in acknowledgement, but he hadn't stopped ravaging my neck. "It's about our daughter."

That did the trick. He drew back, steadying his eyes on me, alarmed. "*Which* daughter?"

"Miss Eva Diane—our eldest daughter. All-star high school student," I beamed, laying it on thick. He saw right through me, narrowing his eyes and waiting for me to elaborate. "She texted me at work today. It was why I left the office earlier than usual."

"Oh? What did she need?"

"Well, she wanted to um—talk to me about something."

His eyes were just slits. Feeling anxious, I hurried to fill the quiet space with more words before he could speculate on anything negative. "You remember Knight Thibodeau? Nice young man. He's good friends with Ford. They were baseball teammates in high school." My husband was frowning at me, and I couldn't understand why. I just kept talking. "You know... Knight. He used to come over here and play video games with Ford and their other friends. You met his parents. The Thibodeaus own a chain of pharmacies. They've contributed to several of the charities we work with."

"O-kaaayyy?" he drawled, shrugging his shoulders. I was taken aback by his indifference but resolved to close the deal, advocating for Eva and her desire to go out on a date with a nice young man.

"Well, Knight asked Eva to go out with him this Saturday, and she'd like to tell him *yes*. I told her I'm fine with it, only if you agree."

Mason's lips tightened in a line as he tilted his head over to one side, nodding in contemplation. Even after twenty-plus years, I still couldn't read this man. After several beats of silence, he finally spoke.

"I appreciate that our daughter was mature enough to ask you first."

Mason's reaction astounded me. I felt a bubble of pride for our daughter growing inside, itching to burst. "I know, right? But that's just how Eva is. She's never been sneaky or underhanded. She's always been open and honest with us."

"Exactly," he nodded. His expression was still unreadable, until it turned sour. "Unlike that knuckle-headed older brother of hers—"

"Mason!" I was sick of him taking cheap shots at our son. Ford was a really good kid. I didn't feel like starting an argument with Mason about him. It was late, and I was too tired.

"Well, it's true," Mason grumbled. The creases in his forehead began to flatten as forced calm settled in. "Eva has shown a lot of maturity for her age."

"Agreed. I'm astounded by our big little girl. She is going to do great things."

"Absolutely," Mason concurred. He didn't smile. He rarely did.

But I saw the pride in his olive-tinted eyes. I felt the presence of relief just around the corner.

"So, you agree? I can give Eva the good news in the morning so she can confirm her date for Saturday?"

His frown returned with a vengeance. "Wait—I didn't agree to that. The answer is *no*. Absolutely not."

I gaped at him. "Excuse me?" I was convinced he was joking. If not, he'd just pulled a world record breaking one hundred and eighty degree turn in a matter of nanoseconds. I considered getting Guinness World Records on the phone. "Mason, you just said Eva was mature. She's at the age now to start dating. She'll be going to senior prom next year—"

"The answer is still *no*, Liza," he interrupted. "She's not going. She needs to focus on her studies, not boys. Besides, isn't that kid in college? He's way too old for her."

I was livid, seconds away from slamming my hand into my husband's good-looking face. "Knight is only a college freshman. Eva is a junior in high school. It's not even in the realm of a May-December romance."

"First of all, there is no *romance* here. Eva is a child. Secondly, I'd be damned if *my* daughter goes with some punk named after the motherfuckers who sang *The Right Stuff*. I don't know what that *stuff* is, but it had better not go anywhere near my kid."

"Mason…stop. You're sounding crazy right now."

"I'm only crazy for you, Mrs. Pope," he said, tugging me into his arms.

I pushed him away, clenching my teeth in extreme frustration. "Look, I'm fine with Knight. I *like* Knight. Please, Mason, let our daughter go out with him. They're just doing pizza and a movie at the mall. They don't plan on going anywhere else."

I sounded so desperate defending our wonderful daughter to my overbearing husband. We had a solid partnership, but looking back, it seemed as if I'd been the only one doing all the compromising. Mason had always gotten his way.

"Eliza, I don't know how many other ways there are to say the word *no*. Non? Nein? Niet? Either way, the answer is still *hell no*."

My teeth ground together, and I mentally counted to ten before speaking. "Mason, you're being unreasonable."

"Am I?" he shot back, sounding indignant.

"Yes, you are. Eva is a good girl, and Knight is a nice young man."

"He's an eighteen-year-old college kid and an athlete. That makes him extra horny. Meanwhile, our sweet and innocent daughter is sixteen and in high school. It's statutory rape."

No—he did not just go there. He, of all people, had some nerve. He was ten years older than I was. I'd been twenty when we'd met and gotten married.

"Do you want to be an accessory to a crime?"

My eyes were so dry from gawking at my stupid husband for so long. "For statutory rape? They are less than two years apart. Do you know how insane you sound right now?"

"Insane? You don't know the half of it. By the way, I'm not talking about being an accessory to statutory rape. He'd never get a chance to touch her. I'm talking about murder, Eliza. Because he will surely die if he even tries to lay one finger on my daughter. I'd kill him with my bare hands, and it would be your fault for agreeing to let Eva go out in the first place. For your sake and Thibodeau's, Eva won't be agreeing to that date."

I'm done. Instead of arguing with him and saying something I'd later regret, I pinched my lips together tightly and lay down on my pillow, facing away from him.

"Liza?"

For several beats, I stewed to a boil before springing up and around with a glare. "I don't understand you one bit, Mason Pope. Eva is a good girl, and she is seriously going to be bummed when I tell her she can't go out on her first date with Knight."

Mason shrugged as if Eva's future sadness and my current anger were no skin off his back. "The boy's okay, so far. But I still don't trust him with my daughter. I don't trust *anyone*."

My mind searched behind his critical glare. I replayed two words he'd just spoken. "*So far.*" Coming from anyone else, it was a harmless statement. But in Mason Pope Land, that meant so much more. I let the thought linger for a bit before my eyes grew round and wide.

He didn't…

"Did you know Knight and Eva were communicating prior to today?" I asked.

Mason said nothing. My stomach dropped to the floor, then rolled.

Here we go, once again.

First me, then Ford, and now poor Eva was getting a bitter taste of her overly zealous father and his penchant for stalking our every move, including the people we were in contact with.

Will the vicious cycle ever end?

Four

Ford

At ten o'clock at night on a Tuesday, the library on campus wasn't necessarily empty. There were many other students present, but they were spread throughout the building, leaving wide gaps in between. I sat in the computer lab, the only one present in the second from the last row of workstations.

I exited out of the classwork portal for one of my courses before launching a new browser in incognito mode. I pulled up a popular social media site and searched for one name in particular. I'd learned from past missteps, no longer perusing this person's profile page using the MacBook my parents bought me.

People on campus may have thought I was a dick because I did well maintaining that front. They assumed I had the entire world right in the palm of my hand. To them, I was just some spoiled rich kid with everything going for me. I was sure some of them might have been eager to trade places with me in an instant. But the moment they realized what they'd be sacrificing just to have the last name *Pope*, they would quickly reconsider.

The 24/7 surveillance.

The constant scolding and the controlling.

It fucking sucked.

But here's the funny thing. As soon as I was right where my father wanted me to be, he'd finally lay off me. He'd let me live the rest of my life how I saw fit.

Sure Pops, I'd run your multi-billion-dollar company. But once at the helm, I'd finally be in control of my life. I'd put barriers in place to make sure no one had a say in where I hung out, who I hung out with… *Or who I fell in love with.*

There she is.

My heart skipped a few beats when I laid eyes on a newly posted selfie of her at the bar with a couple of her girlfriends. She looked like she was having a grand ole time. *Damn, she looks happy.* I felt a pang in my chest, stronger than the chronic one that ached in the background while I was out here living.

This was Harper's final year at UCLD. It was understandable that she was having her last hurrah with a group of friends, including her roommates. In theory, Harper should've graduated a year ago. However, midway into her studies, she switched her major from nursing to hospitality management. This change required her to have to take an entirely new set of core classes.

When she wasn't in class, she worked part-time at the Marriott in Los Derivas. I'd often thought about surprising her at her job. That would never work since I was constantly being followed.

Her aspiration to work in the hospitality field didn't surprise me. She'd always been a natural with helping people. It was why she wanted to be a nurse. Growing up, she'd helped her dad and stepmom with stuff over at the main house, as well as at the house where they stayed. Harper also volunteered to help my parents whenever she came around to hang with my sisters and me.

Hospitality was an admirable profession. If anyone asked my father whether it was a good profession, he'd probably say *yes*. However, when it came to his own children being connected with someone who aspired to work in that field, my father abhorred it. What may be good for someone else's kid wasn't necessarily good enough for an offspring of Mason Pope. My father might have pretended to be down-to-earth to the masses, but when it came to me, there wasn't a girl out there good enough, in his eyes, to be with me.

I couldn't fucking understand why he was such a hypocrite. My grandparents were good people, and they raised my dad well as an only child.

I knew little to nothing about my father's youth. Something traumatic happened to him at a certain point of his life, but nobody would talk about it. Why was everyone so protective of him? I couldn't understand it.

And my mother seemed incapable of making a decision without Dad co-signing it. When she'd caught Harper and I making out in the theater room that day, she insisted on telling Dad about it. She'd known goddamn well he'd lose his shit. Yet, it hadn't stopped her from ratting me out.

When Dad had confronted me, I confessed to being in love with Harper. By the way he'd reacted, one would've thought I'd confessed to being an axe murderer. No way was Mason Pope letting me frolic in the meadow with his estate manager's daughter.

From that moment on, Harper had never come on the property again. Not too long after we were found out, I'd attempted to meet secretly with Harper in Los Derivas. My efforts hadn't gotten very far. My father had eyes everywhere. When I'd finally figured out how to outsmart him by coming up with creative ways to reach out to Harper, the girl had begun to push me away. I'd been brokenhearted ever since.

I couldn't understand for the life of me why she'd had a sudden change of heart. *Did my father get to her?* I kept asking her, but she never would say. From that moment on, my goal had been to find some way to bring her back to me. It was why I decided to go to Stanford instead of out east. For a year, I held my breath, hoping she'd surprise me one day on campus. And even though we managed to reconnect over the summer, she hadn't been the same. Something deep down was screaming at me, telling me that she was trying her damnedest to move on.

That couldn't happen.

I was still stuck in our yesterday, asking *why* over and over again.

Why won't you fight for us, Harper?

Last night, my Project Management professor shot me an email demanding that I meet him at his office today between the hours of one and three. No details, just—"*Ford, it is urgent that we meet. Let me know what time works best for you.*"

I hadn't bothered asking if I'd done something wrong. If I had, he probably wouldn't have been the one reaching out. If I'd royally fucked up, you'd better believe someone from student affairs would've contacted me instead.

As I made my way over to Professor Ship's office at the Graduate School of Business building, a few familiar faces stopped me along the way. Mostly female faces.

"Hey, Ford, I haven't seen you hanging around Rebecca since we began fall classes. Did you guys break up?" one overly enthusiastic girl said.

"Rebecca and I have always been *just* friends," I replied.

"Well, maybe I'll see you around," another girl winked.

"I'm sure you will," I said, quickly turning on my heel.

The fellas I socialized with would often ask me why I never took full advantage of the girls more than I did. They seemed envious at how often attractive females approached me, even though I behaved like a jerk.

"*But see, the bitches love it! They love Pope because he doesn't give a shit about them. Hot girls don't want a nice guy. They want an asshole.*" My pal Zac often said that to our buddies right in front of me. I just sat back with a nonchalant expression on my face. It was one of the few moments I didn't have a witty comeback.

I'm not intentionally mean to women. I *love* women. I come from a household full of them—strong, intelligent, and very open with their feelings. I'd never intentionally treat a woman badly.

Rebecca the cheerleader was a different story. When I'd first come to Stanford, she'd hounded me for months at various parties. And when she hadn't been making good enough progress with me one-on-one, she sent her sorority and cheerleader friends after me.

"Hey, you like Rebecca? I think she really digs you."

And—

"I think you and Rebecca would make such a cute couple! You guys look perfect together. She's hot, you're hot…"

Then, some of those *friends* Rebecca would send my way on her behalf would secretly throw her under the bus.

"Between you and me, Rebecca's a hoe. I'm nothing like that. I'm an old-fashioned girl. Something tells me that's more your speed. I can tell that fast girls don't hold your attention for very long."

Sure, a traditional girl was my jam. The problem was, there was only one *traditional girl* I was interested in, and she didn't go to Stanford.

I wasn't sure why all these girls continued to chase after me, even after I'd shown that I wasn't the least bit interested in them. I enjoyed getting my dick sucked like the next guy, but after a while, it was just a blowjob. And sex was just sex. None of that shit meant anything to me unless it was someone I truly cared about.

I thought about couples like my parents. Anyone could see that even after over twenty years of marriage, Mason Pope and Eliza Cooper were just as in love now as they'd been back then. When they didn't think anyone was watching, I caught the way their eyes lit up when they gazed at each other from across the dinner table. The subtle way my dad would place a hand right at the dip in her back. The way she tilted her head and leaned against his shoulder blade, looking up at him like he was the only man in the world… No doubt, these were two people in love.

As a kid, I'd often asked my mother to tell me stories about when they first met. Hearing her tales about how Dad would randomly surprise her with trips to St. Kitts and Sydney had absolutely blown my mind. He was totally different with my mother than he was with anyone else. He was vulnerable with her. She was his safe haven.

It was said that men gravitated toward women who were very similar to their mother. For some guys, that would've been a total nightmare. For me, it would've been a dream come true. My mother was my dream girl. However, she was taken, and not to mention, that would've been beyond sick. I wasn't down with the Oedipus scene.

Thankfully, I'd spotted my mother's kind, benevolent spirit in Harper. Like Liza, Harper was always willing to help others in need. She was always willing to sit down and listen instead of making everything about *her*. That was the opposite of Rebecca. Harper Benton was the only girl I knew who came remotely close to my mother, but she was so much more. She was the complete package for me.

Finally making it to Professor Ship's office, I approached the open door, and he waved me in from behind his desk. "Ford, welcome. Please shut the door and take a seat." I complied.

Ship looked like he was closer to my grandfather's age than my father's. Rumor had it that he was in his early fifties, like Dad. Ship obviously lived a rough life. To be fair, not too many people were as ridiculously lucky as my father. Not only had he been born into the right family at the right time in order to claim an empire, but he had the right genes. The only thing that dated him was the gray in his hair. Other than that, Mason Pope looked slightly over half his age. Same with my mother, except she didn't have the grays.

Professor Ship wore a dated plaid shirt and matching brown corduroy pants. I could've sworn he'd come out of a time machine—straight out of the decade when my parents were born. His dark-rimmed glasses were the only fashionable thing about him. His balding hair, fuzzy gray and brown, was cut close to his scalp. He'd been on staff for about five years, mostly teaching classes at the graduate level. Before that, he'd worked as a top executive at a Fortune 50, taking a buyout during the downturn and returning to California with his family so he could work at his alma mater.

I'd had him as a freshman on a fluke. He normally didn't teach brand new business students. He'd been filling in for another professor who'd had to bow out due to health issues. I could tell at the time that Ship wanted to be in that intro class even less than I did. *Intro to Business* was a colossal waste of time. I'd been born with business aptitude. Hell, my parents were the ultimate global business power couple, for crying out loud. I'd interned part-time for them during my junior and senior years of high school for co-operative educational credit.

But as time had gone on in intro class, Ship was happy he'd taken a step backward. He'd underestimated the new talent entering Stanford, especially me. By the end of the semester, Ship had come up to me personally and asked me to be a part of his special advanced project management course at the beginning of sophomore year. At the time, I hadn't known he and the leadership at the School of Business had handpicked all the students for that class. The class wasn't even listed in the catalog.

"So, Ford—just like the previous time, we started the first day of class on the wrong foot."

Oh shit.

My lips tightened as sweat began to form on my skin. *Is he kicking me out of his class?* I was internally going haywire, yet I remained quiet and attentive.

"You always come across as extremely arrogant to your peers. A know-it-all. You can be an educator's living nightmare. I've actually spoken to a few of your professors here about you, both past and present."

Double shit.

That didn't sound good. Although, I shouldn't be worried about getting kicked out of a class that doesn't technically exist on record. Sure, the course credit would appear on my transcript at the end of the semester—that's if I didn't get kicked out of class. But if I did get kicked out, my parents wouldn't have any way of knowing I got released. As long as there wasn't a negative letter grade recorded on my transcript, everything would be peachy.

That small consolation didn't make me feel much better, though. I dug Professor Ship. I'd even managed to turn some of my classmates' impressions of me around in the past couple of days. Don't get me wrong, I was still a smart ass, but I'd like to think I've backed up some of my words with action.

"You are the quintessential shit-talker, Pope. You use this mean persona to build this wall around yourself that's difficult to penetrate. I don't know what your deal is," he said, gazing up to the ceiling as if searching for the answer to drop in his lap.

He was reading me, and I didn't like it. I didn't need a shrink. Reluctantly, I let him continue on his tirade.

"Despite that smart mouth of yours, your work truly speaks for itself. Question for you."

I shrugged, not knowing where he was going with this. "Sure."

"If you came over to my office of your own volition, sitting where you are seated now, and you asked me, 'Ship... What do you think I should do with my life? I need your unfiltered advice.' How do you think I'd respond to that?"

I blinked, not necessarily feeling all that comfortable with what was happening. Honestly, I was afraid to hear his response. I had a hunch what it could be. He'd tell me to lay off the self-imposed accelerated program and take my time to graduate. He'd encourage me to find out who I really am without the strings of my family. I already knew who I was. I was going to cut the strings anyway.

With a shrug of my shoulder, I prompted Ship to humor me with his unsolicited advice.

"I'd tell you to pack your shit now, leave Stanford at once, and return to Arcadia's Crest immediately."

My mouth was agape. *What in the hell is he talking about?! I thought I was kicking ass here!* I'd just turned in one of the best papers I'd ever written. It was all about managing vendor/supplier relationships and how to resolve conflict and unmet expectations. It was such a masterpiece I'd been tempted to send it to Dad before thinking better of it. I was still pissed at him for watching me get my dick sucked.

"You don't belong here, Ford," Ship said. "Mason Pope is one of the most masterful businessmen of our time who only found himself after dropping out of Yale after his freshman year. This is your second year here, and you're completely wasting your time. You are cut from the exact same cloth as your father."

To someone else, that would've been the highest praise. I was so pissed at Ship I could've turned his desk over on top of him. I. Was. NOT. My. Father.

"I can tell you're frustrated sitting through these classes," he continued, "learning things that are seemingly useless to you. It's not just me who sees it. All the professors I've talked with feel the exact same way. You are being restrained. Held back. You have a very powerful and innovative mind, Ford Pope. You don't need boundaries that institutions, such as this one, often impose on brilliant minds like yours."

I was floored. "Wh—what? Are you telling me to drop out?"

"Well… I'm not telling you to do that. I'm just saying *hypothetically*… If you asked me what you should do with your life, that would probably be my response to you. I can't force you to drop out. Do I *want* you to leave? No. You are a thrill to teach, Ford. That paper you turned in last week—I've read it over five times already. I haven't even posted a grade on it yet."

"I've noticed," I chuckled. He's normally quick to grade our work.

"I couldn't imagine ever grading a paper like that, Ford. It's far beyond anything I could teach from a textbook. That shit is something your peers will never learn if they are stuck here reading textbooks written by people who have never bothered working at some of the top corporations that they expect their students to study up on. You'll be thrilled to know that your international marketing course, which I presume you'll be taking next semester, has updated their textbooks to include an entire chapter on LRPI as a spotlight organization and a case study. I say that it's about damn time," Ship beamed.

I closed my eyes. I was pained, not honored by Ship's words. *Dammit, I've fallen into the shadows of my father once again.* Sure... I was in college because I wanted to be, and yes, also at my parents' urging. Dad often stressed that I should do what he failed to do, which was finish his degree. At the end of the day, I was doing it for myself. Not for Dad. Not for Mom. ME. I needed to prove to myself that I was not my father. What better way than to do something he'd hadn't done? Yet in that moment, I had a professor telling me I was literally too cool for school.

Just like Daddy.

"Look, Professor Ship... I appreciate your kind words, but I am here to learn. I might act like a prick sometimes, but I understand that I don't know everything there is to know about business. That's why I'm here."

"I know that, Ford. Even though you may seem disinterested at times, I can tell you are very eager to learn. Like I said, I'm not urging you to drop out, nor do I expect you to. But if you do decide to go that route, I have no doubt that you'd do exceptionally well in the business world. What I do regret is not being in the field anymore and having the opportunity to work with the likes of you." A look of pride spread across his face.

It should've been touching that he felt so strongly about my potential, but I wasn't moved one bit. I kept the same unreadable, stoic expression on my face. Ironically, it was the same look my father was famous for. I moved my lips to speak back, but Ship stopped me before I could.

"I hope you don't mind, but I shared your paper last night with my boss, the dean of the School of Business. He read it immediately and wants you to expound on it. He'd like to publish it in the next GSB Journal."

My mouth and eyes were agape. "But I'm not a graduate student. That's a graduate publication, and I'm only a sophomore."

"It's unheard of, I know," he smiled with pride. "But that's just how much the dean loved your work. It's unlike anything he's seen from an undergrad. You have an unfair advantage over your peers, Ford. All of this shit we teach—you can recite it in your sleep. I'd feel comfortable enough to sit out a class and let you teach it," he laughed.

But I was feeling beyond uncomfortable. How did Mom and Dad deal with people kissing their asses all the time? I could never enjoy this. It made me feel uneasy.

"I had a feeling that paper was far beyond the original scope when I wrote it," I told him. "But I never expected it to grow legs. I still have a lot to learn, even if my attitude doesn't always show it. If you think I'm doing way too much, I promise to dial it back."

"Never!" he growled. "Don't ever shortchange yourself *or* your educators. Just like you learn from us, we learn from you. I am no longer out there in the field. As a man in my fifties, my circle of friends is as big as it's going to get. Without the insight of young, brilliant minds like yours, I'd never learn anything new. Times and technology are constantly changing. Your generation has a handle on that, and it's your job to keep us old fogies honest and in line."

But why did he feel the need to share my paper with the dean? I had a hunch that I still didn't know the half of why he called this meeting.

"So, your vendor relations paper that I absolutely refuse to grade. I will give you some additional bullet points to help you expand your composition for the GSB Journal. It will probably end up being ten to fifteen pages max. How long do you think you'll need to wrap this up?"

"Maybe a week? I'm taking more than a full load of classes right now, but I'm not working part-time or anything. I can swing it in a week's time."

"Alright... good. I'll give you two weeks, just to be on the safe side. Again, I'm not going to grade your paper. Just keep showing up for class. Take all of the exams, which I'm certain you'll ace. Since you're doing the journal article, you won't have to do the capstone case study for a final grade in my class. As far as I'm concerned, you already have your *A* from me. And I'm saying this at the very beginning of the semester. You should be very proud, Ford," he said with a smile.

That was good to know. Anything less than an *A* from any class wasn't an option for me. Even a solid B+ would give cause for my father to say, "*What the fuck are you even doing at that school, Ford?!*" Nothing less than an *A* was allowed in the Pope household. Fuck a tiger parent, my father was a rabid grizzly bear.

"There's one more reason I asked you to be here today. I have an opportunity for you next semester," Ship prefaced.

I knew it. Was this another one of his invitations to join some special class? Hell, he just tried to talk me out of staying in school! Then, he proceeded to share my paper with the head of the college of business, who wants me to publish my paper in the *Graduate School of Business Journal*. The entire office visit had been overwhelming. I wasn't sure I could take another moment of Ship's kudos or praise.

"The assignment you turned in was twofold. I had no doubt you'd be the one sitting before me when it was all done. But as policy would have it, I'm still required to screen all potential candidates for every position."

"Position?"

Like a job? I wasn't looking for a job. I was there to plow through all my requirements, take my degree, and bring it home to Arcadia's Crest as soon as possible. I refused to waste precious time instead of hurrying the fuck out of here in fourteen months. Besides, there was no position here on campus or elsewhere that would pay me what I'm already getting in my stipend from my parents.

Ship read my perplexed expression and tried to ease any doubt. "There's an active learning internship program where selected students can leave the university and work full-time an entire semester. You'd actually be working in your field of study. Many top firms from across the globe have partnered with Stanford by putting some of our brightest students to work, giving them the exposure they need, as well as enriching their resumes. Some of these companies are extremely hard to get into as an entry-level employee, so having any sort of exposure with them gives you a leg up above the competition."

I narrowed my eyes, ready to cut to the chase. "What company are we talking about?"

"Zinfinite."

Mic drop.

The expression that once resided on my face—the one that said to the world that I couldn't give a shit less about getting *kudos* and an article in the graduate school journal? Well, it just left. I fucking lit up like a kid on Christmas.

"Zinfinite? Like, corporately headquartered in Los Derivas, *Zinfinite?*"

Zinfinite was Amazon's number one competitor. They were located right in my backyard back home. I would be a hop, skip, and a jump from UCLD.

Looks like I'll be paying someone a visit. Many visits.

"Do I finally have your attention now?" Ship chuckled. "Yes, that would be the place. There's an internship spot available from January to May of next year. You'd go back home and work a forty-hour a week paid gig as an intern dealing with vendor/supplier relations. Then, you'll present your senior honors thesis based on your internship. You're making the connection now?"

Ship smirked, and I laughed. "Oh, yeah. Loud and clear."

Did I mention how much I loved that fucking paper I wrote?

Harper, I'm coming home, baby.

"So, what do you say? You interested?"

"Hell, yes."

Professor Ship chuckled before leaning over his desk to shake my hand. "Congratulations, Ford."

"Thanks, sir."

"You up for making the five-hour trek down to Los Derivas for the day to meet with the Zinfinite vendor management group early next week? They want to introduce you to the team now before putting you to work after New Year's. Will that work for you? You'll receive an excused absence for the day, of course."

"I can do that. I have a question for you. Even though the internship will count as four courses, I've been regularly taking six to seven a term in order to keep up with my accelerated graduation plan. Could I possibly tack on two more remote courses to my internship? Or perhaps I can even take them at the UCLD campus for transfer credit?"

The same school Harper attended. *I'm a sly devil.*

"Absolutely," Ship nodded. "I'll get you a list of available transferable courses remaining on your graduation plan so you can continue plowing away. In the meantime, I'll narrow down a date and time for your introductory visit to Zinfinite. I'll have the dean's office email you the congratulatory letter as soon as we wrap up here. Feel free to share the good news with your folks."

I had time to plot and to visit Harper to give her the good news. I'd be coming home for four months and taking some night classes at her school.

Hopefully, she's just as anxious to see me again.

Five

Liza

Yesterday, I told my sixteen-year-old daughter that she couldn't go out on her first date... *yet*. And although I'd promised profusely to keep working on her dad, Eva had stormed off in tears. It was something she'd never done.

"Eva—don't be that way!" I'd called out. *"I told you I'd keep talking it over with your Dad! I'm on your side!"*

She'd spun around from across the room and glared angrily at me. *"No! You're not on my side! If you were, you wouldn't have told him in the first place!"* Recalling her words made my heart break all over again. It hadn't been the first time a child of mine had said that to me.

Eva had locked herself in her room, refusing to join us for dinner. No matter how many times her father and I had knocked on her door, she wasn't coming out. I had to talk Mason off the ledge. He was seconds away from breaking her door down. I told him that she needed time to cool off. We'd give her that.

Whether or not Mason agreed with my method, he had no other choice but to comply. He hadn't been playing fair because he'd known about Eva being in touch with Knight. Mason finally came clean in bed after I withheld sex. I'd been the one blindsided in all this. I hadn't a clue the other night when Eva was so eager to take her sisters to the mall for some *skirt*, Knight had just happened to shoot her a message about being at the very same mall with friends.

Mason had known all along.

Discovering Eva's true motive hadn't bothered me. Sure, she hadn't been completely honest with us, and I'd never encourage that sort of behavior. But how many times growing up had Jessie and I told our parents we were hanging out with our friends, only to omit that we were meeting up with some guy? As teenagers, we'd all done it. Like my parents, I could have gone a lifetime without ever finding out what Eva was really up to. Her sisters had been in on it. They'd known all about Eva and Knight's flourishing *like* for one another. The twins were willing co-conspirators.

Eva's absence at the dinner table had been loud, and her twenty-four-hour silent treatment toward her dad and I had been even louder. Our soon-to-be thirteen-year-old twins were beginning to feel hopeless about their future state of dating. Mason had stepped away to grab a corkscrew for the wine when one of them spoke out.

"Dad is crazy strict. Why won't he let Eva date Knight? Will he be as crazy with us, too?"

It had been heartbreaking to hear that from Beth as Brie nodded in total agreement beside her. I needed to fix this immediately before it tore our family apart. It was bad enough that I'd had the incident with Ford hanging over my head for almost two years. It was an incident I was certain his sisters weren't aware of. If all were revealed, neither Eva, Brie, nor Beth would have any hope for their futures.

Mason was being unreasonable, and there was no talking him down. He'd die on that hill no matter how many times I tried to convince him that our children were not him. On top of showering our children with so much love and self-worth, both Mason and I made sure they remained safe. They were stronger and better protected than he'd ever been at their ages. More importantly, they had each other. Mason had been the only child. How could I get him to see it?

Harper Benton was not a predator, so why had Mason given her the predator's treatment? We'd known her since she was four.

That beautiful girl had been raised right before our very eyes. We knew exactly where she'd come from. She was a sweet girl who'd grown up to be a wonderful young lady. The age difference between her and Ford was just four years. Way less than the ten years that separated Mason and me. But Mason hadn't cared.

I'd only caught Ford and Harper kissing in the theater room. If they were having sex, I hope Ford had remembered all our safe sex lectures. He'd been seventeen at the time, so it hadn't been abuse. At six-three with an athletic physique, he was more than capable of defending himself against a petite five-five girl. If our son had been inappropriately touched before that, his father and I would have known about it. As a child, Ford had been open about everything under the sun.

Now at eighteen, going on nineteen, I had no doubt he still held a grudge against me. I never forgot the look of sheer disappointment in his eyes when I told him I'd have to tell his father. For me, it hadn't been about *who* he'd been with. What had mattered was that he was supposed to be in school. Instead, he'd played hooky to be with a girl. I'd never cared that the girl was Harper. If he was going to skip school with anyone, I was secretly glad it was with her, because I knew Harper. I'd known her father and stepmother since I began dating Mason. The Bentons were a wonderful little family.

If I'd known Mason would overreact as he had and pull Russ, Harper's father, right along with him, I might've done things differently. At the time, all Mason would talk about was how Harper had *"lead Ford astray."* He'd called her a bad example and blamed her waywardness on the influence of her biological mother, whom I'd never met. Then, he said that Russ had assured him Harper would never set foot in the main house again.

I remembered my heart sinking when he'd told me. Harper had grown up with our children. She'd babysat the twins. All our kids loved her. *I* loved her. Back when she'd been very young and in her curious phase, she'd asked me many questions. It hadn't bothered me in the slightest because I'd loved entertaining her inquiries. Spending time with her in those days had made me look forward to the age when all of my children could ask me questions like that.

The last time I'd seen Harper was that day in the theater room. What had taken place between her and Ford two years ago had cast a dark shadow over the next Pope child in line. It wasn't fair. I had a mind to give Mason the same silent treatment our daughter was giving the both of us.

At least this time, Eva joined us for dinner. Unfortunately, she still wasn't speaking. A spirited back and forth took place between the twins and their father over various subjects—school, band, sports… I'd normally joined in, but not this time. My heart was heavy. I felt distant.

Eva was quiet as well, but instead of looking all sad like me, she appeared slightly annoyed. Bitter. It seemed she'd rather be cleaning up pig slop than sit in our presence. It broke my heart to see my strong, good girl display such an angry adult emotion. An extreme emotion she didn't deserve to experience at such a young age.

Eva Diane Pope had always done what her parents told her to do. She'd been the model daughter, sister, and student. And for all of the good she'd done, she never asked her father and me for very much. The only time she had was to ask to go out on an innocent date to the mall with a nice young man with a good reputation.

This was how we repaid her?

If we woke up one morning and discovered Eva missing because she ran away, should we be surprised? Every time I considered that outcome, I was on the verge of tears. I had to have been thinking about it when my husband called me out of my reverie from across the dinner table.

"Mrs. Pope? What is your deal today?" he frowned.

I sighed, but I didn't say a word. I resumed nibbling at my cheesy potato casserole like a sad little mouse.

"Mom's upset too... just like Eva. You won't let Eva go out with Knight," Brie bravely answered for me. *That's my girl.*

I looked and caught Mason flashing Eva a stern look. She stared blankly at her plate, not touching a morsel on her plate.

"Eva, you'll get over it soon. You'll be speaking to us again. School always comes first—you know that."

Bile rose up, and my face twisted. *That's all you have to say for yourself, Pope?! Was that supposed to make Eva feel better?* Unlike me, Eva had no reaction. She just sat there away from everyone at the table, saying nothing.

"Eat your dinner, Eva. This is not a request," Mason demanded. Her eyes rose to meet his, and she seemed nearly unshakable. I knew right then that things were about to get *really* ugly.

"If I eat this, will you let me go out to the mall with Knight on Saturday?" she said, not missing a beat.

Right before my eyes, I started to see myself in her.

Leverage. That's my girl. I slowly cracked a smile mid-chew.

"No. *Eat*," Mason barked.

I curse at my husband in my head. *Pope—what on earth is wrong with you?!*

In an instant, Eva leapt to her feet and stormed out.

"Eva! Get back here and finish your dinner! You were *not* excused!" Mason yelled after her.

I blinked in slow motion and pressed my mouth in a flat line.

Well—what did he expect?

As if reading my mind, my husband's critical eyes bore into me. "You encourage this type of disobedient behavior, Eliza?" Now that he didn't have Eva to yell at, I was the next best thing.

Uh-uh, Pope. You aren't turning the tables on me. This was all you.

Sensing that a storm was brewing, I decided to clear the room before it got any nastier. "Brie, Beth... please go to your room. I need to speak privately with your father."

The twins did a double-take before gaping at their father with a look that said: *You've really done it now, Dad.* The girls quickly stood and vacated the area.

"Why did you excuse them?" Mason glared. "They weren't done eating."

Unbelievable. He had some nerve confronting me in front of the kids, which he's never done, and expecting me to just sit back and take it. He had another thing coming.

"Mason—cut the crap," I growled through clenched teeth.

"Excuse me?" He had the nerve to be appalled.

"You heard me. You're making us the villains here. I don't want to be that to anyone, much less our own children."

"We are not their friends. We are their parents. It is our job to guide and protect them."

"And we've done that. But what you fail to understand is that parenting doesn't involve treating our children like babies all their lives. Eva is *sixteen*. Yet, you treat her like she's *six*. She has more than earned the right to be trusted out on a date with a trustworthy young man," I growled.

"Liza," he sighed. He wore a smile that barely masked his frustration as he shook his head in total disagreement.

"Eva and Knight are going to be in public, Mason."

"Yeah. This time. What about the next?"

I shrugged in response.

"What the fuck is that supposed to mean?!" he roared.

"Shhh..." I urged him with my eyes to lower his voice and watch his language.

"Are you telling me you don't care if that boy puts his hands on our daughter?"

"If she's prepared to have safe intercourse, then—"

"The fuck she is!"

"She will make the best decision for *her*. We've armed her with all the knowledge she needs. She will go on making smart and safe choices."

"Liza, she's a kid!"

"And there you are, being unreasonable," I sighed, rolling my eyes.

"There's that word again—*unreasonable*. You always throw that in my face when things don't go your way."

Feeling indignant, my head tilted over to one side. "Really, Pope? And what about when you don't get *your* way? Oh. That's right. That *rarely* ever happens!" I sprung to my feet, then turned on my heel to leave the table.

"Where are *you* going?!" Mason bellowed.

"To speak to my daughter!" I shouted back.

"*Our* daughter!" he shouts in correction.

Now, she was *our* daughter. She'd been *his* daughter until then. I turned to look at him for a brief second. He was seated at the large table, all alone. *How fitting.*

If he continued being a jackass, that would ultimately be his future.

I knocked on the door twice and paused before reluctantly twisting the knob. I pushed open the door, stunned that she hadn't locked it. I found Eva in the brightly lit room, lying upside down over her made bed, duvet and pillows still intact. She held a book in her hands.

"Whatcha reading?" I shut the door behind me, taking a seat on the bed right beside her. Her still pretending that I didn't exist was like a dagger to the heart. "Eva—"

"I heard you... Yelling at Dad," she said. She placed her book off to the side before looking up at me with pensive blue eyes. *Had she been eavesdropping?*

"I didn't mean for you to hear any of that." I sighed, ashamed.

"I appreciate you siding with me now. But if you *really* were on my side, you would have never told him about Knight in the first place."

Her sharp demeanor caused me to flinch. Eva had always been

a good girl. She'd never talked back to me. But no matter how upset she was, I wasn't going to tolerate that sort of behavior.

"Eva, I'm going to let that slide because I know you're upset. I am on your side, but I'm not going to let you speak to me in that tone again. I get it—you're mad because I told your father. But as I explained before, we don't keep secrets. Your father and I are a team when it comes to you and your siblings. Together, we raised you to be the strong young woman you are today."

"I'm sorry, Mom," she murmured dejectedly. "I was just being honest. You taught us to always be honest. Right?"

"Yes. Honest *but* respectful," I qualified.

"Well, with all due respect, why does being a part of a so-called *team* seem to be only one-sided? It's like one person's voice matters more than the other."

My daughter hadn't been off base. All our children were extremely perceptive. "My dear—in marriage, there will always be areas where the husband and wife won't always agree. That is where compromise comes into play," I explained.

"Where's the compromise in this instance?" she asked, her voice almost cracking. I silently prayed that my sweet little girl didn't break down.

"It's a process, sweetie. If you don't understand anything else, just know that I trust you. You've done nothing to make me feel otherwise. I only need to get your father to see things from the same lens that I'm looking through. He'll get there," I assured her.

"*When?*" she pleaded. "When I'm twenty? Thirty? How long do I have to wait to be free?" Tears began streaming down her beautiful face.

I instantly wrapped my arms around her, pulling her to my bosom. I stroked her long, soft hair like I used to when she was a little girl. "I want you to always feel free to be exactly who you are. I don't want you being anyone else. I love you just as you are." I was trying hard to hold it together—for her. I needed to be strong for my big little girl.

"Mom, it just sucks. I get awesome grades. I've never been in trouble at school. I receive awards all of the time. I made all-star band, and I was just nominated as president of our STEM club."

I gaped as she sprung the big news out of nowhere. *Wow, my brilliant daughter was just nominated to be president for the Science, Technology, Engineering, and Mathematics club for the entire school.* "Eva, honey, that's fantastic! I didn't know you were running for office."

"I wasn't, but I think I'm going to run now since I've been nominated and all. Besides, it'll look great on my college resume."

"Absolutely, you should totally run. You'd make an awesome president," I said proudly, kissing her softly on the forehead.

"Anyway... I do all this good stuff. I always get home before curfew, and I hardly ask you and Dad for anything. Then, when I finally ask to go out, Dad says I'm too young to be thinking about boys. Is he kidding?! I'm sixteen! Tons of girls my age have boyfriends!"

"Honey, I know. I'm so sorry," I cooed, rubbing the back of her head and her back gently as she cried. "I'm not going to give up working on your dad, sweetie. I promise."

Eva peeled away from my chest and turned her wet, disappointed face toward me. "Yeah, good luck with that."

As she sobbed uncontrollably, I began wringing my hands. *This has to stop!* I tell myself that I'm putting my foot down the moment I'm back in Mason's presence. I wasn't letting this go.

Five sexless nights had done the trick. Eva was going out on a date.

At five o'clock, I knocked on her door to stealthily deliver her the good news. I'd told her we were all going out for dinner, which was true. But Eva wouldn't be joining us.

When I opened the door, she was dressed but lying across her bed like a starfish. I could tell by her expression when she looked up at me that she wasn't looking forward to going anywhere.

"You're wearing that?" I asked. She wore a plain t-shirt and jeans, and even though the clothes were hers, it wasn't her usual daring sense of style.

"Yeah," she mumbled.

"I'll let you know when it's time to go. Mr. Donner will drop you and Knight off at the mall," I said matter-of-factly.

Eva practically fell out of bed as she stumbled to her feet. "*Wh*... What did you just say? Knight's here?" she gasped.

Exactly the response I expected. I beam at her. "Yes. Your father invited him over. He had Mr. Donner pick him up from the UCLD campus. They're going to have a brief discussion, then you two will be on your way."

"You're kidding?!"

It was the first time I'd seen her smile in almost a week, and I had to do everything to keep from bursting open with joy. "Nope."

My sweet daughter's loving personality made a triumphant comeback. Without saying another word, she pounced and wrapped her arms tightly around me. I melted into her, pressing my nose against her hair and taking in the scent of her mango shampoo. I started to feel whole again.

"Thank you, Mommy!" Eva gushed.

"My sweet girl... You're growing up so fast." I was on the verge of tears, which I tried to hide when she released me from her embrace.

"You're going to make sure that Dad doesn't say anything crazy to Knight, right?" she asked, quirking a brow.

I chuckled. "Of course. I'll be in the room, rest assured." She quickly grabbed me again for another strong hug, and I kissed her on the cheek.

"I need to find something to wear!" she squealed in excitement.

"I don't like this, Liza. Not one bit."

I sat calmly on the sofa, watching my husband pace his study like a maniac.

"Relax, Mason. Just talk to him. Besides, Greg will be close by. It's going to be fine," I reassured.

"No—not *close by*. Donner will be *right fucking there* with them at all times," he growled.

I sighed. "Don't be ridiculous. Sit down."

There was a knock on the door, and Mason stopped mid-pace and took a seat beside me on the sofa. "Come in," he called out. The door opened, revealing Greg Donner, a handsome, fit gentleman in his early thirties. By his side was Knight, a young man with dark blond hair and the same height as Ford, but a tad leaner to my son's more muscular build. Wearing jeans with a light blue button-up under a black jacket, he had an expression that looked hopeful. I silently prayed my husband wouldn't change that.

"Sir, ma'am... Mr. Thibodeau," Greg introduced.

I started to rise, but Mason held me in place with one hand while gingerly waving Knight in with the other. I turned to him on my left and flashed him a displeased frown before shifting ahead to greet Knight with a genuine smile. I felt Mason's hand going slack, so I stood quickly, throwing him for a loop. He unwillingly stood up with me.

"Mr. and Mrs. Pope, thanks so much for inviting me here," Knight said in a strong, confident tone. He'd surely grown since I last saw him. In fact, he'd grown a lot.

Dare I say he's a cutie? Way to go, Eva!

"It's good to see you again, Knight. It's been a long time," I said as I took his extended hand and shook it.

"Yes, it certainly has been, Mrs. Pope," he smiled. He then extended his hand to my husband. "Mr. Pope, good to see you." Mason glared at his hand, then at him.

Sweet Jesus, Pope—give it a rest.

Thankfully, Knight wasn't swayed. He kept his hand out there until Mason reluctantly took it. I saw the flinch at the corner of Knight's mouth before glancing at their joined hands. I could tell by the way Knight's fingers curved that Mason was squeezing him tighter than a regular firm handshake. It was the handshake of a skeptical father afraid of letting go of his little girl. Perhaps Knight had already witnessed this with his own father when his older sister had started dating. Something told me he was empathetic to Mason.

"Have a seat," Mason said after releasing his hand, gesturing to the matching burgundy leather sofa facing him and me. We all took our seats.

"Thank you. So, how's Ford doing at Stanford?" Knight asked, breaking the ice. I cringed internally. Ford was a sore subject for Mason. I didn't even bother looking next to me as I took the liberty to rave over my only son.

"Ford has another full load of classes this term. He's still excelling in all of his courses," I beamed.

"He's a brilliant guy. Kinda bummed I didn't get a chance to hang out with him over the summer. My family and I spent time with my grandma in New Orleans. She recently passed."

"Oh no, I'm so sorry for your loss," I said regretfully. I turned to Mason, who looked stern, but I could tell he's softening just a little. I had no doubt he knew about Knight's late grandmother since that would've been something he'd shared with Eva through text.

"Thank you. She was ill for a long time. We're relieved she no longer has to suffer. I'm just glad we had a chance to spend time with her."

"Of course," I compassionately remarked. I glanced at Mason, who nodded quietly.

The three of us sat in awkward silence for a few beats, and I grew eager to hop into the topic of the date. I wanted to get it over with. I had an anxious sixteen-year-old waiting in the wings.

"So... Eva," I prompted. The mere mention of my daughter's name turned the once confident, self-assured young man into a bashful young boy.

Aw! He really likes her!

Mason cut in, breaking his silence. "Why do you want to date our daughter?" I frowned at him.

"Well, sir, I like Eva. A lot, actually. I've always liked her. I've been wanting to ask her out for a while," Knight responded. I fought back a grin.

"And there are no girls your age at UCLD who you can date?" Mason lobbed.

I turned to my left, seething. *What in the hell are you doing, Pope?!* He ignored me, keeping his eyes trained on Knight.

"Mr. Pope, Ford and I are the same age, but he graduated before me. I just started going to UCLD. With the exception of maybe a former classmate or two from high school, I haven't had a chance to meet anyone. And besides, I only like Eva. There's no other girl quite like her."

I'm swooning on my daughter's behalf. He checked all the boxes—handsome, polite, not shaken by my husband, and he was totally smitten by my daughter. I didn't care what Mason thought. They were going on that date tonight.

"I agree, but surely there's someone else you'd better connect with. I mean—what interests do you even share with Eva? Do you play an instrument?" my husband interrogated.

I wondered why he was asking questions he'd already known the answer to. Maybe he wanted to see the young man sweat. Who knew what was floating around in that thick skull of his?

"Well, no—I don't. But I dig that Eva does—"

"What about books?" Mason asked, cutting off Knight. "Eva read one hundred and fifty books last year and is well on her way to reaching two hundred this year."

I closed my eyes to try and will away the uncomfortable exchange.

"Sir... I'll admit—I don't read a lot for leisure. Over the summer, when I wasn't in New Orleans with my grandmother, I was training hard for baseball. I understand that books are Eva's thing. Yet another thing I admire about her. She's unlike any girl I know."

Knight remained composed after everything Mason threw his way. Now, I completely understood why my daughter was so eager to go out with him. A huge smile took over my insides and gradually made its way to my face.

"What's your major?" Mason grilled again.

My grin was wiped clear off, and I began screaming at my husband internally. *Pope—hang it up! You already know all the answers! You did a background check on him!*

"Sir, I'm undecided at the moment."

"*Undecided?*" Mason scoffed. "Surely you don't believe you'll be guaranteed a contract with the National Baseball League?"

Jesus, please take the wheel.

"Of course not, sir. Out of thirty-five thousand NCAA baseball players at any given year, only two percent of them will go pro. I know the odds are definitely not in my favor. Therefore, education is a number one priority for me. I'm leaning between three different majors at the moment. I've decided to take all of my gen-ed courses first before narrowing my major down to one."

Score one for Knight. Mason didn't show his hand, but I knew Knight hadn't struck out with him—no pun intended.

"Look, Mr. Pope—I totally understand your reluctance with me taking out your daughter. But I want you to know that I care for Eva, and I would never take advantage of her."

I sighed after he directly addressed the elephant in the room. Knight had pricked Mason right in the chest, and he reacted accordingly.

"Oh, I know you won't. I'll see to it," Mason snapped.

Classic, Pope. Real classic.

"Mason..." I placed my hand on his lap to placate him. He paid me no mind, keeping Knight in the crosshairs.

"Here's what's going to happen," my husband said with authority. "Donner will drive you and our daughter to the mall. He will know your whereabouts at all times via the tracker on Eva's phone. You will see your movie. You will have your pizza. After pizza, Donner will take you back to your dorm, and our daughter *will* be home by ten-thirty. Is that understood?"

I tried to mask my baffled emotions but failed. I turned to look at Knight, amazed at how he remained calm and understanding. Whatever he was smoking, I wanted some of it. Drugs were probably the only way to tolerate Mason Pope and his overzealous ways.

"Absolutely, Mr. Pope," Knight nodded in gratitude. "I appreciate the opportunity to take out your daughter."

My eyes grew wide, and I clenched my mouth shut to keep it from doing the same. Knight was willing to take scraps, adhering to my husband's outlandish demands just for the chance to take Eva out on a date. I was astounded. I had even more respect for the young man.

"Very well," Mason acquiesced. "I'll be keeping a close eye on you. One misstep—"

"Mason... *enough*," I scolded in a whisper. I'd had enough of his intimidating demeanor, insane demands, and compounding threats. "Knight, I trust that our Eva will be in very good hands. It was nice seeing you again. Wait here, we'll go grab her." I forced a smile past my irritation toward my husband as we proceeded to leave the study.

Once Mason and I were on the other side of the door, I pounced, slapping him hard on the arm. "Cut it out!" I whisper-yelled.

"What?! I had to let him know he can't be fucking around with our daughter, figuratively or literally," he whispered back.

I shook my head in exasperation as we made the long trek toward Eva's room. "As if he'd have the chance. Donner will be there, for goodness sake."

"I don't want him even thinking about sneaking our daughter off to some dirty restroom to... *do his deed*," he said in anger. The man was impossible.

We continued with our back and forth concerning what he

thought Knight would try with Eva, and I countered him each time. "You are being ridiculous. Knight would never do that." We finally reached our daughter's bedroom door. After all these years, I hadn't gotten over how enormous our house was. I swore we were downsizing once all the girls moved out.

"Like I said, I don't want that asshole even *thinking* about trying anything," Mason growled quietly.

"He's not an asshole, Mason. He's a very nice young man."

"Anyone who wants to take out any daughter of mine is an asshole."

"*Our* daughters. And I disagree. I really like this one," I smiled. Mason glowered, and I couldn't help but chuckle. Before I could get out a good laugh, the door swung open, revealing one of the most beautiful sights I ever saw. I was rendered speechless.

No longer in jeans and a t-shirt, my angel was clothed in a red skater dress, denim jacket, and knee-high stretch black boots. Her beautiful brown hair was propped up in an adorable messy bun. Her light makeup was subtle and age-appropriate with just a touch of gloss on her lips. She was simply perfect.

"Mom! Dad!" she exclaimed. Her resurrected glowing smile melted my heart. Before I could speak, she threw her arms around me, and I hugged her tight. Taking in her scent yet again, I suddenly longed for that rambunctious little girl I once knew. My sweet little girl was growing up fast, and the thought depressed me.

"What in the hell are you wearing?" Mason griped, pulling me from my reverie. I rolled my eyes.

"Clothes, Dad," Eva smirked as we released one another. She approached her father on her tippy toes and kissed him lovingly on the cheek, smearing lip-gloss there.

He observed her with a skeptical eye. "That dress is way too short. And those boots..."

"Yes, the dress is shorter so you can actually see them," she countered.

"Those are hooker boots," he scowled.

I shook my head. He was too much. "They are not hooker boots. And you had no problem with her wearing them before now. You've seen her in them many times," I reminded him.

Eva nodded in agreement. "I wore these to Sunday dinner at Grandma and Grandpa Pope's more than once. Even Grandpa said he liked them."

Mason was clearly outnumbered, and I could tell he didn't like it one bit. I wanted to laugh in his face, but by no means did I want to anger Senõr Ego Maniac enough to change his mind. Not to say he'd make Eva stay home to spite me, but I didn't want to chance it. Countless tears were shed, and many loud arguments were had to bring us to this point. I wasn't going to let my pride ruin Eva's night.

"Well, the boy is waiting in my study," Mason said with a gruff voice. I knew he was pouting. He didn't want her to go, but Eva only saw victory. Freedom.

"Thank you, Daddy," she sighed. She hugged him tight, squeezing him hard like a snake. His stubbornness had no other choice but to give in as a semblance of a smile finally surfaced. He kissed her twice on the forehead, and I exhaled in relief, happy that he was letting her do this.

"No funny business—you hear me?" Mason staunchly warned her. "Donner will be close by."

"I know," she replied, unshaken in her excited state.

"And if he touches you inappropriately, I've instructed Donner to shoot first and to *not* ask questions later," he said matter-of-factly.

"Mason!" I snapped. Eva laughed.

"I am not joking," he said, stone-faced.

Indeed, I'd known he wasn't joking, but Eva had just caught on. Her smile dissolved. "Dad! Calm down—*geez!*"

"I want you safe and at home in one piece at ten-thirty. You got that?" he ordered.

Eva closed her eyes and shook her head before hugging him one last time. *Gotta love him, right?* "Dad, I'll be fine. Promise."

Minutes later, Donner was holding the front door open for Knight and an excited Eva to go through it. Knight stood aside to let Eva walk out first. *Such a gentleman.* Once the two were out, Eva spun around to face her father and me. She mouthed "Thank you" to us, and we returned a smile.

I blew her a kiss. "Have fun!"

"But not too much," Mason grumbled with a scowl.

Eva brushed away her father's rude remark as Knight turned back to face Mason and me. "Thank you, Mr. and Mrs. Pope. It was a pleasure speaking to you both. I hope to see you again soon."

"Take care, Knight," I beamed. I made the mistake of looking at Mason and caught him giving Knight a death stare. I was sure the young man didn't catch it. He'd already turned on his heel and headed to the car with Eva.

Lord, help us all.

The twins and I wanted to go to a nice little Italian restaurant for dinner. Mason insisted we go to the pizza place at the mall. It didn't take a genius to know what he was up to. Thankfully, he was outnumbered. The twins and I couldn't dream of ruining this night for Eva.

At nine-thirty, Mason positioned himself on the sofa nearest to the front door. He was like a guard dog, waiting for his eldest daughter to return. All I could do was shake my head. He needed to let our little girl grow up.

I left him to it, walking to our room to change out of my jeans and into loungewear. Just as I was headed back to the main room, my phone rang on the bedside table. I was surprised to see it was Ford. He'd never called me that late. I was on high alert when I picked up.

"Ford?"

"Mom—*hey*. Did I catch you at a bad time?"

"No, not at all. What's going on with you?"

"First of all, how are *you?*"

His question took me aback. I couldn't remember the last time he'd asked about me first. I was really worried. *Did something happen at school?*

"I'm doing well. Earlier today, we saw Eva out on her first date," I smirked.

"You're kidding!" He sounded beyond stunned, and I chuckled. "Oh—you're serious! Dad actually let Eva go out? On a date? Who is this mythical creature?"

"Knight Thibodeau."

"No freaking way!"

"I know, and it wasn't an easy feat. However, your dad finally gave in. I like Knight. He's a really nice young man."

"Knight's a cool dude. Very down to earth. If I had to pick anyone for Eva, it would be him."

"I agree. He's well-mannered and smart…"

"He's an all-around good guy. I just feel bad for him. And for Eva," Ford said soberly.

I blinked several times. "Why do you say that?"

"You know why. Dad. You know how tough he can be."

I could tell Ford was holding back, but I didn't want to press him. He'd called me for a reason. "Is everything okay with you?"

"It's great," he said. "I just got selected to take part in an internship program. I get to work full-time with pay in the spring and earn twelve credit hours in the process."

"Wow, that's fantastic news, Ford. Where will you be working?"

"At Zinfinite."

"Zinfinite? In Los Derivas?"

"The very one."

My heart leapt for joy. "God—Ford, that's wonderful!" My son was coming home… at least temporarily. I was ecstatic.

"I know, I'm stoked. They want me to come out there for the day this Wednesday to meet with the vendor relations team I'll be working with."

"That's great! Do you think you'll have time to have a meal with your folks before you head back?"

"I think so. I'll keep you posted. One last thing..." From the way his voice dropped, I braced for something bad. "I'm still on my accelerated track to graduate in a year and a half. In order to do that, I'll need to take some transferable courses." He paused. "At UCLD."

My eyes narrowed in confusion. "Why is that a problem? You can handle working along with the course load, right?"

"I can. But who else attends UCLD, Mom?"

His tone suggested that I already knew the answer to his question. I pondered for a beat. "Knight goes there." It would be nice seeing the two of them hanging around the house again, just like old times.

"Besides Knight," he said. I had no clue who else he was referring to. I was genuinely at a loss. He tried helping me out. "I'll just say Dad is going to have a problem with me taking classes there, even if it's only for a semester."

Realization hit me like a tidal wave. I knew exactly who he was referring to. I felt a pang in my chest. "Ford, we need to sit down—the three of us. You, your father and me. We need to put this whole Harper thing to rest. We've moved way past that incident from high school. It's been two years."

"That's just it. *You've* moved past it. Dad hasn't."

I hated seeing Ford walk on eggshells because of his father. I didn't want him living like that. I missed carefree Ford. I wanted my son back.

"Look, I won't tell your dad the good news about your internship at Zinfinite. The three of us will do dinner or lunch when you get here next week and talk about it then. We'll also broach the UCLD situation. I'll back you up. And if it's any reassurance, your father supports your accelerated graduation plan. All we need to do is get him to think logically. Taking these classes at UCLD is something you must do. And if you happen to see Harper while you're here, you're an adult now."

"Mom, I appreciate the optimism, but I don't see this ending very well. That's why I'm telling you first. Maybe you can prime Dad before I get there. You know how much he hates surprises. Tell him about the internship and the classes at UCLD tonight. He'll be less pissed if he's had a few days to mull it over."

With the phone propped on my shoulder, I massaged my temples with both hands. I'd just gotten over the hurdle of getting Eva out on a date. Now, I have to open up old wounds and usher in the healing between Ford and his father. It was something I'd been putting off.

Being a wife and mother caught in the middle positively sucked.

Six

Ford

I was grateful my dad hadn't freaked out about me taking classes at UCLD like I thought he would. My mother had smoothed things over ahead of time, so I didn't have to walk into a storm when we met for lunch at a restaurant near LRPI headquarters. I'd explained to my father that the transferable courses I needed to take were available in the evenings at UCLD, allowing me time to work my internship during the day. My very informative visit with my future team at Zinfinite and a pleasant meal with my folks had made it a good day.

Once Mom and Dad had returned to the office, I headed over to UCLD. I'd been nervous to reach out to Harper ahead of time to let her know I was coming. Instead, I decided to go with the element of surprise. I had been certain I'd find her roaming around the building where most of the hospitality courses were held. So, after stopping by the admissions office to get the ball rolling for spring registration, I roamed the area where I'd suspected she would be. I waited. I waited some more. Time definitely wasn't on my side because I'd have to leave Los Derivas soon and drive back to Stanford.

Right as I contemplated giving up, I looked up as several students crossed the nearby courtyard. One of them, a familiar silhouette in my periphery, made me do a double-take. My eyes set on a young girl with long, light brown hair wearing a white skirt decked in dark flowers, a long-sleeved blue jacket over a black top, and a white scarf. It was a unique style that only one person I knew very well could pull off. She walked fast, looking distraught. I tried to tell myself it wasn't her but couldn't. It *had* to be her. To be safe, I yelled out a name to rule her out. *If she turns toward my voice, it's her.*

"Eva?!"

She stopped dead in her tracks and spun my way.

What in the world is my little sister doing here?! She's still in high school!

"Ford?!"

She was just as stunned to see me. We met each other halfway in a jog.

"Why are you here?" I blurted out in an accusatory tone.

"I should be asking you the same thing!" she countered.

"You first."

"Nuh-uh… You don't even go to school here. You're supposed to be at Stanford."

I shrugged in resignation. "Mom and Dad wanted it to be a surprise for you and the twins. I'm coming home in the spring to work an internship at Zinfinite. I'll be taking night classes here for the semester." She squealed, knocking the wind out of me when she jumped and threw her arms around my neck. I laughed in amusement.

"That is so awesome!"

"Yeah—it's a sweet deal. Now, your turn. Why are you here?"

When her gaze dropped to the ground, I quickly recalled that she'd been crying before I spotted her. It was obvious she was ditching school, something Eva Pope had never done. This was not good. She was going to fuck it up for the twins and me if our parents found out their perfect daughter was a juvenile delinquent. Here I was, thinking my father was finally in a place to lay off me when it came to Harper…

"You're skipping class to see Knight, aren't you?" I smirked. She sighed, defeated.

"Look, our first date last weekend was bad. Dad had Donner

on our ass the *entire time*. Knight didn't even kiss me goodnight! He couldn't!"

This wasn't good. It meant Mason Pope was taking his level of intrusion to another level with the next crop of Pope kids. Despite her grim state of affairs, I wanted to cheer my little sister up. I hated seeing her this way.

"You wanna go grab a milkshake?"

Not long after, the two of us sat in a booth at a fast-food spot on campus with our strawberry milkshakes in tow.

"I switched cell phones with Cynthia at school so I could sneak here," Eva confessed, unprovoked.

Both of my brows raised. "You did *what?*"

"Dad tracks our whereabouts on our cells. You know that, right?" I answered with a single nod as she continued. "Look, I had to see Knight. I felt awful about Saturday night. I don't want him to stop seeing me just because Dad's a pit bull."

"You need to talk to Mom."

"I did talk to her!" she raged. She toned it down when others began staring at us. "It got me nowhere. She's always going to side with him."

"Listen to me. Mom trusts you. As long as she does, she will be your ally. Eventually, Dad will cave. But once you lose her trust, she will let him run loose. That's when you're screwed."

"He never caves," Eva hissed. "Mom's voice doesn't matter in that marriage, Ford. You know I'm right."

"False. You obviously haven't been paying attention. When Mom's not happy, nobody's happy—Dad included. You just need to give her time to work things out on your behalf. You may not see it, but she's working behind the scenes."

Eva grunted in frustration, rubbing her face in her palms.

"Yeah, I know," I commiserate. "That's the cost of being the prized daughter of two wacky billionaires in Arcadia's Crest. You'll get over it... Brat." My little sis leaned over the table and bopped me across the forehead for that.

"I almost wish for a normal, working-class family. At least I'd be able to date who I want," she pouted.

"No—fuck that. You don't want to be normal. Struggling to pay for school and catching the Metro everywhere. You have a driver and a trust fund, Eva. And this summer, you can just walk into Pope Tower without an interview and work for one of the largest multinational companies in the world. How many of your peers can say that?"

Eva rolled her eyes. "Whatever. I don't care. I just want a life, Ford. Don't you want your own life? Aren't you sick of having to live up to some unrealistic expectation Dad has set for you?"

I shrugged. "Any good parent wants their children to do better than them. Yeah, Pops can be hard, but it's all in love."

She groaned. "I used to think that. I'm not sure anymore."

"Get out of here. You just don't know how good you have it. This is your first hiccup as the star child of the family. Eva Pope could do no wrong."

"Whatever," she brushed off.

"Change of topic. Why were you crying? Did you find Knight?"

Her expression fell flat. "Yep. He was just as shocked to see me as you were. He did give me a hug and a stupid peck on the cheek before telling me to go back to school."

Did little sis just get dumped? I wondered. "Did he say anything else?"

"He said he likes me entirely too much to piss off my folks," she uttered in exasperation.

I responded with a shit-eating grin, delighting in the fact that Knight Thibodeau was the strait-laced do-gooder I'd always thought he was. "Who would've thought Knight would be so smitten by you that he tells you to return to school instead of bringing you straight to his dorm room?"

"Maybe he just wanted to get rid of me. What if he's dating some girl on campus? That would explain why he was so shocked to see me," she said sullenly.

"Nope—I don't think that's it. He wasn't expecting to see you here. You live and attend school in Arcadia's Crest. His reaction was to be expected. Between you and me, I think he really likes you. We talked a few months ago. He wanted to know if it was okay to ask you out."

"He told me about that."

"And did he tell you that I told him good luck getting through Mason Pope?"

For the first time since we ran into each other, Eva laughed. "Yeah, he did. When I asked him how his talk with Dad went, he brushed it off like it was nothing. He said Dad was cool. Dad? Cool? No, Dad is fucking nuts."

This time, she made me laugh. "He can be high-strung at times, but Mom balances him out. That's why they're perfect for each other." Eva responded with an eye roll before I switched topics. "Back to what I was saying earlier about Mom working behind the scenes. She'd spoken to Dad about me coming home to work the internship and to take classes here. At lunch today, Dad took the news surprisingly well."

My sister scrunched her nose, looking perplexed. "Why wouldn't he be okay with that?"

"You were young and oblivious when all hell broke loose a couple years back. You know... With Harper Benton."

"Right—the infamous Harper incident," she nodded.

"The very one where I got shit on for skipping school. The same as you're doing now."

"I'll be back before final period, Ford," she groaned.

"How'd you get here? You mentioned switching phones with your friend, but you know Dad tracks—"

"Yeah, yeah—Dad tracks our cars. He hardly lets me drive myself anyway. He has Donner chauffeuring me everywhere. Not only did I borrow Cynthia's phone, but her car, too."

Although I shook my head at my sister's newfound mischief, pride swelled up in me. "Anyway, after I ditched class to be with Harper, she'd pretty much been banned from the estate."

A few beats had gone by when Eva's eyes opened wide in what appeared to be sudden realization. "I think I just saw her here on campus not long before I ran into you. She was holding hands with some guy. Well, at least I thought it was Harper. You know... Honestly, I'm not all that sure. I was too upset and couldn't see through my stupid tears."

I ignored the last part because my entire world had just bottomed out. The way I held myself together in front of my sister even impressed me, since my head was on the verge of exploding. *Maybe Eva was mistaken. Maybe she saw someone else.* No matter how hard I tried to counter my worst fears, my heart remained wedged in my gut.

Had Harper moved on? But we'd never officially broken up! Did she cheat?! Okay, fine... I got my cock sucked at school, but I never slept with or kissed anyone but *Harper.*

I asked my sister one of the many pressing questions cracking my skull. "Did she recognize you?"

"No, because if it was her, I didn't want her seeing me. She'd probably tell her dad, who'd tell our dad—"

"She wouldn't have."

Eva shrugged. "I wasn't chancing it, so I hid behind a building until she passed."

I needed to find Harper. My sanity couldn't take the uncertainty that took residence.

I'd thrown in the towel after over an hour of roaming aimlessly around campus. My plan of surprising her didn't pan out as I'd hoped. I had to let her know I was here. Back in my parked car, I took my other smartphone from the glovebox. No one had the number to this phone. A month ago, I'd created a fake social media account. I was going to finally reach out to Harper using it.

Harper would get a kick out of my alias. She'd never let me live down the time when I was a little kid and confused a penguin in a documentary with a puffin that we'd seen in person when Mom had taken us to the zoo, Harper included. From that point on, Harper would call me Puffin every now and again. I smiled at the memory as I drafted her a direct message.

Puffin P: Harper, it's Ford.

I sighed in relief when I saw her read receipt. She didn't respond right away, so I held my breath. I pondered the notion that my sister was mistaken when she thought she'd seen Harper. With each passing second, I grew more anxious. *Give her a minute, Pope. She might be in the middle of class.*

Staring at the phone while nothing was happening was worse than standing over a pot and waiting for it to boil. To kill the hair-pulling tension, I lay the phone face down on the passenger seat and waited with my head resting on the steering wheel. I took several deep, calming breaths. Before I knew it, the device finally pinged. I couldn't get it fast enough.

Harper B: Hey, you! What's with the name, haha! How are you?

Ilit up like Christmas, seeing her words show up on the screen.

Puffin P: Doing good. I'm in town.

Harper B: You home?

Puffin P: Yep. I'm doing an internship in Los Derivas next term.

Harper B: At LRPI?

Puffin P: No, Zinfinite Corp. Also taking night classes at your school to transfer back to Stanford in the fall. Are you on campus now?

As soon as I hit send, I second-guessed my approach. It had taken her what felt like ages to reply.

Harper B: Yes. Are you here?

Puffin P: I'm parked on campus. Are you free to meet?

I waited on pins and needles. It was as if she took her sweet time, plotting each solitary word. Harper had never been a calculating individual, which is why it was an easy fear to brush off. She was probably sitting in a lecture or something. I was relieved when the bubbles began to appear by her name as she typed.

Harper B: I'm in my service management class right now. Will you be around in two hours?

Hell, I was supposed to be halfway to Stanford by then. Traffic was going to suck something awful if I didn't leave in the next fifteen minutes. If I remained in Los Derivas for a couple hours, then spent time with Harper, there was no telling when I'd be on the road. Because of that, I decided to remain in town until the morning. I'd get a hotel room and hope Harper would join me…

Puffin P: Yes. You wanna grab dinner?

I couldn't wait to see her. It had been two months since I'd touched her. I missed that girl like crazy. I hoped she was ready for me.

She'd taken way too long to respond again.

Harper B: I have dinner plans. You're welcome to join us. I'll introduce you to Aiden.

I swore I heard tires screeching. I even searched out the window to catch someone doing donuts in the visitor parking lot. *Who the fuck is Aiden?!* My sister's earlier words echoed in my mind, ripping my chest wide open.

"I think I just saw her here on campus not long before I ran into you. She was holding hands with some guy."

Puffin P: Who is Aiden?

I hit send, hoping for the best but anticipating the worst. Nothing could prepare me for what would come next.

Harper B: Ford, when was the last time you spoke to my dad? Aiden is my fiancé. I'd like you to meet him.

I remember completely shutting down as opposed to reacting with rage. Instead of replying, I turned on the ignition and made the five-hour drive back to my dorm at Stanford.

My rage was delayed, but it came.

How could she so casually invite me to join her and her *fiancé* for dinner! Did she honestly think I'd agree to that bullshit? How dare she pretend that what we had never mattered?! She'd known what lengths I was willing to go through just to be with her, yet she'd dropped me like a bad habit without warning. She'd *really* moved on.

She was fucking engaged and still in college.

Who was this chump, anyway?

I sat in an empty section of the campus library on a Saturday to find out. My emotions had been running rampant, with restlessness taking over for the past three nights. Finally, the person I've been waiting for showed up. He was late.

"Gerts, what took you so long?" I said, exasperated.

He took a seat across from me at the table. "My bad, dude. It's been a busy day," the gangly blond geek muttered.

I swallowed down the tension lodged in my throat. "I've heard good things about you."

"I'm the best, especially for the money. What can I do for you?"

"I need you to pull intel on someone in Los Derivas. Whatever you can find."

"Easy enough. What details do you have to get me going?"

"Name is Aiden Cramer. Senior at UC in Los Derivas."

"Good enough. I'll handle the rest and give you a summary of what I come up with. If you want more, then we can talk price."

"If I like what I see, I'll give you five grand to move forward."

Gerts broke his laid-back character, sitting forward in his chair with wide eyes. "Whoa—dude. You serious? I normally charge a few hundred here and there. We're struggling college kids for Christ's sake."

"I hate to be *that asshole*, but five grand to me is like a hundred bucks to you," I said, nonchalant.

He actually slapped a palm across his forehead. "Hell, you're Mason Pope's kid. Doesn't he have someone on payroll that does this, but with better resources? Why aren't you going that route?"

"I have my reasons."

Gerts smirked. "So, you're tracking someone Daddy wouldn't approve of? Who is he?"

My eyes narrowed in irritation. *He'll just dig and find out anyway.* "My ex's new fiancé."

The dipshit was beyond amused. "A lost love, huh? Someone Pops don't approve of? If that's the case, I got you."

"Good. When can you report back?"

"Let's meet here again Monday night. I'll have something for you then."

Shortly after my meeting with Gerts, I made the trek back to my dorm. It's a standard sunny day in Cali, but my insides are anything but.

Why couldn't she wait for me?

Why didn't she fight for me like I've been fighting for her?

Why was she able to give up so easily and move on without me?

I felt so betrayed and couldn't see past it. Harper had known how much I loved her. The last thing I'd said to her before Dad swooped in and blocked me from ever contacting her again was: "*Wait for me.*" She couldn't even do that.

Hell, I'd just seen her over summer break! I'd managed to sneak away from my family for a few hours and go to the Marriott in Los Derivas where she worked. Based on our time together, I thought everything between us was just fine. Hell, had she been engaged then? Was she fucking around with this Aiden fool and hadn't bothered telling me?

I tried thinking back to two months ago. It hadn't occurred to me that anything out of the ordinary was going on. Harper was just as sweet and as loving to me as she'd always been. She even said she couldn't wait to see me again next time.

We'd even made love.

My heart stilled at the bittersweet memory. While taking a lunch break to see me, she'd managed to get her hands on a master key. We'd spent quality time talking in an unoccupied suite in the sitting area up front. Talking had soon led to kissing. Eventually, we could no longer fight the feeling. I'd ended up carrying her to the bedroom and made her come three times.

I hated leaving, but I knew my Dad would be suspicious if I'd stayed away for too long. He was always riding my ass. Thoughts of lunch with my parents last week flooded my mind. Dad had been nonchalant over the news of me taking classes at UCLD. It was unlike him. That made it apparent that he'd known about Harper's engagement. It was why he no longer cared about me going to Harper's school for a semester.

"When was the last time you spoke to my dad?"

Of course, Mason knew. I felt like the biggest tool. *Fuck!*

I could've done one of two things: play the hand I was dealt and try hard to move on or fight for what was mine, regardless of where my father stood.

I believed in my heart of hearts that she and I belonged together. This wasn't a fling. Harper Benton was the absolute love of my life.

Seven

Ford

On my phone, I had a folder of images just for her. There were pictures of her from when we were together. There were pictures of her taken way before we professed our love to one another—snapshots from our childhood. For good measure, I'd also lifted photos from her social media account... Beautiful photos. Of course, every image of Harper was very beautiful. Beauty was something she never had to fake. It was something she couldn't turn off if she wanted to. It was her very essence.

That digital photo album had gotten a workout for the past ten days, even more than normal. I clung to it as my lifeline in an attempt to diminish feelings of betrayal. If I could see Harper as I always had, perhaps I wouldn't feel the innate desire to scream out my pain in her face or cathartically punch out the asshole who'd taken my place.

Why couldn't she have just waited for me?!

She said she would!

I'd arrived twenty minutes early and sat in the very spot in the library as Saturday. Five minutes before ten, Gerts slid into the seat across from me. Wearing his usual bum-like frayed sweatpants and ratty maroon Stanford t-shirt, he pulled a manila folder from his backpack and placed it on the table facing me. Sliding the papers out, they were upside down from where he sat, but the words faced upright for me. He began speaking discreetly, pointing to lines as he went along.

"So—our girl, Harper, apparently doesn't mess with broke dudes. Aiden Cramer… originally from Henderson, Nevada. Son of Steve Cramer, owner of a chain of automotive dealerships. Baby boy is an art major, going against the grain of his Pops." Gerts snickered as he pounded his index finger on a photo. Staring back at me on the page was a dickwad hipster with long blond hair and a lumberjack-looking, button-up long-sleeved shirt. I scoffed. *I thought that look went out of style when I was a baby!*

Harper, Harper, Harper. For shame!

"Needless to say, he's not aiming to get into the family business. Unless the fam has a street pharmacy side gig I'm not aware of," Gerts snorted. I rolled my eyes as he flipped the page. "The irony of that is *little Aiden* apparently got away with some major shit growing up in Nevada, including avoiding a drug possession charge back in high school several years back."

I gaped at him, stunned. *You've gotta be fucking kidding me.* Russ had to have known about this. Hell, did Harper even know?

"That's right, man," Gerts smirked, accurately picking up on my extreme shock.

She had to know who she was engaged to. I honestly couldn't see Harper intentionally ignoring the fact that her new fiancé had a history with drugs. It was inconceivable.

I sat outside the commons area with my secret phone in tow. With her cell phone number already cued, all I needed to do was hit the call button. A charge of fear rushed through me in waves. Before the end of this call, I'll either be a hero or a total villain. Either way, she needed to steer clear of him. He was bad news. I finally bossed up and called her. She picked up just before the fourth ring, setting my nerves ablaze.

"Hello?" said a sweet, familiar voice.

"Harper? This is Ford."

"God, Ford… Are you okay? I've been messaging you all week—"

I felt sick to my stomach all over again but decided to play it off with a bullshit response. "Sorry about that. I had issues with my phone and couldn't reinstall the app, so I decided to call you now instead. Did I catch you at a bad time?"

"No—not at all. What's up? How have you been? How's Stanford?"

Really? Small talk? If she wanted to play that game, I'd play it, too. "Stanford is Stanford. Are you doing well?"

"Not too bad. Classes are already kicking my butt. I'm just glad it's almost over. Oh… sorry. I know you have a ways to go," she laughed awkwardly. That made me glare straight ahead as if she were in the room. She knew I was on an accelerated program, so why had she said that?

"I'll be done three semesters from now."

"Wow, really?" she gasped. "Aren't you just a sophomore now?"

"No, I'm essentially a junior and a half. The accelerated program. I've told you this."

"That's right—I'd forgotten you were on the fast track. Anxious to run the family business, I see."

Her seemingly light-hearted wisecrack stung like hell. Not only because she had clearly been a part of my future plans and had known it, but her tone had taken me aback. I'd known this girl my entire life, and she'd never been bitchy to me or anyone. That had to have come out of her mouth wrong.

"Who knows, maybe I'll be the future CEO of Zinfinite instead," I volleyed.

"I have no doubt you could do it. You've always exceeded everyone's expectations," she praised. "But why would you want to climb up the corporate ladder elsewhere when you have LRPI on a silver platter?"

The girl was twisting my heart without even knowing it. Or

maybe she didn't care. She'd known I'd always wanted to make a name for myself, away from my father's influence and control.

Part of me hoped the whole Aiden thing was her idea of a joke. Next fall, we were supposed to be together once and for all. Instead, I sat there trying to figure out the best way to tell her about her drug-possessing paramour who was occupying my rightful place.

Harper was supposed to be marrying me.

"Well... Between you and me, I'd like to try out my own thing and see how it goes," I finally responded after taking a pause.

"I totally get that. And you should get out there... spread your wings. I'm so proud of you, Ford."

Her patronizing tone made her sound more like the mature older friend she would've been had we'd not fallen in love. I had to get to the bottom of all this bullshit. "You were telling me over DMs that you were engaged to someone named Aiden. How did that happen?" The instant I said the words, my heart started to thump. It was as if my body's natural defenses were on high alert, preparing for the worst.

"I met him a year ago on campus. We started—"

A *year ago?! Is she fucking kidding me?!* I cut her off mid-sentence. "Were you seeing him when—"

"No! We didn't start dating until recently!"

That didn't make me feel any better. She and I just had sex six weeks ago, so how did she get engaged to someone else so fast? "None of this is adding up, Harper," I tell her.

"Look—I know what you're thinking. Aiden was courting me hard the entire time, but I didn't want to hurt him. I didn't want to hurt you."

"Too late for that. Does he even know about me?"

"He—he knows there was someone back home and that we were having a difficult time being together due to complicated family issues," Harper carefully replied.

Was? Was I now in the past tense? It was obvious, since she'd gotten engaged. "We never discussed this. I thought we were together?" I fought hard not to raise my voice at her, but I was beginning to lose the battle.

"Ford, we have to be realistic here. We are worlds apart—"

My blood started to boil. "I was coming back for you! I'm even taking classes at UCLD for a semester! Why is distance suddenly an issue now?!"

"It's not just the distance in miles, Ford," she sighed. "It's everything else. You know what I'm talking about. You're calling me from a weird number. I can't even come to your family's house anymore, the place where we grew up together. Did you really think things would eventually work out if I can't even sit at the same dinner table with you? Meanwhile, I've already had a number of dinners with my future in-laws. They have welcomed me with open arms."

Is she fucking kidding me right now?!

I was beside myself. "You obviously don't know how much you mean to me—"

"Ford—I *really* have to go right now. I'm late for my study group. Let's finish this discussion tomorrow. We really needed to talk. I'm so sorry I've waited so long to do this."

I was dumbfounded when we ended the call, feeling like someone was playing the cruelest practical joke known to man. She was right. We needed to have this discussion because she was out of her goddamn mind, and I still had to tell her that her so-called fiancé was nothing but trouble. Hopefully, the revelation would knock some sense into her head and bring her back to me, where she belonged.

I had a plan for us that included heading east, and instead, she'd fallen for some hippy burnout and would be pulled in another direction. Would she move to Nevada to help him run his family's car business? Not on my watch.

Love always wins, and I was still madly in love with Harper. Therefore, I would fight.

I was sitting impatiently in my dorm room when my second phone rang at the appointed time. I picked up after the first ring.

"Ford?"

Her voice was reluctant, and I immediately knew whatever she had to say wouldn't fix the unending ache in my belly. I had to be in class after this call. Would I even be in a mindset to attend, or would I be obliterated beyond the point of functioning? I decided to rip the fucking Band-Aid off at warp speed.

"Last time we talked, you mentioned that you'd moved on. Meanwhile, you failed to mention that fact to me prior to that. We were together not even two months ago, and now you're engaged to someone else? Did you just start dating six weeks ago, and that led to his fast proposal?"

"I never said we started dating six weeks ago."

The edge in her voice wasn't lost on me. I frown harshly, as if she could see me. "You said you weren't with him when we were together last. That's what you said."

"It's true… I didn't sleep with him, but we were still spending time together."

I was confused. Were they running around in the same circle? Is that what she meant? That was hard to fathom, being that he's a senior art major, and she was a senior hospitality major. Certainly, at this stage of the game, they weren't taking any of the same courses together. They were about to graduate.

"What am I not getting?" I asked in a confrontational tone. "You said you've already met his parents. You claimed they like you more than my parents ever did. Isn't that what you implied?"

"Well… Yes."

She stayed silent, not adding anything more to her harsh statement. My mother adored her. How could she say that with a clear conscience? She was being dishonest, and I needed clear answers. Spouting off one-word responses wasn't going to cut it. Why was she with this guy and not with me? She'd said she loved me. Had that been a lie?

"I'm not understanding what's going on here, Harper. I asked you again weeks ago after we made love to wait for me. You said you would. You. Said." I made it a point to utter the final two words carefully.

"Ford, you're not being realistic here," she sighed, exasperated. "It never would've worked out. You know it wouldn't have."

I saw nothing but red. "This is a fucking joke!"

"Ford—"

"I had a plan! You were good with the plan—so you said!"

"Ford—"

"I was doing the accelerated program for *you*! For *us*! As soon as I graduated, we were going to take off to Chicago! You said that you wanted to work at the Hyatt Hotels... and I was going to shoot for Boeing! We'd rent a room Downtown until we landed our dream condo in Lincoln Park! Then, I'd launch my business! That was the plan! You agreed!"

"Ford! That's unrealistic!"

What in the hell happened to her? I didn't know this girl anymore. This wasn't the same girl who had encouraged me to stay the course. She wasn't the same one who'd been as desperate as I was for us to finally be together without outside forces flying over our heads.

"What are you talking about?! That's not what you said, Harper!"

"I know what I said," she started in a calm voice. "But reality finally set in. Things were never going to work out between us. Do you want to know what would've happened the moment you pulled the bait-and-switch on your father and took me to Chicago after graduation? Heck, your dad only agreed to your accelerated graduation plan after you promised you'd return to Los Derivas and help him and your mom run the business."

She may have calmed, but I was still worked up. "I said

exactly what I needed to say to set our plan in motion! Once I graduate from college, I no longer have to deal with him! You knew that! You couldn't have waited?!"

I was hyperventilating, tightly clenching my bed quilt with my free hand so I could stay rooted. Once I stood, I knew I'd take out my frustration on the wall or some other object, alarming the other residents.

Why is she doing this to me?! Doesn't she know I love her?!

"I know I told you I'd wait, but I couldn't anymore. I'm sorry. I didn't know how to break away from you. *This*—isn't good for me. This isn't healthy for me or you. I'm going on twenty-three, Ford. I can't keep playing the star-crossed lovers… teenage-love games. It's time for me to grow up," she said in a trembling voice.

And there it was.

Harper had just told me any feelings she may have carried for me were simply out of immaturity. She'd finally outgrown me. My heart dislodged from my stomach and dropped right to the floor.

I couldn't wrap my head around that fact after we'd shared all those years. She had to be a heartless bitch to drop everything we had and take on something so new, with a guy with a fucking police record. I couldn't believe for one second that the Harper Benton I knew could be so heartless and stupid.

Something wasn't right.

"Harper, what's really going on here? Did your father tell you to do this? Was it *my* father? You can tell me. I won't be upset."

"Ford—no. I realized we weren't going anywhere living like this, so I finally allowed myself to move on with Aiden. I am genuinely happy now. Isn't that what you've always wanted for me?"

What in the actual fuck?

"This is all bullshit!" I seethed.

"I want you to be happy, too!" she pleaded. "You are drop-dead gorgeous… A great catch. You're brilliant—probably the top of your class at Stanford. And you're a *Pope,* for crying out loud! You have so much going for you. One day, you'll be running the top firm on the planet. What on earth would you want with the daughter of your family's longtime estate manager? You have your pick of any other girl you want. Prettier. Smarter. Better connected—"

"But I want *you,* Harper!" I roared. "Why are you doing this?!" My voice began to crack, and I felt my whole body following suit. If only the floor could swallow me whole and put me out of my misery. It was the worst thing I'd ever felt. She was killing me softly.

"I apologize for taking so long to explain. I don't deny I had feelings for you. But now, I understand my feelings were all inappropriate. I babysat you when you were ten. I did the same for your little sisters for years. I'd let things get too far between us. Now, I'm with someone my own age."

I couldn't listen to this shit anymore. "We're only four years apart!"

"Four years is a long time at our age. You're not even nineteen yet. You have so much more to experience in life."

She was speaking to me like she was my mother, and it grated every single nerve. She hadn't said anything like this when I'd fucked her multiple times. "Are you saying I'm not man enough for you?" I scoffed.

"I get it," she sighed. "I was your first love. But trust me, you'll get past it. You'll forget all about me once you've moved on. I care so much for you, Ford... but as a friend. I'm engaged now. I love Aiden."

Fucking Aiden! Up to that point, I'd never wished serious harm on anyone. In just two sentences, she'd strapped a bomb to my chest and detonated it while trotting off into the sunset, holding hands with her brand new lover.

"I'm not sure how you expect me to respond to that. By the way, I called you yesterday to tell you all about some research I'd done. Your supposed fiancé has a history dodging illegal drug possession charges. Is that what you want to be with?"

Silence spread between us, thick and heavy like mud. It had me wondering if she had already known. "Harper?" I said, checking to see if she was still there.

"Unbelievable," she snapped. "You're becoming the person you swore you'd never be—judgmental and intrusive. You're turning into your father. Bye, Ford."

When she hung up, my world ceased moving.

Eight

Liza

After a trying morning, I'd returned to my office from lunch relaxed. I'd caught up with Lola, laughing about the joys of raising children. It was refreshing talking to another mother. My kids were older, so I often gave her feedback on what to expect with teenagers. Needless to say, Lola wasn't looking forward to her turn.

Just as I settled peacefully behind my desk, I got word of two executive fires I needed to put out. Over the years, certain issues came directly to me because people believed I was more understanding than my husband. In a crisis, I had the ability to resolve things calmly without resorting to spewing a series of *fucks* like my co-CEO did. Whenever I heard bad news, I sat back, swallowed, calmly reflected, then devised a logical solution.

After wrapping up the second issue of the afternoon, I used a manila folder to fan myself. My hot flashes from this morning had returned with a vengeance. When my cell shook the desk, I groaned when I caught the name on the screen.

Do I even have the energy to talk to my mother right now?

I'd just seen her over the weekend at the twins' birthday party. She was back home in Texas, yet she still couldn't keep away from meddling with me and the kids. On social media, she constantly replied on everything the kids and I posted with the most random things. Things like stupid cat memes and a boatload of smiley-faced emojis with heart-eyes. Then, there was the nasty habit of her *liking* her own posts. It was disturbing. Someone needed to shoot me if I ever started doing that to my kids.

"Mom."

"Liza, dear. How are you?"

"I'm fine. Did Jerry survive the three days without you last week?" Jerry was husband number four, her longest.

"Just barely. You know how he gets when I leave to see you and the grands. The party for the twins was simply wonderful."

"They loved it," I responded." I'm so happy everything turned out great."

"You and Diane, Mason's mom, always throw the loveliest parties. I had such a good time, I thought it was *my* birthday," Mom chuckled.

"I could tell you were having a ball." I smiled.

"So, I guess that's it for at least two years, huh?"

"Big parties for milestone birthdays, only."

"The next one isn't until Eva's eighteenth, right? Then, Ford turns twenty-one the year after that."

I groaned. "Mom, please don't remind me. Let me enjoy the kids while they're still young." I slowly sank into my chair at the depressing thought of getting old.

"I meant to call you the second I got back, but I was sidetracked with Jerry. I'm growing sick of his retirement. He needs to find a part-time job or take up a new hobby when he's not golfing," my mother lamented. "But enough about me. Oh—I just saw photos from the party on Eva's and the twins' pages. I went ahead and tagged myself in every single one so all of my friends can see them on my page."

Oh, joy—I'm sure the girls will love that. No doubt, she *liked* and commented on each and every image as she tagged herself.

"The only reason I even have a clue as to what's going on with my granddaughters is because of social media," my mother said. "And that Knight fella... He is such a sweetie! I love all of the pictures of him and Eva together on his page!"

Yes, Julia, I know. The second my mother had met Knight on Saturday, she friended him on social media.

"I don't understand why Ford refuses to be online. He hardly ever calls me anymore. I have no clue what he's been up to lately. I miss my oldest grandchild… my only grandson," sighed Mom.

Unfortunately, Ford had to miss his sisters' party because he had a paper due, so my mother hadn't been able to see him. He'd done video chat with his sisters the morning of their birthday and managed to mail them a present ahead of time, which I'd kept under wraps until the party.

Ford wasn't a fan of social media, but something told me it had more to do with his father's penchant for snooping around than anything else. The very thought made my stomach curl in knots.

"He's been extremely busy with his accelerated program. You know he's coming back for his internship at Zinfinite in the spring. Why don't you and Jerry come up and stay in the guesthouse for a month while Ford is home?" My mom may have been a handful, but I'd be lying if I said I didn't enjoy her when she was here.

"That sounds like a good idea. I have a feeling it'll just be me, but I'll talk with Jerry."

"It'll do you some good to spend a month with all of your grandkids under one roof."

"I would really love that. I'm so proud of all of them," she said, oozing with joy. "So, what's going on with you? I feel every time we talk, it's always about the children. How's my Liza doing?"

I didn't realize I'd stopped breathing until I exhaled. "It's going okay. Business is great."

My mother remained silent for a beat, which disarmed me. She was usually *always* talking. "Liza?"

"What?"

"What's wrong? Spill it."

Busted. I take in a deep breath, not knowing what to say in the moment.

"Go ahead… spill to Mama."

I decide on the truth. "My hormones are all out of whack. One minute, I'm moody and the next, I'm burning up and sweating. Then, there's the crying for no reason—"

"Liza, *sweetie...*" Mom interrupted. She had changed from the woman she'd been two decades ago. She no longer told my sister and me what to do with our lives. She was now a free spirit who encouraged us to trust and follow our own hearts. As I waited for her to speak, I silently hoped she didn't revert back to the old her. I didn't need her to tell me what to do with my life. I only wanted her to listen.

"I was in my early forties, just like you, when I became premenopausal."

I wasn't expecting her to say that.

"Everything you're describing is exactly what I went through. Sounds like you have of touch of what I had. You may want to visit your OB/GYN," Mom advised.

"Mom, this is the first I'm hearing this."

"I know," she hummed. "At the time, you'd just given birth to Ford. I was so happy, I just brushed off what was going on with me. By the time Jerry and I got back to Texas, I couldn't take it anymore, so I caved and went to my doctor. That's when I found out what was going on. Believe it or not, my mother had gone through the same thing in her early forties."

Reality had come crashing down. *I could be menopausal, which means that's it; I can no longer have children.* I rushed the thought out of my head. I'd done everything I ever dreamed of doing, including having four wonderful children. I regretted nothing.

"I'll set an appointment with my doctor. I'm glad I talked to you about it," I tell Mom.

"That's why you need to speak to your mother from time to time. I've walked in your Jimmy Choos, dear."

I laughed. "I love you and miss you. Please see if you can come down for a month after New Year."

"I will, my love. Call me as soon as you've seen your doctor."

"Will do."

My sister had surprised me at the office late that afternoon. Although she only lived two hours away in LA, we rarely got to spend much time together due to our demanding jobs. She'd managed to get a couple of days off from the news station.

Mason insisted Jessie and I have our girl time that evening away from the house, while he kept the twins company. Eva would be out having dinner with Knight before they joined Mason and the twins at home for a Friday night movie in the theater room.

I had to pinch myself at how far things had come in a short period of time. Getting Mason to let Eva date in the first place had been like performing a root canal without anesthetic. Weeks prior, I couldn't have fathomed a day when Mason would have actively included Knight in our family plans.

I remembered staring in shock at him over the dinner table the other night when the following conversation took place between Mason and Eva…

"Eva, will Knight be joining us at Bethany's fall recital a week from tomorrow?"

"I told him all about it. He was pretty stoked. He's been itching to hear Beth play her guitar."

"Keep me posted. Sherry needs a final headcount for our dinner reservation after the recital."

It had been as if I were living in an alternate universe, but that was nothing. On a couple occasions, I'd witnessed Mason and Knight set off together—either to Mason's study or elsewhere in the house. No, he hadn't threatened Knight within an inch of his life. They'd been having a genuine back and forth, a very calm and casual dialogue between two men. In passing, I'd heard Knight asking Mason questions about LRPI. The young man appeared to be weighing his options. Knight had yet to declare a major at UCLD, so he'd done the right thing by asking questions to someone who could give him solid career advice. Mason was more than happy to oblige:

"We have an excellent summer internship program for full-time college students. I'll send you all of the details to look over if it's something you're interested in. Take the three months to discover if business is something you'd be interested in pursuing once you return to school for your sophomore year. Eva plans on being at LRPI next summer under a specialty program for exceptional high school students."

"She told me all about that. I'd really appreciate the opportunity, Mr. Pope. By the way, I have an appointment next week with my advisor to explore some intern opportunities. Not sure if I should go through with it—"

"Cancel it," Mason interrupted. "You won't find a better opportunity than this. Most internships will have you running out to fetch coffee or setting up lunch meetings. At our internship program, you'll learn more about business and economics in three months than you would in an entire year at school."

"Wow... That's great, sir. I'd definitely be interested in exploring something like that."

Again, what was going on? My husband, who'd once called the same young man an *asshole,* was practically begging him to intern for us. I could hear the eerie theme music from *The Twilight Zone* playing loudly in my head.

Part of me wondered if this is my husband's way of plugging Knight into some Ford-shaped void. In the past, Mason had tried to push our son to work summers at LRPI. However, next year, Ford would be a part of a coveted internship at Zinfinite on the vendor/supplier relations team. It was an opportunity of a lifetime that our brilliant young man earned all on his own. Ford hadn't landed the spot because he was Mason Pope's son.

I had doubts about Mason being on board with Ford interning anywhere else other than at LRPI. And I swore Mason would blow a gasket when Ford mentioned he'd be taking classes at UCLD. Harper was there, and we all knew how Ford felt about her.

I didn't have a clue what Harper had been up to these days,

other than school. Ford no longer spoke to his father and me about her. I'd asked Russ and Trisha about her from time to time. I really missed her. Being that Harper had been around since we'd made Arcadia's Crest our home, she was like a fifth child to Mason and me. I was heartbroken that those days now seemed so distant.

I recalled the time Trisha and I helped Harper get ready for senior prom. I felt a pang in my chest at the memory, then wondered if I should reach out to Harper myself to see how she was doing. *Or perhaps I should just wait until Ford saw her around and have him tell me.*

My sister pulled me out of my reverie when she emerged from the restroom and approached our reserved table at Club Sahara. Jessie was as gorgeous as ever. She had a fit body that hadn't been worn by childbirth. And although she was well into her forties, she'd made a pair of jeans, V-neck tee, and long beige cardigan with matching booties look New York fashion runway fabulous. I frowned at my Isla Cole jeans and blue blazer over a boring black blouse. Clothes had always liked my sister better.

"That is one fancy bathroom," Jessie exhaled, taking a seat. I nodded.

We were surrounded by wide teardrop archways, sprawling chandeliers, jeweled table lamps, and dark marble floors. The club embodied the romantic essence of the old classic film *Casablanca*, but more vibrant with color.

"Aren't you and Pope majority owners here?" Jessie inquired.

"Yep. By the way, the twins loved the nail polish and manicure set you sent for their birthday."

"I can't wait to see them tonight. At first, I was thinking we'd do each other's nails tomorrow. But I think this weekend calls for a day of pampering at the spa for the five of us girls."

"Eva won't be joining us," I announced. "She'll be at the UCLD football game with Knight."

Jessie groaned. "Man, where has the time gone? My niece has a boyfriend now. I'm getting old."

After we ordered salads and appetizers, my sister started on about my visit to the doctor this morning.

"Is everything okay?"

I took in a deep breath. "Well, I spoke to Mom earlier in the week and told her what was going on with me. She suspected I was enduring what she had at my age."

"That's right—she was premenopausal."

"Right. I've been experiencing random hot flashes and crazy mood swings. So, this morning, my doctor ordered a series of tests. Her first observation was that I'm a classic case of rapid perimenopause."

"Wow, I'm sorry. That totally skipped over me," Jessie sighed in disbelief.

"Ain't genetics grand?" I said, rolling my eyes. "Anyway, I'm off birth control now. Hopefully, that helps to even out my hormonal episodes."

My sister's eyes sprung wide. "No way. The last thing you want is to be over forty and pregnant."

"Tell me about it," I blinked, horrified by the thought.

"The kids are all nearly grown. You're so close to freedom," she said, shaking her fists for extra emphasis.

"Exactly. But my doctor doesn't think it's likely I'll get pregnant. I've endured three pregnancies, one of them with multiples. After that, I have been on birth control for thirteen years straight. Couple that with wacky hormones and the likeliness of me falling in line with grandma and mom with the early menopause thing—"

"Shouldn't Pope get clipped or something before you quit birth control?" Jessie argued.

"I'm sure Mason would if I suggested it. Although, he's been bugging me for years to have one more. Nope—I'm not going to be pushing sixty with a teenager."

Jessie laughed. "You know how people are having kids much later these days and living longer to enjoy them."

The longing gleam in her eye wasn't lost on me. I started to wonder if she'd rekindled things with Tom, her estranged husband. That thought was short-lived once I quickly remembered Tom was a cheating asshole. I didn't call my sister out on her mood shift because I knew she'd deny it.

"I should have my lab results in a week. Then, there's more bloodwork after that. Getting old royally sucks," I pouted.

Nine

Ford

For the past eleven weeks, I'd been functioning on autopilot. I refused to let myself feel anything as I focused one hundred percent on excelling in all my courses. The semester had ended a week ago for me, but I stuck around campus to partake in a few activities. One of them included having *a lot* of sex.

As soon as my heart got crushed weeks prior, I'd let Rebecca the BJ Queen do more than just blow me. But first, I'd apologized for lying about being gay, explaining to her that my situation was complicated. I was no longer fucking with *complicated*. I wanted easy.

The only bad thing about fucking Rebecca was that she didn't understand boundaries. She blamed it on the earth-shattering orgasms I gave her.

"I've never felt that before. Only you know how to speak to my body, Ford," she'd purred into my ear when we were naked in her bed one morning at her sorority house. That had happened shortly before I hopped in my car and started the journey home to Arcadia's Crest. I'd be there for the next few months.

It had taken Becky no time to spread the word that I was her boyfriend. Meanwhile, I hadn't been as quick to give us a name. As far as I was concerned, we were just in a monogamous friendship that included lots of sex. I'd stopped giving a shit about titles many weeks ago.

Rebecca had reached the level of delusional when she tried convincing me not to take the summer internship at Zinfinite. She was obviously out of her damn mind if she'd thought I'd pass up the opportunity of a lifetime for some ass. She'd sworn that she wouldn't be able to function next semester without me. I, in turn, had explained to her that the next good-looking guy that came along would take her mind right off me.

Six hours later, I pulled my car up to my parents' grand circular drive. As I unloaded my luggage from the trunk, my blood pressure rose the instant I saw Mr. Benton surface.

"Welcome home, young Mr. Pope."

"Mr. Benton," I said, forcing a smile. "Are my folks around?"

He gently nudges me and claims the task of gathering my luggage. "They are. Why don't you go in? I'll handle this."

Part of me had wanted to take my pain out on him and my father. They had everything to do with driving Harper and me apart. But the fact remained that no one had forced her to get engaged to that burnout. If I knew Mr. Benton—and I think I did—he'd never have approved of this Aiden dipshit.

"Go inside. I've got this."

I hadn't realized I'd been staring mindlessly at Mr. Benton as he unloaded my trunk. I shook off the trance and walked toward the double doors of my family's mansion by the sea. First thing I noticed was that the blinds were drawn. Not only was it still daylight, but the blinds were never closed.

Another strange thing I noticed stepping into the grand foyer was that it was dark, and the silence was deafening. It was almost too weird. As soon as I hit the lights in the main room, a group of bodies leapt up with a cacophony of whistles, cranks, shakers, and cheers.

"SURPRISE!"

They nearly scared the shit out of me, but I managed to stay cool. I panned over my surroundings, taking in the 'Welcome Home Ford' banner above. When my eyes dropped back down, they landed on Grandma Julia. *What's she doing here?* Grandma and Grandpa Pope were also there. Next to them were my parents and my sisters, all wearing guilty grins. Knight stood right beside Eva. Behind them were my closest friends since grade school. *What the hell's going on here?*

"We missed you, big bro!" Brie sang, pulling me out of myself. Both she and Beth had their arms around me before I knew it. I smiled and hugged the gruesome twosome tightly.

"We were bummed when we heard you were back in town and we didn't get to see you," Beth pouted.

"Hey kiddo, I was only back for part of the day. I only had a chance to see Mom and Dad while you were still in school," I said in my defense.

"*And* Eva," Brie added.

I stare stunned at her since the entire room heard her say it. No one was supposed to know about me running into Eva at UCLD. She'd been skipping school to see the guy standing next to her. I braced myself, expecting Dad to lose his shit. In three-point-two seconds, Knight would be flying out of the front door and landing on his ass like Will's friend Jazz on those *Fresh Prince* reruns. Before things could get more awkward, Mom puts me out of my misery.

"We already know where she saw you," she said with a smirk.

"Hey—that was my one and only time ever skipping class," Eva said in her defense.

I caught the grumpy expression on our over-projective father's face, and Knight swiftly defended himself.

"For the record, I didn't encourage her to do that. I told her to go to class." Laughter filled the room, coming mostly from the guys Knight and I went to school with.

My youngest sisters pulled me aside, much to the chagrin of everyone eager to greet me. Brie and Beth immediately flooded me with what's been happening with them while I'd been away. The varsity volleyball coach at the high school Brie would be attending had reached out to our parents about her bypassing junior varsity. Meanwhile, Beth had been busy jamming on guitar with the high school ensemble. Like her twin, she couldn't wait to go to high school. Then, she'd be able to apply for one of the coveted CYS spots—the California Conservatory program for high school students at UCLA. Beth was an insanely talented musician.

"You'll be a shoo-in, no doubt," I told her.

"Thanks, big bro," she said, hooking me into her with one tiny arm.

My sisters finally released me to the masses, and I moved across the room like a politician. It was all so strange. I hadn't expected a grand reception. I wondered whose idea this was.

"And what are you doing here, gorgeous lady?" I beamed as I pulled Grandma Julia in for a big hug. She'd come all the way from Texas.

"I haven't seen my only grandson in forever." She pulled me down to her and planted a kiss on my cheek. "Your mother thought it would be a great idea if I stuck around for a month while you're here working your internship. I'll finally get to spend quality time with *all* my grandchildren."

"I'm so glad you're here," I said, hugging her once more. She proceeded to tell me that Grandpa Jerry, her current husband, was home in Texas but would be here for Christmas. She also mentioned that my biological grandfather, Grandpa Chuck, was on his way. I still couldn't get over how many times she'd been married. That was some scandalous shit.

I heard a different feminine voice speak from behind. I turned to hug both Grandma Diane and Grandpa Lyndon at once. I'd been a shitty grandson to all of them—too busy wallowing in my own self-pity. I was pissed at Harper and my parents and ignoring the fact that I was fortunate to have all my grandparents still here. I had so many people in my corner who loved and cared for me. I used to call my grandparents for no reason at all, just to hear their voices. Lately, that had all changed.

When my mother walked up, I shook a finger at her face in a playful scold. She laughed, letting me know that the party was entirely her idea. I embraced her, and she kissed me on the cheek

"Mr. Benton said you were caught in traffic. *Mom,*" I scold with a smirk as I pull my mother into a squeeze. She kissed me on the cheek.

"Welcome home, son," my father said, patting me on the back.

My relationship with him was odd. He'd never been a touchy-feely guy where I was concerned. The moment I'd hit thirteen, he had stopped hugging and started doling out handshakes. I had to watch old home movies to remember how he'd been with me when I was a little kid. Back then, he'd been gentle and affectionate.

I casually transitioned over to a waiting Eva. She was quick to jump and yank me into her arms. "Double trouble, together again!" she said, as her eyes landed on Knight. That's what she used to call Knight and me when we were in high school together.

I clapped hands with Knight before we pulled in for a bro-hug. "Dude—you're dating my little sister," I said with mock disgust.

He barked out a laugh. "It's all good, BP. Nothing has to change with us. We're still boys. At least, I hope we are."

"Of course," I said, slapping five with him again. "But what's even more weird is that my Pops lets you in his house." Both he and Eva laugh.

"Crazy, right?" Eva said, amused. "Believe it or not, Dad loves Knight now. He'd rather hang with him now than me and the twins."

"You've gotta be fucking kidding me," I murmur between my teeth.

"Your Dad is pretty awesome," Knight beamed. Eva and I looked at him in disbelief.

"You're not talking about Mason Pope over there, are you?" I said as I eyed my parents chatting with his.

Knight chuckled. "Yep. And starting next month, guess who's

going to be interning twice a week at Pope Tower during baseball season?"

No. Fucking. Way. "You *can't* be serious," I groaned. Knight nodded in the affirmative. "Dude, you'll be attending classes and practicing for the new season in February. You plan on working an internship at LRPI on top of that? That sounds next to impossible."

"It's quite doable, actually," Knight said confidently. "I talked it over with coach and everything. Also, during summer, I'll be interning full-time."

I couldn't believe what I was hearing. It sounded like a disaster in the making. Something would have to give. It was going to either be work or baseball. My gut told me it would be his internship that would lose the battle. I couldn't help but wonder if he was doing this at my father's urging. He'd been trying nearly all my life to control me, and in comes this guy who wants to impress him so badly that he's willing to interfere with his dream of playing baseball.

"So, where will you be working?" I asked, humoring myself.

"The data analytics group, the same place you interned."

Why the analytics group? Why not marketing, logistics, or finance? Again, I wondered if that had been my father's doing. Was Mason Pope using my sister's boyfriend to get to me? Irritation was running rampant, and I had to keep my emotions at bay. Then, my sister chimed in.

"I'm interning, too. In the afternoons starting next month, I'll be in the mailroom."

I couldn't hold back that time. I rolled my eyes hard, finding it odd how everyone was going to be interning at LRPI. It was almost cult-like. I knew Dad couldn't wait until the twins were old enough to join the fold.

I didn't care who else my father threw in my face; he wasn't going to see me sweat.

My existence wasn't predicated on being Mason Pope's heir.

"Did you see my pic?" she asked.

My eyes rolled at the dimly lit ceiling as I lay in my childhood bedroom. The phone was placed loosely to my ear, although it could've been flat on the pillow, and I would have still heard the shrill coming through the phone.

"I did," I murmured.

"You didn't respond," whined Rebecca. "Did you like it?"

"Well, I was with my family when I saw it, so forgive me for not answering you right away," I snarked.

"Okay, but you had what—like ten hours to reply?"

"Rebecca, I was with my family the whole time." I was getting really irritated and prayed for the day she got tired of me and found another boy toy to keep her company. True, she was super-hot and pretty good in bed, but she was more trouble than she was worth.

"I know. I'm sorry. I just miss you, is all," she pouted. "Can I call you right now on video chat?"

I was bored, so I caved. Moments later, Rebecca's made-up face filled my screen. She lay in a sea of pink and white with all kinds of furry, fluffy shit. Her long blond hair was swooped to one bare shoulder. Right away, I wondered if she was naked underneath where the screen had cut her off.

"Where are you?" I asked. I knew it wasn't her room at the sorority house. I'd been there often since Harper had broken me.

"At my parents' in San Diego."

There she was, all naked shoulders, and her folks probably weren't too far away. I instantly thought about my own parents bursting into my room but relaxed as soon as I remembered that I had locked the door.

"Did you just get there?" I knew San Diego was a seven-hour drive from Stanford, and she hadn't alluded to going home that day. The semester didn't technically end until the following week.

"Nope. Decided to catch a last-minute flight instead of waiting a week. Most of the girls were headed home after finals today. And plus, my guy left, so I had no real reason to stay," she purred.

It boggled my mind how she functioned as if she and I were a thing. Rebecca was well aware of her reputation on campus. Her lips and the dicks of Stanford's finest on the football field went way back.

No joke—one of the guys on the team who I tutored couldn't contain his laughter when he'd told me Rebecca had recently turned down blowing the quarterback because she was *'dating Ford Pope exclusively,'* end quote. Even he hadn't believed that line of bullshit.

"Rebecca, why are you calling me? I mean... What is this?" I maintained a semblance of humor in my tone, eliminating any trace of malice. My attempt to shield her feelings was a waste of time since she appeared more concerned with how great her pout looked on the screen than any word I said. I continued speaking anyhow.

"You and I have been screwing around for about a year. Only recently, a little friendly fellatio transformed into full-blown sex... Which, I have to admit, has been great. But we'd both be foolish to think this is more than just sex." I instantly regretted my words when she winced in pain.

"Love Bug, I told you that you were different. You're not like any other guy I know. I don't want to be with anyone else."

This conversation was a complete dumpster fire.

"Rebecca, you have a ton of..." I didn't have a kinder way of saying BJ recipients, so I went with "admirers." I then proceeded to tell her that no one believes her when she tells them that we are a thing and that there isn't one guy who can keep her attention. She disagreed.

"The only person I'm interested in convincing that I want more between us is *you*." There was fire in her brown eyes, which made me more uncomfortable.

"Look, Rebecca—you are very sweet and pretty. I thought you just wanted to have fun. I'm honestly not looking for a relationship right now. I've got way too much going on. Any other guy would totally jump at the opportunity to sweep you off your feet."

"But I don't want anyone else. I want..."

Her soft sobs took over, and I actually got mad. I bring the camera phone close to my face to plead with her to leave me alone. That's when she took over and started begging.

"Ford, you're all that I think about. I know we're going to be long-distance at least until the fall, but we can make it work."

"Rebecca," I called her name once more, hoping she'd finally snapped out of her delusional trance. She was headed for the deep end, and I wasn't sure I'd be able to pull her out.

"*Shhh*. Don't you say it," she pleaded, the sound of tears in her throat. "I don't want to hear it. Look—we'll take things slow. We'll talk on the phone every day. It's obvious this relationship is one-sided. Maybe over time, you'll grow to feel the same way about me. In the meantime, I'll wait for you to catch up with me, alright?"

I wanted to ram my head right into a wall. No matter what I said, it wasn't getting through to her. I couldn't be rude and hang up, nor could I change my number. Eventually, I'd have to face her again on campus. *Dammit!* I had no idea what to do.

"Rebecca," I tried for the last time.

"Don't you dare say another word, Love Bug. Let's just go back to the beginning as good friends. We'll work our way back up to where I want us to be."

Jesus Christ. I was getting major psycho vibes from this bird. Her Glenn Close/Fatal Attraction impersonation was on point. I began quietly humming the melody of an old song made famous by the band Buckcherry.

And yes, she did *fuck so good* on top of being totally nuts.

"How about I give you one last treat before we slow things down a bit?" Her tears were all dry, and the sex kitten returned in full force. Slowly, the camera began panning backward, exposing more than just her shoulders.

Yep—and there are her tits…just…there.

And there went my cock, awakening in my pajama pants.

"You remember touching me here early this morning?" she moaned as her free hand glided over each breast.

"Yeah," I groaned.

"I know we're just friends now, but this body belongs to only you, Ford Pope. I promise, I won't let anyone else touch me. Okay?"

I was stunned stupid, unable to respond. My eyes bore through the screen as her camera continued its journey downward, exposing smooth, bare skin. Skin I instantly recalled sliding all over on and *in*. The panning didn't stop until the screen reached her glistening sex. My breath caught in my throat. *If she were here right now, I'd…* I dropped my thought before venturing over to the point of no return.

She's batty, Pope. Don't you dare fall for those big, soft tits and that tight, warm…

"This body is all yours," she breathed. "You're the only one who gets to see it from now on."

Before I knew what happened, I was licking my chops and asking her to play with herself for me. I had no doubt I'd live to regret giving in to temptation.

Ten

Ford

A brand new year. 'Out with the old, in with the new,' as they say. The mantra was becoming easier to stick with internally. But on the outside, things weren't going as smoothly.

For one, Rebecca wouldn't stop calling or texting. For Christmas, one of the things she'd sent was a box of homemade peanut butter and chocolate chip cookies. The package had also included an eight-by-ten glossy of her draped in a festive apron with massive cleavage, happily posing with a baking sheet full of cookies she'd prepared just for me. Fortunately, Mrs. Benton had delivered the package directly to me. It would've been awkward if anyone in my family mistakenly opened it and saw not just the photograph but the note that came with it.

Merry Christmas, Ford!
I know you really love my cookies, but hopefully, these ones will suffice until we meet again.
Love,
Your Rebecca

She'd planted a bright red kiss beside her signature. As far as the baked goods were concerned, I had no desire to eat them. According to Knight, who did eat them, Rebecca was a pretty good baker.

I'd been hoping to leave her in the previous year, but she'd been on me like white on rice. There was no plan in place to deal with her, but at least I had a few months to figure it all out.

Rebecca wasn't the only pain in my ass. My baseball crew from high school had threatened to wreak havoc on my new year. Excluding Knight, the rest of them were a band of fucktards. They even tried to pull me away from my own welcome home party to go out clubbing, but that wasn't happening. My grandparents were all in town, and my father would've had a conniption.

Christmas and New Year's Day had come and gone, and I'd successfully managed to avoid them. But the second I had a Saturday night to myself in an empty house, I started to cave. My sisters were spending the night over at my parents' spare penthouse in Los Derivas with Aunt Jessie. Grandma Julia was catching up with local friends. I had no idea what my parents had planned when they'd returned from their dinner date. I was going to stay home and get a head start on some pre-work for my UCLD classes that started in two weeks, but I quickly gave up on that. There's that saying about an idle mind and how it's the devil's workshop, and all that jazz. As if on cue, my old baseball teammate, Monty, gave me a ring-a-ding just after nine.

"Sir Douchelord!"

I laughed out loud. "Monty Carlo! What's up?!"

Carlos Montague, definitely no relation to Romeo, had been my friend since junior high. He's always been *Monty* to those who knew him well. He's *Monty Carlo* to the select few who made it to his inner circle, particularly those who played on our state championship-winning high school ball club.

Like me, Monty had hung up his bat and glove after high school. Today, he's a quarter of the way through with his two-year culinary arts program in Santa Barbara. As long as I'd known him, he'd aspired to be a chef. As a kid, he'd often promised to *hit me up* when he was ready to work as head chef at one of my parents' many establishments.

"The fellas want to hang tonight and prowl for thotties," Monty sang.

"Geez," I sighed with an eye roll. "Who's all going?"

"ACYC, baby!"

That meant Dave, Mark, Ty, Monty, and me. "That lineup sounds awful," I groaned. Back when we were kids, we'd often get into trouble. I had no desire to call my folks later and ask them to bail me out of jail.

"You're not boo'd-up, are you?" Monty taunted.

My oldest friend's faux-street vocabulary was cringeworthy, but everyone else found it amusing. He'd grown up in one of the wealthiest towns around, yet he spoke as if he hailed from South Central.

"Nope," I answered, popping the P.

"Well, then. Why don't you go out tonight and get laid and help your friends get some in the process?"

"I've taught you guys everything I know about picking up girls," I smirked.

"But when we put it in practice, that shit just doesn't work the same."

I busted out laughing. "In all fairness, most girls I attract are glorified gold diggers."

"They don't care about your money, Pope. I see the look in their eyes the moment you spit game to them. Birds have no clue who you are at first, yet they are instantly hypnotized and desperate to fuck you."

I laughed louder. "I'm not participating in your tomfoolery."

"Come on, man. You're probably not doing shit anyways but chilling in that huge-ass castle by the sea. I'm pretty sure you're sick of your family by now. Why don't you come out and hang with us? Take a break from the fam and bust one over some hot chick's massive tits."

My friends were lewd and very immature. Yet, I'd be lying if I said hot sex with a hot stranger didn't sound amazing at the moment. I was bored out of my mind, so anything sounded good. If I stayed home and did nothing, I'd be dragging the lovesick puppy into the new year. I needed to shoot the bastard and put him out of his misery.

So far, I'd been doing a decent job erasing Harper from my consciousness. Granted, it hadn't been easy. For one, I was spending my days at the very place we'd met. Across the field was her dad's place, where she had lived. There were so many memories of Harper all around. On the flip side, I'd been too busy with my family to do much wallowing. Now that everyone was out and doing their own thing, my mind began to wander. I needed something to do.

"Man, are you coming or what?" Monty challenged. "Shit's about to get crazy—"

"Alright, alright," I conceded. "Where are we going?"

"*So*... Dave wants to go to Genesis."

"Hell, no. Out of the question," I said firmly.

"Why the fuck not?"

"My parents are part owners. They'd never serve us alcohol."

"Shit. What about Déjà Vu?"

"They own that too," I sighed.

"Fuck!" Monty growled. "Do the Pope's own every fucking joint in Los Derivas?!"

"Yep—just about."

"Alright, what about Wonderland? Do they own that?"

"No, but one of our security guys has associates who moonlight there as bouncers. They'd narc on me in a heartbeat."

"Where in the hell can we go and not get caught with fake IDs?" Monty was at his wits end, and I didn't blame him.

"Cosmos," I suggested. "I don't believe I know anyone there."

Monty sighed, relieved. "Cosmos it is. Damn dude, I swear," he chuckled, and I laughed right along with him. "I'll call the boys and have them meet us there. You think Thibodeau will want to tag along?"

"No way," I snorted. "Knight's a choir boy."

"Thibodeau's a bit uptight," Monty agreed. "I hope, at least for his sake, your sister is giving him some."

"Fuck, Monty..."

"What?"

"That's my little sister you're talking about, man!"

"So, what? Eva Pope is bae. Everyone wanted to smash that back in high school," he said matter-of-factly. I was thoroughly disgusted.

"Monty, cut it out."

"Alright, alright," he chortled. "I'll swing by your place in an hour since I don't trust you not to flake on me."

"Yeah, yeah..."

"Don't forget your fake ID."

"Duh."

"And don't forget the rubbers, playa. As Confucius once said: 'It don't mean a thang unless you bang-bang-bang.' You feel me?"

I howled. "You're a fucking nut, Monty Carlo. You know that?"

"Well, at least I hope to bust one tonight, son," he crowed.

"Not if you talk to the ladies like that, creep. Settle your ass down."

"I'm cool, Pope—I swear. See you in an hour."

"Daaaaayyyyummm!" Monty bellowed with his eyes nearly ejecting from his skull. As we entered the club, my friend, Dave Franco's long-lost twin, admired some doll seated at the bar. Unfortunately for him, one of our friends had beaten him to the punch.

Cosmos was a massive nightclub with the bar itself taking up the entire perimeter of the interior. There was a DJ booth and a vast dance floor located dead center. Seated across the way were our friends, Ty and Mark. They hadn't noticed when we walked in because they were busy spectating on our friend named Dave. Monty and I passed him while he attempted to mack on the girl Monty had been staring at from the entrance.

The girl's dark mane was thick, wavy, and swayed all the way down her back. Her hair was so dark that it shimmered in the dim light. Her short red dress exposed two fit and smooth-looking light brown thighs that taunted the eye when she absentmindedly crossed her legs.

Her gorgeous face was overtaken by a blasé expression, and her body language read, 'Not this cocky, overly aggressive bullshit again.' It made me wonder why girls like her went clubbing in the first place. Douchebags and awkward men with liquid courage were the status quo in places like this. If women were *really* unlucky, they'd end up with a drunk-douchebag hybrid trying to press his luck.

My friend Dave was a good-looking guy. Tall with raven-black hair and lily-white skin, he had the sexy vampire thing going that all the chicks loved. He owed the movie *Twilight* a huge thanks for getting him laid on a regular basis.

Dave rarely struck out on the field or with girls, so this was rare. He'd already lost the moment he decided to walk across the bar and speak to this girl in the first place. I'd just arrived, but even I knew he failed to read the room before assuming he had her in the bag. *Poor bastard.* I laughed to myself as Monty and I met Mark and Ty. At the bar, the four of us high-fived and patted each other on the back. ACYC was together again.

Jokers in grade school gave us the ambiguous acronym which stood for Arcadia's Crest Yacht Club. I was surprised the town's country club hadn't bagged the name first. Now, it was synonymous with Mark, Ty, Dave, Monty, and me.

Mark was biracial, but the nickname 'Casanova Brown' had stuck since high school. In our gang of pretty boys, I'd always thought he was the best looking. But just as Carlos Montague wasn't Romeo, Mark Fielding was no Casanova. Mark only went for the low-hanging fruit. In other words, he was shy. He would wait for a girl to speak to him first before making a move.

Next was Tyler Shaw. With his signature part on the left side of his dark brown hair, he had the puppy dog look down pat. The son of a politician, you rarely saw Ty anywhere without a sports coat. Voted the guy in ACYC most likely to marry first, he was still going strong with his high school sweetheart.

After shooting the shit for a few, Dave finally joined us with his tail stuck between his legs.

"I saw you over there, striking out," I teased over the booming bass.

"Dude—she's a piranha," Dave agonized, wiping his brow with the back of his hand.

"I told you!" Ty squawked in exoneration. "She is snobby as hell!"

"I believe the word you're looking for is *sadítty*," Monty swaggered.

"Sa-*wha?* Anyway, no man could ever satisfy that girl. It's chicks like her who cling to their four hundred-dollar vibrators and swear they *don't need no man* to take care of them," Ty mocked with a sassy head roll and finger snap. The rest of us hollered with laughter.

Monty gazed across the bar at the woman in question, practically drooling as she obliviously worked her phone. "That bird is hot as fuck," he growled. "She didn't come here alone, did she?"

"She came with friends," Mark said.

"Well, fellas, her kryptonite has just arrived," Monty ceremoniously announced. We all laughed at him.

"Well, it most certainly ain't *you,* asshole," ribbed Dave.

"She will eat your dumb ass alive. I'd actually pay to see that," Ty snorted.

"Hell, no—not me. Pope," Monty clarified.

Oh—no, no, no… I'd just gotten there and was already being thrown to the wolves. I hadn't even had a drink yet.

"I'll admit Pope, you are *El Play-yore Extraordinaire-roe*. But that female over there is impenetrable," Ty declared.

"Bullshit. All females are penetrable."

The other three boneheads laughed at Monty's lazy double-entendre. I started to regret my decision to go out. I should've gone with my gut and stayed the fuck home.

"Not *this* girl," said Dave, echoing Ty.

"My man Pope got this," Monty said confidently. "I believe in him so much, I'm willing to put my money where my mouth is." To everyone's surprise, he pulled out his wallet, fanned through the bills, and took one out.

I gaped at him. "What the fuck are you doing, man?"

"Twenty bucks right here says Pope will at least get her real phone number."

Monty flung the bill on the bar's counter like a playing card. I could only shake my head repeatedly. I was beyond perturbed. *This is not happening.*

"What if he goes home with her?" Mark snickered. I turned my head toward him in shock, willing him with my eyes not to feed the animals.

"One hundred dollars," Monty blurted.

The other three laughed while I rolled my eyes in sheer annoyance. "I'm not interested in your stupid-ass bet," I asserted.

"Hey, you'll be doing the dirty work, so you don't need to contribute to the pot. If you succeed—and I know you will—you and I will split the winnings down the middle. If you strike out, the three of them will split it," Monty proposed. I vehemently shake my head in refusal while he continued to plead his case. "You have more game in your pinky than any of these clowns have in their whole body. Prove the non-believers wrong, Pope. You have absolutely nothing to lose."

"Well… I'm in," Mark said after a beat of awkward silence. He threw a twenty on top of Monty's.

Once again… Why am I here?

"Take your money back, fellas. I'm not taking part in this," I said firmly.

Both Monty and Mark jeered in disapproval, while Ty and Dave laughed.

"Pope, we're well aware of your legendary playa status in high school," Dave started. "You'll definitely go down in history as the guy every hot girl wanted to bang. But we're playing in the big leagues now. These are women we're dealing with, not girls. That same shit from your old playbook won't work with her over there," Dave ribbed, pointing his chin to the girl in the red dress.

This asshole couldn't get laid if a naked chick was spread eagle on his twin-sized bed. My eyes formed narrow slits as a sinister grin took form on my face.

"I sense your apprehension, Pope John Balls. Maybe you ain't got it anymore. Whatever *it* was," Ty heaped on.

I'd had enough.

Fuck this. Watch and learn, kiddies.

I rose from my barstool. "Cast your bets, bitches," I said, throwing the gauntlet down at Dave and Ty. "Watch and learn. By the way, there's an ATM up front. You're going to need more than twenty. Get your Benjamins ready, fellas. I'm taking Saditty Alice to Wonderland."

"*Ooooohhh* shit! *Ooooohhh* shit!" Mark and Monty chanted excitedly and slapped palms with one another.

"That's my motherfucker!" Monty declared proudly.

Ty and Dave just laughed and waved me off like the haters they were.

They both were about to be one hundred dollars poorer.

I claimed the vacant seat next to her and swiveled the stool in her direction. Still emersed in her phone, she hadn't even looked my way. I used the time she spent ignoring me to have a better look at her picturesque profile. I had to admit, she was the most beautiful thing here, and there were quite a few tens in attendance tonight. Her looks surpassed them all, by far. On top of that, she had an air of confidence that radiated. Based on that, I could tell right away that she didn't suffer fools gladly.

I knew her kind. I saw the likes of her gracing the halls of Pope Tower and walking around Stanford's campus. Girls like her had no time for male macho bullshit. A *hey, baby* wouldn't even get you past the screen door with someone like her. What she was looking for is someone who could make her think. She desired someone who could make her genuinely laugh. I understood her because she reminded me of my mother, but twenty years younger.

I took aim.

I fired.

"Can you imagine a time when we didn't have portable mobile devices? No way to take selfies. No way to answer texts. No way to laugh-out-loud at dank-ass memes," I mused.

She continued on her phone, not once acknowledging my presence.

"Believe it or not, there was a time during our parents' lives when they actually had to use a payphone. The idea of portable mobile technology wasn't even conceivable until around the nineties. Today, we can't imagine life without a phone in our pocket. Hell—we can't even use the toilet without one anymore. Can you believe that?"

She didn't budge, so I kept going. "I, for one, would like to go back to the day when we simply turned-off and unplugged. Let's finally live in the moment for once," I cogitate out loud. Once more, she paid me no mind.

"I hope you're reading a lengthy joke and haven't quite reached the punch line. It would be tragic if you were wasting your time reading the phone at a club, and no laughter was involved. If that's the case, I can point out a couple of stiff white people doing what looks like the Harlem Shake on the dance floor right now. It's pretty hilarious."

She finally broke character and stifled a laugh, but more importantly, her pretty eyes left her phone and landed on me. Her smoky eye shadow provided the canvas for a pair of gorgeous hazel eyes. I turned from her gaze and focused on the glass of ice sitting in front of her.

"What are you drinking?"

My question caused her eyes to drop back down to the phone in her hands. If there were a medal for the sport of playing hard to get, she'd capture the gold every time.

"Let me guess," I said. I lifted her tumbler, and the sweat of the glass tickled my fingers. When her eyes met mine again, she looked displeased. I paid her irritation no mind as I floated the glass around my nostrils and took a whiff.

"Gin and tonic?" I guessed.

She did a double-take. "How'd you know?"

My, the angel doeth speak. Her voice was warm and husky. I wanted to break her open and see everything inside—all the things she didn't want anyone to see. I wouldn't stay long enough to watch her put it all back inside again.

"You ever drink it on the rocks with a cucumber?" I asked.

She frowned. "I hate cucumbers."

"Trust me, you've got to try it. It will change your life."

I waved over the bartender with clear instructions on how to prepare the lady's next gin and tonic. He's back with the order in no time, placing it on the square napkin in front of her.

The beauty appeared to be fighting a smile as I lifted the glass to her. "I'm serious. I *really* want you to try this." She shook her head, turning it down cold. "Why not?" I ask.

"I told you, I don't like cucumbers."

"And yet, you're sipping on a Hendrick's and tonic."

"Yeah, *so?*" she shrugged.

"Hendrick's uses rose petal and cucumber botanicals in the distilling process. For someone who hates cucumbers, you were certainly drinking the hell out of this," I teased, pointing at the empty glass.

"I had no clue there was cucumber in that," she chuckled.

"Adding a cucumber slice does something special to it," I tell her in a low voice.

All of a sudden, her eyes transformed into satin orbs, and her body leaned just a bit closer to mine. In that moment, I prayed the boys were watching this. *This is how it's done, fellas.*

"You obviously know your stuff. So, tell me..." she purred.

"Mm-hmm?" I hummed sensually, leaning in her direction slightly to hear her better.

"Are you even old enough to drink?"

Fuck. She'd caught me red-handed, but I refused to let her see me sweat. I'd figured she was much older than me.

"I'm here at the bar, aren't I?" I challenged.

"Well, if you are old enough, the band of idiots you rode in with couldn't possibly be over twenty-one," she blasted.

Goddammit—she'd been low-key looking at me. How else would she have known those dipshits were with me? I didn't have much game left in my arsenal, so I braced myself for defeat. I hated losing, especially to my asshole friends.

"I'm sorry about that. My friends can be a bit immature. I'm sure your company is more civilized," I said smoothly.

Her skeptical smirk melted away, then she motioned her head toward the dance floor. There, I saw two ditsy girls in skimpy black dresses, grinding on three rowdy frat boys. The girls were quite tipsy.

"My friends," the looker at my side deadpanned. I laughed out loud.

"Your friends and my friends would get along great."

"Sure would," she smirked.

After one last attempt to make her sample the gin and tonic, she reached for the glass. Before her fingers could reach it, I snatch it away from her. "Are *you* old enough to drink?" I teased.

She brandished a shy smile and fluttered her long lashes. "Like you, I'm here."

"How old are you? And don't lie to me. I'm a human lie detector."

She answered with an adorable grin. "Not-quite twenty-one," she confessed.

I smiled victoriously and brought the drink back around, placing it back on the napkin in front of her. "What does that even mean—*not-quite* twenty-one?"

"My birthday is in March. I'll be twenty-one then," she came clean.

I slid the glass with napkin closer to her, and she took it. Bringing it to her lips slowly, she took a sip. After savoring the taste, she put her plump red lips back on the glass and began chugging the whole thing.

"You like?" I murmured, doing my best to disguise my triumph. She nodded, still drinking.

"Are you not-quite twenty-one as well?" she asked after placing the empty vessel back on the bar.

"Something like that." *More like not-quite nineteen.*

I could tell she was still tasting what lingered on her tongue. It was a turn on.

"Wow, I didn't think I'd like it."

"You're welcome." I extended my hand, and she took it. "Ford."

"Alana," she said softly.

My head tilted to one side. "I like it. You look like an *Alana*." Her answering blush told me I was headed in the right direction. "Where do you go to school, Miss Alana?"

"UCLA."

"Major?"

"International Marketing."

I nodded, impressed. "Junior?"

"Yep. You?"

"Almost a senior," I said, sipping her gin minus the cucumber from earlier. I ingested the watered-down drink and took a thin ice cube into my mouth.

"*You're* a senior?" She looked surprised. Shocked, even.

"Almost. I'll be completely done with my degree after the fall semester."

"Where at?"

"Stanford."

The expression on her face read, 'well la-di-da!' before she asked, "What brings you to Los Derivas?"

"I grew up not far from here. I'll be working on my honors thesis."

"You're working an internship?"

"Yes."

"Business major?"

"Economics."

"Impressive," she smirked. "I'll be starting the second round of my internship as well. Looking forward to it."

"What do you like about it?" I said in my attempt to make small talk. Before answering, she was distracted by the bartender moving in her periphery.

She placed two fingers in her mouth and whistled like a champ. I'd never seen a woman do that. When the bartender's eyes landed on her, she pointed to the nearly empty tumbler in her hand. "Two more, please—*with* cucumber." The bartender hopped to it.

"This round is on me," Alana smiled.

The idea of women paying for men's drinks was borderline emasculating, but something told me I didn't want to piss this woman off. I let it fly but told her she wouldn't be doing that again.

"I asked you a question earlier," I reminded her. "What do you like best about your internship?"

"I admire the spirit of teamwork where I'm at. I love seeing a room full of brilliant minds coming together," she responded.

"That's admirable. Do you see yourself as a leader in the business world, or do you see yourself in a supporting role?"

"I'm not one who desires the limelight. I like to think of myself as a secret weapon," Alana uttered. When she reflexively licked her lips, her words took on a whole new meaning.

Well… that's what my dick told me, anyway.

"What about you, Ford? Something tells me there's not a second-fiddle bone in your body."

"Why do you say that?"

"I just can't envision you in any sort of supporting role. You'll probably be on the cover of Forbes in five years."

I grinned, casually smoothing my stubbly chin in my hand. "It's funny you'd say that. The first day in my honors class last fall, the professor went around the room asking us what we saw ourselves doing in five years."

"You said you were going to take over the world, didn't you?" I laughed hard, and she beamed triumphantly. "I'm right, aren't I?! Tell me… Who's your ideal business leader? Past or present," she challenges.

If she wanted the real answer, it was my father. My mother had been right up there with him, but both answers were out of the question. I enjoyed conversing with someone who didn't know who my parents were. I didn't feel like removing the mask.

"Steve Jobs."

"Really?" My answer took her aback. "Why?"

"A person that can take a company going nowhere and make it rise from the ashes is to be admired. Not only that, but the very company he helped start is now woven into the fabric of global society. But most of all, it was his ability to evoke passion in the people who worked for him. They wanted to be the first to create and innovate. It's unlike anything we've seen before or since."

I took a glug from the new glass of gin. When I looked up, Alana was staring right at me.

"Like I said… Five years," she grinned, satisfied.

After chatting a while, I found out Alana was originally from Missouri. Her family had moved to the Los Derivas area when she was in high school. Alana had one sibling—a younger sister Eva's age. When she asked about my life, I remained as vague as possible. Since she'd been a resident of the area for seven years and a business major, there was no doubt she knew who Mason and Eliza Pope were.

Midway through our conversation, I was enchanted by her beauty and intelligence. And because of that, I no longer fancied having a one-night stand with her. She wasn't hook-up material. Like my mother, Alana was probably a keeper.

Unfortunately, I wasn't in the market to *keep* anyone.

So, imagine my surprise when Alana mentioned her car being parked outside, then asked if I wanted to leave the club with her. Instead of going with my gut, I stood and took her by the hand to help her out of her seat. The club was filled with ear-shattering bass, so I couldn't hear anyone more than three feet away. After placing a palm to the small of her back to lead her toward the exit, I turned on instinct.

I saw my four former teammates going bonkers like I'd just hit a home run with bases loaded. Dave and Ty enthusiastically slammed more bills on the table, while Monty happily collected it. Monty hoisted the cash in the air and waved it in my direction. I shook my head and quickly turned before Alana caught on.

She didn't live far from my parents' pre-marital penthouse in downtown Los Derivas. With a press of an app, Alana opened the door of her studio and flicked the lights. I took in my new surroundings and noticed a pristinely made bed straight ahead and to the left. The bedroom was only separated by a white curtain that could be drawn for privacy.

The small sitting area adjacent from her bed featured modest Ikea-inspired furniture facing the television. Directly to my left was her kitchenette. It was obvious that she lived alone.

I turned to face her. "Nice place."

"It's walking distance from downtown and much closer than where my family lives," she told me.

I nodded and took one step closer to her. Her prominent floral scent invaded my nostrils, which surprised me. I hadn't noticed it at the bar or on the car ride here.

"You said you've lived here for a few years. How well do you know the area?"

She blinked in contemplation. "I haven't really explored downtown, to be honest. I'm not much of an explorer. I'm quite boring."

"You need to visit the art museum. Oh—and the symphony. Los Derivas has some of the best culture around. I come down here all the time."

"Oh?"

She didn't really seem all that interested in what I was saying as she rocked on her tiptoes and began sliding her lips across my neck. Needless to say, this girl was ready for business. However, I remained a gentleman.

"There's this awesome little French bistro near here that I always enjoyed growing up. They have this lamb burger that's *to die for*," I murmured.

She suddenly grabbed me by the chin and pulled me toward her.

"Stop talking, unless you're telling me naughty things," she demanded.

I didn't argue. My lips hurriedly engulfed hers in a rough kiss.

"Honestly, that lamb burger is so fucking good, it's obscene," I groaned into her mouth. She giggled.

As we kissed wildly, I ran my hands up and down her back, and she threaded her fingers through my hair. I carefully walked her backwards to her bed, then removed my phone and wallet from my pockets to place on her nightstand. She stepped away from me before proceeding to roll her tight red dress over her hips, revealing a pair of sexy black lace panties and her bare breasts. *That escalated quickly.*

I removed my light blue dress shirt and t-shirt under it. As she sat on the edge of the bed, she stretched out her arms until her palms glided across my chest. Her hands traveled downward until they reached my belt. Right away, I removed two condoms from my front pocket.

I made quick work of removing my shoes and jeans as I watched her slide on her back to the center of the bed. I got a little excited when I noticed she was still sporting her black high heels. Alana was very beautiful, but it didn't negate the fact that she was simply a one-night stand.

I joined her in bed, but before she could touch me, she squealed as I flipped her around on her stomach. My lips languorously traveled across her bare back several minutes until reaching her panty line. I glided the garment down her thighs until it was over her shoes and completely off.

It was then that I lifted her waist and wreaked havoc on her sex with my tongue and fingers. She vocalized her pleasure the whole way through. After she climaxed, my boxer briefs came off, and the condom went on.

After two in the morning and two condoms, I lay on my side. I was trapped by Alana's naked body, held tightly in a spider monkey's hold. All four of her limbs had practically come around me in a full circle. From my angle, I couldn't tell if she was asleep.

In a perfect world, someone like Alana would be my ideal girl. Beauty, brains, confidence, drive... And she was great in bed. She'd done this thing when I was inside her. Her little love-pocket had suddenly turned into a pulsating fist that violently jerked my cock. It was fucking unreal. She'd had me gibbering like an ape.

I figured some lucky bastard was really going to love his life the moment she decided to stride into it. A part of me wished that bastard were me, but I had way too much shit clouding me. She'd be better off with someone less complicated.

No matter how much I tried purging my nagging thoughts, I still felt a certain way about a blue-eyed, blond-haired girl. And though she'd made it perfectly clear she no longer felt the same way about me—if she ever truly felt anything for me in the first fucking place—my mind, heart, or whatever-the-fuck-it-was couldn't unfeel the pain of losing her for good.

When my thoughts sat still for a beat, I was reminded that

my phone on the nightstand had been lighting up the room for the past fifteen minutes. I finally reached for it.

Rebecca again. She was getting more ridiculous by the minute.

Monty.

Rebecca again.

Ty.

Rebecca attempted to video chat. *I really need to block her.*

Mom.

Dad.

Fuck me.

And that was just in missed calls. There were about fifteen texts, and the majority of them had come from my father. That was my sign to leave. Last thing I needed was for my crazy father to come bursting in and making me look like a glorified adolescent in front of the independent, mature young woman I'd just had sex with.

"Whatever happened to wishing you were *turned-off* and *un-plugged?*" Alana croaked.

Apparently, she wasn't asleep. I twisted in her arms to face her. She appeared to be exhausted, but in the best way.

"Is that your girlfriend?" she murmured cautiously.

"No girlfriend. But I do need to head out. I *really* had a nice time with you, Alana." My smile was genuine, and she answered with a lazy grin of her own.

"Me too. You need a ride home?"

"No, thank you. I'll order a ride share. It's downtown Los Derivas, so it'll be here in no time."

"You sure?"

"Yeah, I'm good," I told her.

I rolled out of bed and got dressed while she sat up, wrapped tightly in her duvet. She watched me intently, and I didn't think much of it. She was wide awake, so what else was she supposed to do other than check her phone? Once my ride was approximately two minutes away, I leaned down and kissed her softly on her forehead.

"Stay sweet, Miss Alana. It was a pleasure meeting you."

"Likewise, Mr. Ford," she answered with a smile reaching her eyes.

As I turned to walk toward the door, the phone in my hand made a strange radar sound. On the screen, I saw someone in my immediate area named 'Alana Faust' had just airdropped me her contact information. I smirked, accepting the drop before spinning around to catch her secret smile. Normally, I'd get the girl's phone number before taking her to bed. Her volunteering it after the fact told me it had been as good for her as it'd been for me. Still, I told myself I'd never call or try and see her again, but what a fun distraction she was.

In the backseat of the rideshare, I fell in and out of consciousness with no clue what drama awaited me at home.

Eleven

Liza

Just after three-thirty in the morning, I realized my husband wasn't in bed. I knew exactly why. I checked my phone on the bedside table. Nothing. Mason and I had been trying to get ahold of Ford ever since arriving home from date night five hours ago.

Our son hadn't so much as left a note, text, or anything else to let us know where he was or that he was safe. Mason had come close to hunting Ford down himself. This, of course, wouldn't have been difficult for him to do. Mason continued to use what he referred to as his 'tried and true techniques,' or some new variation of them, which he had done ever since he took over the Pope empire.

After I exited the master bathroom and slipped on a bathrobe over my nightgown, I made the trek toward the main room. The entire time, there was an unsettling charge radiating in my chest—a mixture of exhaustion and dread. I knew with each passing minute, my husband was getting angrier and angrier. The instant I arrived in the main room was like the cruelest of jokes. I heard the door swing open before I saw it, followed by another set of footsteps inside. It was Mason marching to the door to meet our son.

Great, just in time for a showdown.

Thankfully, I beat Mason to the door as he emerged from behind me, still in the dark jeans and blue buttoned-up shirt he'd worn to our date night. Ford, dressed similar to his father, looked like he'd gotten rammed by a train.

"Where the fuck were you?!" Mason growled quietly.

His question came as no surprise, but if my mother weren't sleeping in the main house for the night, he would've screamed at the top of his lungs. To ensure no one's voice got any louder, I wedged myself between the two men, acting as a buffer.

"Ford, honey—we were worried sick," I said as calm as I could.

"Sorry... I was out with Monty and the guys—"

Mason interrupted his impending excuse. "It's nearly four o'clock in the fucking morning. Your mother and I called and texted you nonstop, yet you didn't have the decency to tell us where you were." Mason wasn't even *red* at this point. He was more like *mauve*.

"You obviously knew where I was. Don't you track me?" Ford said in a snarky tone. Even *I* felt like bopping my beloved son across the mouth, so I could only guess what his father was feeling. I didn't bother turning to see Mason, keeping my eyes on Ford.

"While you're living under our goddamn roof, you *will* follow the same rules as your sisters. Do I make myself clear?" When Mason's voice cracked, I shuddered. Bad was turning into worse.

"So, I have a curfew now?" Ford scoffed.

"Since you apparently have difficulty calling and texting people back, the answer is *yes*. Your ass had better be inside of these doors before midnight, or you can forget coming back."

Although my heart sank at my husband's threat, in his defense, he was being fair. Ford coming home in the wee hours of the morning without checking in was beyond irresponsible. The Popes were a prominent family. Anyone could've used Ford as a pawn to shakedown Mason and the empire.

Would Ford ever see past his own selfishness and take in the big picture, or would he simply call his father's bluff and leave the family for good? The worst-case scenario terrified me. It had only been a month since I was on cloud nine because I had all my children under one roof again. Now, my peace of mind was in jeopardy.

When Ford shut his eyes, I could tell he really wanted to say something stupid. He was exhausted and not thinking straight. Mason recognized the same thing. "Don't try me, Ford," he hissed. "Unless you've forgotten that your academic scholarship at Stanford only covers tuition and books and not room and board. Believe it or not, I'd been considering getting you a comfortable apartment off campus for your final semester. You pretty much just shitted all over that."

Ford turned to the side, facing away from his father and me. He was visibly frustrated.

"Ford—" I started, before he interrupts.

"Sorry, Mom. Dad. I promise to text next time." There was no substance ringing from his promise. He said the words as if out of obligation and not genuine remorse. "I'm going to bed."

As Ford headed for his room, I turned to face my husband. The pounding in my chest made it feel like I'd just escaped a hurricane. There was no doubt in my mind things could've gone way worse.

"It took everything in me not to strangle him with my bare hands," Mason pushed through gritted teeth.

I placed my hands on his shoulders and kneaded them. "I know."

"He's the reason my hair's so gray."

A smirk curled on my lips. "Um… excuse me, Pope. I resent that remark. I thought *I* was the one who brought on your gray hair."

His gaze was hooded as he snaked his arms around my waist, pulling me into him. "Don't mistake me. You're the root cause of much of my affliction," he teased before pressing a kiss on the corner of my mouth. "But you're also my remedy." He kissed my mouth, and I laughed into it. "You don't think I was too hard on him?"

His question floored me. He'd never questioned himself before when it came to how he dealt with our son. "No," I breathed.

"That boy has a lot of growing up to do," Mason declared with a clenched jaw.

"Ford will be fine. He's a typical eighteen-year-old male."

"He'll be nineteen next week, but he's never been *typical*. He's a Pope, and he'll have a degree from Stanford before he turns twenty. He'd better grow the fuck up fast, or this world will squash him like a bug."

My brows drew together in disapproval. College degree or not, Ford was still a teenager. I didn't want him growing up too fast like I had. I wanted him to slow down and enjoy his youth before he blinked and completely missed his moment.

"You saw how he looked—like shit, coming in at damn near four in the morning. I have no doubt he spent the night drinking and screwing some random girl."

"Mason," I sighed. I didn't want to imagine my son in some sordid one-night stand. I hadn't raised him to be that type of guy.

"It was written all over his face, Eliza. Not to mention, his location on GPS was parked in the same spot in downtown Los Derivas for hours before coming home. He'd crashed somewhere not far from where his sisters were staying for the night. He'd better not ruin his life by getting some girl he just met pregnant. Gold-diggers in this town are itching to clamp their legs down on a Pope and take his inheritance."

Mason's cruel words had me balling my fists at my sides. Had he thought that about me? Sure, I'd come from a well-to-do family, but he hadn't known that when I was collecting the trash from his office. I pushed the knot down my throat, knowing that Mason's problem wasn't with me, but with anyone he didn't trust with our children. He didn't have the same confidence as I had that we'd done our best in teaching our children the importance of safe sex.

Always use a condom.

YOU provide the condom.

"That boy needs to get his fucking head on straight," grunted Mason. "That brief Zinfinite internship is just a bump in the road. His rightful place is at LRPI. He knows he's next in line once we retire."

"But do we know if that's what he really wants?" I countered.

"He doesn't have a clue what he wants or what's good for him. If you recall, there was a time you hadn't a clue about that for yourself."

Although a smirk teased his mouth, I frowned in disapproval. "What's that supposed to mean?"

"Exactly what I said. Tell me, Mrs. Pope... What was the career you told me you'd always wanted? Then, tell me what you ended up doing."

Oh, no you didn't, Pope.

Mason looked so pleased with himself, and it took the patience of Job for me not to pour water all over his flame. "It was *my* choice to finally leave Isla Cole and to join you in the front office. And if you recall, *Mr. Know-It-All,* I was able to experience my dream job and work in fashion for a time. At the end of the day, I made the best decision for *me*. You need to give our son the same chance to find himself."

The argument did nothing to sway him. Mason was hell-bent on Ford taking over the business. My only hope was that our son didn't end up resenting us in the end. I hadn't a clue what he wanted out of his life. It was something he'd never shared with me. Numerous times, I wanted to have a heart to heart with him to gauge where his head was. Unfortunately, that approach didn't necessarily work well on Pope men. Like his father, Ford internalized a lot of his feelings.

"I don't want him fucking up his life," Mason said as we moved away from the front door. "It's a good thing he's no longer infatuated with Harper."

That was a name I hadn't heard him say in a while. I'd often wondered if the change in Ford had anything to do with her. My eldest's shifty display as he'd strolled in after three was concerning. If there was something wrong with him, I hoped he'd eventually open up to me about it. I'd repeatedly reminded him that he could tell me anything, and I'd never judge him. Sadly, he'd probably never take me up on my offer. After some prodding over the summer, Ford had said he trusted me, but his actions over the past two years said otherwise. Ever since I'd told his father about his relationship with Harper, all bets were off.

"She's been making a series of bad decisions lately," Mason said.

My tired eyes were now wide open. "What do you mean? What's going on?"

"She's stopped speaking to Russ and Trisha altogether—insistent on marrying some burnout," Mason hissed in disapproval.

Harper? No, not sweet, blonde angel Harper.

I didn't believe it. "Are you serious?"

"Russ suspects the main reason they're in such a rush to get married is because she's pregnant."

My jaw nearly hit the floor. "Does Russ suspect she's pregnant?" I felt myself shaking saying the words.

"No—that part has been confirmed."

My God. My eyes widened in disbelief. "Wow," was all I could say.

I wondered if Ford knew and if that news was eating him alive.

Ford

Being at Zinfinite was surreal. A crystal-like tower of the main building highlighted the mammoth state-of-the-art campus. On my first official workday, I sat through hours of orientation in a conference room that was more like a small auditorium. After finally being dismissed, I made the trek from the main tower to one of the adjacent buildings and convened with my team, the vendor/supplier relations group. My boss, Barry Issam, and his assistant, Sandy, greeted me right away just outside a conference room.

"Ford, welcome! How was orientation?" Barry asked with a kind grin.

"It was good," I answered.

"Glad to hear it. We gathered the team together for a quick update on all of our major accounts. How about you sit in? I'll start the meeting by reintroducing you to those you've already met, as well as acquaint you with the new faces."

"Sounds good," I replied.

I followed Barry and Sandy into the conference room, which was quite packed. I managed to find an empty chair at the giant round table. Several individuals seated nearby remembered me from last year's meeting. They greeted me, and I returned the favor.

As soon as Barry started, the chatter stopped. "Everyone… Joining us on his first day of interning is Ford Pope. He'll be with us until May. Please give him your warmest welcome."

The entire room applauded, which made me somewhat uncomfortable, but I smiled and nodded graciously.

"You wouldn't, by chance, be related to Mason Pope?" one guy called out from across the room.

Growing up, I endured the *are-you-related-to* ordeal countless times. It had been annoying as fuck. This time around, I understood that it was human nature to want to identify someone new with someone who was familiar.

"I am. My sisters and I call him *Dad*," I quipped. The room buzzed with laughter.

"Have you interned at LRPI?" a feminine voice inquired.

"Absolutely. It's a rite of passage in our household," I said, tongue in cheek. That line was met with even more laughter.

"So, you know a lot about what you'll be doing here?" the lady followed up. "LRPI is heavy on the supplier relations front."

"I have a solid foundation, but I am adaptive to any corporate culture. It's great that I have prior experience with a major global entity, but I'd never be foolish enough to assume the way I was taught is the best way. I'm here to learn from you and hopefully contribute something positive to the team in the process."

I panned the room, witnessing approving smiles and nods all around.

"Very good, Ford," Barry said warmly. "We're excited to have you with us."

As soon as my new boss transitioned into the first item on the agenda, my eyes halted on a dark-haired brown skin girl in a teal blouse. She was sitting diagonally from me and had been studying me the whole time. As my eyes locked with hers and saw she was visibly fighting a grin, my brain registered who she was. The running blood had chilled in my veins before my brain accepted what my eyes were seeing. Reason being, this person was in a different environment than where I'd seen her previously.

Fuck—out of all the joints in Los Derivas.

Why hadn't it come up in conversation during our time together that Alana Faust was a second-year intern at Zinfinite? If I'd known we'd be working together, I wouldn't have had sex with her this past Saturday.

Twice.

Twelve

Ford

When the meeting dispersed two hours later, I was no better off than I'd been two hours before. I had no clue how to approach a new colleague, who I'd be seeing daily, after labeling her as an obscure person from my sordid past. I'd intended her to be that person I would bring up years from now while reminiscing with ACYC over beers about our player past. We'd tally the number of girls we each had sex with. I'd recall that one Saturday night from years ago—the first Saturday after New Year's.

"*What was her name? It's been so long...*" one of my friends would say.

Then, I'd follow up with,"*That girl who decided to take me home over you assholes. Yeah... She was hot. Standoffish at first. But she ended up being really sweet.*" Then, I'd wondered if she was married with kids and call her husband a lucky dude.

Never in my wildest dreams did I think I'd ever see her again. But, as I sat in that meeting for the most agonizing two hours of my life, I realized something. My intentions were one thing, but what happened after the fact always had the potential to knock intent right on its ass.

Case in point: never thought Cheerleader Rebecca would be such a royal pain. When we first met at a frat party during freshman year, we were both buzzed. I started flirting with her a bit, which is what I did with any girl in my proximity. She laughed. We talked. She laughed some more. She blew me.

As time went on, we'd done that tango many times. I'd seen Rebecca around on campus, and if she wasn't in class or blowing someone else, she blew me. Everything was fine and dandy. I'd been fixated on Harper and hadn't thought much of a harmless blowjob. To me, it hadn't been cheating.

I'd also figured I wouldn't keep the attention of someone whose end goal was to score the quarterback. Rebecca was fun, but Harper had been the end-goal for me. I hadn't planned for a scenario in which Harper dropped a nuclear bomb. She hadn't just burned the bridge; she'd obliterated it.

"I don't deny I had feelings for you. But now I understand my feelings were all inappropriate." Harper then had the audacity to say I was turning into my father before hanging up on me. From that moment on, I hadn't been the same.

Later that day, I'd run into Rebecca on campus. She'd known I was out of it. I didn't know what had fucking possessed me to tell her that the love of my life had just trampled my heart, but she was there. She'd listened.

That was the night I'd decided to have sex with her.

And that was the night Rebecca had lost her goddamn mind.

"I wish I had someone who loved me like you loved her. Maybe one day, you can love me like that."

The fuck?!

I'd known point-blank that I wasn't going to be the guy Rebecca hoped for. I told her this daily, yet she refused to give up on me.

"You'll come around, Love Bug. You'll see. I'll be here until you do. I don't want you to miss out on a good thing."

Like my father, Rebecca frightened me in an *unhinged* kind of way. I only ignored her calls and texts for so long before throwing her a bone. I didn't want her constant threats of paying me a surprise visit in Arcadia's Crest to materialize.

Now, I had one more headache involving a woman.

I didn't know much about Alana, but she didn't strike me as the *Cheerleader Rebecca* type. Like me, I was certain she didn't want drama. I assumed she wanted to finish her internship in peace and head back to UCLA in the fall without incident. If that was the case, she and I would get through the next few months static-free.

As the meeting attendees made the slow exodus to lunch, one of the other male interns tapped me on the shoulder. He invited me to lunch, along with a group of other interns. Once outside of the conference room, those who were tagging along gathered together. Alana joined the fold.

"Welcome, Ford," the beauty smiled kindly.

I figured our exchange could end up being totally weird if I let it. I decided not to let it go there and answered her with a smirk. "Thank you."

"I'm Alana Faust. Nice to meet you."

I smiled even wider.

Yep—she's cool.

The first day of my Zinfinite internship was now in the books. I slung my leather carrier over my shoulder and across my chest and started my way toward the elevators. As soon as I pressed the down button, I heard a set of fast clicking heels trampling behind.

"Ford."

I turned to meet Alana. "Hey."

"I have an hour and a half to kill before I'm scheduled to meet friends for dinner. Would you like to grab a quick drink?"

Her expression told me there was no pretense, so I accepted her offer. "Sure."

"There's a bar just up the street," she suggested.

After exiting the building, we started the three-minute walk there.

"How awkward was it seeing me in that conference room earlier?" Alana posed with an ironic smile.

"Very unexpected," I chuckled. "We talked a lot last Saturday, but it never occurred to me to ask where you interned."

"I know! We knew about where each other went to school... What we majored in... Tons of stuff. But I didn't think to ask you about your internship either," she laughed.

"Same here. I knew about your sister and where you grew up. But for some reason, I hadn't thought about asking you where you worked," I added.

"I found out hours before you showed up today that we'd be working together. I saw the intern roster sitting on Sandy's desk. The line 'Bradford 'Ford' Pope—Stanford University' jumped right out at me. I thought it was a strange coincidence," Alana said with amusement.

We eventually made it to our destination—a hole-in-a-wall called *Alibi*. Once inside, we took our seats right at the bar.

"Hey—what can I get you?" an attractive female bartender greeted us.

Alana gazed at me with a conspiratorial grin, and I knew exactly what she was thinking. I shrugged in response, and she proceeded to order two gin and tonics with cucumber.

"Sure, I'll just need to see your IDs."

In unison, Alana and I retrieved our fake IDs and handed them over to her. I was nervous for a second when the bartender studied the cards in her hand before handing them back to us.

"I told you when my birthday was," Alana murmured after the bartender had left. "When's yours?"

"A week from today."

"Nice. You'll be twenty-two?"

I shook my head.

"Twenty-one?"

I shook it again.

"Not twenty-three?" she frowned in disbelief.

I took my thumb and pointed downward.

Alana winced. "Twenty?"

This time, I laughed while shaking my head.

"Nineteen?" she gaped.

That time, I smiled and nodded.

"You're only nineteen?" she whispered in shock.

My smile grew wider as the bartender placed our drinks in front of her. I quickly threw down a few bills before she left and instructed her to keep the change.

"Hey!" Alana rebutted.

"It was my turn," I said with a wink.

"I can't believe you're only nineteen and a few courses away from earning your degree. From Stanford, no less." It was obvious Alana was having a hard time processing the news.

"Accelerated program."

"I knew you were smart, but *man*. I wondered after you told everyone who your father was why you were interning at Zinfinite and not at LRPI."

"Been there, done that," I chirped as I took a sip of my drink.

"You don't like working for your dad?"

"No, I liked it. It's just… Let's just say it's good to have the Pope name and all, but I want to be my own man."

"I get that. But you know LRPI is slated to grow as big as Zinfinite in terms of revenue. You also have a greater chance of landing CEO there," Alana argued.

"Sure, but I'd like to build my own empire from the ground up. LRPI has been in my family for generations. I'd like to start something of my very own."

"That's admirable," she beamed.

"I have a question for you," I offered, shifting the conversation. "At what point is it appropriate to address the elephant in the room?" She gave me a puzzled look, and I elaborated further. "About last Saturday?"

Her gorgeous brown cheeks turned blush. "Oh yeah… *that*."

I didn't know what was coming over me, but my eyes itched to take the journey from her heels and up her skirt. Thankfully, I held back, keeping my line of sight on her gorgeous face.

"We'll be working together in the same department for at least four months," I prefaced.

"Yep."

"I don't want this to be weird."

"Neither do I."

"Can we both agree that what happened on Saturday can't happen again?"

I had some gall putting that out there, but what the hell. Her response was unexpected. Her mouth had flattened, yet it turned up at the corners in a conspiratorial grin.

"Agreed. We're colleagues now. It's for the best."

I sighed in relief. *I knew this girl was reasonable.* If only all women were like her.

"Agreed," I echoed her. We actually shook hands on it.

"I'm curious about something," she began. "I promise—this will be the last time I ever bring this up. What is the deal with your friends?"

I cracked up laughing. "What do you mean?"

"Were they butt hurt because I took you home instead of them?"

"I'm sure they're over it by now. If not, they'll be laughing at my expense once they find out we're working together."

"You have to spill what they told you before you decided to come by and speak to me."

I really dug our light vibe. Alana was a cool chick with an amazing sense of humor. I knew we'd make good friends.

"Want me to be truthful?" I teased. She nodded adamantly, beaming bright. I hoped she wouldn't slap me once I said the words. "You were accused of being too good for anyone. They even speculated you didn't need a man because you were the proud owner of a four-hundred-dollar battery operated boyfriend."

To my delight, she howled in laughter. "As a matter of fact, I do own a four-hundred-dollar B.O.B. Funny enough, my best friends chipped in and bought it for me after I broke up with my boyfriend three weeks ago."

I sobered up quickly, blinking at her. "Seriously?"

"My friends were trying their best to get me out of my funk. They were the ones who dragged me to that club in the first place. I didn't feel like being bothered but had gone anyway."

"I'm sorry." I felt like such a douchebag using her like that. She didn't deserve it.

"No-no-no," she chanted, holding out both hands. "I needed Saturday night, Ford. It was the first time in a while I felt like I deserved better than the two years I had with Terrence." I was rendered speechless. "You were the only person that night who treated me like a human being instead of a slab of meat. I appreciated that."

"It wasn't hard. You were extremely easy to talk to. That is, when you finally decided to speak," I smirked.

"I'm glad you didn't let up. By the way..." she said, inching closer and dropping her voice. "You may still be a teenager, but you certainly don't screw like one."

My brows rose to my hairline. She wasn't making the *abstaining from your coworker* thing any easier. Shamefully, I was morbidly curious and wanted her to elaborate.

"How do I, then?" I crooned.

"One of your lovers must have been older. She had to have shown you everything a woman enjoys in bed. That was no *boy* I was with Saturday night," Alana exhaled.

The wrong nerve was plucked. It had to have been, because I suddenly swiveled my barstool so that I was facing away from her. Numb, I lifted my tumbler and swished it around so that the ice and the cucumber danced in the liquid. Silence stretched between us, save for the background bar noises and the clinking of ice against glass. Alana broke the stalemate by bearing all.

"Terrence kept pulling me back in, but he was never really serious. I'd make all these life plans for us, which he'd immediately agreed to. Then, during an argument, he would bring them up only to tell me how stupid they were in the first place."

Damn. This guy sounded like the biggest asshole known to man. Who'd do such a thing to her?

"After two years too long, I decided to end it before coming to Los Derivas. I changed my number and everything, refusing to be strung along until something better showed up for him."

She knew exactly how I'd felt, and it had hurt.

"After that, I was angry at all men. You were the first one I'd been intimate with since him. A one-night stand had never been my forte."

Her honesty sent a jolt straight through me, opening me up to vulnerability. It was an emotion I hadn't felt since...

"Harper. Her name's Harper."

Her name came spilling out of me like bitter poison. Speaking it out loud made my chest want to cave in. I could hear Alana moving, the sound of her stool inching closer to mine.

"Did she break your heart?" she murmured.

I finally lifted my head and took in her empathetic brown eyes. My heart yearned to tell her everything. "I saw her a few weeks before the start of fall semester. I thought everything was perfect between us. We had a solid plan in place for once we finished college. My whole world fell apart when I came home from Stanford six weeks later to meet the team at Zinfinite. I couldn't wait to see her, but when I reached out, she told me she'd gotten engaged."

"No way!" Alana's mouth fell open in disbelief. "That is low. How long were you together?"

I felt like such a dumbass for loving Harper Benton for as long as I did. "I loved her my whole life. We didn't get together until four years ago."

"Wow—four years?"

"She was my everything." Feeling like the ultimate chump, I glugged the rest of my drink and waved the bartender down for another.

"I'm sorry, Ford." Her hand cupped my shoulder, but her attempt to comfort me did nothing for the storm raging inside.

"What can I say? *All's fair...*" I couldn't even finish the shitty old cliché.

"She will regret it if she doesn't already," Alana assured me. "You're a *good guy*, Ford."

Reliving the pain made it all fresh. It was as if Harper said *our love wasn't really love* again for the first time.

"Look, Ford, I'm not trying to fill some empty space, and I don't expect you to do the same. Hell—we even shook on it. We're strictly coworkers. But that doesn't mean we can't be friends. What's wrong with being there for each other? No one knows what we're going through better than us. Who better to talk some sense into our heads but us, especially if our crappy exes try to jump back into the picture?" Her sweet chuckle wasn't lost on me, but the brick wall surrounding my heart didn't budge.

"There's a better chance of your ex coming back than mine," I snorted. "She's about to marry someone else."

"What if she woke up one day and realized she doesn't love this guy because she only truly loves you?"

I scoffed. "I won't hold my breath. Even if she did, I'd never trust her again."

Alana studied me for a beat, then a resolute expression took over her. "How about this... From now on, happy hour at Alibi will be our thing. It beats spending money on a shrink, right? All we need is alcohol and honesty to lift our burdens, am I right?"

I met her cute smile with one of my own. "So, do we just send out an S.O.S. whenever we need to have a therapy session?"

"Absolutely. The second you need to vent about Harper, send out an S.O.S. No other explanation will be needed."

Ford

Age 17

I stood in the center of the pristine hotel lobby without a clue. It had been a couple of weeks since I'd laid eyes on her, and I was homesick. I approached the check-in counter where an older man stood, tapping away on a green screen terminal.

Her sweet voice from behind startled me before I could ask the man where she was. I turned on my heel and locked eyes with the love of my life. Her signature long gleaming blond hair was pulled back into a ponytail and tossed over her right shoulder. I took in her uniform—a black skirt and a matching blazer over a white blouse. On her lapel was a gold-plated name badge etched in black font with *Harper Benton* and *Arcadia's Crest, CA*. The most beautiful thing my eyes ever saw appeared to be baffled.

"Ford—you can't be here," Harper whispered in haste. Her eyes bounced around frantically, surveying the area.

"I had to see you," I pleaded with urgency. It had been too long.

She hooked my elbow in the crook of her arm and led me over to a more private area of the lobby. "You're skipping school again. We were caught two weeks ago because you did that."

"I know, "I groaned, confessing to the boneheaded move. "I fucked everything up. I had no idea my mother would be home so early."

Harper and I had been able to keep our relationship under wraps for two years. Over time, I'd grown cocky. When my mother had caught us necking in the theater room two weeks ago, I'd been startled but not alarmed. I'd assumed that Mom would have my back. It wasn't until she'd broke it to me gently that she was going to tell my father that I finally received my wakeup call.

That was when my world had gone to shit.

"You think our dads aren't having us followed now?" Harper snapped. "Think again."

"I have my ground covered this time. It won't happen again," I promised.

Her expression turned melancholy. "It *can't*. I'm not allowed to see Dad and Trisha on the property anymore."

"What?!" I barked. She hushed me as her eyes combed our surroundings yet again.

"They thought it would be *for the best*," she said regretfully.

"It's all my fault," I groaned, mussing up my hair. "The twins have a new sitter now. They miss you. *I* miss you. I *love* you."

I attempted to close the chasm between us, but Harper stepped away immediately, taking my heart with her.

"Not here. I'm at work."

I shook myself back to life. "Where can we talk in private?"

"You need to go to school," she countered.

"I told you, I have it covered. I'm way ahead in my next two classes, so I have solid coverage. My cell phone is with a classmate. I also didn't drive my car here, so I can't be tracked. I borrowed Monty's Honda," I snorted. A semblance of a smile bloomed across her face, but I could tell she was conflicted.

"You'd better hurry back, or Monty will go drifting in the school parking lot with your Mercedes," she smirked.

Her light-hearted jab didn't feel genuine because of the uneasiness venting from her pores. I wanted to wrap her in my arms and tell her, repeatedly, that everything was going to be okay. Nothing or no one would ever have the power to tear us apart.

"Like I said, I'm covered. I know you're off the clock right now, which is why I'm here. We need to talk. We've gotta stick to the plan, no matter what."

Harper's eyes blinked rapidly as if trying to hold back tears.

"Baby…" I pleaded.

As if something clicked in her mind, her sight widened. "Wait here," she instructed before walking away from me toward the front counter. The gentleman nodded at Harper as she spoke discreetly. Moments later, he reached down then handed her a key card before Harper headed back to me.

Forty-five minutes later, I was holding her tight against me as we lay naked underneath the sheets. We were both sated after our intense lovemaking. I kissed her soundly, reassured about us.

This is what I came here for.

To reconnect with her.

To reaffirm what we have.

"Angel," I exhaled.

"Puffin," she giggled.

I snorted at her tease. "You didn't answer my question from earlier."

"What question?"

"Are we sticking with the plan? You'll move to Chicago two summers from now and start working at Hyatt HQ. I'll follow behind you that December," I reminded her.

"You think you'll be finished with your degree by then? That's just two and a half years from now."

"I already have a significant amount of credits right now on my transcript. I'll attend classes year-round. I estimate that six classes a term will get me there."

"Holy crap, Ford. That's *a lot*."

"Not for me. I've always managed my time well. I'm early to hand in assignments, always going the extra mile. Hell—I'll even volunteer my tutoring services for some of their more problematic students for extra kudos points with the professors. They love that shit."

Harper laughed. "You seem to have it all figured out. You are more of a grownup than I am."

"We have our roles in this relationship. You're the looks… I'm the brains." She chortled and playfully swatted me on the chest. "I want you doing what you've always dreamt of doing, and I want to be in your life while you're doing it," I added.

Harper gently swept her soft hand across my chin. "My life would be absolutely perfect. The perfect career. The perfect guy," she cooed, pecking my lips.

"And the only thing I care about is your happiness. I want to take care of you," I exhaled, returning her kiss with one of my own.

"You do?" she murmured. I nodded in response. "I want to take care of you too, Ford. No matter what, I will always love you and protect you."

With that, I kissed her like there was no tomorrow. Little did I know at the time, tomorrow would wither away.

Ford

(The Present)

She fucking lied to me.

I was emotionally spent as I switched off the car's ignition inside of the garage at home. For two days, my dreams and waking thoughts had been filled with Harper. It was becoming unbearable. And to think, I'd have many opportunities to run into her at UCLD starting the following week. The thought alone made me ill. Part of me wanted to rip the bandage off quickly and get the awkward face-to-face reunion with Harper over with. However, I had no idea how I'd react if I saw her holding hands with her so-called fiancé.

I can't believe she left me for him.

Did I believe Harper ever loved me in the first place? Something deep down said she couldn't be so cruel as to fake something for that many years. My gut told me she had just gotten tired. She no longer had the strength to fight for us anymore. It was all too much—fighting her dad, fighting my dad.

Harper understood more than anyone how complicated my life was. I hated sounding like a whiny little bitch, but being the son of two people running a multi-billion-dollar global empire wasn't all it was cracked up to be. Part of me related to Eva when she'd ranted about not being able to date Knight once upon a time.

"I almost wish for a normal, working-class family. At least I'd be able to date who I want."

I never thought my folks particularly cared about me dating in general. They seemed more concerned with *who* I was dating. For them, me dating Harper was just weird since she had practically grown up with my sisters and me.

I might've been rash lumping my parents together. My mother—she'd always adored Harper. If I were to take off to be with her, I had a hunch that Mom wouldn't even bat an eye. It was my father who had a problem with every fucking thing I did outside of his perfectly set boundaries. He was dead set on me being molded into his image as if he were God, and I were the first man.

Mason Charles Pope wouldn't be caught dead with an older woman. Fortunately for him, he needn't worry about Harper any longer.

She had succeeded in severing us beyond repair.

Thirteen

Liza

"Damn, baby," he lazily chuckled.

I laughed under my breath in the darkness of the early morning. I turned in bed to face my husband's silhouette. Rapt, I watched the deep rise and fall of his chest. Yet out of nowhere, I casually struck up a conversation as if we hadn't just partaken in hot, steamy sex.

"Are the plans for the Japanese facility completed?" Though I could barely make out the shadows in our dark bedroom, I could tell my husband was dumbfounded by my instant shift. "Mick asked yesterday evening," I added.

"*Shit*—I guess," he sighed, still catching his breath.

"Is hard sex finally getting to be a little too much for you, old man?" I teased.

"Uh… no. It's just…" he stalled.

I took the opportunity to change the topic. "You think Ford might want to spend next summer in Japan to help set things in motion? Perhaps I can bring the girls along, too. You could stay home and keep the ship afloat, so to speak."

"Not a chance. I can't have you spending an entire summer away from me, Mrs. Pope. Although, I don't think it's a bad idea to send Ford. He'll be finished with his degree by then. He'd be our eyes and ears."

"That's if he wants to work with us," I added.

"What do you mean *if*? As *if* he has a choice," Mason scowled.

"We can't force our son to work at LRPI after college. It has to be his decision and his alone."

"I figured you of all people would be confident in our son to make wise choices. He knows LRPI is his birthright—his destiny," he said while he glided his hand across my hair. He hummed a sweet kiss on the corner of my mouth.

"What if he wants to make a name for himself?" I argued.

"It would only be to spite us. We've given that boy too much for him to just turn around and spit in our faces."

"It wouldn't be like that, Mason. Him dreaming of something other than running LRPI wouldn't be out of spite. Who's to say Eva or one of the twins wouldn't be more willing to take over when the time comes?" I suggested.

"Or maybe our next child," he said in a humorous tone.

I snorted. "What are you talking about, Pope? This baby shop is closed, thanks to perimenopause."

Although as of late, I hadn't been experiencing those pesky hot flashes. Instead, a more interesting symptom had taken its place.

"You sure about that, Mrs. Pope?" he murmured.

I arched a brow. "Of course. My doctor said so. Mom, my grandmother… They all went through early menopause."

"I thought lack of sexual desire was a symptom of early menopause. Looks to me there's no *lack* in sight," he purred.

"I've been the same," I squeaked in defense.

"Bullshit. I wouldn't be surprised if you were pregnant right now."

"Give me a break. You're exaggerating. My sex drive is normal." I gawked at him. Why in the world would he even say that? It was preposterous. I'd been pregnant three times and knew the symptoms. The entire first trimester and some of the second had been hell. I was sick all day and night and extremely sensitive to smell and sight. That wasn't happening now.

"Not that I'm complaining, but you've been vise-gripping my

dick for the past few minutes, trying to get it hard again," Mason said with a devilish grin.

I gasped at the delayed realization and released him immediately, blushing. "I… I didn't realize—"

"I know you didn't," he laughed. "For the past few nights, you haven't let me sleep."

He was right. I'd been keeping him up at night. I'd also been waking him up in the middle of the night to scratch my itch. That wasn't like me. Mason was right, my sex drive had been growing out of control lately.

"I'm sorry," I whispered, ashamed.

Before I could breathe, he quickly rolled his naked body on top of mine. "You've always been wild, but you haven't been *this* wild since you were carrying the twins," he teased before planting a bevy of kisses on my neck.

"Stop messing with me, Mason. I'm not pregnant—I'm hormonal," I pouted.

Ford

When I was alone in my dorm room for most of the year, I was never really *totally* alone. There was the background noise of the other residents to contend with. Still, there was the concept of personal space… a certain protective radius where I could reflect without outside interference.

But inhabiting a large compound with tons of wide-open space and my ever-present family, I didn't have the same freedom. For one, my little sisters were constantly underfoot. There was my mom's constant nagging, making sure I ate something for lunch earlier that day. Then, there was Dad, checking in for no apparent reason at all. I knew that was his way of making sure I hadn't snuck out without telling anyone.

Dinnertime wouldn't be for another hour, but I thought I could go for one of those tasty salted caramel cupcakes Brie had baked the other night. I stood from my bedroom desk, leaving the pre-reading for tomorrow's class idle on my laptop.

On the way to the kitchen, I saw Knight and Eva sitting side by side in the main room, sharing a secret laugh. They were free to roam Pope Manor like a happy little couple, free to whisper and cuddle in plain sight. I shook off the envy as best I could and proceeded onward before Knight stopped me in my tracks.

"Yo, Ford!" He rose up to meet me.

"Thibodeau." The two of us greeted one another with our standard hand slap and partial bro-hug.

"Mom says dinner's almost ready," Eva called out while joining us.

"I was just on my way to grab another cupcake," I fessed.

"Might as well save it for dessert. Dinner will be served in a minute. Let's head to the dining room," she suggested.

When we got there, I saw that the rolls, salad, and glasses of water were already spread out. Starving, I pulled the nearest plate from one of the place settings and filled it with Caesar salad, topping it with a buttered roll. Knight followed suit and sat in the chair beside me. My sister went to the kitchen to help Mom, leaving Knight and me alone.

"Dave told me what happened last weekend when you idiots were hanging out," Knight whispered humorously.

"Assholes," I sighed, rolling my eyes.

"They claimed you left the club with the girl. Is she still in the picture?" he said in jest. I knew it was in jest because my answer surprised him.

"Yes."

"Seriously?"

"Not how you think. Come to find out, she's interning over at Zinfinite with me. In the same department, no less."

"Holy crap."

"Yeah, I know. It's all good. We're just friends."

"That's cool. How's Zinfinite coming along?" Knight asked.

"It's going great. I'm learning tons about their corporate culture and how they do things. It's a very laid back, very creative atmosphere."

"Sounds a lot like LRPI," Knight assessed.

"Pretty much."

"Dude—I'm telling you… My internship at LRPI is the best thing ever."

I winced, watching Knight beaming brighter than the sun. Before I could dig deep, oncoming footsteps pulled me out of our conversation.

In walked my father. "Gentlemen. Don't let me interrupt."

"You weren't interrupting, Mr. Pope," Knight ass-kissed. "I was just telling Ford about my internship at LRPI."

My father took his rightful place at the head of the table, which was separated from me by one seat.

"I've been hearing great things from your managers about you," Dad smiled at my sister's boyfriend.

Already? Seemed rather soon for Knight to be garnering the praises of his superiors. It normally took a couple months to decide if a new employee was worth a damn.

"Thank you, sir. I discussed with my immediate supervisor about how I think the regular forecasting data pulling process can be improved. The way it's currently being handled is a bit counterproductive. The current method taints the data set," Knight said.

I frowned, perplexed. "I worked in that department last summer."

"I know," Knight acknowledged.

"I was able to parse the data just fine. It's complicated, but it can be done. All that's needed is a slight front-end fix," I argued.

"The meta data is convoluted. There are tons of redundancies. I'm actually in the process of putting together a change proposal document," Knight revealed.

I couldn't hide my appalled expression. No way in hell were they giving this kid carte blanche to make major process changes. He'd *just* started working there! I started to refute him. "I think that's a complete waste—"

"That's fantastic, Knight," my father said, cutting me off. "Why don't you get in touch with my executive assistant, Sherry, tomorrow and set up a meeting with me in a week to go over your process proposal," Dad said, looking through me and focusing his gaze on Knight.

He can't be fucking serious.

Knight wasn't the first person to make such a claim about the data process, and he was just as wrong as the rest of them had been. Dad had even agreed with me the last time we'd talked about it. He'd also had me put together a document of work instructions for the interns who would follow me.

"Absolutely, Mr. Pope."

Knight looked so pleased with himself, and it took everything in me not to roll my eyes until they bled.

"What's the deal with Thibodeau?" I said, immediately getting to the point of my visit.

An hour after her boyfriend left, I sat on the edge of my sister's bed. Wearing reading glasses, she glanced up from her book to look at me in question.

"He's already trying to make a major move. He's a two-day-a-week intern," I chortled.

My little sis closed her novel and slid her readers from her face. "Knight loves working there."

"Obviously."

"So much so, he wants to quit the team."

My mouth fell open. "He wants to quit baseball?"

Eva nodded. "He finally declared a major—business. He wants to focus on school and working at LRPI."

"What about his athletic scholarship?" I asked, still in shock.

"Something tells me LRPI will pick up his tuition and expenses moving forward."

This had to be a joke. But also, this bullshit had my father's name written all over it.

"Knight loves baseball. He lives and breathes it," I argued.

"Well, so did you," my sister countered. "But even you passed on athletics. They would've given you a scholarship for that, but you didn't need it. However, you still took the academic money—"

"And Dad has given back to Stanford tenfold—"

"...but Knight didn't have that choice. At the time, that baseball scholarship was the only way he could get all his tuition covered."

"It's not like he's poor," I scoffed. "He lives in Arcadia's Crest, and his folks run a chain of pharmacies, for fuck's sake."

"His parents are in big time debt, Ford. They've been living way above their means and are on the verge of bankruptcy. If they were faced with covering Knight's tuition, they wouldn't be able to swing it," Eva said soberly.

The revelation hit me hard. I had no idea my friend was in such a financial dilemma. Suddenly, I felt like a jackass.

It was a brand-new workweek at Zinfinite. The difference this time around was that my routine would be altered, starting this evening. It would be day one of class for me at UCLD.

Happy Birthday to me.

I'd pleaded with my family not to make a big deal out of my nineteenth birthday. As far as I was concerned, it was just another day. I had agreed, however, to partake in a late dessert tonight when I got home from class. I'd never turn down dessert, especially if my mother, Mrs. Benton, or one of my sisters made it.

Harper was also a great baker.

I quickly dismissed the aching thought. It would be just my shitty luck if I ran into her on campus today, of all days.

After a very productive day at work, I exited the office building. I had two hours to burn. Unfortunately, Alana couldn't make it to happy hour this time. Her younger sister had an S.O.S. of her own. Bridget had just broken up with her boyfriend for the fourth time. I figured I'd go home for an hour or so before returning to Los Derivas for class. But as I headed for the employee parking lot, I heard a familiar voice squeak out my name.

Fuck. Me.

Even though the voice was out of place, I instantly knew who it was. I turned slowly and found a surprisingly modestly dressed Rebecca walking toward me. She wore blue jeans and a pink cashmere jacket. Once we stood toe-to-toe, she casually handed me an envelope, which looked to have a card inside it. I took it, dumbfounded.

"Happy Birthday, Love Bug!" she cried out before pouncing with outstretched arms and leaping into me.

How the hell does she know it's my birthday?

"Geez... uh... thanks," I stuttered. "What are you doing here?"

"I wanted to see you. I'm only here for today."

She drove all this way just to see me? "Wow... well—I mean..." I was utterly speechless.

"Did you have plans with your family? If so, I hope you don't mind if I tag along for a bit. I can't wait to meet your parents and your little sisters," Rebecca sparkled.

I was more than convinced the girl had completely lost her mind.

"Actually, I'm taking classes at UC Los Derivas in a couple of hours."

"That's right! Gosh, I'm sorry—I totally forgot about that."

"Aren't you supposed to be in class at Stanford today?" I frowned.

"Yeah, but I told my professors I had to be home today for an emergency," she winked.

Rebecca had lied to be here. Although I was mostly disturbed, I was a shred flattered.

"Look, Rebecca—I'm sorry you came all this way, but I

only have a couple hours before class starts," I said with insincere remorse.

"I wanted to give you both parts of your present. The first is in your hand. As for the second part, all I need is an hour of your time, Love Bug," she purred, pressing her body against mine.

So, she came all this way to give me some booty, eh? Who was I to turn down a little birthday sex, especially if the girl could suck and ride a cock like she could?

"Did you drive here from Stanford?" I asked.

"No—I've been taking an Uber everywhere."

"Damn, that's expensive as hell."

She waved me off. "Daddy's got it covered."

That's right, she'd been a rich kid like me.

"I've been waiting out here for about an hour," Rebecca said as her eyes admired the state-of-the-art architecture of Zinfinite's world headquarters. "It's really nice here."

"I know," I answered shortly. "Look, I have an idea. You wanna hang out at the Meridian for a few?"

Rebecca frowned. "What's that?"

"The Meridian Grande, a five-star hotel here in Los Derivas. I can only stick around for about an hour and thirty," I told her.

"Does that mean we're getting a room? That way, I can give you the second half of your gift," Rebecca beamed.

"Sure, why not," I shrugged. It was my birthday, after all.

I arrived on campus just in the nick of time. If I hadn't known better, I would've assumed Rebecca was literally trying to break my dick off. She rode me like a wildebeest, bringing me to the verge of admitting her gift might've been the best surprise birthday present I'd ever received.

Still, I couldn't ignore how nerve-wracking it was being with her. Rebecca was now under the impression that she could insert herself into my life whenever she wanted. Breaking a sweat with her had been all fine and dandy, but I didn't want her making these visits a habit. The last thing I needed was Dad or Mr. Benton catching me with her.

The first night of class had ended smoothly, ending in just an hour and a half instead of two. I ran into a few familiar faces, mostly from high school, on my way to the commuter student parking lot. I stopped for a few to chat, letting them know why I was here for just the spring. We exchanged contact information and vowed to keep in touch before I resumed my journey to my car. I finally saw it in the distance but froze in my tracks when I heard someone else call my name. This time, the very sound made my stomach bottom out.

It's my fucking birthday. Not today, Satan.

I wasn't ready to face her, even though I assumed I had my emotions under control. Everything I'd pushed down had buoyed back up to the surface. It was the shittiest feeling. Ignoring her, I popped the car locks open and tossed my bag into the back seat. The sound of footsteps became louder.

"Ford—hey."

I shut the back door and turned to face the voice's owner. My heart nearly stopped beating, and my breath was stuck in my throat. It was Harper, and she was as beautiful as ever. As I stared at her, time stood still.

I knew seeing her here at some point would be a given, but I wasn't prepared for it to happen so soon. Foolish me for assuming that if it rained, it wouldn't pour.

First Rebecca, and now this.

"*You...*" It was evident she was alarmed by my hesitancy to speak.

"Hey."

There was no bitterness present in my monosyllabic response. I was essentially a robot. Perhaps my automatic response system had kicked in once my normal coping mechanism had checked out. I silently hoped it would reboot soon.

"Welcome to UC Los Derivas. You look *really* good," Harper said casually.

"I'm only here for the semester," I answered in a hurry. The swirling in my stomach told me that was probably an inadequate response.

Maybe a simple 'Thank you' would've sufficed.

"I know," she replied. "Did first day of class go well?"

I had no idea what was going through her head. You'd think the simpler task would be to figure out what's going on in mine. Yet, I couldn't seem to decipher my own thoughts. To kill some of the awkward time, I decided to take one good look at her. I regretted it right away.

She wore an ankle-length, baggy pea-green dress underneath an unzipped studded leather jacket. Her entire right leg was exposed through the slit of the dress. Anchored to the ground were two beige suede high-heeled boots. When my eyes moved back up, they landed on her gorgeous blond hair, which was tucked behind her ears.

My brows met my hairline once I snapped back into reality. It boggled my mind how she could carry on such a casual conversation after our last exchange. She'd hung up on me.

"Class went okay?" she asked again, completely ignoring the stare-down I was giving her.

"Yep. This is your final semester here, right?" I awkwardly asked.

"Yes—thank God," she breathed. "I'm looking forward to being done. You're quite close, too, aren't you?"

"I'm shooting for December."

Yeah, Harper, I'm still sticking to the plan.

Even though you have plans of your own nowadays.

"That means you'll be attending classes in the summer, right?"

"Back at Stanford," I said dully.

I leaned against my car with my palm on the roof as we stood in uncomfortable silence.

"I won't keep you," she said, glancing down at her wristwatch. Her eyes opened wide all of a sudden. "Crap—it's your birthday..."

I hadn't expected for her to care. Hell, even I didn't care tonight.

"It's no big dea—"

Before I could complete the sentence, she approached me for a hug. Surprised by the gesture, I fumbled my arms around her just before she let me go. I released my hold, and she stepped back, but the damage was done. The familiar sweet scent of her hair invaded my nostrils, making my shoulders slump.

"Happy Birthday. I'm sure you have to head home for the festivities. I know how your mom is. She lives for her kids' birthdays." She chuckled nervously and smoothed out the invisible wrinkles in both her jacket and dress.

"Yeah," I sighed, opening the driver's door.

"I guess I'll see you around," she exhaled. "Take care."

"You too, Harper," I responded. As I climbed inside my car, I caught a glimpse of the modestly sized diamond reflecting the streetlamp on her left ring finger. My entire soul disintegrated.

That girl used to be mine.

After closing the door, I watched her walk away from my rearview mirror. There was a glimmer of hope within me that she would turn around to see me one last time. She didn't give me a second glance. Disheartened, I cranked the ignition. The second she disappeared between two buildings, my forehead met the steering wheel and lightly tapped it five times.

I fucking hated myself for still loving her.

Liza

I headed home from work early to help Trisha with Ford's birthday dinner. I was grateful she'd made the red velvet cupcakes earlier in the day. They were Ford's favorite. I was glad to be busy, but it hadn't kept Mason's words from the other night out of my head. It had played over and over again like a broken record.

"You've always been wild, but you haven't been this wild since you were carrying the twins."

My paranoia was in full effect. I'd passed on wine with dinner last night, even though I was certain I wasn't pregnant. My cycle was as erratic off birth control as it was on it. According to my doctor, my chances of getting pregnant were slim to none, yet I couldn't help but feel anxious. That was why I'd stopped by the grocery on my way home from work. I'd grabbed a few necessities as well as something else.

Once home, I greeted Trisha in the kitchen, and she immediately took the shopping bags from me, along with my jacket. I promised her my swift return before heading to my bedroom to change. Trisha said to take my time.

By some miracle, I managed to get to my room without being intercepted by any of the girls. I locked the door behind me and grabbed what I needed from my purse before entering the master bath.

I ripped the box open.

I knew the drill. I'd done it at least two other times before.

This time, I prayed *not* to see a plus sign.

I did my business, washed my hands, and waited.

Fourteen

Liza

I lay in bed, my eyes glued to the ceiling.

Earlier, we'd had Ford's birthday dinner... *without* Ford. Mrs. Benton had made sure to set aside a nice helping of his favorite—bowtie pasta with grilled chicken and sundried tomatoes. When he arrived home after class, he'd reheated the dish before topping it off with an insane amount of freshly grated parmesan cheese. Before that, Mason, Mom, the girls, and I sang *Happy Birthday* to him before he blew out the candle on his cupcake.

I couldn't help but notice my dear son hadn't been himself today, even though he'd insisted that both work and class went well. It later dawned on me that he could have possibly encountered Harper on campus. I wondered if Ford was still hung up on her. Perhaps discovering her pregnancy did him in.

Was she showing yet?

My stomach fluttered at the thought.

Well, if that's what has him down, I have another humdinger for him.

Before I could wallow in my anxiety, Mason strolled in.

"You're still awake?" he murmured as he climbed into bed. I hummed in response as I turned on my side. He spooned me from behind, pulling aside my hair to kiss the nape of my neck.

"Ford seemed distracted tonight. He wasn't his usual joking self with his sisters," Mason reflected out loud. Still in his grasp, I twisted my body around to face him.

I wanted to bring up the notion of Harper as a possible reason for Ford's distant demeanor. Instead, my own pressing issue practically somersaulted from my belly and spewed out of my mouth.

"I'm pregnant."

I even shocked myself at how the words just came tumbling out. It was mind-boggling because I'd been pregnant three other times before. I should've been a pro by now. What made it worse was that Mason's expression gave nothing away.

"I took a home pregnancy test today. The results were as clear as day," I murmured.

He finally showed some emotion, and I wanted to punch his lights out. He hadn't exploded or yelled. No. Instead, his mouth curled into a slow smirk, looking rather pleased with himself.

"I'm a steed, baby. A stallion. Your eggs simply can't resist my virility," he boasted.

My doctor was going to get an earful first thing in the morning. I hated liars.

Mason rolled me onto my back and climbed on top of me. He looked down, beaming from ear to ear. I was pissed but couldn't help but be amused by his giddy expression. His glee had eased the tension in the room, but I needed to give him some perspective on why I couldn't bask in his glory. I arched a brow at him.

"I'm forty-two, and you're fifty-two. We have four teenagers. Before the year ends, we'll have a newborn. You don't find this odd?"

"We fuck a lot, hon. I'm surprised we don't have more than five." I rolled my eyes at him, and he narrowed his in reply.

"It's been a while since I've changed diapers. It's going to be crazy starting all over again," I sighed.

"You're the perfect mother, Eliza," he crooned softly before planting kisses on my throat. "I'm looking forward to you being even more insatiable than you already are. Right around the seven-month mark, you'll insist my dick stay in you at all times," he growled. I slapped him across his back, and the ass had the nerve to laugh.

"I am freaking out, Mason."

"Why?" he shrugged. "We're rich as fuck, baby. If you want to keep working, we can hire a full-time nanny. Hell—a team of nannies."

I adamantly shook my head. "No, silly. I'm freaking out about how the kids will take the news."

"They'll be fine. The twins are going to be fighting over who will spend the most time with their new baby sister or brother," he uttered with his lips pressed against my shoulder.

"What if it's twins again?"

"Great. Bring it on."

I scoffed. "What about Ford and Eva? They're at the age where they might feel *really weird* about this."

Mason gently stretched the neckline of my gown to expose more skin at the base of my neck. He traced my skin with the tip of his tongue, and I shivered.

"They'll get over it," he exhaled before flurrying hungry little kisses across my shoulder blades. He craftily eased up my night-gown at the hem.

"Mason," I sighed his name in a laugh.

"*Shhh,*" he vocalized, tugging the silky garment all the way off. I was now naked from head to toe. I'd learned after twenty-plus years of going to bed with a highly sexual man not to waste a good pair of clean panties after a shower. In haste, Mason yanked off his shirt, boxer briefs, and pajama pants.

"What is your deal? Why the rush?" I breathed.

"The moment you uttered the words 'I'm pregnant,' my dick got instantly hard," he rasped right before rolling his naked body on top of mine.

Twenty years ago, I'd had no idea how Mason would be as a father. But with each child we'd brought forth together, his heart had expanded just a little bit more. Mason loved being Dad. And as a husband, he was dynamic. I loved living life with him.

Liza Pope, you are such a lucky broad.

"Pope—what am I going to do with you?" I giggled.

"You're going to lie there and take this dick like the champ you are," he growled.

I bellowed so hard my stomach started to ache. He ignored my mirth and remained focused on attacking my neck with his mouth. All humor went away as I became turned on to the highest degree.

"You're such a freak," I moaned.

"I'm *your* freak," he whispered as our lips touched, and he pushed his erection inside me.

Ford

My eyes sprung open, and I instantly reached for my phone on the bedside table. I groaned in exasperation because it wasn't even midnight. Heart-wrenching dreams invading my sleep had stopped me from reaching tomorrow. Dreams that combined real memories with a future that would never come to pass between Harper and me.

I couldn't understand why she continued weighing so hard on my psyche. As of late, dreams of her had been a constant occurrence. I knew I had to get it through my thick skull somehow, my subconsciousness, to drive home that she and I would never be.

Here were the facts...

Harper was engaged.

Harper had moved on without me.

It had been nearly three months, yet in my mind, reality hadn't absorbed past the first layer. Over and over again, I tried to figure out how to scour this woman from my every thought. Desperation practically had me down on both knees, pleading for mercy. I'd been on the verge of seeking outside help. This was madness, and I needed a way out.

With my brain running one hundred miles an hour, I knew I

had zero chances of falling back asleep right away. Feeling defeated, I put on my slippers and journeyed quietly to the game room, where I attempted to blast away my shitty insomnia.

Hours later, I was at my desk at work. Alana showed up ten minutes after me and glanced in my direction on the way to her workstation. I quickly mouthed the three letters we'd agreed to use when we required an ear and a shoulder. She paused in place and winced before mouthing back, "Lunch?" I nodded, and she mimicked me in conformation before gracefully gliding to her desk in her very high heels.

A short time later, my manager, Barry Issam, stopped by my desk to praise me for my vendor price analysis efforts, which one of the purchasing managers used to negotiate a lower price with two of his main suppliers. He also invited me to start attending his supplier management meetings, which interns or lower-level Zinfinite Corp employees never sat in.

The rush of endorphins I had due to Barry's bombardment of accolades invigorated me, because for once, they had nothing to do with my last name or my parents. From that moment on, I knew burying myself in work would be the key to drowning every single waking thought about Harper Benton. Getting through spring and returning to Stanford in the summer in one piece was my primary goal. I had two graduate-level courses, an exciting internship, and my family and friends to keep me busy. I had no time to mope over the past or a future that would never be.

At lunch, Alana and I walked over to Alibi, our watering hole of choice. Instead of gin and tonic, we stuck with iced tea and water.

"That's awesome news, Ford." Alana seemed just as excited as I was about my recent inclusion in the company's high-profile supplier meetings.

"I was floored when Barry told me," I exhaled, still stunned by the news from earlier.

"They are going to be begging you to work for them after you graduate. Mark my words," she beamed as her plump cherry-red lips curled around the tip of her straw. I quickly shook off my wayward thoughts.

"Honestly, I don't know what I'm going to do. I'd planned to move to Chicago and define myself without the help of the Pope name. Now that Harper's out of the picture, I can be pretty much anywhere," I mused.

Alana's eyes rounded in realization. "You called an S.O.S. first thing this morning. Did you see her last night on campus?"

I shut my eyes in despair, regretting calling out an S.O.S. before making the decision to no longer meditate on my ex. Still, Alana doesn't let up.

"What did she say? Did you talk?"

I proceeded to tell her how Harper met me at my car and how we made small talk for a few before I headed home. "She wished me a happy birthday," I said under my breath as I took another swig of water.

"That was nice—I guess," she said awkwardly.

"It was hard seeing her," I admitted.

"I'd bet. On the bright side, you only have to get through these next couple of months. After that, you'll never have to see her again."

I took in a deep, calming breath. "Right. It's best I continue to play it cool and not lose my head every time I run into her."

"Exactly. Be cool and cordial when you see her, but keep it short," Alana advised.

Forty-five minutes later, we were walking back to work, joking about a high-strung intern who works with us. Alana's imitation of him was spot on. Her laugh was so adorable and contagious, I couldn't help but join her. As we stood outside of our building, we were in stitches. She gripped both hands around my bicep, presumably to keep herself from falling to the ground. A sudden high-pitched shrill from behind staggered us.

"Who the fuck is this, Ford?!"

Alana and I turn in unison and face an angry blonde in a

pink cashmere jacket, tight dark blue jeans, and black stilettos. My stomach twisted in knots.

Rebecca.

"What the hell are you still doing here?" I snapped. "You're supposed to be at Stanford." The sight of her standing outside my job, yet again, without notice made my blood boil.

"Is this Harper?!" Rebecca growled in disgust. Before I could yell back, my lunch mate calmly corrected her.

"I'm Alana."

Rebecca answered with a scoff. "Well, *Alana*—I don't know if Ford told you, but he's my boyfriend. So, I'd appreciate it if you didn't flop yourself all over him."

"Stop it. We are *not* together," I hissed.

Her anger quickly morphed into desperation. "You can't be with anyone else, Ford!"

I was done—no longer able to deal. So, I yanked Rebecca by the arm, pulling her in the opposite direction. Once we were a good distance away from Alana, I laid into Rebecca.

"You're fucking out of line. Alana is my coworker. You're not supposed to be in Los Derivas," I seethed.

"I had to see you—"

Due to lack of sleep and the emotional rollercoaster of facing Harper, I'd run out of patience. "We'd already established that you and I were *just* friends. Because of what you just pulled back there, we can no longer be that. You've completely blown my trust."

"Ford—*no*," she begged, weeping.

"You've left me no other choice. You can't just show up to my job and yell at my coworkers like that. You are putting my internship in jeopardy."

"I didn't mean to! I love you!"

Fuck me.

"You're psychotic, Rebecca. You need to leave," I said, exasperated.

She fell apart right there on that busy downtown Los Derivas street, hysterical. Yet, I knew I couldn't console her because it would only encourage her to keep behaving like a lunatic. So instead, I served her a cold expression until she finally buckled and left. As she hopped in the taxi I called, I felt the heat of disapproving stares from spectators. I couldn't have cared less. Rebecca was completely in the wrong.

I was surprised to see Alana still there when I walked back toward the building. She held an unreadable expression for a long while before it slipped into a smirk. That smirk then gave way to laughter. I closed my eyes and shook my head in embarrassment.

"Alright, playboy. We still have a few minutes left. You must dish," Alana beamed, hungry for the sordid details about my intruder.

"Please, don't make me," I grimaced.

"Park bench," she ordered, pointing to the nearby seats perched in the center of the lawn. I reluctantly followed her lead. There, I explained how the occasional BJ with a cheerleader became hot sex. I even spilled about the hour of passion that took place on my birthday.

"She wants more and obviously can't take the hint," I told Alana. "It boggles my mind how she's so focused on me when she's known for being loose around campus."

Alana's disappointed reaction chilled me instantly. "Loose or not, she still has feelings."

Right away, I felt like a massive dick for leading Rebecca on. Sure, she couldn't take the hint, but she didn't deserve to be treated like a toy to put away after I was done playing with her. I, of all people, should've understood how it felt to love someone and not be loved in return.

Fifteen

Ford

Twenty minutes after leaving work for the day, I sat alone at a tiny table inside of a nearby coffee shop. After Alana had talked some sense into me earlier, I'd decided to text Rebecca with an apology. Eventually, she'd replied, letting me know she hadn't left town and agreed to meet me.

When she sauntered into the coffee shop, she spotted me right away. Her eyes looked extremely puffy as she dragged her small suitcase behind her, making me feel like a complete jackass. I stood to greet her and pulled out the chair on the other side of the table for her. I'd already bought her one of those frothy caramel latte thingies she liked so much, which she took right away after sitting down. I reclaimed my chair and my plain black coffee.

"Rebecca—I'm sorry for the way I spoke to you. I wish you would've called before surprising me again at work."

"I'm sorry," she whined. "I can't help myself. I always want to be near you."

In an instant, I started to regret calling this meeting. I had no clue how to get her to see that we would never be an *us*, but I tried. "You knew I didn't want to be in a relationship. I told you this from the beginning, and you said you were fine with that," I reminded her.

"I know—I know. I thought I could handle it, but I obviously can't," she answered with a shaky voice.

"I told you all about my past with Harper. I am still dealing with that breakup. In fact, today, I decided I was going bury myself in my internship and my coursework. I'm putting love on the back burner for a very long time."

Rebecca's laser-sharp eyes bore into me, and I saw something so familiar. She and I shared a similar pain, but hers didn't come from me. I decided to take a shot in the dark.

"I don't know who he was to you. Maybe he was your high school sweetheart or someone you've known since elementary school. From the moment he broke your heart, perhaps you started to lose your way. That's when you decided to hide your own pain by bringing pleasure to other guys. But did that *really* heal the hurt?"

I couldn't believe I'd said that to her. Someone else should've been reciting those same words to me. I was grateful for the extra napkins on the table because Rebecca had them clutched in a ball to dab against her face. I'd obviously struck a nerve.

"We used each other to dull the pain," I said point-blank.

"I really do care about you, Ford. I seriously thought I was over that guy. Hell, I can't even say his fucking name without wanting to hurl," she sniffled.

"You need to put *you* first again. Stop relying on someone else to make you happy. Don't fuck up your opportunity at Stanford for some dude, even if that dude is me. Get back there and kick some ass. Move on and take over corporate America, or whatever it is you want to accomplish in the future. That's what I'm going to do."

After over an hour of consoling and encouraging her, we hugged it out.

"Promise we'll still be friends when you get back to Stanford," she softly pleaded.

"Just friends—*no* benefits," I smirked. I could tell she didn't like my answer at first, but understanding eventually surfaced across her sweet face.

"I promise to be better. I won't go down in history as the campus Head Queen," she declared.

I grinned. "Good girl."

Soon after, we shared one last cordial smile before I closed the rear door of her ride share that would take her back to Stanford.

I ran into Harper again on campus, but this time, I didn't stop to talk.

She'd yelled my name across the courtyard, and I simply waved at her with an artificial smile. She waved back, but her disappointed expression told me she had expected me to stop and shoot the shit with her. Instead, I kept walking with long strides as if I were late for class. In reality, I arrived fifteen minutes early.

As I took my seat in the practically empty lecture hall, my short encounter validated that keeping a physical distance from Harper was the right way to go.

I was now more determined than ever to get this girl out of my system.

I'm sick of constantly thinking about her.

I'm tired of always dreaming about her.

Until then, I'd thought a no-strings-attached sexual relationship would do the trick to erase all signs of Harper from my being. Instead, I ended up with bat-shit crazy Rebecca on one hand, and cool-ass Alana on the other. That was the universe's way of telling me there was no safe way of engaging in a sex-only arrangement. Eventually, someone would want more.

I couldn't use sex to mask the pain anymore.

If my friends, colleagues, and schoolmates thought I was an asshole now, they hadn't seen anything yet. I reiterated my promise to myself to go above and beyond in every aspect of my life. If there wasn't a challenge, I'd make one. I was given the opportunity to sit in Zinfinite senior management meetings, so I would take advantage of it as much as possible and garner the attention of all the higher-ups. My thrill-of-the-chase drive ignited a spark that had me eager to play and conquer the corporate game. When I was done with them, they'd more than feel my absence. I might've felt horrible about leading a girl on, but I had no bones about taking everything I wanted from these corporate America big-shots before leaving them high and dry. My family's company included.

As the lecturer addressed the now full room, I pondered the question: Had I learned everything there was to know from my father, one of the masters of our modern economy? For the past few years, he'd been single-minded about taking me under his wing. His end goal was to sculpt me in his own image. He wanted nothing other than for me to take over LRPI after he and Mom were done. Unbeknownst to him, I had no intention to stay in Arcadia's Crest or to run his company. However, I couldn't help being curious about every single facet that made Mason Pope tick in the business world.

Maybe I'd go to LRPI and work for him after college after all. That way, I'd be able to get inside my father's head and learn all the things that made him the brilliant businessman he was. You see, the only way to take over the world is to start under the tutelage of a master.

I knew I had what it took to work my way up to being on a first-name basis with the CEO of Zinfinite. But let's be real—this guy may be a billionaire, but he lived at the mercy of a board and shareholders. In contrast, Mason Pope was his own man. *He* made all the rules and called all the shots.

That's exactly who I wanted to be.

After class, I maintained tunnel vision as I marched toward the parking lot, praying not to run into *her*.

"Yo! Ford!"

I was grateful it was only Knight.

"You just get out of class?" he asked, adjusting his backpack over one shoulder.

"Yep," I exhaled.

"I was on my way to my dorm. You wanna grab a coffee or something?" Thibodeau offered.

"Sure, man."

At the on-campus coffee spot, we caught up while drinking our tall cups of black coffee.

"I probably told you this before, but your dad is amazing," he gushed. I winced at him. "Working at LRPI is a dream come true. I never thought I'd ever love the business world more than I love baseball."

"Eva told me you were looking for an alternative to your sports scholarship," I said matter-of-factly. "Any luck?"

"It's already done. Coach wasn't happy about it, but I have to think about myself and my family. A career in baseball isn't a sure thing for me."

Holy shit, I thought. *He actually did it. He quit baseball.*

"How are you—"

"I received a scholarship from LRPI," he said, answering my unasked question. "I get to work a minimum of thirty hours a week while finishing school. It's going to be tough, but I'm focused, man. I'm sure you understand since you're doing the same thing—working and finishing school."

"Sure," I agreed.

"To top it off, your father has decided to mentor me personally. Isn't that great?" Knight said gleefully.

It didn't sound *great* to me. I knew my father was using Knight as a substitute for me. With baseball now behind him, Knight could be everything Mason Pope wanted him to be. But in reality, Thibodeau's climb to the top at LRPI would be limited. He was dating my sister, but he'd never be family. The one with the keys to Pope Tower must have Pope blood running through his veins.

I wouldn't shit on his parade, though. He looked too excited to be my father's pawn.

"I still can't believe it. I've already learned a great deal from your dad," Knight gleamed.

"You have a chance to show him your proposal for the data set problem?" I asked.

"I officially meet with him in two weeks, but he's already reviewed my draft. He wants me to spend time with the data architecture team. That way, I can make a more informed suggestion."

I still believed Knight was wasting his time, but hey—whatever floated his boat. He would figure it out for himself. Instead, I showered him with praise. "That's fantastic. The data architecture team is top-notch. It's good you'll be spending time with them and my father."

"I may even enroll in a few database classes in the fall."

That was a bad idea and a total time suck. Especially if it wasn't what he was going to school for. Still, I bit my tongue. "Not a bad idea."

"Enough about me. How are things at Zinfinite?"

"Not bad. I was able to impact a couple of major vendor accounts and in turn, got pulled into some high-profile management meetings."

"Whoa—you are a force of nature, my friend. Just like your pops. When you're all done at Stanford, you have to bring that tenacity to LRPI. I'd love to work with you, man," he grinned, looking full of hope.

If he'd said that to me a day earlier, I would've shot him down immediately. But now, I saw clearly that working at Zinfinite after college wouldn't give me the knowledge and the freedom I needed to innovate and elicit change across the board. Working anywhere other than LRPI after college would ensure I remained under someone's thumb. Even if working for myself was the end goal, I still needed to work in order to build my initial capital. As a stipulation, I wouldn't be able to use my trust toward any independent business venture. It was a safeguard to ensure no Pope offspring would run off to become the next Bernie Madoff and soil the family name. We'd have to do that on our own dime.

The only logical choice for me was to begin my post-educational career at the very company my great-great grandfather started. My dad may have been a tyrant when it came to my career and love life, but if I were to come on board at LRPI and positively impact the bottom line, he'd let me soar. My experience working beside him would take me anywhere.

"We shall see," I finally responded, flashing Knight a secret smirk.

Before my drive home from campus, I saw I'd received a text earlier from my mother, which I replied to before starting my car.

Mom: Are you on your way? We'll wait before having dinner.

Ford: Yes, but don't wait for me. Go ahead and eat.

I thought that was odd because they'd never waited on me before, not even on my birthday. I had questions. Without warning, a frazzled Eva appeared as soon as I pulled into the garage.

"Finally, you're here. Something fishy is going on, and I have no idea what in the world is happening."

Even though I'd arrived safe and sound, I felt whiplashed. "What do you mean?"

"We haven't eaten yet. The twins and I are starving," my sister griped while I yanked my backpack from the backseat.

"I told mom not to wait for me. Everyone knows I'm in class until late," I frowned.

"She texted me, asking if Knight was coming for dinner. It's Friday. He only does Saturday or Sunday. Mom knows that."

I couldn't decode these random-ass clues that evidently screamed something significant. Something my sister wasn't telling.

"I just left Knight. We had coffee on campus. What's the deal?"

My sister hemmed and hawed before coming clean about what was truly bothering her. "I have a bad feeling Mom and Dad are calling a family meeting."

"Shit," I sighed in disappointment.

"I know," Eva whined.

The last time I'd sat through one of those dreadful meetings, it was my parents informing us that Harper would no longer be over to the house. That had been the worst night of my life, up to that point.

God only knows what shit show my parents would dish out tonight, along with the meat and potatoes.

Sixteen

Liza

I sat amidst my family at the silent dinner table, wishing my news had happened a few days earlier while my mother was still in town. If Julia were here, the kids would be less tempted to scream, and Mason wouldn't be so compelled to unleash insurmountable wrath in response. I was bracing for World War III.

Unable to focus on the contents of my plate, I surveyed the room. At the head of the table and to my left, Mason was devouring his meal. Ten minutes earlier, he'd been annoyed that I kept everyone waiting for so long. He didn't understand my reasoning for insisting that Ford be present for our announcement.

I observed the twins seated across from me, and they looked moments away from falling face first in their plates. I couldn't blame them since it was their bedtime. My oldest two, Eva and Ford, were seated on my right. It was obvious they were studying their father and me between bites.

I'd thought about waiting until tomorrow to break the news, but the kids were often busy on Saturdays, doing their own thing. I couldn't chance having any of them hearing the big news second hand. They needed to hear it from their father and me, and they needed to hear it now. I was unsure how I'd drop the bomb, but it had to be done.

Finally, I decided to put them out of their misery—*and* me.

"So… I'm sure you're wondering why we're all here eating

dinner *really* late," I prefaced. In response, the twins groaned in agony.

"It's not my fault," Ford mumbled through a mouth full of bread. "I told Mom to let you guys eat."

"I'm *so* tired," Beth moaned.

"Me, too," echoed Brie.

I stared helplessly at my husband, who, as usual, looked calm and cool. *Damn him.* Thankfully, he took the hint and the reins.

"Since the family is all together, your mother and I have some news to share."

The sudden rhythmic clanking of silverware to porcelain followed by silence let me know we had everyone's undivided attention. Four pairs of young eyes that were a composite of Mason's and mine stared at the two of us. I started tasting an acidic version of my meatloaf rising in my throat. I gulped my glass of water to chase it down before taking a deep, calming breath.

It was now or never.

"We... We are..."

Why was this so hard?!

Just say the words, Liza.

"Oh, my God—are you guys getting a divorce?!" Brie shrieked in utter horror.

Her way-off-base assumption most certainly threw me for a loop.

Why would she even insinuate that?

"No freaking way that's happening!" Eva snarled at her little sister. "Those two are constantly slobbering all over each other."

Just when I thought we were doing a stellar job hiding our canoodling from our kids.

Ford laughed, and I felt the heat rising in my cheeks. Mason was definitely getting a kick out of my discomfort and didn't even pretend not to smile. From there, the conversation continued to get further and further away from me.

"Our friend, Missy Draper at school... Her folks told her and her sister last weekend that they were getting a divorce. Missy is devastated," Beth explained. "I told Brie that would *never* happen to us."

"You don't know that!" Brie struck back.

It was obvious that a dash of anxiety mixed in with hours of hunger and *a* lot of fatigue is what caused Brie to assume the worst. We made it a point to never argue in front of the children, but it was evident they weren't as blind to our private disagreements as we thought. The *Eva dating* argument came to mind.

By now, all of the kids were speaking out of turn about the impending divorce between their parents, and my brain became as mushy as the mashed potatoes on my plate. This late family meeting had been a terrible idea.

"Quiet!" Mason roared. The kids instantly hushed. "No one is getting a divorce. We don't believe in that word in this house. I love your mother very, very much." He took my closest hand and pressed it to his lips.

"Sick," I heard Eva mumble beside me. Ford reacted with a faint snort.

"And I think your mother loves me too," Mason said, winking at me. I answered with a smile of my own. "Which is why..." Mason lobbed the ball up in the air and looked at me to slam it into the hoop. So, I did.

"We're having another baby."

My eyes shifted from Mason to the kids. Brie and Beth were wide awake now. The identical twins mirrored one another, and their expressions conveyed identical levels of shock. Their eyebrows were close to their hairlines, and their lips had parted into near-perfect Os. Then, their shock changed into something else.

"Oh, my God!" they screamed before leaping to their feet. "We're finally going to be big sisters!" No matter how old they got, their identical twinning thing would never cease to amaze me.

As the two extremely excited sisters hugged each other in victory, Mason leaned over to me with a satisfied smirk. "See—I told you there was nothing to worry about," he murmured, planting a kiss to my temple. I closed my eyes as the same nausea whooshed down into the pit of my stomach. A few beats later, I opened my eyes and turned my head to the right. Both Ford and Eva looked the polar opposite of the twins.

I knew it. They hate this.

Ford

I gawked at my mother, who anxiously chewed a mouthful of bread while my father squeezed her hand. Dare I say my old man looked proud? I had no fucking idea why. Dude was over fifty and about to have a newborn. Obviously, Mason Pope's pullout game was atrocious, and Eliza Cooper-Pope didn't know the meaning of birth control. I wanted to facepalm. Meanwhile, Eva couldn't hide her outrage.

"Are you freaking kidding me?!" she screeched.

"This was not planned, believe it or not," Mom defended. "Regardless, you will have a new baby sister or brother come this summer."

"Yaaaaassssss!!!" Beth cheered triumphantly.

The predicament was weighing more heavily on Mom than Dad. In contrast to her seeming on the verge of a breakdown, he sat there sporting a shit-eating grin. Mom would be the one enduring pregnancy and all its side effects while Mason Pope made plans for his new spawn to take over the planet. It was going to be a boy—I was sure of it. I'd started believing the online Illuminati rumors about my father long ago and was certain he and his co-conspirators had already sacrificed to the gods in hopes of a son who'd finally get shit right.

A son who wouldn't argue with him at every turn.

A son who would do everything he wanted before he even asked.

A son who fell in love with the girl he wanted him to fall in love with.

A son who was just like him, willing to pick up the LRPI mantle once he stepped down.

My sister's venomous voice yanked me out of my self-pity. "This summer?! You've known you were pregnant for months?!"

Mom gazed empathetically at her eldest daughter, but Dad wasn't as patient. "Eva—settle down."

His warning was glacial. Eva wisely took the hint, closing her eyes and taking in a few deep breaths to collect herself. As children of Mason Pope, we knew we were at level one of MP's explosion index. There weren't many levels left before we'd face a nuclear event, so we knew better than to chance it by pushing him to the edge. When it came to our father, the fucking needle could skip from a *one* to a *ten* in a matter of seconds.

"I only found out yesterday," Mom said in her defense. "I didn't think I could have any more children after the twins. This was as shocking for me as it is for you."

"Mom—I'm sorry," Eva said after cooling down. Mom soberly nodded, and Dad's smile from earlier was restored.

"This baby will be a blessing, just like all of you," he said. He squeezed Mom's hand over the table as he fondly looked at each of his children. When his eyes landed on me, a thought crossed my mind.

I have a feeling he didn't actually mean that as a blanket statement.

The longer he stared, the more I felt like a fraud. I shifted my gaze over to my mom out of nervousness. The concept of a couple who's less than five years away from being complete empty nesters, yet starting all over again, was absurd. Yet I refused to give Mom any crap about it like my sister had. Mom seemed more worried about our reaction to her news than anything else.

At this point in her life, she should be able to take spur-of-the-moment trips with Aunt Jessie around the world. But with a new baby on the way, it would be difficult for her to drop everything. Dad, on the other hand, wouldn't break a sweat. He'd have Mom right where he wanted her—at home with him, along with a new fan to worship the ground he walked on.

If anyone could hear my thoughts, they'd assume Mason Pope was the world's worst father. False. When I was a little kid, my dad was fucking amazing. He was an awesome father. The problem was, the shine wore off the moment I started making decisions outside of his perfect will. Perhaps the new addition was a blessing in disguise. They were going to be spoiled more than the four of their siblings combined. It would also take the heat away from us.

"Congratulations, Mom—Dad," I finally said. "I might not be here when the baby comes home, but I'll make it back as soon as I can." I gave them a genuine smile and saw the weight visibly lift off my mother's chest. I saw my sister scowling in my periphery. She might've assumed I'd freak out more than she had, justifying her earlier outburst.

"Thank you, sweetheart," my mother answered, now smiling.

"I'm in charge of decorating the baby's room," Beth called dibs.

"No way—I have the best decorating taste," Eva argued.

Wow, that was fast.

"All of us will have a say," Mom declared lovingly. She and my sisters began their excited chatter on how the new baby's room should look. Meanwhile, Dad and I exchanged a look of amusement.

"We need to find out what Mom's having before we finalize anything," Eva ruled.

"Are you having more twins?" a hopeful Beth interjected.

Mom's face shifted in horror, and everyone laughed.

I woke with a start, unable to recall what I'd dreamt about. The heaviness in my gut told me Harper Benton had been all over it. I checked my phone on the nightstand for the time after a trip to the bathroom. It was only a quarter 'til two.

I'd just eaten dinner four hours ago, but I was seriously craving something sweet. So, I navigated through the quiet, dark house and into the kitchen, where I only activated a small fraction of the recessed LEDs embedded in the high ceiling. On the counter, I spied a clear glass dome encasing a glorious chocolate cake. I could've sworn I heard the *Hallelujah* chorus playing in my head.

Right away, I took a small plate from the cupboard and reached into the utensil drawer for a cake spatula. As soon as I lifted the dome, my father entered the kitchen, startling me.

"I see we both had the same idea," he smirked.

I flashed a guilty grin. "Want a slice?"

He narrowed his eyes in a *what the hell do you think* gesture before reaching into the cupboard for his own plate. Sauntering to the silverware drawer, he retrieved two dessert forks. *Good thinking, Pops.*

I cut us each a sizable helping of chocolate bliss, and the two of us sat at the breakfast bar to indulge.

"Your mother won't be happy when she finds out someone inhaled half the cake while everyone was sleeping," my father said. He wasn't all that concerned since he proceeded to take a guilt-free chomp of it from his fork. I chuckled as I licked the rich, thick icing from mine.

"By the way, nice going on how you handled your mother spilling the beans at dinner. She was very worried how you kids would react."

"I could tell. So... How does it feel to be starting all over again? You and Mom ready to lose sleep?" I teased.

"You know I hardly sleep anyway. And I'm certain the Bentons missed taking our baby barf covered suits to the cleaners."

I chuckled. "At least it's not double the load this time. I vaguely recall the chaos after the twins arrived."

"Yes—it was chaotic, but I wouldn't trade it for the world. I've learned over the years never to take anything for granted. I cherish all those moments—with the twins, with Eva... with you."

My father's words pricked something within. I couldn't recall a time when he'd bared his soul in such a way. Normally, he was guarded with his emotions. To this day, I didn't know why. Whatever it was had something to do with his childhood. There was a period of time that was missing because no one ever spoke about it—not even our grandparents.

"Being a father changed my life. It was one of the best things that ever happened to me, after marrying your mother. You'll see one day." He smiled then winked, and I winced. "No time soon, though," he added.

"Hel—I mean *heck* no," I quickly corrected myself. Dad tried to look stern after my near slip. Although he cursed like a sailor, my mother had taught me never to swear in front of elders.

"With the new baby coming, I'm counting on you to lead the way by setting a good example. Your sisters look up to you, so the little one will eventually follow suit," Dad said, foreboding.

I glanced at what remained of my cake. *So much for the brief, heartfelt talk.* He was back to heaping that good ol' fashioned *eldest Pope child* burden over my head.

"How are things coming along at Zinfinite?" he asked, changing topics.

"Pretty good. I managed to get two major accounts to reduce their costs and got invited to take part in some management-only meetings," I told him.

"I'm not surprised," he said, expressionless.

One thing about being labeled *the fuckup*—others usually weren't moved by any blunder you made. They always expected it from you. On the flip side, being pinned as *the overachiever* had its pitfalls as well. Whenever my father heard about any of my great accomplishments, he never batted an eye. At least Mom treated my victories as if they were all special. I guess that's just what moms do.

"Do you see yourself working there after college?" my father asked all of a sudden.

His question stunned me. I thought me working at LRPI after college was a foregone conclusion for him. I fully expected a knock-down, drag-out fight the moment I told him I wouldn't be a part of the family business.

It now seemed as though he was presenting me with an out.

Should I take it?

Or is it a trap?

"Zinfinite is a fantastic company," I told him. My father was impossible to read in general, but even more in that moment. I resolved to tell him where my head was and brace for the aftermath.

"When I'm done at Stanford in December, I hope to be working at LRPI."

I observed my father's expression transform from a look of uncertainty to unmistakable pride. "Son, I always knew you'd come to your senses. I'm just happy you figured out sooner than later where you truly belong. You are too fucking gifted to be restrained, which is what every other company would do to you."

"Yeah," I nodded in agreement.

"I've waited a long time to hear you say that. Your mother and I will be more than happy to welcome you to your rightful place next January." My father stood and motioned for me to join him before stretching his arms out to me.

Dude wants a hug? Seriously? Who in the hell was this man?

Bewildered, I embraced my father, and he squeezed me tight, kissing my hair. My verbal declaration to begin my career after graduation at his company obviously meant a great deal to him.

Seventeen

Ford

On the first of April, my parents were preparing to leave for Cancun the next day to celebrate twenty-two years of marriage. Mom, not quite six months pregnant, was sporting the cutest little baby bump. It served as a constant reminder that I'd soon be the eldest of five.

Eva's explosion from months ago was a distant memory. Both she and I were looking forward to meeting the little guy or gal. Yep—my folks had no idea what they were having. My father wanted it to remain a surprise until the very end, which drove my mother insane. They'd have to come up with both a boy's and a girl's name for the arrival in four months.

Last month, Eva had a killer seventeenth birthday party at the house. She'd initially expected fifty people, but over one hundred and fifty had shown up. Buddies of Knight and mine had come through, including Monty, who'd hung out with us at the pool long after the parents and grands had called it a night. Alana, my friend from work, had even stopped by.

I'll get back to her in a moment.

I was two weeks away from scheduled final exams, but one had been waved. My Business Strategy professor told me not to even bother taking his final once he read a draft of my honors thesis. It would be smooth sailing in my Operations Management class. I'd simply show up in two weeks, ace the final, and be on my merry way back to Stanford.

I was almost done with my thesis, which covered supplier management based on my experience at Zinfinite. The end result would have Professor Ship at Stanford jizzing in his pants. I'd planned to go the extra mile, having the final report printed and bound at the Pope Tower print shop by finals week.

Back to Alana...

Until recently, I'd been doing quite well with staying focused on work and school. I'd sworn I wouldn't let sex interfere with the prize. My father had been making plans for me to make the rounds and learn even more about the business to prepare me for when I returned for good next January. He'd even piled on some additional reading material to indulge in my scarce spare time.

Yet, with a full schedule, my old baseball pals had tried to convince me that I had plenty of time left to take Alana Faust back to *Ford Land*. The boys gave me so much shit when she showed up at Eva's party. It didn't help that she spent most of her time hanging around me. The boys ignored my numerous pleas that Alana and I were *just good friends*.

After all that, I couldn't help but wonder if I'd made the right decision to not sleep with her again. I remembered that night in her apartment like it was yesterday. The girl was supreme in bed. However, I had to remind myself on a regular basis that I couldn't mix business with pleasure. In a month, we would no longer be interning together.

Alana was a cool chick and a fantastic friend. After work and before night classes, she and I would hit our spot at Alibi's and partake in gin and tonics for old time's sake. She was so fucking real and a joy to be around. She was becoming one of my best friends.

Despite that, I continued to have nagging thoughts about Harper. It had been months since she'd broken my heart, but it didn't hurt any less. I'd seen her a few times on campus from a distance and managed to remain cordial, but I'd never stopped to speak. And although the weather was getting warmer, her outfits seemed baggier. Perhaps her fiancé had her on his stupid hipster kick.

Oddly enough, I had yet to see Harper and her fiancé together on campus. If I hadn't run a background check on him, I'd have sworn he wasn't real. I had no clue what this Aiden Cramer joker looked like outside of the mugshot Gerts had shown me.

After a productive day at work, I was relieved to grab a drink with Alana. One drink turned into two, and soon we were ordering burgers and fries. I knew I'd have to text Mom so she or Mrs. Benton wouldn't bother setting a plate aside for me tonight.

Later that evening, I left class and headed for the parking lot. I saw Harper leaning against my car, and all my senses were on high alert.

What is she doing there?

She stood upright and eyed me intently when she saw me approaching, tugging her baggy jean jacket closed, covering up most of her long black dress.

"Harper?" I said, perplexed. As we stood four feet apart, her oh-so-familiar scent filled my nostrils. The cocktail of nostalgia and longing made my stomach churn. I'd been able to handle seeing her from afar—but this close, I felt myself slowly melting away.

I studied her, awaiting her explanation for stalking my vehicle. Right then, I noticed her face was much rounder than normal.

Was she pregnant?

Fuck.

Perhaps she was just happy, hence she was eating more. That would mean she was way happier living without me.

Double fuck.

And it was then that I decided to pray for her to put me out of my misery so I could run home and sulk over her like a little bitch.

"I've been wanting to talk to you for a while now, but every time I see you, you always seem to be in a hurry," Harper criticized. I let out an uncomfortable sigh, making it obvious I'd been avoiding her on purpose. "Look, Ford—I know this is weird. I don't want things to ever be like that between us."

The nervous trill in her voice wasn't lost on me, but I didn't care. As I started to move my mouth to say, 'it is what it is,' she spoke again.

"I'm sorry for what happened between us. You are so important to me."

No fucking way. This has to be a joke.

I checked my watch, and sure as fuck, it was still April Fools' Day. I frowned. Her words had completely contradicted her actions for the past seven or eight months. If I were so *important* to her, she would have waited for me like she'd promised. Instead, she'd abandoned me.

"You and your family will always hold a special place in my heart. Your mom and sisters accepted me in my most volatile state. And Ford, you mean *so* much to me that it would mean the world if you finally met Aiden."

She had some fucking nerve. I wasn't having any of it.

"I'm not interested," I snapped.

"Ford—*please*. Aiden's a great guy, and I want him to meet someone in my life who means the world to me."

Harper's beautiful blue eyes started to glisten, and I sensed her disconnecting from her plea. Had she believed what she was saying to me? I wondered what her game was. What she was doing was downright cruel. I stood there, dumbfounded, hoping she'd get a clue.

"Other than my mom, no one else cares to know Aiden. My father isn't interested. He has his own assumptions, but he doesn't know Aiden like I do."

The truth had come out, finally. Russ was against his daughter marrying the stoner kid. The sadistic part of me wanted to witness the train wreck live and in the flesh—Harper Benton's living, breathing mistake. But the other part of me didn't want to face the fact that Harper could be happy without me.

I had to leave, or things could get ugly in this public lot. I couldn't yell at her like I did over the phone last year. If I could just walk away and continue to ignore her for two more weeks, I'd never have to worry about seeing her ever again.

"Just say you'll meet him," she begged. "Please."

"No, Harper. I don't want to meet him."

Despite her stupid request, she was smart enough to clear the way for me to hop in my car. I burned rubber as I got the hell out of there.

"Pope?" Alana called out across the table during lunch.

She and I shared a pizza not far from work. I'd been out of it all day due to a lack of sleep. The more I tried writing Harper out of my life, the more she continued to affect me in the worst way. I narrowed my gaze at Alana, urging her to say whatever it was she had to say. I pulled another slice of pepperoni and prosciutto pizza from the tall tray propped between us.

"What is going on?" she drawled with concern riddling her hazel eyes. "You look like hell."

"And yet my looks aren't remotely close to how I feel. I was tempted to call an S.O.S. earlier, but I figured I needed to be a big boy and handle things on my own for a change," I expressed mid-chew.

"You know that's not how this works. We've been doing this friend thing for what... three months now? We've become each other's sounding board in the process, in *all* things," she reminded.

I blinked rapidly, knowing she'd spoken the truth. Regardless, I didn't want to tell Alana what was eating me. Saying it out loud would make the situation more real.

Since leaving campus last night, I'd been endlessly rationalizing the scenarios in my brain to the point of losing sleep. I'd arrived at work at five-thirty in the morning because I was getting *nowhere*. I'd managed to exceed all my deadlines for the week, just this morning. There was no feeling of accomplishment. I felt as empty as I had when I first arrived at the office. I planned to go on a seven-mile run to see if that would help, but I knew it wouldn't. I had no other choice but to come clean.

"Harper tracked me down last night," I started, after taking a big gulp of water.

Alana's eyes grew wide. "Really?"

"She wants me to meet her fiancé."

Her jaw almost fell on the table. "What?! She has some nerve!"

"I know," I agreed.

Silence allowed the reality of my words to sink into both of us. Suddenly, Alana appeared to be enlightened. A morsel of clarity dawned in that pretty little head of hers.

"What did you say to her?"

"I told her *hell no*," I said in disgust.

"You should call her bluff."

I gaped at her. "Huh?"

"Something tells me she believes you're bitter. Prove her wrong. Invite them to lunch on Monday and show her you've moved on, too."

"Faust—are you on crack?" I laughed sardonically. "I am *not* meeting the dude she left me for."

"I say you ask them out for lunch and take me with you."

Whoa—was she suggesting we pretend to be a couple? That didn't seem like a bad idea. It wouldn't hurt to find out if Harper gave a fuck that I'd potentially moved on with someone my family would deem more worthy. Alana was more Eliza Pope than Harper could ever be. Not only that, but Alana was closer to my age and more my equal.

The more I pondered it, the more the prospect of accepting Harper's asinine offer to meet her new lover seemed tempting.

"We don't have to lie about what we are," Alana prefaced. "We're good friends. I'd only be there for support. That way, they'll know you're not in this alone. And I'd bet you'll see a whole new side of Harper with me on your arm. She'll regret ever asking you to meet her new guy."

She made a solid point. If I wasn't there alone, it wouldn't be a situation where the ridiculously happy couple ambushed the lonely loser. Alana's presence would neutralize the situation. But I still had doubts.

"I'm not sure if that's a good idea. Having you there—I'd be playing her little game."

Alana shrugged, then challenged me to reconsider. The whole situation had my stomach in knots and my emotions in flames, but I appreciated how Alana clearly had my back.

I can't believe I'm actually going through with this.

When I'd left work last Friday, I hadn't been able to stop thinking about what Alana had said. The whole drive home, I'd weighed all of the pros and cons of doing lunch with Harper and her *Aiden*. When I'd pulled into the garage, I had decided to bite the bullet. I figured this would be all the closure I needed because the Harper of old was no more. She wasn't the same girl I'd fallen in love with many years ago. That Harper would never have brought me to such a devastating place.

Right in that garage, I had texted Alana and told her that Monday lunch with Harper and Aiden was a go. I had then texted Harper and told her that we'd meet at a restaurant in downtown Los Derivas.

Harper B: Sounds great! Look forward to seeing you there!

I rolled my eyes, recalling her misplaced giddy text and instantly regretting my decision to go through with this bullshit. On top of that, my parents were in Mexico, and I had no clue if my father was still tracking my every move when it came to her. Something deep down told me he'd quit giving a shit a long time ago because if Russ had known about Aiden, I was certain Mason knew, too.

Monday had come too quickly, and so had the lunch hour.

More than anything, I wanted to get this sham of an introduction over with. Thankfully, my good friend made it easier. There wasn't a day when Alana Faust didn't show up to work looking like a total knockout, but something told me she had intentionally kicked her game up a few notches for my benefit.

She wore a sexy, fitted, all-black pants suit with gold high heels as we waited at our table in an Italian restaurant for the future Mr. and Mrs. Cramer. I had settled for a button-up dress shirt with dark blue and white check print, a solid navy tie, and gray pants. I hadn't noticed I was nervously twiddling my thumbs on the table until Alana laid her hand down to still them.

"You'll do fine. Stop worrying," she soothed.

I placed one hand in my lap and used the other to reach for my glass of half-and-half tea and lemonade. Just as my eyes went up to meet the door, in walked a stunning blonde in a black dress riddled with sunflowers.

Harper. The very sight of her caused my appetite to dissipate. I was heartbroken all over again.

Holding the door behind her was a blond ponytailed hipster in black jeans, black t-shirt, and dark suit jacket. Aiden's beard looked way neater than it had in his mug shot from years ago. *Asshole.*

"Is it them?" Alana whispered, gesturing her chin toward the door. A greeter intercepted the couple as Harper scanned the room—perhaps searching for me.

"Yep," I muttered.

Alana moved her chair closer to me and whispered, "She pregnant?"

I blinked really fast as every vital organ in my body pulsed with the realization. I pushed the words through the knot in my throat. "I noticed the other day she's gained some weight on her face. I really never saw a belly." My eyes honed right on Harper's midsection, and Alana's assessment appeared to be true.

"Really—you hadn't noticed? Because the girl looks like she's about to pop at any moment," Alana murmured scandalously.

Harper beamed from across the restaurant when she spotted me, then she let the greeter know she located her party. With Aiden by her side, she made her way toward the rear of the restaurant. The closer she got, the more I felt the sensation of bile rising up to my throat. The huge sunflower-covered bump wasn't obscured under a jacket or baggy clothes. Every question as to why she was in such a rush to marry this dude was answered immediately. She was pregnant as hell.

I fought with all my might to mask my shock as Alana and I stood up to greet them. Harper's earlier smile waned the instant she shifted her gaze from me to Alana. My ex's mutual jealousy was palpable. I was devastated to see her with child, but half of me was glad to see that I caused her to feel something—even if it was jealousy.

Harper put on her very best fake smile. "Ford."

"Hello," I answered, nonchalant.

My guest introduced herself, taking the opportunity away from me. "Hey, I'm Alana—Ford's friend."

"I'm sorry… I didn't know Ford was bringing someone along." I could tell Harper felt slighted, but she shook Alana's offered hand apologetically anyhow.

"My bad," I uttered half-heartedly.

"I certainly hope I'm not intruding," Alana tagged on.

"No—it's fine," Harper said, appearing to dismiss the awkward introduction.

"The more, the merrier—right?" Aiden chuckled, speaking for the first time. The guy was nauseating.

Harper formally introduced herself to Alana before announcing the man standing next to her. "And this is my fiancé, Aiden," she said, now looking at me. "Aiden, this is Ford," she chuckled nervously.

Aiden shook Alana's hand first before offering the same to me. Reluctantly, I took it.

"Harp told me a lot about you, man. Glad to finally meet you," he smirked.

Harp? This motherfucker.

"I see that congratulations are in order," Alana said, motioning down at Harper's expanded belly.

I literally wanted to kick myself for never noticing that before. If I'd known she was pregnant, I wouldn't be standing here playing friendly with the asshole who'd knocked-up the one person I couldn't live without.

"Yes—thank you," Harper said without looking in my direction.

I shot down the nagging thoughts with a much-needed pep talk.

Settle down, Pope. Just get through this. After this, you'll never have to see her again.

I pulled out Alana's chair, and Aiden followed suit with Harper at the other side of the table. The waitress took the new arrivals' drink order before setting off.

"So, when are you due?" Alana asked. I scowled at my friend.

Really, Alana? Really?

"The end of May, which works out great," Harper twinkled. "Graduation takes place the end of this month, and our wedding happens the day after." Aiden draped his cruddy hipster arm around her shoulder, but strangely, Harper didn't move into it.

"Wow—that's great," Alana responded. "Where are you having the wedding?"

Faust, stop it. Stop it now. I was getting perturbed with her. She was supposed to be here making me feel better. Instead, she was bringing every anxiety to the surface. She was shining the light on my worst nightmare, and it was uglier than it had ever been in the dark.

"We're doing the courthouse thing," Aiden chimed. "We didn't want to bother with all of the family politics that come along with planning a wedding. We just want to get married and start our new life together with our baby boy."

As he pulled Harper close, I felt like throwing up all the food I had yet to eat.

Harper is having a boy, and it's not mine.

Harper is getting married, but not to me.

This hurt... *Bad.*

"I see," Alana responded with pursed lips, taking in a sip of water.

I wanted to stand and storm out of there. My whole life was literally across the table. Harper should have been seated next to me. If someone had told me a year ago that this would be our fate, I would have bloodied their nose.

"So, you two are just friends?" Harper casually asked.

"Yes," Alana and I answered in unison.

"We intern at Zinfinite," I mentioned.

"Oh." Harper's expression was unreadable.

"Well, you two make a very handsome pair," Aiden said with humor.

When Harper shot him an annoyed look, it made me wonder why she'd chosen him in the first place.

Alana and I took our time getting back to the office after the most uncomfortable exchanges I'd ever been a part of. I had no idea if I'd found the closure I was looking for. That whole ordeal was just... weird.

"You notice something... *off* back there?" Alana said on the walk back.

"Yeah," I acknowledged, still digesting what had taken place earlier.

Aiden was obviously happy to have Harper. Who wouldn't be? The woman was drop-dead gorgeous, even at nearly eight months pregnant. But for some reason, I wasn't getting the same vibes from Harper toward her so-called *fiancé*.

"Harper wasn't all *lovey-dovey* with him," Alana said, stating the obvious, "but there's something about Aiden. He looks like he has issues."

"Fuck yeah, he does," I growled. "He was arrested back in high school for drug possession."

"Ah—that totally makes sense," Alana said, wide-eyed. "My uncle was on all kinds of stuff, so I know precisely what that looks like."

The thought of Harper being caught up with a potential drug addict made me queasy.

"I can't believe she left me for that," I groaned.

"Look, I could be totally wrong about him. He's graduating with Harper this month, right?" she asked, and I nodded. "He's obviously competent enough to stay on track and earn a degree at a good school. Maybe he just looks like a stoner, even after kicking the habit long ago."

I didn't think Alana actually believed that. Something deep down told me she was just trying to make me feel better about leaving Harper behind in my past where she belonged.

Eighteen

Ford

Age 22

(Three Years Later)

"When do you think you'll start eating cheeseburgers?" I inquired with a smirk.

My regular Monday lunch companion was seated in the booth opposite me in one of the best burger joints in downtown Los Derivas, propped up by his knees.

"Stop making me like what you like," he ordered while masterfully dipping half of a torn, battered chicken strip into a small cup of honey barbecue sauce. "I'm a little kid."

"But you just had a birthday. You're a man now, Toph. Men eat cheeseburgers, not chicky nuggets," I teased. I take another bite of my stacked burger, careful not to spill grease on my favorite tie.

"I'm only *three*," he giggled with a mouth full of chicken.

"*Three?* Well—you could've fooled me."

My kid brother, Mr. Christopher Charles Pope, or Topher—as he insists on being called—is three-foot-four and about thirty pounds soaking wet. Wearing a retro Iron Man t-shirt with blue jeans and his favorite light-up Minions tennis shoes, Topher exuded far more confidence than a man ten-times his age. The boy liked what he liked and didn't share his toys with anyone, thank you very much. He was one of my most favorite people in the whole wide world.

"What's my new big sister doing?" he asked in his commanding little high-pitched voice. I snorted. He was just as bad as our father.

"Having lunch with friends."

"Why couldn't she eat with us?"

"Because... This is Topher and Ford time."

"Man time," he added in the cutest little machismo voice.

I crack up. "Yes, man time."

I loved this kid.

Topher Pope was sculpted after greatness. Even his initials, *CCP*, looked badass as a monogram. I'd say my baby brother was created in our father's image, but Topher possessed something that Mason Pope didn't.

A personality.

"Can I take my chicken home? My driver's coming to get me," Topher told me.

I confirmed the time with my watch. "So soon?" I said in disappointment. Being that I no longer lived at home with my parents, I sorely missed spending time with my little buddy on a daily basis. Mondays with Topher seemed so few and far between.

"The lady took too long to bring the food. You shouldn't tip her good," he said with a look of displeasure. The boy had me in stitches. "Daddy will be mad if you're late back to work."

Again, he'd just turned three and was way smarter than I'd been at his age. If this trajectory continued, he'd probably start college at thirteen.

"I'm in the middle of a lunch meeting with a very important person. By the way, Dad and Mom aren't my bosses. I work for Miss Natalie," I reminded him.

"That's okay, Ford. You'll be working for me one day," Topher said nonchalantly as he dipped a fry into a lake of ketchup.

"I don't doubt it," I grinned. "Maybe we can work together? As equals?"

"Okay, but I will be the big boss at Pope Tower when I grow up," he beamed with his mouthful of little teeth.

At Pope Tower, I'd worked in the cosmetics division for a little under three years. Recently, I'd been told I would be replacing Natalie Harrison as VP of cosmetics after she retired early next year.

Things had panned out better than I'd expected at my parents' company. At only twenty-two years old, I was making significant moves. But part of me wondered how much more I'd accomplish if I were in business for myself. I'd have to wait just a little longer to see that come to fruition. In the meantime, things were going well for me at LRPI.

Knight Thibodeau, my sister's longtime boyfriend and one of my best friends, had landed a full-time gig there as well after completing his degree at UCLD one year ago. In a short time, he'd quickly moved through the ranks and into a management position, where he worked as one of the leads in the analytics division.

Thibodeau and I crossed paths in meetings on a regular basis. He got a kick out of it anytime I got bored at someone's meeting and decided to take over and steer the ship. Nothing was more of a pain than a meeting organizer who didn't have their shit together. Don't get me wrong—I wasn't a total prick. I despised the boring and mundane and opted to keep meetings purposeful and lighthearted.

Thibodeau's already-full plate had recently received another helping in the form of a major project. He was slated to give a presentation to my parents' executive staff. Even I wasn't privy to sit in such a meeting. I wouldn't be among that company until I made VP next year. As a guest presenter, Knight's project would kick off the new *Propel the Future* initiative. The PTF buzzword was sweeping through the entire global organization. If anyone's job description or performance goals included those words anywhere, they were sitting pretty. Knight was already among the *who's who* in the company.

When my old friend and I weren't touching base about LRPI business, we were touching bases at the nearby park for old time's sake. Our corporate softball team was undefeated so far.

Knight's girlfriend—my sister—was an upcoming junior at UCLD. She moonlighted part-time in the data analytics group, helping Knight and his team as needed. The young couple had taken the department by storm.

People may have had the impression that I was jealous of my best friend. I wasn't. Despite how things looked on the exterior, my father was grooming *me*, not Knight, to take over our family's company. Yet, even that didn't move me. I hadn't gotten butterflies that day in his massive office when my father had taken me under his arm and said: *"Son—one day, this will all be yours."*

I didn't build LRPI, therefore, I didn't want it.

I wanted something I could call my own.

Liza

I'd been going back and forth with this nagging issue for a long time. My OB had been hounding me for the past three years. She figured once I had a hysterectomy, it would solve all of my problems.

I was naïve to think the hot flashes and pain would suddenly stop after giving birth to Topher. Instead, my health had gotten progressively worse. My uterus and I had been a team for almost forty-six years. It had helped me bring five wonderful children into this world.

But my womb was now tired. It started fighting me something awful. Things were so bad, even Mason had begun pushing me to schedule the surgery. So, one morning, I finally did it. I hung up the phone, scared to death.

Getting older was already terrifying, but the threat of having major surgery made it even worse. All that aside, it was good to get ahead of this thing before it became something more devastating. I had my children to consider, as well as my husband. It was important for them that I take care of myself. I wanted to be alive to see my youngest get married and start a family. Sheesh—that would mean I'd have to be here at least 'til ninety! What on earth Mason and I were thinking having a child in my forties and his fifties, I'll never know.

November was when I'd have the surgery and take the rest of the year off from work to recover. The thought of getting cut wide open for a purpose other than having a baby made my spirit plummet, but things quickly turned around the moment my youngest pride and joy barged into my office. All the joy in the world flooded me when he ran up to my desk, full of excitement.

"Mommy!"

"Topher! What are you doing here?" I said, squeezing him tight. He wrapped his tiny arms around my neck as I slid from the chair and down to the floor with him in my lap.

"You have to watch me until Mr. Russ picks me up. Ford took me to work so we can finish eating in his office," my baby boy beamed.

"Oh?" I said, astonished.

"Yup. We had to eat the rest here so Ford won't be late for his meeting. The stupid waitress lady took a bazillion years to bring our food," Topher said with a little bravado.

"Christopher Charles… What did I tell you about calling people bad names?" I chastised lovingly.

"Like when Daddy called the Starbucks man dumbass for messing up his coffee?"

"Topher!" I gasped.

"Daddy said that, not me." He waved his hands in placation.

"I don't care *who* said it. You can't say words like that. And Daddy knows better." On cue, the door that joined my office and Mason's swung open.

"I thought that was you, son," Mason beamed down at our youngest.

"Daddy!" Topher scurried away, leaving me hanging on the floor. His father scooped him up in his arms and smacked a loud kiss to Topher's cheek.

"What was your mother just yelling at you about?" Mason sweetly asked our brilliant little boy.

"I wasn't yelling," I frowned.

"Yeah, you were," Mason egged on.

"I said a bad word," Topher admitted shamefully.

Mason flashed a scolding look, making him shudder. "You know that's not allowed."

"I know—but I was only saying what you said. You said the Starbucks man was a dumbass."

Mason snorted involuntarily.

"Christopher!" I shouted in mortification.

"It's *Topher*," the boy whined.

"Well, he was a—" my husband started to say under his breath.

"Mason," I scowled in stern warning.

"Looks like we're in big trouble with Mommy," Mason winked to his mini clone.

"We're sorry, Mommy," Topher said in the cutest voice, making it difficult to stay mad at either of them.

"How was your weekly lunch with Ford?" Mason asked, putting our son down on his little feet. Mason settled on a nearby sofa, and Topher climbed up to join him. I took a seat on Topher's other side.

"They took too long to bring the food."

"I hate when that happens. You should've told them who you were," Mason replies. I shake my head at the both of them.

No, Pope—we don't raise our children to act entitled, I scolded in my head.

"Next time, me and Ford will have Monday man-lunch at one of your restaurants," Topher resolved. My three-year-old was absolutely a handful.

"Great idea. Our staff knows better than to keep the owners' sons waiting," Mason said, egging the little egomaniac on.

Good grief.

"Me and Ford can eat lunch at Sahara. Can Monty make me chicky nuggets?" I laughed out loud at my insanely witty little man.

"Absolutely. Make sure you tell Ford to have his former roommate treat you real special," Mason said as he ruffled Topher's already messy head of hair. Like the overzealous mother I was, I started to tame our son's hair with my fingers. He didn't like me hassling with it all that much, so he shook his head until my hand fell.

"Mommy, we going to swimming school this Saturday?"

"Yep—we sure are," I said, pinching his cheek.

"*Mommy & Me* swim lessons are almost here, huh?" Mason grinned.

My shoulders slumped in disappointment. I should've had Topher in the class a year ago, but things had been hectic at work. Now, life was much easier due to the lighter load on Mason's and my shoulders, thanks to some strong recent hires. I included Knight and Ford in that group.

I finally had the time to take my son to swim class, but I'd have to break for my surgery in two months. Someone else would have to fill in during my recovery. I considered asking Eva soon, but that involved telling her about the surgery. No doubt, she'd freak out. When it came to me, she was the worry-wart. It was as if we swapped roles—she was now the mother, and I was the child.

My, how times have changed.

My beautiful daughter, who lived in a dorm at UC Los Derivas, had told me an hour ago over lunch that she and Knight wanted to get an apartment together. Mason was still having a hard time dealing with the idea of them having sex. Them wanting to live together wasn't a conversation I looked forward to having with my husband. Our daughter was a very mature twenty-year-old woman, but she'd always be Mason's little girl. He needed to be reminded that I was her age when he and I first moved in together.

"I learned a new trick from Mr. Russ," Topher squeaked.

"Please, show us," I urged my baby boy.

"Okay." Topher removed a quarter from his pocket and held it up in his tiny hand for his father and me to see. Propping his small frame on his knees on the sofa, he held the quarter by my ear. He then flicked his wrist and brought his arm back to show us his hand. There was no quarter in sight. Mason and I gaped at our miniature Houdini.

"Son... Where did the quarter go?" my husband asked in astonishment.

"It's gone. It's magic, Daddy," the three-year-old explained proudly.

"That was wonderful," I praised. "Mr. Benton taught you very well."

"I will be the best magician in the world," Topher declared.

"Yes, you will," I beamed, pinching both of his cheeks.

"Do that again," Mason smirked.

"Alright, Daddy. This time, you give me a hundred dollars, and I'll make it disappear, okay?" I laughed so hard my stomach started to ache.

"No way, but nice try," Mason chortled. "I think your sisters Bethany and Brianna can make Daddy's money disappear faster than even *you* can."

Our twin daughters were upcoming high school seniors and an absolute handful. I was so ready for the two of them to leave for college and free the household of their daily teenage drama fest. If I had been half as bad when I was a teen, I owed my parents a sincere apology.

The two of them combined made Eva's teenage years seem like a walk in the park. Eva had actually been the perfect kid. We'd had a minor altercation when she rebelled over her father refusing to let her date. But once he'd had some sense knocked into him, we hadn't had any more problems out of Eva. She had graduated high school a semester early and was able to jump right into UCLD on a full academic scholarship. She worked part-time some evenings, helping Knight's department with some extensive data mining in preparation for Propel the Future.

In contrast, my youngest daughters were a challenge. While their eldest siblings had done part-time stints at LRPI during high school, the twins had made it clear they wanted nothing to do with Pope Tower. I supported their decision. I, for one, didn't believe in forcing the kids into a job they didn't want. The problem was, they didn't want to do *anything*.

Because they'd never had jobs, they could not empathize with Mason, Ford, Eva or me. We'd all been hard at work on the PTF initiative, sometimes staying late at Pope Tower. Had Brie and Beth been there working alongside us, they'd know how important this project was to the company.

They didn't want to understand. Instead, they'd rather we drop everything and be there at their every beck and call. It was our fault for spoiling them. When they were little, we jumped whenever they asked us to. Brie chipped a nail—Eva was there. Beth stubbed her baby toe—Mason would carry her around like a wounded veteran.

I'd taken many days off from work when Brie had broken up with Jesse Rogers two months before homecoming dance. I shuddered at the memory of that unbearable time in our home. Brie had constantly been in tears, and she'd brought all of us down with her. Never mind that the two would eventually get back together and have the time of their lives at the dance, only for Brie to dump Jesse again a week later for no reason at all.

It wasn't until Mason and I saw the confused expression on our youngest son's face in response to the twins acting out that we declared, 'No more.' The change kicked off with Mason grounding Brie for two weeks. She had gotten snarky with me about the new curfew. From that point on, Mason and I were their enemies.

Don't get me wrong, it wasn't all fire and brimstone at home. There were more good days than bad. The seventeen-year-olds could be as sweet as pie if they wanted to, but when their hormones kicked in—and thankfully, their cycles were in sync—things got brutal.

Mason's salt-and-pepper hair was no more. It was *all* salt. Thankfully, Topher took it easy on his old folks. We couldn't handle *three* demon children.

A soft rap on my main office door startled me at first, but then I relaxed. I alerted the guest to enter, knowing exactly who it was, but Mason seemed irritated. He calmed once the open double doors revealed a trusty Russell Benton.

"Mrs. Pope—Mr. Pope," he bowed in greeting. "Mr. Topher Pope, you ready to head home now?"

"No—I wanna stay here and work." Topher rocked back from his knees, landing on his butt. He folded his arms in protest. I'd known this would happen. Once Mason and I showered him with all the attention he deserved, he wouldn't want to leave.

"Son, you know you can work from home, right?" Mason said sweetly, reaching out to pat him on his little back.

"I can?" Topher said, wide-eyed.

"Absolutely. Mommy and I do it all the time."

"Can you and Mommy come home and work with me now?"

I laughed at his charm. "I'll be home two hours after you. Promise," I said as I kissed him on his cheek.

"And I'll be there an hour after that," Mason added on.

"Okay. What should I work on?" Topher asked his father.

"I'm running low on Topher Pope original artwork. How about you have Mrs. Benton help you to construct a new masterpiece for my office?" Mason proposed.

"Yes! Mr. Topher Pope will do that!" I cackled every time my sweet boy referred to himself in the third person. "You want one too, Mommy?"

"Of course. It would make Mommy very sad if Daddy got a new picture and I didn't," I piled on with a pouty lip.

"You'll get one. Let's go, Mr. Russ—I have work to do," Topher announced as he made his way toward the door.

"Don't forget to ask Miss Lola for your jacket," I said. The order was mostly for Russ to handle, which is why the older man nodded in acknowledgement.

Mason and I kissed Topher goodbye before he and Russ headed out.

"So," Mason started once the door closed.

His eyes were like beams of truth on my skin as he slid closer to me on the couch. This man had known me for over two decades and could sense my distraction a mile away. He was about to interrogate me.

"Ford volunteered to fill in for me at the late auditing meeting. That's why I'll be home at a decent hour tonight."

My eyes grew round because it wasn't what I expected him to say. Still, his revelation didn't please me. I didn't want to seem ungrateful, since I was always glad when my husband came home at a decent hour. I just didn't like it being at our son's expense.

Ford had been working late every night for the past two months. I didn't want him to become the workaholic his father was. It was good that our son had recently decided to settle down with one girl. But if he wanted to keep her, he needed to be home at an acceptable hour. And he also needed to stop working every single weekend.

"Why, Mason? Why is Ford working late again?" I groaned.

"He takes after us," he answered with pride beaming in his gorgeous olive eyes.

"I know, but don't you think that's unhealthy for such a young man? What about his girlfriend?" I countered.

"Knowing her, she's probably working later than he is." Mason pulled me into him and planted his lips on my forehead.

I decided to change the subject. "By the way, I'm scheduled for surgery on November 9th."

Mason dropped his arms and searched me. "Baby, it's going to be fine. You know that, right?" The look on his face wasn't so sure. My eyes fell in fear, but his fingers pushed my chin back upward. His eyes locked onto mine.

"I'll be fine," I answered, saying what he wanted to hear. He saw right through me.

"You have multiple fibroid tumors, Liza. Surgery is for the best."

"I know," I replied softly. His arm snaked around my waist, and he pulled me close. His lips softly touched mine before taking the kiss deeper. I hooked my wrists behind his neck.

"I love you so much," he exhaled after pulling away briefly.

"I know," I whispered before kissing him once more.

It was great having my sister over for dinner. As soon as she walked in the door, she followed the savory aroma directly into the kitchen. She stood over the stove in awe.

"It's Trisha's special marinara recipe. We've got meatballs cooking here," I said, pointing to the massive frying pan adjacent to the sauce. "Trisha will plop those bad boys into the sauce while I get the fresh noodles going in the pasta press," I tagged on, gesturing to a large covered bowl containing the rising dough. I tell my sister all about the fresh bread my fabulous housekeeper had baked this morning that would be sliced and turned into garlic bread.

"Me thinks I just died and went to heaven," Jessie drooled. "Can I take you and Mrs. Benton home to LA with me?"

"You'll have to battle my husband and our three youngest first," I winked, clicking my tongue before monitoring the meatballs.

"Anything I can help you with?" Jessie insisted.

"No!" I reflexively shouted. My big sister couldn't even boil water correctly. When she and I were slumming it in LA after moving there from Texas, I'd done all the cooking.

"Ooookaaaayyy," said Jessie, seemingly slighted.

"Auntie Jessie!" Topher squawked after padding into the kitchen. His flailing arms brought our attention to the sheet of paper gripped in his hand. Like the wonderful aunt she was, Jessie bent down and scooped her nephew in for a great big hug.

"Topher—what's that you got there?" Jessie asked.

"I was at the office today, and Daddy let me leave early and work from home."

"Is it a big project?" my sister said, playing along.

"Yep. It's the biggest project. Here's one I designed for Daddy's office at Pope Tower, but I can't show him yet."

"Why not?"

"It's not finished." Topher proceeded to show Aunt Jessie the big building he'd drawn. I snuck a peek, and it absolutely looked like an adorable little three-year-old had drawn it. When Topher caught me snooping, he snatched the drawing away and hid it from view.

"You can't look, Mommy," he scolded.

"That's for Daddy, right? It's not for me. So, why can't I see it?" I asked in a sad voice.

"You aren't s'posed to see it until the meeting. I'll show you and Daddy your projects at the meeting." My son poked out his little bird chest, exuding authority. He was Mason Pope's clone—no question.

"Okay, then. I look forward to our meeting, Mr. Pope," I said with a kiss on top of his head.

"I'll be back for dinner. Gotta hide this before Daddy sees," he called out before scurrying out of the kitchen.

"That kid's a riot," chuckled Jessie.

"It's the cutest thing. He wants to start wearing suits now, just like his father." I sauntered to the pasta station, and Jessie followed.

"It's *cute* now. Let's just hope he doesn't turn into a little douchebag."

"Jessie!" I gasp.

"Well..."

"I won't allow it. I'm determined to keep him grounded. If I'm well enough to work the soup kitchen on Thanksgiving, it will be Topher's first time doing it with us."

Jessie arched a brow. "*Well enough?* What do you mean?"

That's right... She doesn't know yet. I had to break the news.

"I'm having a hysterectomy the second Friday in November."

I heard the wooden spoon cease from stirring. I turned to the stove and saw Trisha hovering over it, frozen. That was her first time catching wind of the news.

"Liza." My sister pulled me into a one-arm hug.

"It's fine," I assured her. "It's necessary. My fibroids are getting bigger, and the perimenopause is progressively getting worse. Mason knew it was bad when the doctor showed him the results of my MRI. He insisted on surgery along with the doctor. At first, I thought, *why couldn't they just remove the tumors?* But it's way too bad now. They fear it could potentially become… something else," I said, avoiding uttering the scariest word on the planet. If that word ever came up in any diagnosis of mine, Mason would go completely insane.

"Oh, honey," Jessie sighed, bringing me in for another hug. This time, I hugged her back.

"Recovery is only three to four weeks. Everything is going to be okay."

At the stove, Trisha's sunken expression wasn't lost on me. I held my hand out to Jessie, letting her know I'd need a minute, then approached my friend and longtime housekeeper. Trisha and Russ were family. When the Popes hurt, the Bentons hurt, and vice versa. I surprised Mrs. Benton by wrapping my arm around her apron-clad waist. She slumped then leaned her tied-back blond head on my shoulder.

"I'll be good as new, Trisha. No worries. Okay?" I reassured her. She nodded, but I could tell she was holding back tears. She cleared her throat and tried shaking herself back to life.

"My sister had the same surgery years ago, and she came out of it just fine. It's just… I had no idea anything was wrong," Mrs. Benton murmured. "You are so healthy, Liza. I guess it goes to show it can happen to anyone."

"Life happens. Genetics… The environment… The doctors are going to shut down this baby factory for good, which isn't entirely a bad thing," I jested with a smirk.

Nineteen

Ford

In life, one thing was true: Change is a constant.

I'd been roommates with Monty until two weeks ago. These days, my good friend worked as a junior sous chef at Club Sahara, one of the many establishments my family owned. I knew not living together wouldn't mean I'd never see him. There'd always be lunch with Topher and the occasional romantic dinner with the girlfriend.

I'd opted to move out and get my own place close to the office. For the first time ever, I felt like a grownup. Although, my dad owned the penthouse I now lived in. It was the very spot my parents occupied before I was born.

The charm of downtown Los Derivas couldn't be denied. For one, I no longer had to worry about the often-hour-long drive to Arcadia's Crest due to heavy traffic. And though I adored the ocean view, I loved the view of the bustling city just the same.

As I stood in the main room, admiring the skyline through the floor-to-ceiling windows, the dinging elevator snapped me out of my reverie. When the elevator doors parted, I smelled her sweet scent before I saw her.

"Hey."

"Hi," she beamed with gorgeous red lips. She sauntered in my direction and greeted me with a lingering kiss to my mouth. I eagerly returned the favor.

"Mmm… cherry," I groaned, sampling her flavored lip-gloss.

"What's for dinner, honey?" she purred.

"You."

"Well, what's for dinner *before* you have me," she qualified, kissing me once more.

"Whatever you want."

"I thought you'd have dinner ready since I had to work late."

"My bad. I thought we'd grab a quick bite somewhere."

"We do that on Friday. It's Monday," she reminded me.

"I had to sit in a late meeting for Dad. I just got home myself. We need a housekeeper," I bellyached. "Grilled cheese and tomato soup won't take long. Let's do that."

"Sounds good. I'll change and help." I stole one last kiss from her tempting red lips, and she protested. "Stop, or we'll both starve," she laughed.

"I don't think I'll ever starve tasting you."

"Ford, you're so bad." She does a poor job warding off the biggest smile ever. I slapped her on the ass, and she groaned before heading to our bedroom to change.

If someone had told me three years ago that I'd fall for someone and eventually move in with them at the ripe age of twenty-two, I would have called them a liar. Back when I'd been obsessed with a blonde angel, I hadn't believed I'd ever let another woman in again. That so-called angel had ripped my heart into a million pieces, yet there had still been some shadow of hope that wanted her to come back to me.

I'd kept my promise after finishing my internship at Zinfinite three years ago. I'd buried myself in school until I graduated that December. The moment I took my diploma from the dean, I made a beeline back home and began working full-time at LRPI in cosmetics, where I kicked ass and got on the fast track to management. That whole time, I kept in touch with my good friend Alana Faust from Zinfinite. We'd talked at least once a week over the phone and texted daily.

A year and a half ago, Alana had finished her degree at UCLA and started working at LRPI. She'd done a stint in finance before moving to her latest role as a lead analyst in the data analytics group, with Knight as her boss. Miss Faust came from a good family and was smart as a whip. She was as gorgeous as when I'd met her in that club three years ago, yet we'd only had sex once—that night.

That was until six months ago.

One night after hanging out, we'd started reminiscing about the night we met, and things had gotten a little steamy. We'd ended up reliving that memory five times over. She'd come countless times, and I'd given her another refresher when we'd awoken in her bed the next morning.

Since then, we'd been going at it constantly. The girl was stimulating in so many ways, body and mind. So, I hadn't been surprised when I'd started seeing myself in a monogamous situation with her. I'd been getting tired of the random booty calls. I wanted to be able to put one face and one name to my life outside of work.

Alana and I were very good friends, so she was well aware of my sexual exploits. I'd randomly find girls on hookup apps and embark on a series of one-night stands. Alana would ask about them, and I'd tell her. She'd never judge me, though I'd judged myself. I knew I wasn't any good.

Then, six months ago, I'd finally asked Alana out on a real date. Her response?

"I was wondering how many years it would take for you to ask me out. You know… If we start going out together, you'll have to call all of your little admirers and tell them the *Bradford Pope Fun Shop* is now closed."

I'd laughed at the time. I knew it was the beginning of something really special. Our lives somewhat mirrored that of my parents. It was why Dad had dug Alana from the second he'd met her. He told me she was as feisty as Mom when they'd first met.

These days, my girlfriend and I lived in the very place where my parents had started their lives together. I'd happened to mention to my folks one day that Alana and I were looking for a place together, and my father had immediately offered up his Los Derivas penthouse. Things were going good with him and I. Well—when he wasn't pushing work or my relationship in my face, saying shit like…

"You know, son—I'd proposed to your mother two and a half months after we started dating. You've been dating Alana for what… six months now?"

I had no doubt my father was anxious to set his legacy in motion, starting with Alana and me. He desired us to be the next Mason and Eliza Pope. Seeing how hard the two of us worked at the company that brought him so much pride and joy.

Mom, on the other hand, told me to ignore Dad altogether. She urged me to *take things slow* and to *just enjoy the moment…*

"There's no rush to get married," she'd said. "There's plenty of time later for that. You're both so young. Just have fun and enjoy one another."

That was exactly what I planned on doing.

I'm going to enjoy the hell out of my girlfriend tonight.

The two of us lay prone in bed, side by side, after Alana's intense orgasm.

"Pope…," she panted, "…you're a *god* in the sack."

"And that's why you're with me. You love my huge cock and what I can do with it." I hovered over her and landed a kiss on her mouth. I felt her smile as she kissed me back.

"You know, you can be a pompous prick sometimes, but you tell no lies." I tugged her into my side, and she rested her head on my shoulder after planting two kisses on my bare chest.

"Don't you like it when I'm a pompous prick?" I teased.

"Sometimes, it's hot. Other times, I want to strangle you with my bare hands."

I laughed. "Making you want to strangle me isn't a top goal of mine. Call me out the moment I head in that direction."

"You know I will," she beamed up at me. "I forgot to ask… How did *man lunch* go with Mr. C. Pope?"

"Fantastic, as usual. He asked about you. Wondered why you didn't join us. He wanted you to ditch your regular lunch crew for us."

Alana laughed out loud. "I just love that kid. I hope my future kid is like him."

"Everyone needs a Topher Pope in their life. He gave me some solid career advice before breaking the news that he was going to be my boss."

Alana cracked up even louder. "What did he say?"

"He gave me his thoughts on a few things. Oh—he did say I could have Dad's office, and you can have Mom's after we're married. He plans on constructing another floor where his entire office will reside," I chortled.

"What!" she gaped, fighting a huge grin.

I nodded in sheer amusement. "He's as bad as his father, that one." Alana's expression immediately fell, and concern brewed in my gut. "What's wrong?"

"Nothing," she murmured.

"You know, you're a terrible liar, Faust. You're way too honest. Just spill. You know we don't keep secrets." She sunk deeper into me, and I pulled her naked body in tighter.

"Sometimes, I get the feeling you have something against marriage."

I winced at her words. "Why do you think that?"

"It seems you hate it every time your father brings it up."

"I don't want him to control us. We'll get married at our own time—that's if you want that," I backtracked.

She kept silent, only burying her head in my chest. That was when it dawned on me that this girl actually wanted to marry me.

Holy shit.

"Are... Are you wanting to get married soon?" I asked with a stutter. I was a barrel of nerves.

Her gaze flitted upward, revealing her stunned face to me. "No—not now." Relief rushed in, and I felt at ease. "But one of these days, I'm going to snatch you up for good, Playboy Ford," she proclaimed with a twinkle in her eye. I leaned in to kiss her soundly.

"I'd want nothing more, Alluring Alana," I moaned. "It'll happen when the time is right. You'll see. Just stick around."

"I'm not going anywhere," she purred before rolling her sexy naked body on top of mine. She claimed my mouth with hers.

Liza

"Ready, Topher?" I asked, taking my little boy by the hand.

"Topher was born ready," he answered in the cutest little grown man voice.

Our flip flops clacked against the tile floor as we entered the child pool area of the aquatic center in our swimwear. Up above, the massive skylight beamed the Saturday sun into the blue water.

"Wowwwww," Topher gasped, mesmerized. His blue eyes telescoped right at the area where tall spouts sprayed the excited children running through them. Next to the spouts was a big slide leading into a wading pool. On top of the slide, a huge blue bucket gradually filled with water and dumped a tidal wave onto those who dared to be underneath once the bell sounded. I felt my son's gentle tug.

"Topher, swim class is over here."

"But Mommy, I wanna go over *there*!"

"We're here to learn how to swim. Just forty-five minutes of swim class. Then, we're free to do whatever you'd like. Okay?"

We lined up with the other moms and kids while a young lady

checked each attendee off on a list. Once our names were found, I followed instructions and got Topher settled in a life vest before we got into the two-and-a-half-foot deep section of the pool. I was taken aback by how careful these people were. My son was taller than the water level and in a life jacket. The main instructor blew the whistle, and all moms and kiddos joined her in a circle. We began with kicking exercises on the edge of the pool, the mothers holding their children steady as they became acclimated with the motion. Topher was having a good ol' time splashing water in my face. At the fifteen-minute mark, the instructor called a ten-minute break.

"Can we go over there?" one little girl asked her mom.

The instructor overheard and smiled. "Yes—everyone can go to the play area. But when I blow the whistle, you need to be back here."

A chorus of kids squealed in glee, mine included. Quickly, Topher climbed up the ladder and scurried toward utopia.

"Topher—don't run!" I yelled.

He ignored me and plunged into the play area's pool like a missile. I sat back at the edge, watching him go down the slide a few times. I wished I had my phone on me to take pictures for his father, siblings, and grandparents. The kid was having a total blast.

"Look, Mommy!" he squealed from afar.

"I am! You're doing so great, sweetie!"

I silently wished I'd taken off his life jacket before he ran off. I didn't want the straps to get caught in the slide. Thankfully, he abandoned the slide once he started chatting with another little boy. The two took off running through the water sprouts. In the middle of them playing, Topher held the boy's arm and said something that made him throw his head back in laughter.

Not far from where I stood, an older blonde woman watched the boys with a small smile on her face. I recognized she was with the little boy in class who was now fast friends with Topher. Going by looks alone, she could either be the child's much older mother or his young grandmother. It was really hard to tell. To settle my curiosity, I walked over to speak.

"My son Topher is really good at making friends."

She faced me with a smile. "It's funny, because Ronan isn't. He's very shy."

"How old is he?" I asked

"Three."

"So is Topher," I beamed. "How long has Ronan been in swim class?"

"Two weeks. He loves it here. Is it your son's first day?"

"It is."

"He seems very sweet," she complimented.

"Thank you. He is. He's my fifth child."

"Wow… five. Does he have younger siblings?"

"No. He's our youngest. Our oldest is twenty-two."

"Geez," she said, then quickly covered her mouth in embarrassment.

"No worries, I get that reaction all the time," I giggled. "After our twenty-two-year-old son, we have three daughters—ages twenty and seventeen. The seventeen-year-olds are twins."

"Unbelievable," she said in awe. "You don't look old enough to have grown children."

"You're too kind," I blushed.

"Topher must've come by surprise, huh?" the kind lady beams.

I smirked. "And how."

"He is so well behaved."

"You must've missed it when I told him to stop running, and he ignored me," I chuckled.

"Boys will be boys. You should write a book on raising well-behaved children. I don't know about the others, but if they're like Topher, you must spill all of your secrets," the woman laughed.

"Ronan seems well-behaved, too. Maybe you can co-write that book with me." I don't know what triggered it, but the woman's countenance fell. Right away, I wanted to take my words back. Then, she dropped a bombshell.

"I just hope to get it right this time. Ronan's actually my grandson."

The reveal made my stomach lurch. *Where was his mother?*

"I'm looking at Ronan right now, and he seems like the sweetest little guy," I said to reassure her.

"He has a long road ahead of him. His father's been in jail for about a year now."

My heart ached for her and her grandson. "I'm so sorry. Is Ronan's father your son?"

"God no," the woman frowned.

I was mortified. This woman, who I'd just met, was telling me some very personal information. I felt intrusive. Then, I realized as she spoke that this might've been the first chance that she had to lift some of the burden off her chest. All I had to do was stand there and listen.

"My daughter is Ronan's mother. Right now, she's in a bad predicament. She's not in jail, but I do have temporary custody of Ronan until DSS clears her."

My heart broke for this woman. I prayed she had others helping her while Ronan's parents were sorting their lives. All I could say as I studied the beautiful brown-haired little boy playing with mine…

"Ronan—what a handsome name for such a handsome little boy."

The two of us just stood there in silence, watching him. Wondering about him. The loud pitch from a whistle shook us out of our thoughts. It was time to gather the boys and return to class.

"I'm Liza, by the way." I offered a handshake to the grandmother, which she accepted.

"Nice to meet you, Liza. I'm Shannon."

I wished there was something I could do to help the kind stranger and her adorable grandson. It would destroy me if any child of mine had to endure such misfortune. But instead of jumping the gun and helping a total stranger, as I was known to do, I decided to give it time. I could get to know her better each Saturday and gather more information about her situation. That way, I could better assess if helping her would do more good than harm.

Twenty

Ford

"My—don't you look handsome in that suit," raved the young, very attractive hostess.

"Thank you," I smiled. She narrowed her eyes at me, and I laughed. "Oh, you mean *him*." I gestured to my little brother. In pure Topher fashion, he ignored her compliment and hopped into the seat of his choice. I claimed the empty chair across from him and scooted it toward the table.

My baby brother had decided to go *all-business* for our Monday man-time lunch meeting, sporting a heather gray vest and pants, blue dress shirt rolled at the sleeves, and a Yale blue and white striped tie. It was safe to say he made up his mind where he'd be attending college in the next decade. But out of everything Topher wore, the pièce de résistance had to be…

"Oh, my God! Even your little shoes light up!" the hostess squeaked.

Those God-blessed Minions tennis shoes. No matter what he wore, Topher always threw them into the equation. Once more, he ignored the hostess and focused on the menu placed before him. I was certain he couldn't read yet. I figured he was on the hunt for a sign of chicken nuggets. I doubted he'd find it on a Club Sahara menu. It was one of my parents' higher-end establishments.

"Your waiter will be right with you," the blonde beamed at the two of us.

"Is Monty Montague working the kitchen today?" I asked.

"I believe so."

"Tell him Ford's here."

"And Topher!" my companion excitedly chimed without taking his eyes from the menu.

"Topher is such an awesome name," the blonde gushed. "Is that your real name, little guy?"

Topher doesn't respond, so I speak on his behalf. "It's short for Christopher." The blonde placed a hand over her heart and sighed with stars in her eyes. Apparently, it was cuteness overload for her.

"It's Topher! Topher Pope," the boy insisted. "Where's the chicky nuggets in here?"

"Well, *Topher Pope,* I'm not sure, but I'll send your waiter right over while I check for Monty, okay?" she smiled big. Topher nodded absently, still combing the menu far and wide.

My bro had better watch his back because this bird wanted to take him home. She wouldn't be the first hot girl to fall for the Topher Pope charm. My kid brother macked on chicks better than I ever could, and he did so without trying.

Just then, the blonde turned her attention to me. "You're Ford *Pope,* I presume?" she inquired with flirty eyes. I caught those same eyes slyly searching my left hand on the table.

"That would be me," I said with a smirk.

"Topher's dad?"

"Uh, *no.* He's my brother. You think I look old enough to be his father?" I teased.

She blinked and blushed. "I figured you were quite young, but you never know. I knew you had to be related. You're both so cute."

"Thank you."

My lip twitched, and she blushed even more. "Are you two related to the owners?"

What is this? Twenty-one questions? "Yes," I said, simply.

"Mason Pope is my Daddy, and Liza Pope is my Mommy," Topher interjected. He was finally looking at the hostess.

Appearing embarrassed, she cleared her throat. "*Oh*—well… Welcome back to Club Sahara. I am new here, if you couldn't tell. I'm Laura, by the way."

"No worries, Laura. You're doing just fine," I murmured with a lopsided grin.

I heard the air sucking through her mouth before she cleared her throat again and readjusted her posture. "Um… I'll get your waiter and check on Monty," she said before scurrying off.

"She talks too much," Topher spoke once the hostess was far away enough.

"Easy, tiger," I smirked. "She's just nervous. She's new."

"She likes you. Her face was changing colors."

I laughed. "Actually, I think she likes you more. She spoke to you first, then you gave her the cold shoulder. You shouldn't do that to the ladies, Toph."

"Girls are yucky," he frowned. "She's a thot."

My eyes grew wide. "Where in the world did you learn that word? That's not a nice thing to say." Part of me wanted to laugh, but I couldn't encourage him. He'd bring the word home, and Mom would blame me for teaching it to him.

"Dude!"

I searched for the source of that voice and saw my boy Monty approaching. He was decked out in all white, looking pretty legit as a junior sous chef, but I knew better. Monty was and would always be the wisecracking asshat, regardless of what he wore. I stood, and we high-fived before pulling each other into a one-arm bro hug. Then, he gave Topher a fist pound.

"Topher, my man, Laura tells me you had a special request?" Monty said, kneeling down at my brother's side.

"Chicky nuggets?" he said as if it were a question. Anyone who knew Topher, knew that he never asked questions; he gave orders.

"Piece of cake, son. I got you," Monty said, pounding his chest. He turned to me. "What about you, douchebag?"

I narrowed my eyes and discreetly made a slicing motion to my neck. *Not in front of the kid, Monty.* "I'll have the chicken, sun-dried tomato penne thing," I said, unsure of the exact name of the dish.

"Excellent choice, sir," he joshed in a faux regal accent. "Make sure you relay your order to the waiter, so he knows. I'll get it started."

Ten minutes later, Topher and I were digging into lunch. Monty was the man. He'd even stopped to check in on us after our waiter left and decided to take a break with us. He pulled in a chair next to a booster-seated Topher.

"How's the chicken tenders? I made them especially for you." With a mouth full of chicken, Topher mumbled something unintelligible, making Monty and I laugh.

"No complaints here," I snorted.

"Another satisfied customer." Monty's eyes honed in on me. "So—where's *Miss Booty for Days?* I was hoping to lay eyes on her today."

"I appreciate your concern for my girl, but chill on the objectification," I said with a smile not reaching my eyes.

"Bro, you know I'm just playing. All joking aside, she does indeed have a nice fatty," Monty said, letting his voice trail off.

Topher started laughing out of nowhere, and Monty and I stared in amusement.

"Alana has a *big butt!*" the kid giggled.

Monty practically lost it. I wanted to join him, but I fought to maintain my composure. After all, I was supposed to be the big brother and the positive influence. Plus, I thoroughly enjoyed Alana's voluptuous derriere, so I couldn't be mad at Monty for looking. It had gotten slightly larger over the months as I made it an area of focus in our all-night sexcapades. The key to a round ass? Two words: Doggy. Style.

"How do you know what a *fatty* is, Toph?" I asked with a pursed lip.

"Monty told me. He told me what a *thot* is," he said matter-of-factly.

Monty snorted, then covered his mouth, and I shook my head in disappointment—at myself. I should've never left my kid brother alone with that asshole for longer than a minute when we were roommates.

"Don't tell that to your parents," Monty begged. "They might fire me."

"No, *tell them*," I urged my brother.

"Thanks a lot, Ford," Monty smirked. "So—you two love birds have been settled in at that lush love nest for about three weeks. When should I expect my invite to the wedding of the century?"

"Don't," I groaned.

"What?" he countered, feigning innocence.

"I get enough of that from the old man. Answer me this: When are *you* getting married? Let's talk about that," I hissed.

"Last I checked, you needed at least two people to do that," Monty winked, thinking he's clever.

"You can marry Samantha," I drawled with a devilish grin.

"I don't think Santa Barbara County issues certificates of marriage to inanimate objects," he pretended to ponder with an upward tilted head and a finger to the chin.

"Love is love, Monty Carlo. If you want to marry your blowup doll, then who's to say it's wrong? I'll fight for your right to marry who you'd like."

"You're an a-hole, Pope," Monty chuckled under his breath.

I checked on Topher, who was coloring in between bites. He wasn't paying attention to Monty or me.

"Since Alana the Hottie isn't here, I can give you this," Monty whispered, sliding over a piece of paper.

"What's this?" I frowned.

"It's Laura's phone number—the hostess."

"Nope. Not getting caught with that," I said, forcing the paper back into Monty's hand. He blocked me, refusing to take it.

"Dude, I won't say anything. Just call her. She's hot as hell."

"Fool, are you insane? I'm not cheating on my girlfriend." I balled up the slip of paper and placed it on the table.

"Don't leave that here. She'll see it, and her feelings will be hurt," Monty said with a pouty lip. He tried his best to flatten the paper to its original state, folding and placing it into his chef's coat.

"Yeah—*you* call her," I hissed.

"By the way, I've been trying for weeks to get her number. Leave it to you to score in five seconds," he said with an eye roll.

"If it makes you feel better, she hit on my brother first."

"Topher is definitely a babe magnet supreme, but so are you. Believe me when I say that girl had her eye on you the whole time. She told me."

"When you call her, you can pretend you're me," I volleyed.

"I'll need you to fill up my checking account with a few more benjis in order to convince her," Monty smirked.

"I'm sure you make more than enough here to get by. You're paying the rent at the apartment all on your lonesome."

"Life's been good—I can't complain. Thanks to you and your pops for getting me in here."

"Don't sweat it."

"I envy you. You're kicking ass at Pope Tower, doing what you were born to do. The only way I'd bring home the big bucks doing what I love is if I owned my own Michelin three-star restaurant."

"Make a plan and set it in motion," I advised. "Don't keep fulfilling someone else's dream. Bring yours to fruition."

"That's sound advice, Pope. But does that mean you and I are living your pop's dream right now?"

It was rare, but sometimes, my old friend dropped knowledge on your ass and left you speechless. This was one of those moments.

"You and I are on a bridge to the promised land. We need to stay the course until all our ducks are all in a row. That's why you need a plan," I told him.

"Do *you* have a plan?" he lobbed back at me.

"Right now, I'm stashing money away. I recently landed another raise and I no longer pay rent," I said. Monty nodded his approval. "Also, I'm soaking in all I can at LRPI. I've been shadowing many departments when I'm not busy with my regular job. I've even started filling in for my dad in some capacity." I added.

"All you have to do is hang in there for ten years or so, and LRPI is yours," Monty declared with a wide grin.

My mouth pressed into a straight line. "Yeah, I *could* do that. But why wait ten years? What if I can make my dream come true in ten months?"

"Honestly, bro, I don't know if it's a good time to start a new venture. Right now, you have it made in the f-ing shade," he said with envy. I was glad he had enough sense to filter his language in front of Topher.

"That's true, but there's no better time than the present to take calculated risks. It's easy to jump ship when the economy is good. But returns are greater if a new venture can succeed during a downturn," I argued, taking a swig of water.

"Your pops is literally grooming you to take over the world. Why would you turn that down?"

Monty wasn't seeing the greater picture. "Who says I'm turning it down?" I sounded off. "I'm taking every single thing my parents give me."

"Yeah, but at some point, you plan on bringing everything to someplace else. Why not just ride it out until you become CEO at LRPI?"

"Yes, I *will* be CEO… just not there. Besides, Topher called dibs on LRPI," I smiled.

"I'm going to be the big boss," Topher chimed, breaking his silence.

"You certainly look the part," Monty said, popping Topher's collar.

"I'm going to be *big boss number one,* and Ford will be *boss number two.* Alana will be *medium boss number three,*" Topher ran down.

Monty cracked up, and I simply grinned in acknowledgement. "Is that right?" Monty challenged.

"Yep—and I won't share being the big boss," Topher declared with a poked lip. "I'm not getting married. No thots."

Monty and I couldn't hold back. We laughed our asses off.

"Ain't nothing wrong with a little thottie action every now and then, Sir Topher. In fact, I'm quite fond of that particular female species myself," Monty poured on.

"Topher, buddy—you can't use that word anymore," I pleaded, trying my damnedest to not laugh again.

"Why not?"

"Because. It's not a good word."

"Is it a bad word?" Topher was trying hard to grasp understanding.

"Yes, it is. It's a word that objectifies women," I calmly explained. I knew he wasn't old enough to conceptualize *objectification,* but whatevs. No one could say that I didn't try to steer him in the right direction.

"Brie said Jesse's new girlfriend is..."

My teeth clenched as I prepared for the worst thing possible to exit his mouth.

"...that bad word," Topher said, completing the sentence.

Phew. "She would say that," I replied with an arched brow.

"Your sister is a man-eater. I need to see this Jesse Rogers character with my own eyes. Brie ripped that sucker's heart to shreds, from what you told me," Monty chortled.

"The poor chump," I groaned.

I used to be that guy.

Liza

Mason was on top of me, ravishing my neck. I fought underneath him, trying to garner his attention.

"Hey—I told you I wanted to talk..."

He was so good at getting me to forget—him and his hypnotizing mouth.

"So, *talk*," he murmured in between kisses.

I didn't know if the looming conversation would ruin the mood. I hoped not because I wanted his hands all over me afterward. He seemed to be getting a head start. His hands began inching up my nightgown as his lips slid from my neck to my jaw before reaching my mouth.

"Mason," I giggled. "I need that to talk."

"You don't need to right now, baby. You can use it to do other things," he purred like a lazy lion. The junction between my thighs pulsated rapidly.

I laughed. "Stop that. I need to tell you something."

"So...tell me," he exhaled, shifting his mouth back down to my neck.

"You know I had lunch with Eva today."

"Mm-hmm," he mumbled before his lips made a smacking sound against my skin.

"She wants to leave her dorm for an apartment near campus." He stopped kissing my neck, and I froze. I looked into his quizzical eyes. *This isn't going to end well,* I thought. "She wants to get a place. With a roommate."

"With her friend, Cynthia?" he prompted.

Shit. This is painful.

I braced for the storm and shook my head reluctantly.

"Then *who?*" Mason asked in a rough voice.

I practically shook in my boots. He was about to go insane momentarily.

"Her boyfriend."

Mason stilled for a beat before rolling his body off mine. *So much for a sexy Monday night with my husband.* He propped himself on his elbow and watched me intently.

I babbled in a flurry. "Look… They've both saved enough for first and last month's rent for a decent place by UCLD. They've thought this through. Eva has outgrown her dormitory. She's a junior now."

"Settle down," he said, holding up both hands in placation.

"I know you're about to lose your shit, Mason. I'm just covering all bases before you say *no*." His eyes narrowed. "Say I'm wrong," I demanded.

He continued staring at me in silence. With each passing second, the compacting in my chest grew more uncomfortable. Suddenly, the corners of his mouth twitched.

Wait, is he joshing me?! Jerk! I slapped him on the arm, and he winced.

"You knew!" I accused.

"Knight and I had lunch while you were with Eva," he spilled.

"You're such a jackass," I hissed. Still, I couldn't help but smile. He'd gotten me worked up all for nothing.

"But you still love me," he cooed, inching his puckering lips in my direction. I swatted him away.

"So—what did you tell Knight?" I prodded, begging him with my eyes to yank me out of misery.

"After Knight told me their plans, I chewed on it for a bit before giving him my blessing. I then put him in touch with my broker."

I gaped at my husband. *Seriously? Am I hearing him correctly?*

He continued. "I believe the two of them are mature enough to handle this together. Knight's the same age as our oldest, and Ford recently moved in with his girlfriend. Thibodeau has a bright future at the company. Eva is an excellent student and hard worker with a good head on her shoulders. They have my blessing."

I fell back into bed and dragged a pillow over my face. I

couldn't believe what I was hearing. Mason climbed back on top of me, yanking the pillow from my clutches.

"What is your deal, Mrs. Pope?" he said with a smoldering look that always made me weak.

"What have you done with my husband?" I crooned.

"Baby, he's still in there," he said, pointing to his chest. "He's just older and more tired," he quipped, and I laughed. "I'm learning how to pick my battles. I also know our daughter is dating a trustworthy young man. Knight has more than proven himself over the years."

Amazing. My sweet, reformed asshole.

Twenty-One

Ford

"Thanks a ton for watching your little brother tonight."

"Are you serious right now?" I smirked at my mother. "Really—it's no bother. Topher is my number one ace."

"We're going to have a blast with this guy," Alana eagerly chimed as she ruffled the man of the hour's hair. Topher managed to get away and ran through the main room and into the kitchen, all while waving his arms and making fighter plane sounds.

My folks needed to attend some fancy midweek fundraiser, so they'd asked if we could watch Topher. The Bentons were tied up with something else, and the twins had a midweek AP Calculus study group happening. Alana and I were up for the challenge.

Dad looked like a billion bucks in his navy tux. And Mom? Holy shit. Dad had better keep his woman on a leash. She slayed in a gown that had a single strap on her right shoulder that began black on top, then faded into a royal blue when the skirt reached the bottom. Her hair was styled in an elegant bun, exposing her back in between four black straps with intricate beading.

"Liza, you're a total knockout. That dress is simply to die for," Alana gushed for the third time in five minutes.

"And I see I'm chopped liver," Dad smirked, making me laugh.

"Your handsomeness goes without saying, Mr. Pope," Alana sweetly said. Mom chuckled at the merciful compliment.

"Hey! Stop flirting with my old man," I teased. My girlfriend brushed me off with a flick of her wrist.

"We shouldn't be more than three hours. It is a work night for crying out loud," Mom sighed.

"We've got you covered," I reassured.

"Call us if you need anything at all," Dad added.

"Leave," I snickered at the two of them. *Overprotective parents, I swear.* They relented and pinned down Topher long enough for a kiss before hugging Alana and me on their way out.

"So, bud—what did you want to do before you go to bed in an hour?" I asked our little guest.

"Bed?! *Noooo!*" he cawed before darting around Alana and me in a circle. Alana reached out in an attempt to grab him, but he was lightning fast.

I teamed up with her and tried to nail down the slippery little monster as he made his way through the main room and into the kitchen.

"I'll get you, Topher!" Alana roared playfully.

"Don't let her catch you, or you'll have a wet-willy coming your way!" I called in warning.

"*Ewww!* No way!" he shouted in a fit of giggles. He was dashing to and fro, non-stop.

Suddenly, I heard the chirp of a phone. It was Alana's. "Time out," she called, out of breath. That didn't stop Topher from running and me from chasing him. I'd almost had him in my hands twice, but he'd wiggled his way out.

"Crap, it's work," Alana announced from the breakfast bar. "I've gotta take this."

"Tell Thibodeau to stop torturing you with that *Propel the Future* debauchery," I heckled.

When Alana left to take her call, I finally grabbed Topher by the arm and tackled him on the floor. He wailed in defeat.

"Got you!" I proceeded to tickle him relentlessly, and he giggled uncontrollably.

"Stop tickling me!" Topher cried in a fit of laughs. I granted his midsection clemency but moved my torment to his head of hair. He tried blocking me with his skinny little arms. We each caught our breath after a while.

"I forgot to ask about your swim class."

"I go again Saturday," he told me.

"Sweet. You like it?"

"Yep—It's fun! I learned how to kick my feet. Then, I got to play on the water slide and had lots of water dumped on me," he rattled off animatedly.

"Dude, that sounds pretty amazing. I'm jealous."

"Me and my friend Roman had so much fun," he smiled brightly.

I narrowed my gaze. "Your friend's name is *Roman*? Is he a centurion guard or something?"

"No. I don't even know what that is."

"Didn't think you did," I winked.

After Alana concluded her brief call, the three of us indulged in my delicious homemade bread pudding. It was my Mom's recipe. If I do say so myself, it came pretty close to Eliza Pope's perfection. An hour later, all engaged in a highly competitive game of Hide and Seek. Twenty minutes later, Alana and I gave up looking for Topher.

"Seriously, where did he go? We've looked *everywhere*," Alana sighed.

"I should've warned you. Topher Pope is the family's Hide and Seek champion. He'll pop up. Eventually."

Not long afterward, my parents surfaced from the elevator, escorted by Greg Donner.

"Is he in bed?" Mom asked Alana and me.

"Funny you ask. I think we've lost him. We were playing Hide and Seek," I admitted, thoroughly embarrassed.

Mom sighed. She was well aware of how crafty her youngest could be in the masterful game of lost and found.

"I'll be back," Dad smirked, marching off in his Gucci loafers. Two minutes later, he emerged with a sleeping Topher dangling lifelessly in his arms. "You two must've worn him out."

I dusted off my hands. "Well, my job here is done."

Alana was flabbergasted. "Where did you find him? We looked *everywhere*."

"Mason has mastered all the champ's prized hiding spots," Mom answered instead as she lifted Topher's bag of toys from the floor.

I was in my office having a productive video conference with the folks at Pifany Natural Cosmetics in New York City. We were close to making a deal to acquire them. With Pifany in our portfolio, LRPI would be able to make inroads in our quest to making the world a greener place.

I was focused on the group of ten men and women on the screen when my desk phone buzzed quietly. I checked the screen and saw it was the reception desk on the main floor. I frowned, wondering what on earth they wanted. I never received calls from the main desk. My boss' assistants, Tara and Marie, usually filtered those sorts of calls. I ignored the phone.

Two minutes went by, and the meeting was starting to wind down. My desk phone buzzed again. Once again, it was the front desk. Now, I was concerned.

"Ladies and gentlemen, I hope we're all squared away on this next phase," I said in closing.

"We are, Ford. Thanks so much for your time. Sounds like your phone's ringing off the hook over there," the VP of Pifany chuckled.

"Yeah, it's never a dull moment here," I sighed.

"We'll let you go, then."

"I'll circle back with your team next week before the meeting with Natalie and the rest of my leadership team," I told them.

"Excellent. Please give our best to your parents. We look forward to working with them, as well as yourself," the president of the company tagged on.

"Sure thing. Take care, everyone." Once we said our goodbyes, I immediately dialed the front desk.

"Mr. Pope?" the female receptionist uttered before I could get a word in edgewise.

"Yes, did someone just call?"

"Sir—you have an unruly visitor here who refuses to leave unless she sees you. We can call security if you'd like," she said in a discreet tone of voice.

The last time I'd had an *unruly visitor* at work, I'd been a student at Stanford. It had damn near taken an act of God to get Cheerleader Rebecca off my junk. I couldn't imagine her relapsing after all these years.

"Who is it?" I asked in a sharp tone.

"She says her name is Harper Benton."

My heart felt like it stopped pumping mid-beat.

Harper? Why is she even here?

I was feeling things I didn't think I'd ever feel again... Lightheaded and woozy, sick and lost. I tried to gauge what my physiological state was enduring in that moment, then something hit me dead center.

Harper Benton... not Harper Cramer?

Why had Harper told the front desk her last name was Benton? Perhaps it was purely for my benefit. Maybe she assumed I wouldn't know her as *Cramer*. Little did she know, I didn't know Harper Benton either. At one time, I'd thought I did. At the moment, I didn't want to face either Harper.

"Mr. Pope—you still there?" the receptionist asked. I heard muffled sounds in the background that sounded like a woman shouting.

Holy hell. I immediately thought about my father seeing my ex raising a stink in the lobby. What about Alana? *Shit.*

"I'll be right down."

With my heart pounding out of my chest, I made it down the elevator from the nineteenth floor. I took long strides toward the main desk. Then, I saw her. She leaned against the sandstone with her hands covering her face. I scanned down her length and assessed her.

Thick, long blond hair.

Open red flannel shirt with black t-shirt underneath.

Over-washed jeans.

Tattered sneakers.

Harper didn't look the same. This new person looked battle-weary. She was torn down and ravaged. This girl before me wasn't the same bright-eyed angel I'd once known—the one who had run with me through our meadow and beach with a smile plastered on her face.

The girl standing before me had obviously gone through some serious shit. But through it all, the essence of her beauty remained intact. I hated seeing her in such a broken state and feeling sorry for her. It wasn't fair. She had earned every stripe on her back because she'd inflicted the same on my heart.

The receptionist cleared her throat when she noticed me standing there. Harper lifted her head and turned in my direction. Those tortured blue eyes locked with mine, and I felt completely lost. She wasn't wearing any makeup, so I could tell she'd been crying, a lot.

I didn't know what to say to her. I had no words. I'd been dreaming of this moment for over three years, and I had *no fucking words*.

"Ford?" she trembled.

I stood there, frozen in time. Soon, I felt her arms wrap around me.

Why is she here?

I finally came to and pulled away from her, holding her at arm's length.

"Harper, what's going on? Why are *you*—"

"Ford… *I*… I need to talk. Can we please talk?" she rattled off with urgency and despair.

"Calm down. What happened?" I murmured, making sure she doesn't lose it again in front of onlookers. I needed to get her out of there before someone we knew saw us.

"I… I…" she stuttered as her otherworldly blue eyes pooled with tears.

"Come with me." I guided her gently by the arm and led her down the hallway and into a small conference room tucked in the back. I locked the door behind us. She began to shake before falling on my neck.

Jesus, why is she clinging to me like this? It's unbearable.

"Harper… tell me. What is going on?"

A small part of me wanted to yell at her. *The nerve of her walking back into my life after all these years. She decimated my soul.* But there was a voice within that called out on a deeper level. It was the only space inside of me that had compassion for her.

"I can't help unless you tell me what's wrong," I voiced through her audible sobs.

She began easing away until she stood on her own two feet. I reached into my suit pocket and handed her a handkerchief.

"I'm sorry for coming here," she wept. "*I*… didn't mean to interrupt you at work."

"What happened? Sit," I urged, taking her by the arm and helping her into a swivel chair. I took the seat beside her and rolled in closer.

"I'm scared. I think I'm about to lose my son."

Stop.

Hold up.

Wait a second.

I was missing out on three years of information. It's as if I'd tuned into the program three seasons later. I needed the CliffsNotes to bring me up to speed.

"Where's Aiden—your husband?"

The question obviously triggered something because it made her cover her face. "I *really* messed up," she said, muffled through her hands.

Yeah, you fucking did. I'd known the guy wasn't shit from the get-go. Her dad had known he wasn't shit. The only person who hadn't known was *her*.

"What did he do to you?"

It was apparent to me that whatever happened to her, it had everything to do with that shitty husband of hers. I searched the fingers glued to her face, and there was no sign of an engagement ring or a wedding band. No tan lines. No nothing. I gave her a few moments to collect herself. Eventually, her hands moved from her face.

"We never married."

The news took me by surprise. "You didn't marry him?"

"No. We lived together. We rented a house together after the baby was born. Then, he started getting into drugs heavily."

"Jesus Christ," I grunted, shaking my head in revulsion. I *knew* that asshole was a druggy. Alana also knew it the second she met him at lunch three years ago.

"I couldn't understand his fascination with drugs. I didn't get it. We had this smart, beautiful baby boy at home. That alone should've made him want to give that child *everything*, but he didn't care. He only cared about his next *gnarly trip*."

She was just a ghost of her old self as she recalled all kinds of horrific things to me. And all the while, I was thinking: *This was the choice that you made. YOU wanted this.*

"Living with him got progressively worse," she murmured. This was so painful. I didn't want to hear anymore, but she kept on going. "And when his money dried up, he began stealing from me."

Holy fuck. It explained why she was dressed like that. The girl had *nothing* left.

"And then, when my money was all gone, he ventured into other things. Him and his druggie friends."

"Dammit, Harper—*why?*"

It was all I could say. I had no other words in response to her allowing all of this to happen to herself. It never had to be this way.

"It wasn't until a stickup at a truck stop had gone wrong that it all stopped. He was already on probation for a possession charge. Last year, he ended up getting a mandatory ten years for armed robbery."

My eyes clamped down, and I shook my head. "*Harper, Harper, Harper…*"

"I know," she breathed and started crying again. I placed my hand on her shoulder and rubbed it gently. She leaned into my touch.

Why am I even touching her? My hand stilled, then dropped into my lap.

"You're a single mom," I concluded.

"I worked two jobs, trying to keep things afloat. It was hard. My mother helped watch my son while I worked. It didn't stop the bills from piling up. Things got pretty bad," she said, shaking through the tears.

The Harper I knew wasn't *this*. The Harper I knew had her shit together. She had a plan and a goal. This was a totally different Harper. A sad, pitiful Harper.

There was a tragic reality that screamed loudly and clearly. My father was right all along to keep us apart. He'd known how fragile I was back then and how fragile Harper was.

Harper and I weren't meant to be together.

I sat there, stoic, watching her. I waited for whatever else she had to say, anticipating the real reason for her intrusion and disruption in the main lobby.

"While I was working all that time, I missed my son. I wanted the simple life with him. A life with no pressure. I wanted to know what it felt like to not feel anymore."

An ominous feeling came over me as she said exactly what I had feared.

"A coworker at the night auditing job I had introduced me to oxycodone," she said with shame riddled all over her face.

"Fuck, Harper… Are you joking?! *Oxy?!*" I bellowed.

"I tried it only once. I wanted to understand why Aiden couldn't kick the habit. I wasn't going to do it again. But that night I took the drug from my coworker, we were caught on camera."

"Jesus," I say, shaking my head for the hundredth time. *The hits just keep on coming.*

"I was fired and arrested. Later on, this woman stops by my mom's place to see me. I'd never met her before. Come to find out, she works at the Department of Social Services. Say what you will about me, but I'd never been a bad mother. I *love* my son. I would *die* for my son." Harper wept loudly for a few moments before pressing on. "This woman must be getting paid by Aiden's parents. There was no reason for DSS to be called on me. But since I was arrested for drug possession, they probably assumed I was doing drugs at home in front of my kid."

I couldn't hear any more of this. It was too much to take in. "Harper…" I started in an attempt to make her stop heaping all her bad shit on me. Why was she telling me this instead of her father?

"They're trying to take my son away from me, Ford! I can't let them do that! They want to take my baby from me and my mom! *Please!*" she groveled through the tears.

"What do you want *me* to do?" I sneered, throwing my hands up in the air. "You come here after three years… I have no idea what's been going on with you. Then all of a sudden, you spring this heavy shit on me. I don't know what to tell you, Harper. Really—I *don't*." The words came tumbling out of me. It was everything I'd wanted to say for the past fifteen minutes.

She sat there, muddling through the tears. I saw the realization on her face as a thought entered her mind. Her lips began to move as if she was wanted to say something, but then thought better of it.

"I'm sorry for coming here. This was a bad idea."

She started for the door, but I stood and grabbed her by the arm, stopping her.

"You need me to help you with legal fees?" I asked. She looked down at her feet and didn't say anything. "Have you spoken to your dad?" She shook her head without looking up. I figured as much. "No one? What about Trisha—your stepmom?"

"They don't know. I stopped speaking to them after Aiden and I got engaged. If they knew everything that happened since I disobeyed them, they wouldn't want to help me anyway."

"That's bullshit, Harper. They *love* you," I snapped.

I hadn't realized I was still holding her arm until she tugged it. Still, I didn't let go.

"It was a mistake coming here," she said, distraught.

"Where do you live? Are you doing okay? Do you need money?" I rattled off, holding her arm firmly.

"I'm fine," she said through a tight jaw. "I was hoping for help to fight for my son. It was foolish of me to come here."

"Just tell me what you need me to do." I pleaded softly in hopes that she calmed down and told me what it was she wanted. However, at this point, she'd already claimed defeat in her head. I could see it written all over her face.

"It's fine, Ford. I'd like to go now. Please."

"One second." I let her go and reached in my pocket for a business card. "My personal cell is there. If you change your mind, give me a call. I'd prefer a phone call over a surprise visit," I added with a bittersweet smirk.

With one hand on the door's handle, she eyed the card in the other. "Bradford C. Pope, Executive Manager of Cosmetics," she read in a whisper. "You're a step away from Vice President. How long did it take you?" I saw a faint semblance of pride on her face.

"I've been full-time since graduation," I told her.

"So, two and a half years," she quickly calculated before sliding the card into the pocket of her jeans. She pulled the door open.

"I'll see you out," I offered.

She held out her hand, petitioning me to stay in place. "That won't be necessary. I'll leave the way that I came in. Thanks, Ford."

Harper walked away without looking back, leaving me standing in place. I was dumbfounded to find myself holding the proverbial bag for her yet again.

You know that feeling you experience when you are expecting that *one* call? Your brain cells interpret a sense of vibration in your front pocket. But when you retrieve your phone and see that you don't have a new call or text, you feel like a moron. It was just a phantom sensation, a figment of your wild imagination.

The idea of Harper contacting me after the manner in which she'd left seemed absurd. The sheer regret of visiting me in the first place was evident on her sweet, tormented face.

I arrived home hours before Alana had planned to leave the office. I was there earlier than usual since there hadn't been much I could do back in my office. Harper had left me stupefied in that small conference room. Her words had continued to replay in my head, sounding just as ludicrous as when she'd first said them to me.

"We never married..."

"He started getting into drugs heavily..."

"Living with him got progressively worse..."

"And when his money dried all up, he began stealing from me..."

I'd thought Aiden was just a stoner. Turned out he was way worse than I ever imagined. Then, things just got worse.

"I worked two jobs, trying to keep things afloat..."

"I missed my son. I wanted the simple life..."

"I tried it only once..."

"I was fired and arrested..."

I didn't know this girl anymore. The Harper I fell in love with long ago wouldn't have even puffed a cigarette. *My* Harper would have never been so irresponsible. She wouldn't have put herself in a position to potentially lose her child.

I recapitulated her words for hours in the main room of the penthouse. I was enslaved to my thoughts and feeling helpless. I feared for her. I wanted to help her. However, the ball was in her court. She had my number, and I no longer had hers.

Prior to leaving the office today, I'd reached out to Cliff Gerts, who was now a reputable private investigator in Los Angeles. After giving him the background details, he'd eagerly accepted the challenge. From there, I'd transferred his retainer right into his bank account. Gerts' mission was to find out everything he could about what had happened with Harper over the past three years. He'd also keep a close eye on her and monitor any sudden moves from the Cramers.

In the meantime, I was able to obtain a copy of the court documents filed by Steven and Allison Cramer, Aiden's parents. They'd petitioned for full custody of Aiden and Harper's son, who so happened to be unnamed in the documents, due to the child's age. Mr. and Mrs. Cramer lived just outside of Las Vegas. If the Cramers were to win custody, that would obviously make it difficult for Harper and her mother to remain in the child's daily life.

Another piece of information I was able to get was arrest documents on two other Cramer offspring. Simply put, the Cramers bred drug addicts. The way these people raised kids wasn't conducive to a positive and thriving upbringing. Armed with these tools, it would be easy for Harper to fight them in court—with the right lawyers, of course.

Because of what I knew, I was more than willing to help Harper and her mom fight to keep her child in Los Derivas. But no matter how much effort I was putting into gathering intel for her case, I couldn't make a move until she picked up the phone and called me. Until then, I'd have to sit, wait, and hope she'd want me to help her like she had in her initial desperate plea.

Later, I decided to reread the court documents over again in my study. This study had once belonged to my father. I could vaguely picture him sitting right where I was, doing very similar things. He'd have called his top consultant to keep an eye on all of the new people who would dare enter our lives. When it came to protecting his family, my father was leery of everyone. Now, I understood how my dad was wired.

I wish I could have protected her.

Two knocks on the door startled me. I hurried to close the document I was in before Alana opened the door. She was home earlier than expected.

"Hey, what's going on? You left work early," she said to me with a concerned look.

"A bunch of shit," I sighed, massaging my temples.

Alana seated herself in one of the chairs facing my desk.

"Darcy said there was a strange visitor at the front desk asking for you. I tried calling you in your office to see if everything was okay."

Fucking Darcy in analytics. Why in the hell had she been on the main level when she was supposed to be helping her boss, Knight, pull materials together for his big presentation? The woman was a busy body.

"Harper came looking for me," I said matter-of-factly. There was no use in hiding it. Secrets always managed to get out. My girlfriend's eyes grew wide.

"You're kidding."

"Nope."

"Why? What did she want?"

I shrugged. "Let's just say that she's been through hell. She wanted my help."

"What does she want? Money?" Alana said, appalled.

"She doesn't have her kid right now and may end up losing custody permanently. Aiden's serving a lengthy prison sentence for robbery, and his well-to-do parents are now fighting to take the child away from Harper. She'd recently gotten into some trouble, and the grandparents might use that against her." I stopped there, not divulging in what Harper did to put herself in such a predicament.

"Wow," Alana winced.

"Yeah," I sighed, trying to take in the reality myself.

"She had a boy?" she asked, and I confirmed with a nod. "Maybe the child being with his grandparents might do him some good. Harper obviously doesn't have a handle on things."

"I don't think it's that simple. Harper used to babysit my sisters, and she's never been neglectful. She's always been a decent, good person. Her only downfall was procreating with a bad guy."

Alana's expression hardened. "But didn't she neglect *you?*" Her words hit me right between the eyes. "Didn't she turn out to be someone other than the girl you thought you knew?" She was absolutely right.

"Yeah, but I can't help but feel sorry for her after seeing her today. Sure, she hurt me years ago, but you should've seen her today. I don't know… It's hard to explain. Something in me wants to help her fight to keep her child."

My girlfriend leaned back in her chair and looked at me sideways. "You don't even know her anymore, Ford. Maybe you should tell your dad and Russ about it. Why don't you let them handle it?"

"Harper doesn't want that. She doesn't even talk to her father anymore. Honestly, I think I'm her only hope."

Alana leaned forward in her chair, placing both hands on the edge of my desk. Her words were clear and succinct.

"It is not your job to help her."

I was caught between a rock and a hard place. On one hand, I couldn't get Harper's tearful face out of my head. On the other hand, I had a very perturbed girlfriend sitting before me. If I went through with helping Harper, it would be the ultimate betrayal to Alana. This woman had been there for me through the worst of times, so betraying her was the last thing I wanted to do.

"You're right," I conceded. "You're absolutely right."

Twenty-Two

Liza

Earlier that morning, I'd been surprised to see a meeting invite from Ford's girlfriend. She'd wanted to do lunch. So, before my assistant screened my mail, I'd gone ahead and accepted Alana's invite. Since she'd begun dating my son, I hadn't had a chance to chat with her one-on-one. It was always a few words in passing at Pope Tower, or five minutes here and there in my home whenever Ford stepped out of the room. Since we never had long chats, something told me this wasn't just a spur-of-the-moment invitation.

Alana had been extremely busy helping her team with data mining for Knight's big PTF presentation he'd be giving to our executive staff. In fact, Knight was slated to do a pre-reading for the CEOs and our executive management team in the next couple of weeks. Eva had told me the team had been having lunch brought in because they needed every possible minute to fine-tune their forecast in the next few days. The fact that Alana wanted to take time out of her very busy schedule to solicit my company spoke volumes. I tried guessing her true objective.

Career advice?

Relationship trouble with Ford?

Goodness—I hope it's something I can handle.

Right at noon, I met Alana with a hug just outside Pope Tower. My driver, Mrs. Gloria Bianchi, led us into the backseat of my sleek black sedan. After securing the door, Gloria began the journey to one of my favorite Greek restaurants in downtown Los Derivas.

My driver was a tiny, no-nonsense, firecracker grandma from Boston who'd been with me for nearly two years. In the past, she'd driven for celebrities and dignitaries. She and her husband had moved to California to be closer to her daughter and grandchildren. Retired life had become too mundane for the lively lady, so a friend of the family had referred her to Mason and me.

I loved driving myself, but as metropolitan Los Derivas grew busier and busier with more corporations setting up shop, the drive home to Arcadia's Crest was becoming a pain. Having my own driver allowed me to take a conference call without the embarrassment of cussing out the jerk cutting me off in traffic. From the back seat, I could respond to a few emails, catch up on voicemails, or read that thirty-page report I received overnight from Japan. It also allowed me to have extra time in the mornings with Topher instead of leaving for work before dawn with Mason and Russ.

In the car, I broke the silence with Alana. "How's Knight's presentation coming along?"

"It's going quite well, actually," she smiled. Alana looked dynamite in her navy-blue dress, and it shamed me to know where she'd bought it. I knew all there was to know about fashion.

"I'm looking forward to seeing it," I told her. "I know Knight will do well. Eva said your team's been working extremely hard on it."

"I don't know how Eva does it. She's a data mastermind and a straight-A student at UCLD," Alana awed.

"My children, I swear," I sighed with the evidence of pride. "I couldn't carry that sort of workload while keeping up my grades in college. I can't imagine doing the stressful amounts of work Eva is doing."

"Me neither. I'm so impressed by her. My sister, Bridget, is the same age as Eva and she can't type and listen to music at the same time," Alana laughed.

"I think Eva wants to accelerate her coursework, just like Ford did. She's eager to work for us full-time."

"She told me that. She's just as determined as her brother," she chuckled.

"It's in their DNA," I simply said.

"Obviously," she smiled. "Any idea what department Eva wants to work in after she graduates?"

"She loves working with data. I think she's just going to plant roots in analytics. However, it would be nice for her to get more exposure."

"I agree," Alana nodded.

At lunch, we waved off the basket of bread (*carbs... BAD*) and opted for a side salad for an appetizer. We had a spirited conversation about food, film and growing up in California. She'd only been in the state since high school, but she considered it home over Missouri. The topic then moved over to college, which prompted me to ask her about her future goals.

"Your major was International Marketing. Any plans on eventually exploring that area in your career?"

"That was my initial plan. I think it's awesome LRPI makes it easy to land an expat position anywhere around the globe."

"You can pretty much write your own ticket. I think you'd really enjoy working at our new facility in Germany. There's also a growing marketing presence at our Sidney headquarters," I suggested.

Alana flashed a kind smile. "That's great."

"Let me know when you're thinking about taking the next step. I'm happy to help."

Her expression turned pensive. "Thank you so much, Liza. I really appreciate it. But unless Ford has a reason to work abroad, I don't think I'll be leaving Los Derivas anytime soon."

Alana's relationship with my son seemed to be getting quite

serious. Mason, for one, would be glad. He'd been a fan of Alana's since day one. He often talked about how she reminded him a lot of me. I knew Alana was a hard worker. She also cared deeply for my son. I'd seen the way she looked at him whenever they were together. But…

There was something else going on underneath the surface. I couldn't quite put it into words. Sure, she adored him, and Ford adored her. They seemed to enjoy being in each other's presence. Yet somehow, they lacked a sort of spark between them. Again, I couldn't pinpoint a single word or a phrase that defined what I felt.

I thought back to my life before Mason. I'd hated going out. I had wanted to stay home and create dresses. When Jessie and I were roommates in LA, she'd had to drag me out of our apartment kicking and screaming. And dating? Forget about it. Sure, I'd kissed a guy or two, but none of them ever took my breath away. There wasn't anyone who had made me want to give more than just kisses.

Then, one day working my night job, I'd met a drop-dead gorgeous god in a suit, yelling on a conference call. He'd suddenly dropped everything—for me. No one had ever done that before, not even my parents. When I met Mason Pope, I'd started believing that fantasies really could come true. I'd hurt anyone who dared to pinch me and wake me from this magnificent dream I've lived for twenty-five years.

When you found that *forever* kind of love, you grabbed it and held on for dear life.

That was precisely what Mason and I had done.

The telltale of a true soulmate connection was demonstrated in the awestruck look Mason gave me each night when we were alone in the still and quiet. It was an ogle that said, 'I'd rather gaze at you for an eternity than waste two seconds looking at the sunset over our private beach.' I felt that same love for him.

I didn't get that same vibe with Alana and Ford. I felt absolutely horrible thinking that, but after many hours of excruciating pain while in labor, I'd better know my son like the back of my hand. Ford was more like his father than he'd let himself believe. I never saw him look at Alana the way his father looked at me.

But he'd looked at Harper that way.

Immediately, I took my glass of water and chugged it to wash away my wayward thoughts. I was having lunch with Ford's live-in girlfriend and wishing she was someone else. Not cool.

"Have you and Mr. Pope discussed retirement?"

Alana's question was off-putting, but I decided to not think too deep about it. She was only having friendly conversation.

"If you asked Mason, he'd say he wants us to retire tomorrow," I smirked, and Alana laughed. "Honestly, I don't know when that will be. Our hope is to keep the business in the family after we've gone. I do believe our two oldest are more than capable of picking up the mantle. Eva has expressed her wishes of taking over one of these days."

I caught a slight drop in Alana's expression. "Really? I didn't know she wanted to lead."

"Oh yes—Eva is a natural leader. She was STEM club president and valedictorian in high school. She turned down four Ivy Leagues so she could stay here and work at LRPI while attending school. Once she has graduated and becomes full-time, she'll be well on her way to management in no time flat."

I was proud of all of my children, each of them bright and driven—all the way down to my little nugget, Topher.

"Ford came in after Stanford and managed to skyrocket up to a guaranteed VP position. He's the most focused person I know."

I narrowed my eyes at her, confused. Why was she trying to sell me on my own son? I knew all his achievements. He'd done great things at LRPI and continued to accomplish a great deal in his career in a matter of three years.

Liza—we're having a friendly conversation.

I tried not to appear offended. There was no reason for hostility since I was sure she meant nothing by voicing her well-placed praise for my son. She was his girlfriend, after all, so one would hope she'd be an encouragement to him. Alana was simply doing her job.

"Absolutely," I said in agreement. "Ford has everything it takes to succeed us. If he wanted the job, he'd be first in line. He or Eva could easily take the reins."

"I think it's wonderful you and Mr. Pope have more than one offspring to continue your legacy. You'll be in good hands no matter what," she beamed.

"Yes, Mason and I are extremely blessed. We even have Topher, who already has ambitions of launching his little empire," I grinned.

Alana laughed out loud. "Topher is awesome. I don't doubt for a second that he'll be running things in a couple of decades."

"What do you mean *a couple of decades*? That kid's running things now," I snorted.

Lunch was served, and we continue to make small talk. Once I stopped second-guessing everything she said, I started to enjoy getting to know her better. At one point, we gave each other a look that said, *I can't take another bite, or I'll burst*. So, we sat there, allowing our meals to digest.

"I wanted to ask you something," Alana started.

"Sure."

"I met Ford before we knew we'd be interning together at Zinfinite."

I smiled knowingly. "He told me the story."

She blushed. "How much did he tell you?"

"Not much," I shrugged.

I wasn't naïve. Two very attractive young people meet at a club while drinking—underage, mind you. Then, after hitting it off, my son doesn't answer his calls and doesn't come home until early the next morning. Yeah, we could all guess what happened that night.

"Good," she giggled and sighed in relief. "Well—when we first met, he was really broken over Harper."

Now, there was a name I hadn't heard out loud in many years.

"Over the next couple of years, Ford and I would become best friends. He knew everything about me, and I knew everything about him. But for some reason, I feel like I'm still missing some vital pieces to him."

The truth of the impromptu lunch meeting finally came out.

"Your son means the world to me, Liza. We've built something solid together. It is my hope for us to continue to grow in our relationship as best friends. As... Everything."

Everything? What does she mean by that?

I couldn't stop my brain from running circuits. Once again, my thoughts were all over the place. Alarms, scenarios, potential motives... I couldn't seem to narrow down what was happening in that moment. I closed my eyes for clarity.

Don't speak. Let her show you who she is.

I opened my eyes and studied her.

"I'd like to better understand the time when Harper was around. Is there anything you can tell me that would help me better understand where Ford's head was at?" Alana pleaded with her gaze.

In my mind, Harper had ended over three years ago. Why was she being brought up now?

If Alana was insecure about Ford's past, I could understand that plight better than anyone. I'd had dozens of Mason's exes to contend with when we'd started dating. If nothing else, I needed to show this dear girl some mercy.

However, my allegiance was first and foremost to my son. I wouldn't dream of ever betraying him or his trust by sharing any information with Alana that he wouldn't want shared.

"Hasn't Ford told you everything about that time?" I finally said.

"He has. I was just hoping to get another perspective," she said in earnest.

"There's a point when you realize that once you really care for someone, you should take them at their word. What has Ford told you about that time?" I asked, turning the tables back on her. She winced before taking in a deep breath.

"He was madly in love with her, and she nearly destroyed him."

Her words stung. You never want to hear second-hand how your own child once felt defeated. I'd always encouraged my children to be comfortable enough to talk to me about anything.

Telling Ford's father about him skipping school with Harper had not only impacted Ford's relationship with Harper, but it had erected an armored barrier between Ford and me. He'd never felt safe enough to share his innermost thoughts and dreams with me since then. The thought of that pierced me. I longed for that little boy again—the one who adored his mama.

Ford never used words, but his eyes told me Harper had meant so much to him. Back then, I'd thought it was just an innocent crush. Now that he was an adult with a live-in girlfriend...

The fact that Alana was bringing this up made Ford and Harper seem more than just an old case of innocent puppy love.

"When I first met him, I'd recently gone through a bitter breakup myself. That was our bond," Alana mused, staring at her cold dish. "At Zinfinite, whenever there was something we couldn't handle, he or I would say *S.O.S.* That was our code word when we could just open up and share what was eating us."

It warmed my heart to hear that Ford had someone to talk to.

"The morning after Harper pressured Ford to meet her fiancé, that was an S.O.S. day."

My eyes widened in shock. I had no clue about any of this.

"Even though I believed it was cruel at the time for her to make him do that, I encouraged Ford to accept her invitation because I'd hoped it would give him some closure. But I didn't let him go alone," Alana said soberly.

Why on earth would Harper do that—especially if she knew Ford loved her so much?

My Mama Bear reflexes were on the fritz. My blood simmered in my veins.

"When Harper and her fiancé walked into that restaurant, she looked like she was going to pop. She was about eight months pregnant at the time. Ford hadn't known until then."

A slow ache began to palpitate within. No one wants to hear about their child being hurt, no matter what age they are. They will forever be your guileless little babies. I buried my face in my hands and breathed in between my fingers.

"I'm sorry, Liza. I'm sure it's the first time you're hearing any of this. I just want to be sure I'm the only girl for Ford. I don't want Harper returning to the picture and playing mind games. There can't be any room in Ford's heart for her to weasel her way back in."

Alana's goal was noble. If her intentions with my son were good, then I'd want the same—*if* Alana was truly the one for my son. Her words and evident devotion to my son told me she was.

But did Ford feel the same about Alana?

I lifted my eyes and looked straight at her. "From what I see, my son appears to be devoted to you. Ford doesn't believe in stringing anyone along. If he's with you, then that means he wants to be with you and *only* you."

"I want nothing but for that to be the truth," she poured out.

I sat in the shallow end of the pool, watching Topher play with his friend Ronan during break at swim class. All the while, I couldn't get yesterday's exchange with Alana out of my head. I had no idea why she'd brought up Harper, or why she'd been fishing for details about Ford's past with his first love. I couldn't help but think something must have happened to resurrect Harper's name.

As far as I knew, Harper had married her college sweetheart, and they'd had a child together. It was my understanding that Russ didn't think highly of his son-in-law, which had placed a wedge between him and his daughter.

I'd be lying if I said that I didn't miss Harper. She'd been like another daughter to me. When she was a little girl, she'd always been full of questions. She'd been equally excited to tell me all about whatever new thing she had learned. When she'd become a teen-ager, my daughters had adored her. Ford had obviously thought the world of her.

I wish I knew what happened to her.

Ronan's grandmother, Shannon, copped a squat next to me on the edge of the pool, lifting me out of my endless web of thought.

"Ronan couldn't stop talking about Topher all week," she beamed, as her words melted my heart.

"Topher has been the same way. Though I've been having a hard time getting him to say *Ronan* instead of *Roman*." Shannon and I laughed.

"It's not an easy name for a little guy to say at first. Even Ronan had a hard time saying his own name for a while."

"I really love that name. It suits him," I said as I watched Ronan go down the slide ahead of Topher.

"Those boys are two peas in a pod."

Shannon's kindness made me revisit the possibility of helping her in some way. Perhaps it would be something small at first—like dinner. Maybe she and Ronan could stop by the house one Saturday after swim class.

"Is it just you and Ronan at home? Is his grandfather in the picture?" I asked on a whim.

"No, it's just Ronan and me," Shannon murmured.

My heart ached for little Ronan. There were no positive male influences around him. I immediately regretted my question. "I'm sorry."

"No worries. I never remarried after divorcing my daughter's father many years ago."

Through the sorrow, I reminded myself about the many strong women out there who didn't mind staying single and happy. And like my father had once said, *"Marriage isn't for everyone."*

I resolved to save the dinner invitation for another time.

Twenty-Three

Ford

At two in the afternoon, I finally took a break away from my office and paid the tenth floor a visit. Once I stepped out of the stairwell, I was welcomed by bulletin board-covered walls littered with multi-colored charts and graphs. It was as if the data beast had hurled all over the joint.

Alana's cubical was toward the end of the hall, but I had to pass Knight's office to get there. His door was shut, and his blinds were drawn. I found that odd. So, on the slight chance he was there, I knocked.

"Yeah?" a faint voice called out. I opened the door and found Knight seated at his desk, rubbing his face in frustration.

"Dude, what's going on?" I asked with a tinge of humor. But when Knight didn't change his demeanor, I knew something was wrong. "Seriously, what happened?" I walked in, shutting the door behind me.

"I really fucked up, Pope."

I'd never seen him like this, and Knight had been through some shit growing up. I approached his side of the desk and leaned against the edge of it. "How bad are we talking?"

"On a scale of one to ten? I'd say ninety."

"Holy fuck, Thibodeau," I groaned. "What did you do?"

"That's just it. I don't know," he said with a sharp intake of air. "All the numbers were primed and ready to go ahead of schedule.

Then, your dad called for a pre-meeting this morning for some reason."

"He does that. I warned you he would."

"But whatever, man—I was ready. Or so I thought," Knight trailed off, hanging his head back down.

"What happened?"

"My whole team combed that entire deck for two days. There was not a single problem with the data. But when I presented it to your dad and part of his executive team, a gleaming error stared me right in the face. I caught it and immediately apologized for it."

"Mistakes happen," I brushed off. "It's no big deal."

Knight was being entirely too hard on himself. He had this unrealistic expectation of showing my father nothing but perfection. Even I knew that was an impossible feat. Dad would always find something to pick apart. He'd been in the business way too long to overlook the small stuff.

If there was a needle in a haystack, Mason Pope would find it.

"This wasn't a small error," Knight uttered. "The slide showed that our facility in Germany was under-ordering. That was incorrect. They were actually over-ordering."

"That's what pre-meetings are for—to catch mistakes," I reasoned. "Just correct the draft and move on. It's fine."

His sad posture didn't change. "Eva shared the draft with Ingrid at the German office. Ingrid turned around and shared it with logistics. Now, supply orders are over budget by fifty million and counting in just *one day*."

"What?!" I reflexively shouted. "It's the fucking draft! The final PTF report isn't due for another month!"

"Dude, I know! We kept telling Germany it wouldn't be ready until next month, but they kept hounding us for a forecast. As soon as they saw a draft from Eva, they jumped the gun. I'm *sooooo* fucked," Thibodeau groaned in agony.

I planted my hand on my friend's shoulder. I was dumbfounded by how quickly everything had gone off the rails. Things were royally fucked up beyond comprehension. It started with a simple error on a draft. Now, we had one of our international offices slaughtering our budget for the next three years.

Eva swung open the door without warning. Her face was blood red with tears.

"I'm *so* sorry! I didn't mean to send Ingrid the file!" she sobbed to her boyfriend.

Knight just sat there, wallowing in shame. Meanwhile, I was trying to make out who was really at fault here. Who had dropped the ball? My vote was Germany. No one told them to open all those purchase orders in one fucking day!

"That wasn't the file Ingrid was supposed to get!" Eva wept.

I stood and took my sister in my arms. "It wasn't your fault. They shouldn't have placed those orders." Before I could say another word, the door swung open again.

Fuck.

Me.

"I've been calling you for the past thirty minutes!" my father roared at Knight. There was nothing but sheer murder in my old man's eyes. He looked seconds away from breaking Thibodeau in half over his knee.

"Sir, I know. I'm *sor—*"

"Your stupid mistake just cost this company fifty million dollars. Fifty. Million. Dollars. Now you think about that for just a second. I have—for *many* seconds."

My father was livid. I'd seen Mason Pope mad before, but never *this* mad.

"Mr. Pope…" Knight pleaded in mortification.

"Daddy! It wasn't his fault!" Eva cried, stepping in between Knight and our father. "I sent Ingrid the wrong attachment! She took the draft as gospel!"

I stood there, helplessly watching the heated exchange between my father, my sister, and my best friend. *Ground, please swallow me now.*

"Both of you are to blame!" my dad snarled at my sister. "Perhaps I made the colossal error in allowing you two to move in together. If you can't help but be distracted by one another, then maybe you need to reevaluate your living situation."

Eva lost it and started wailing loudly before storming out of Knight's office. Knight looked like he wanted to go after her, but my father's fiery glare kept him frozen in place. Knight and I stood there, helpless.

But something happened. My father was about to rip Knight up one end and down the other, but instead, he turned on his heel and left quietly. I stared at the closed door for a beat before turning to a talking Knight.

"I don't want Eva taking the blame for this. It was my responsibility as manager to keep things under control. I think I should pack my things and leave—both here and the apartment."

"Fuck that!" I snarled." Don't you dare leave here *or* home. This is *not* your fault. This isn't Eva's fault, either."

"I swear, Ford—that error wasn't there before. I never saw it," Knight said, shaking his head in disbelief.

In that moment, I was convinced that someone had sabotaged Knight's draft.

Liza

I had to reschedule my two o'clock. R&D needed more time to run testing on a prototype featuring groundbreaking LRPI patented technology. I took advantage of the newfound time and caught up on calls and emails from this morning.

Lola usually emailed me a summary of missed calls, which were automatically routed to an electronic folder labeled *Calls to Return*. But since I had time, and the red message light was blinking on my desk phone, I went ahead and listened to my own voicemails.

The first two messages were from the heads of our New York and Orlando offices. They each had questions about the big LRPI leadership summit coming early next year, which I was helping to organize. Scheduled for January in The Swiss Alps, all attendees would have a chance to ski as well as participate in team-building exercises.

My next voice message was from a woman named Michelle Leahy.

"Mrs. Pope—my name is Michelle Leahy. I'm a producer for MTV."

"MTV?" I mouthed with a frown. *What does MTV want with me?*

"I received your direct number from your daughters, Bethany and Brianna. I wanted to reach out to you about featuring them in a reality show that begins filming there in two weeks called, *The Teens of Arcadia's Crest.*"

Oh no.

"I interviewed your daughters at school after spotting them in the cafeteria, and I think they would be absolutely perfect for the show! Being that they'll only be seventeen at the start of filming, we require your full permission in order to feature them."

This was a bad idea all around. Knowing my girls, they wanted to be a part of this train wreck. Michelle Leahy rattled off her phone number, and I quickly jotted it down on a nearby notepad. Ignoring the remaining voice messages, I dialed the number, and Michelle picked up after two rings.

"Hello, this is Liza Pope. You called earlier. I'm Brie and Beth Pope's mom."

"Oh, *yes*! Thanks so much for calling me back!" she said, excited.

I slumped in my chair, dreading hurting this poor woman's feelings. If not me, it would definitely be my husband—which she wouldn't want.

Really?! A sleazy reality show?! I'd be damned if my daughters were exploited on global television and turned into unflattering memes all over social media.

"As I mentioned in my message to you, we are filming a new reality show that spotlights teens in beau monde California."

Beau monde? So, it was a show about spoiled rich kids. Fine, my kids were rich. And lately, they'd been acting spoiled. But in Mason's and my defense, it wasn't a behavior we tolerated. We were constantly driving humility into our children. I believed Beth and Brie would eventually *get it* once they left the confines of Arcadia's Crest and met people who had much less.

Everyone knew these reality shows were scripted, especially if the 'story' wasn't going in the direction the producers wanted it to go. It might seem like an exciting undertaking at first, but this would be something the girls would end up regretting being a part of. They would be putting their entire lives out on display, leaving room for others to judge them. They'd no longer be able to hide under the anonymity that Mason and I worked so hard to keep them under. They wouldn't be able to go to the mall anymore. We'd have to beef up security.

"Miss Leahy," I began, already sounding regretful.

"Michelle—*please*," she insisted.

She'd obviously picked up on my disinclination. Hell, I couldn't say *no* now. I needed to talk this over tonight with Mason and the girls. That way, the twins would see firsthand how our decision didn't come lightly. Mason and I wouldn't allow the twins to be exploited in any way.

"Michelle. I need to sit with my family and discuss this opportunity in detail. Do you have any documentation you could send me?"

"I gave an information packet to the girls," she said eagerly. "I hope you and your husband decide to let us work with your beautiful daughters. They are both so intelligent and full of life. They'll give our show *exactly* what it needs. I interviewed other students at the school, and many of them agree your twins are very good role models. I believe the world will come to know your daughters in the same light once the show airs."

This woman was obviously very good at her job. The network probably sicced her, like a Doberman, on all of the difficult parents.

"Thank you, Michelle. We'll discuss it over the weekend, and I'll give you a call back first thing Monday." *With my NO answer.*

"Excellent. I look forward to hearing from you. If you have any questions, call me anytime. If I don't answer right away, leave a message, and I'll get right back to you."

"Sure thing, Michelle. Thank you."

After the call ended, I laid my head in my palms and released a deep sigh. I wasn't looking forward to the evening. The twins were going freak once they heard what their father and I had to say about their reality show. It wasn't happening. I contemplated having an entire bottle of wine all to myself after it was all done.

In the middle of another deep, calming breath, my husband barged in through our adjoining door. His pissed expression startled me. Missing his suit jacket, his slightly wrinkled dress shirt was exposed, and his blue tie hung loose. His thick silver hair was all over the place, too.

Had he gotten the call from the MTV producer?

If so, I hadn't expected him to be *that* upset about it.

Mason plopped onto my sofa without uttering a word. I abandoned my desk to join him, smoothing down the back of my cream dress before taking a seat.

"What's wrong?"

"Have you been checking your emails or voicemails? Seems like no one's bothering to do that these days," he clawed.

He was certainly being a dick today.

"I was in the process of doing that before you came barging in. I've had back-to-back meetings all morning and through lunch. My two o'clock rescheduled, so I had time to play *catch up*."

Mason closed his eyes and breathed before speaking. "Your

daughter and her boyfriend just cost this company fifty million dollars. Germany alone blew next year's budget in less than a day."

"What?!" I croaked. "How?!" *Fifty million?!* No, not Knight... and definitely not Eva. They were two of the most thorough people I knew.

"I had Knight's pre-meeting this morning—"

"Wait... I didn't know about this," I interrupted. Mason had agreed we'd have the pre-meeting next week. Why had he bumped it up?

"I heard rumblings concerning things not going all that well with Knight's data-mining practices. I had to see things for myself."

Really, Mason? He, of all people, despised gossip. He should have told me first before he had the bright idea to entrap Knight like that.

"Who did you hear this from?" I said, tilting my head in skepticism.

"It doesn't matter. You know we pride ourselves on our exceptional team satisfaction scores. If I hear something negative, I'm going to look into it."

"And you couldn't warn me ahead of time?" I scowled.

If we'd discussed work after hours at length instead of in passing, Mason would have known I'd been walking through Knight's draft with Knight *and* Eva. But years ago, Mason had put a stop to discussing work at home. He wanted to create the appropriate work/life balance, leaving LRPI business at Pope Tower once we entered Arcadia's Crest. Blowing a fifty-million-dollar budget was why his idea was dumb. We needed to talk about work at home, too.

"I tried. You've been in meetings all morning," Mason growled in frustration.

"Yes, and normally you are too, but you managed to schedule an impromptu pre-meet without my knowledge. *Anyway*," I sighed with an eye roll, "what happened?"

"The current supply forecast for Germany showed they were

severely under ordering and wouldn't reach their target by year end."

"That's ridiculous," I scoffed. "If anything, the Germans have been spending way too much as of late. They would've had to pull back on spending in the last quarter."

"Exactly. But that mistake displayed on the big screen during Knight's presentation as clear as day. That wasn't the worst part of it. *Your* daughter, Eva..."

So, she was just MY daughter now.

Good grief.

"...sent that same draft over to Ingrid Fischer, who in turn shared it with all of logistics."

"Why would Eva send them that draft? I know she regularly sends Ingrid a weekly report on Thursdays. That's what logistics is supposed to go by."

"Well, once they saw the forecasted spend in Knight's draft, they were scared shitless. They thought they'd lose their budget next year if they didn't meet the target for this year. So, like idiots, they issued fifty million worth of purchase orders to the supplier group. Many of them knew it was an unusual event, but like crooks, they hurried and started fulfillment right away so Germany couldn't rescind. FUCK!"

Mason kicked the coffee table, and it fell on its side, cascading the magazines all over the floor. My nerves were all over the place as I watched my husband boil over. After taking in the mess he made, he took some deep breaths, which didn't help.

"I told Knight and Eva if living together is causing them to be distracted at work, then perhaps their living situation needs to be reevaluated."

"Mason! Don't be ridiculous. They've been together since Eva was a junior in high school. Her work has never suffered since they've been together. The same with Knight. His work has been top-notch. I have never seen him make this sort of mistake." I argued.

"Neither have I, but his first mistake cost this company fifty million fucking dollars. I don't think we can afford any more of Knight's *rare* mistakes," Mason seethed.

"It was a *draft*. A draft Germany shouldn't have received, much less processed a large PO from it," I reasoned. "When is Germany going to be held accountable?"

"Oh—don't you worry Liza, I've got HR on the case right this fucking second," he said with a flustered chuckle that didn't match the look of sheer rage on his handsome face. "Ten people are about to lose their asses today."

Hell hath no fury like a Mason Pope scorned.

"Fair enough," I acquiesced. "But I'm still not understanding why Knight and Eva are receiving the brunt of the blame. I've actually been working with them on their draft." Mason's brows raised at the news. "This *so-called* fifty-million-dollar deficit in German purchase orders? I never saw that in the drafts Knight and Eva showed me."

Mason dug his elbows into his thighs and dropped his face into his palms. His hands lifted up and ran through his hair. Whenever he's upset or frustrated, his kempt hair was usually the first casualty.

"It was such a stupid error. Knight would've caught it as an intern," Mason grumbled.

"I *know*," I echoed. On that note, I retrieved my laptop from my desk and brought it to Mason. I showed him a two-week old email from Knight.

From: Knight Thibodeau
Subject: Forecast Draft for Propel the Future

To: Eliza C. Cooper-Pope
Dear Liza,
Here is the draft we discussed. I welcome any additional feedback you may have.

As I said before, I appreciate your help in making this deck perfect before I present the final product to you, Mr. Pope, and your executive team. Your guidance means more to me than you know.

Best Regards / Mit Freundlichen Grüßen / Saludos / Cordialement / Yoroshiku Onegaishimasu

Knight Thibodeau
Manager, Data Analytics – Global Team #3
Lyndon Reginald Pope Industries
Attachments: PTFDraft_v8.5

I opened the file and showed that to Mason, too.

"Did you sign off on his most recent update?" Mason frowned.

"I hadn't signed off on anything. I thought we had more time before his pre-meet," I hissed back. "I also allowed for additional time in case he caught any errors on his own and wanted to submit revisions. However, I did review his draft. See... There's nothing here showing a deficit. This says everything was on par for this year," I said, stabbing the evidence on the screen with my index finger.

His head jutted back ever so slightly. "That's the slide in question. I'm not seeing the same deficit in this version."

"Exactly."

"But he sent you that two weeks ago. Do you have anything recent?"

"That's the latest I have. As I've said, everything he and Eva had shown me looked fine," I reiterated. "They've only added more slides to the deck from draft to draft, not changing any existing output."

"Who dropped the ball, then? How did that fucking error get there?" Mason fumed.

"I don't know. But whatever you do, don't be so quick to pin this on Eva or Knight."

My husband shouldn't have condemned anyone without having all the facts. I'd had my eye on the kids, and from what I'd seen, they'd done exceptional work until now. There had to be a clear explanation as to why this costly gaff had happened.

"As a leader, Knight is accountable for the actions of his team," Mason declared in a stern voice.

I asked a question, fearful of his answer. "Will you fire him, too?"

Fifteen seconds of silence was a lifetime. It was long enough for me to come up with a quick plan to soften the blow. I didn't want Knight to be fired. The young man had been through a lot. He'd dedicated three years of his life to this company. He couldn't lose everything.

"Let me mitigate some of the damage. I'll call Mick in, and we'll get the suppliers on the phone. I'm pretty sure we can freeze some of these orders and rescind the purchase orders," I proposed.

"What about those who already began fulfillment?" challenged Mason.

"We'll ask them to cancel," I countered. "Those suppliers who give us a hard time, I'll negotiate an exclusive deal, guaranteeing our business for the next five years. They'll come out on top if they lock into an agreement for a future commitment versus remaining on our bad side permanently by not refunding us today."

My husband's hooded gaze meant to intimidate was thwarted by the twitch in his lips.

I've won him over.

"We can fix this," I affirmed. I placed my hands on his cheeks, and he leaned into my touch. He planted his hands over mine, holding them steady to his skin.

"I must pull Knight and his team off the project and bring in a different analytics group for damage control."

"I understand," I said soberly. This wasn't going to make Knight or Eva feel good, but it was much better than the alternative. "I don't believe any of the other teams will bring the same freshness as Knight's. I guess the only positive thing from all this is that Knight won't have to work such late hours anymore. Alana will be able to spend more time at home with Ford."

Mason flinched as if I'd just said the magic word.

"What?" I asked, squinting.

"I just had a thought. I'm going to make Ford the project director of Propel the Future."

He'd just ignored everything I said. The key to Alana spending more time with her boyfriend was him being home.

"Ford has way too many things on his plate already. He's overseeing four major cosmetic acquisitions right now," I argued.

"Natalie can handle that. PTF is far more important right now," Mason countered.

"Do you hear yourself? You're talking about bringing our son in as head of the biggest initiative in the history of our company. The same project you removed his best friend, his sister, and his girlfriend from. Don't you think that's a little backhanded?" I said, not skimping out on the irony.

I mean, seriously, Pope. Did he really want to pit our children and their significant others against each other?

"It isn't backhanded. Knight was only responsible for forecasting. Ford would be responsible for *everything*. I'll even let Ford appoint anyone he wants on his team."

"Even Knight?" I asked, hopeful.

"No."

"You said *anyone*," I reminded.

"He can receive input from Knight, but I don't want him as a dedicated resource on Ford's team. It would send the wrong message."

I conceded with a sigh. "What about Alana? Can *she* be on Ford's team?"

"Sure."

"Eva?"

"Liza—cut it out. You're notorious for that."

"*Notorious* for what?" I said, playing up my naiveté.

"Playing ignorant when you're the smartest person in the room," he smirked. "As director of the initiative, Ford will be appointed executive."

"It's a promotion," I guessed.

Mason nodded. "We will no longer have managers or lower handling executive-level responsibilities. As the executive for this project, Ford will have the final say before anything gets to us. He will be responsible for presenting all content to the rest of the executive staff."

My lips tightened in a line. "Fair enough. But will he want the job, especially with all the baggage that comes along with it? Right now, he's guaranteed Natalie's VP position. He's already an executive in training."

"Yes, but this puts him in the role of executive today. PTF will gain traction in the next year or so. At that time, Ford will be invited to do public speaking engagements on the topic of leadership. The media will want a piece of him. Ford will be the new face of the company if he takes the director job. He won't have the same visibility as VP of cosmetics. Nobody gives a shit about that role."

"Mason, that's not true. Natalie's role is extremely vital to our company," I opposed.

"Those on the inside know that, but the rest of the world doesn't. PTF is not only going to revolutionize the way we do business, but it'll change the landscape for everyone we do business with. This project affects the Apples...the Microsofts...the Amazons. It affects government on a global scale. That is what the world wants to talk about. They don't care about the next decaying cosmetic company that LRPI acquires and flips around to turn it into a luxury brand. We've been doing that for decades."

This was heavy—*really* heavy. I wanted to scream, *But he's our baby! He's only twenty-two!* I knew what Mason's response to that would be... *'I brought this company out of the red at the ripe age of twenty-two without a college degree'*...yada-yada-yada.

My hands were tied. The decision lay completely with Ford. I was afraid for him, and Mason saw my reservation right away.

He smoothed the back of his hand across my cheek. "Baby, this will be the perfect opportunity for us and for Ford to see if he can handle taking over after we're long gone."

Twenty-Four

Ford

I'd reached out to Derrick in IT, letting him know I'd soon be in touch regarding a confidential request. One thing about investigating I'd learned over the years from hanging around the likes of Mr. Benton and Greg Donner: Never tell anyone that there is an investigation.

I adored my girlfriend—trusted her, even. But I couldn't reveal what was going on behind the scenes until *I* figured out what the hell was going on. This whole situation with Knight and Eva was so fucked up, and I had to get to the bottom of it.

In the middle of answering an email, I saw Alana standing through the glass door of my office with concern evident on her gorgeous face. I waved her in, and she shut the door upon entering.

"What happened? I heard Knight's pre-read went terribly," she informed, taking the seat facing my desk. "Then, I saw Eva running out of Knight's office, crying. It was after your dad went in there."

"It didn't go well," I said somberly.

"What did your dad say?"

I broke down the disastrous pre-meeting, the fifty-million-dollar error, and the draft sent to Germany. Alana was in total shock.

"They actually placed orders based on a draft?!"

"Yep," I said, popping the P.

"Who does that?!"

"They do, apparently. Needless to say, my dad has been on a rampage. I heard HR's been *very* busy this afternoon," I stated with sardonic humor, feeling anything *but* humorous.

"Is your dad talking about letting go of the entire team that worked on Knight's deck?"

The dread in her eyes was palpable. She ought to know I'd never let my dad fire her. Then, I realized she was probably just asking the question for the concern of the others. I tried putting her at ease.

"I don't see him doing that. Even if he wanted to, Mom wouldn't let him. He's probably talking to her now."

"This is just awful. I feel horrible for Knight," Alana groaned.

"Me too. He doesn't deserve this. My sister doesn't deserve this."

Her eyes bucked. "Eva? What happened with her?"

"The email that went to Germany with the bad PTF draft came from her."

Alana closed her eyes in agony.

"Yeah," I said, validating her guttural response. "It was just a draft, and the shit has definitely hit the fan."

"That's why she left crying," Alana deduced.

"That… and my father pretty much told them to stop living together."

She gasped. "Are you serious?" I nodded.

My girl clutched her stomach, looking as if she was going to be sick. The whole thing was impacting her, too. Not only was Alana a major contributor to Knight's team, but she and my sister had become quite close during their time at work.

"Come here." She slowly approached, and I met her halfway, pulling her to my chest when we met. "It's going to be alright. Knight and Eva… they'll be fine." I kissed her on top of her soft head of raven hair, and she held onto me tight.

My desk phone let out a blaring ring, startling us. I darted to my desk to check the screen and instantly regretted it.

"Fuck—it's my dad."

Alana's eyes widened as I picked up. "Hello?"

"Son, I need to see you in my office."

"Right now?"

"Yes, now. Clear your calendar for the next hour," he ordered.

"Okay. I'll be there shortly." When he hung up, I stood there like a statue.

"What happened?" Alana anxiously grilled.

"He wants me in his office."

"Did he sound upset?"

"I couldn't tell. My father is a difficult person to read."

"Go. We'll talk later," she said before hugging me once more.

As I sat on the other side of my father's seat of power, a million things were running through my mind. It was like a tidal wave hit me. I was left utterly speechless after my father's bombardment of sentences. Sentences I had yet to unravel and dissect.

This is all too sudden.

My father picked up where he'd left off.

"It will take two weeks for your new office on the twenty-ninth floor to be complete. In the meantime, we'll set you up in a temporary office. We'll hire your assistant, and you can start assembling your team. If you need to hire externally, coordinate that with HR."

"Can I think about this?" I finally managed to drag out.

My father glowered at me as if I'd grown an arm in the center of my forehead.

"Son, I've just quadrupled your salary."

"*I*... I know," I stuttered.

"This position will cement your name as one of the world's most innovative leaders," he said rigidly.

"Yeah, I underst—"

"When PTF reaches maturity, there won't be any doubt in the peoples' mind about your legitimacy. You won't be just some kid who got to where he is because of who his parents are. You'll have credibility, all on your own accord. A legacy no one can ever take away from you."

"*Tha*—that's exactly what I want..." I stammered.

"Then what is there to *think* about?" my father volleyed.

"If I take this job, it's going to make some people upset," I said point-blank.

My father sighed and rubbed his temples. "That's the cost of being the boss, Ford."

"Let me think about it over the weekend. I need to have some conversations with the people this decision will impact."

"Ford, don't be ridiculous," he said, exasperated.

"I'm serious, Dad. I need to do this my way. I'll give you my answer first thing Monday morning. Will that work?"

"Fine," he pushed out through gritted teeth.

"Thank you." I smiled with gratitude, and my father rose with me as I walked to the door.

"You sure you and Alana don't want to come by the house Sunday for dinner? You can give me your answer then," he smirked.

I chuckled as I brought him in for a hug. He stilled for a beat before reciprocating. "Monday morning, I promise," I vowed before smacking a playful kiss on his stubbly cheek. I looked in time to see his baffled frown. I couldn't remember the last time I'd kissed my dad, and neither could he. He fought a grin as I stepped away.

"Have a good weekend, son."

"You too, Dad. Tell Mom I'll stop by her office before I leave tonight."

"I will."

Five minutes after returning to my office, Alana was right there, eager for information.

"So?" she prompted.

"*So?*" I teased. She twirled her right hand in a circle, signaling me to *get on with it.* "I'm going to stick around the office for about an hour longer. I need to meet with a few people."

"*Meet?* About what?"

"Since you're here, I'll start with you."

"Really?" she says with wide eyes. "What's going on?"

"My dad wants me to be the project director of Propel the Future."

"That's amazing!" she gushed.

"I didn't take the job. *Yet.*"

She looked shocked. "What do you mean? This is the opportunity of a lifetime. You'll be an executive, right?" I nodded. "A raise, too? For what—twice your current salary?"

"Four times."

"Fuck me," she wheezed, nearly falling out of her chair.

"Oh, I will," I murmured, flashing my best bedroom eyes. She scolded me, and I laughed. "Seriously, I want to make sure the people I care most about are good with me taking this job."

"I'm good with it. Who else matters?" she asked with narrowed eyes.

"Well, there's my sister and Knight."

"The wounds are fresh. But if they truly care for you, they'll understand. This is for the betterment of your career. It's nothing personal," Alana said plainly.

"I get that, but there are other things in play here. For one, I get to assemble my own team. I can choose anyone I'd like. That is, except for Knight and Eva."

"Oh," she murmured soberly, understanding the gravity of the situation.

"So, I need to speak with them first. I'll also be asking certain individuals in the building if they are willing to drop what they are doing and work for me for the next… four years or so."

Alana sat as straight as a rail and bore into me with doe eyes.

Fuck, this is going to be difficult.

"One more conundrum," I prefaced with regret. "I can't pick you."

Her brows reached her hairline. "What do you mean? Is it because I was on Knight's team? My data set is Asia. I had nothing to do with Germany," she adamantly defended.

"I know," I exhaled, bowing my head and raking my hair in frustration. "But bringing you on my team sends the wrong message to Knight and his team. The last thing I want to do is kick them while they're down. *Now*, do you see why this is so difficult for me?"

My harangue left me flustered, while Alana just sat there looking impassive. She obviously didn't understand my plight. I just about threw my hands up in the air in defeat.

"Fuck it, maybe I shouldn't take the job. This is an utter mess," I muttered.

Alana winced. "Ford, don't be stupid. Take the job. It's fine… honestly. I'm okay with not being on your team."

"Are you sure?" I searched her face for honesty and found it.

"Yes. This director position is a really big deal. You *need* this. It's going to change your life. It's going to change *our* lives. Talk to Knight and Eva. We'll discuss everything when we get home." Alana gazed at me lovingly and caressed my forearm.

She was right—this move would push me further along than I'd originally planned at this stage. I'd be in the position to learn the business inside and out in a shorter amount of time.

Before she left my office, I took her into my arms.

"You have to work late tonight?" I murmured. She answered with a nod, and I gave her lips a light peck. "Don't forget, we're going out for Thai. Don't work too late."

"I won't," she smiled sweetly before kissing me back.

I'd briefly stopped by Ford's office before meeting Gloria in front of the building. We were on our way to Eva's apartment. Ford had told me that his sister had been inconsolable ever since the shouting match with their father. Ford had tried getting ahold of Eva to ask for her take on his new job, but he'd been unsuccessful in reaching her.

Earlier, I had managed to salvage thirty million dollars after a dozen phone calls in the course of three hours. Seventeen million more might be rescued by Monday morning. I hoped this good news would soften the blow for my daughter.

"How was your day, Liza?" Gloria called as she shifted the car into drive.

"You don't want to know," I groaned.

"One of those days, huh?" she mused with her thick Boston accent.

"I've gotta talk Eva off the ledge. She and her father had a little spat at work today. I cleaned up most of the mess that caused their riff."

Gloria let out a boisterous laugh. "A mother's work is never done."

"Nope." Her eyes met my smirk in the rearview mirror.

When we reached Eva and Knight's apartment, I rang the buzzer four times. Thankfully, my daughter had provided me with an emergency key fob, so I used that to get through the secured entrance. I moved past the security desk and took the elevator up to the fifth floor.

When I arrived inside the apartment, I saw my eldest daughter vegging out on the sofa. She turned away from the television and looked at me with sad eyes as she hugged a quart of ice cream. It wasn't even six, and she was already in flannel pajamas and wrapped in a fleece throw blanket.

"Eva, sweetheart—I rang the doorbell a dozen times." I placed my Isla Cole shoulder bag on the table in the foyer.

"I'm sorry," she murmured dejectedly.

I took a seat next to her and pulled her into my side. She laid her head on my shoulder, and I smoothed her soft hair.

"What flavor is that?" I asked, pointing to the carton in her hand.

"Salted caramel."

"One of my favorites," I remarked.

"I know," Eva said before handing me the carton and spoon.

What the hay…

I unhooked my arm from under her and dug right in. "This is *amazing*," I groaned with a mouthful of cold, creamy goodness. There was something about the marriage between sweet and salty. It was heavenly.

"I assume Dad has filled you in. Are you here to fire me?" she said pitifully.

"Don't be ridiculous," I scoffed.

"My mistake just cost the company fifty million dollars. And what about Knight? Is he going to be fired or demoted?" Eva huffed.

"Sweetheart—no one's getting fired or demoted. At least not in our building."

Blue eyes that mirrored mine widened. "That means people in Germany are getting the axe?"

I bowed regretfully. "They made a really bad call. We had to let Ingrid go as well as ten others."

"Poor Ingrid. This whole thing sucks," she groaned.

"I know, honey." I placed the ice cream on the coffee table and pulled her back into my side. Memories of my little girl began to flood. I rubbed her side as I'd done many times when my sweet girl had needed her mommy to comfort her.

"I didn't mean to send her that file," she spoke against my blouse. "I thought I sent the weekly forecast. The files got mixed up somehow. I don't know how that could've happened."

"Well, the good news is that I got back thirty million with some negotiation. We're still working on the last twenty. Everything's going to be fine," I assured her.

"Mom—thank you," Eva sighed, squeezing me.

"It's going to be okay. We all make mistakes."

Eva lifted her head and sat up to look me in the eye. "But this is a mistake I don't understand. Not only do I not know how I sent the wrong file, but the PTF draft copies I had before yesterday never indicated under-spending in Germany."

"I showed your father what Knight sent me two weeks ago, and it wasn't what they saw in the pre-meeting."

"This is *so weird*!" Eva groaned in frustration.

"Thankfully, the stress of PTF is over for you. But there's something I have to tell you."

She was terrified. "Oh no—am I on probation? Is Knight?"

"No, sweetheart. Calm down. You and Knight are fine. What I was going to say is your brother tried getting in touch with you earlier. Your father wants to appoint him as director of PTF. Ford will be promoted to executive and will have his own team."

"Wow... I mean, that's great—for Ford," she said with a hesitant look.

"Ford hasn't accepted the offer yet. He wants to be sure you and Knight are fine with him taking it."

My daughter's eyes awaken. "Whoa."

I smiled and nodded lovingly. "He wants to talk to you. He was on his way to meet with Knight before I headed here. He'd already spoken to Alana."

Eva flinched. "Is Alana going to be on his team?"

"No. If he can't have you or Knight, he doesn't think it's fair to bring on Alana or anyone else from Knight's team."

"That's heavy," she mused.

Words couldn't describe how proud I was of Ford. He was always thinking of others ahead of himself. He was going to make an excellent CEO someday.

"I'll call him in the morning," Eva said. "But if you speak to him first, tell him I want him to take the job. He'd be stupid not to."

"That's really sweet of you, honey," I said, kissing her on the cheek.

"I want to run something by you," Eva prefaced.

"Hit me."

"Since Dad seems to think Knight and I are *distracting* one another, I think I should be moved out of analytics."

I gaped at her. "Eva, you *love* working with numbers. You belong there."

"Knight is a good manager, and he has the opportunity to grow into an executive role in no time flat, just like Ford. I still have a long way to go, being that I'm still in school. I'd like to take this time to learn other areas of the company."

My heart melted from hearing how much she cared for Knight and his career. At the same time, she realized she had an opportunity to explore her own growth.

"How about ICF? Are you interested in interning as a clerk?" I proposed.

"Sure, I love Isla Cole. It would be great to see what it is they do there."

"Keep in mind that this assignment will take you outside of Pope Tower. You'll be working fifteen minutes away," I warned.

"I'm good with that."

"Alright. I'll shoot HR an email on my way home and get the ball rolling."

"Thank you, Mom," she said with a tight hug, and I squeezed her back just as hard.

"Are you and Knight coming over for Sunday dinner?"

She smirked. "I think we need a couple of weekends away from Dad to lick our wounds."

"Eva—you know everything will be fine with your father. I want you two over for dinner," I insisted.

"We'll be there. In two weeks," she said stubbornly.

After dinner, Mason and I cuddled on the sofa next to the lit fireplace. I finally had a chance to fill him in on my call with the MTV producer. I'd told the girls not to bring any of it up until after I brought their father up to speed.

The twins were set to arrive shortly, and I wasn't feeling all that hot about the potential outcome of our family meeting. As expected, Mason wasn't sold on the reality show idea. Neither was I.

"I wonder why the producer called you instead of me," Mason smirked.

"They always call the mother for these things. They think we're easier to manipulate."

"I would've cursed her out immediately," he said bitterly.

I laughed. "You wouldn't have cursed at the nice lady. Despite your rough exterior, you're still a complete gentleman," I sassed before kissing his cheek.

Just then, Brie and Beth made their way into the main room with Topher in tow. All three were in pajamas. Beth got comfortable next to her father, and Brie sat beside me with Topher in her lap.

I frowned at the twins. "What's Topher doing here? He's supposed to be in bed."

"No bed!" the youngest Mr. Pope barked.

"He's here as our buffer," Beth grinned.

"It'll be impossible for you to say no to us with this adorable face staring back at you," Brie said, pinching her baby brother's cheeks.

"Try me," Mason challenged, not amused in the slightest.

"Daddy," Beth whined beside him.

"Do you want to hear what I have to say?" Mason challenged. I began bracing for an explosion.

"Only if it's a *yes*," Brie smirked.

I shut my eyes in pain. I knew without a doubt that the twins were about to be inconsolable. We were going to break their hearts.

"Being on this reality show will thrust you into the public eye. It won't end well—I guarantee it," Mason said in stern warning.

You tell 'em, Mason.

"Daddy, you are *so* overprotective," Beth whined.

"Yeah—I mean, shouldn't you allow your children to take

calculated risks? Isn't that how we grow and become mature young adults?" Brie tag teamed.

"This is a once-in-a-lifetime opportunity. We'll have a chance to promote some of the wonderful things that LRPI is doing, such as their contribution toward a better environment," Beth alley-ooped.

Mason and I were floored by the round of bullshit they were serving us.

"We can even have the camera crew follow us to one of LRPI's charity events," Brie tacked on.

"What are you two yahoos even talking about?" I finally spoke up. "You have said on numerous occasions you wanted nothing to do with LRPI."

"Mom, if you want us at LRPI, we'll intern there. It would be great for the show," Beth said with sincere eyes.

"No thanks," Mason rejected. "We don't want you or your television cameras at Pope Tower."

"*Our* television cameras?" Brie gasped with excitement.

"Does that mean we're doing the show?" Beth said, equally as ecstatic.

"Girls..." I moaned in exhaustion. I was ready to get this nuclear explosion over with.

"Here's what's going to happen..." Mason started.

Things were about to pop off. I pictured Topher rocking on the sofa with his hands over his ears as the rest of us engaged in a shouting match for the ages.

"...I'll agree to it..."

Yep, I knew—

Wait a second. Did I just hear...?

"Oh, my God!" Brie cried in glee. She shifted her brother from her lap and met her sister on the floor for a victory dance and shout.

"Stop yelling!" Topher hollered with his little mitts placed over his ears.

"Mason!" I roared.

What the hell is he doing?!

We hadn't discussed this. He was completely going off script, and I didn't like it one bit.

"Wait a second!" Mason interrupted the jubilant girls. They stopped mid-leap, still hugging one another. "There needs to be a clause in the final contract that says your mother and I can pull you out anytime we want. If the show is causing you or this family more harm than good, it's over. Do I make myself clear?"

"Yes!" Beth cheered.

"You two will be the only ones in this house featured on camera. Do you hear me? Not me, not your mother, not Topher," Mason spelled out.

"I want to be on the camera!" Topher whined.

I'd had more than enough. I finally spoke my piece to Mason. "I think this is a horrible idea. I don't want them to do it."

"Mom, *please*!" Brie begged, dropping down to her knees and hugging my legs. I pat her head.

"Honey, this is going to blow up in your pretty little faces. You mark my words," I cooed.

"It will be fine. You'll see," Beth assured. I shook my head at the two of them.

"No clause, no show," Mason reiterated. Beth sat next to her father again and gave him a hug. He wasn't the slightest bit amused.

I could tell this was a difficult decision for him to make, so why did he make it? I thought we'd both agreed they wouldn't do the show. I was so confused.

"We'll both make you proud. You'll see," Beth said to her father. Mason was not convinced.

I foresaw me pulling the twins out of a dumpster fire if Mason didn't beat me to it.

Ford

Early that evening at the penthouse, I sat in my study mulling over the whirlwind that had taken place at work. From my dad yelling at Knight and my sister, to him calling me into his office and offering me a killer promotion…

Although Knight urged me to take the job, I wasn't feeling one hundred percent sold on it. I wanted to know my father's angle. Maybe he wanted to see if I could handle taking over the company at a moment's notice. Still, it was shitty timing to promote me as PTF director right after he'd banned Knight and Eva from the project.

I was dead set on getting to the root of the fifty-million-dollar mistake. I'd be meeting IT in the coming weeks to troubleshoot some potential scenarios. What had happened to Eva's weekly report, and how had Germany gotten their hands on an erroneous draft?

In the meantime, Knight had sent me everything he'd done for the PTF initiative so far. I needed to know what I was getting into before accepting my father's offer.

In the middle of parsing through slides on my laptop, my cell phone buzzed. It was a local number I'd never seen before.

"Pope," I answered.

"Ford—it's Harper."

My heart stopped beating. Her voice sounded timid, which wasn't typical of her. Many of the things that had come from her mouth during her surprise visit at Pope Tower weren't typical of her either.

"Did I catch you at a bad time?" she asked.

"No, not at all."

"So."

"*So,*" I echoed. I realized my once-stilled heart was racing. I slowed my breathing in an attempt to calm my nerves.

"My mom was granted temporary custody of my son two months ago," Harper revealed.

"He's not in foster care?"

"No—thank God. After DSS completes their investigation and comes up empty, I can move in with them until I get back on my feet."

"Where are you staying now?" I asked.

"With my friend, Stacey. She used to work at the Los Derivas Marriott with me."

"I remember her. She was friendly."

"Stacey has been awesome. I'll be glad when I can pay her back for all she's done for me."

"Are you just waiting for the investigation to end? Do you need anything else?" I offered.

"As I mentioned before, Aiden's parents are involved. They've never even met my son, yet they are trying to take him away from me."

It doesn't cease to amaze me how Harper managed to get herself into this mess. Aiden Cramer was the root of all of her problems.

"Have you sought the counsel of a decent attorney?" I asked.

"That was why I came to see you," she admitted, finally.

"I'll put you in touch with some good lawyers."

"I'd appreciate that. But I'd like you to keep that in your back pocket just in case."

My eyes narrowed in confusion. "What are you doing in the meantime?"

"There's this non-profit child advocacy group Stacey put me in touch with a few days ago. I want to see if they can help me."

"Harper, I think we can do better than that," I scoffed. "This is your kid we're talking about. Sometimes, it's the one with the biggest checkbook that wins the game—as slimy as that sounds. Doesn't Aiden's family own a chain of car dealerships?"

"Yes… But I'd like to exhaust my options before bringing you into all of this."

I was confused. Why wouldn't she want me to help if I have the ability to do so?

"Harper, really—I don't mind helping."

"But I *do* mind. This whole thing may turn out to be more than you bargained for," she said cryptically.

What had she meant by that? Was she afraid my father might find out? Or *her* father?

"I'm calling because I know exactly how you are. You're probably working behind the scenes and figuring out how to help me. You can stop now," she scolded with humor in her voice.

She knew me so well.

"Fine," I grinned through clenched teeth. "But I do want to help."

Harper let out a deep sigh. "I know your parents are so proud of you. I don't want to mess that up."

I stared mindlessly at the wall in front of me. "Making sure you're okay is important. You need to be in an environment to flourish after suffering under your ex."

"Yeah," Harper murmured soberly. "I will be. I'm trying to stay positive."

I couldn't for the life of me understand why she'd been with that druggy thieving creep in the first place. The signs had been there the whole time, squarely pointing in the direction of him not being a good dude. Why couldn't she have waited the two and a half years for me instead of hopping on the first train to Nowheresville?

Harper had lost her way at some point. It had seemingly happened overnight. She must've bumped her head when I'd returned to Stanford the fall of my sophomore semester. She hadn't been the same level-headed outspoken girl I'd fallen in love with since then. She'd become this timid person who watched her entire world fall apart and did nothing to save it. The Harper I knew would've spotted an addict from a mile away.

Russ had taught his daughter how to protect herself as a young child. Harper had been brought up learning how to keep away from trouble. But the second she'd left her father's care, she had erased all of those valuable lessons from her memory.

Although she was older than me, it seemed I'd matured over the years while she had regressed. Harper had been the realist out of the two of us. She'd been the overly cautious one. She'd known that if our parents ever caught us together, they'd interfere. Once she left Arcadia's Crest, she stopped being careful.

"Call me the second you need anything. Promise," I tell her.

"Ford…" she hesitated.

"Promise me you'll call. I'm here," I pleaded.

"I promise," she responded under her breath. I had a feeling she was holding back, refusing to share something. "We'll talk later."

"Later, Harper."

Just as I hung up, the door to my study crept open. Alana surfaced, and her expression told me she wasn't happy. She'd just heard me say Harper's name. Alana had never entered a room without knocking first.

"Hey—"

"I don't appreciate you helping her," she griped, cutting me off. Her frame was tense.

"I'm not helping her," I defended. "In fact, she just called to tell me *not* to help her."

"Don't you get tangled up in her drama. You have *way* more to lose than she does," Alana said in severe warning. I winced at her, taken aback by what she was implying.

Something told me it would be *her* I'd lose if I didn't get my head on straight.

Twenty-Five

Liza

"You still upset with me, baby?" Mason purred, feathering kisses on my temple.

Though we were in bed together, I was pissed. I couldn't believe he'd actually permitted our twin daughters to star in a reality television show.

A reality show!

"I'm just... stunned," I uttered aloud.

"I believe the conditions I set were more than fair."

I sighed, exasperated. "Why are we letting them do it in the first place?"

"Because it's better they do it now while we can still protect them. If they sign the contract after age eighteen, it will take us longer to finagle them out of it."

Mason had made a fair point. Still, I was mad.

"It sucks that I had to be the bad guy tonight instead of you," I said with pursed lips. He leaned in and kissed them.

"The twins happened to be in luck today. Their big sister almost cost us fifty million big ones, while their big brother drags his ass in accepting a career-defining position," Mason grumbled. "I was feeling rather generous this evening. Besides, I'd rather have two children hate me instead of four."

"Our kids don't *hate* you. Don't be ridiculous."

"Are Eva and Knight coming by Sunday for dinner?" he lobbed.

"Mas—"

He cut me off. "That would be a *no*." I rolled my eyes, and he narrowed his at me. "What about Ford and Alana?"

"Ford needs time to consider the job," I reminded him.

"That shouldn't stop him from having dinner with his family," Mason said, displeased.

"He knows how you are," I smirked.

He fluttered his lashes, playing innocent. "How am I?"

"You're pushy."

"That's ridiculous," he scoffed.

"Seriously, Mason? You haven't been pushing our son to marry his girlfriend?"

"Nonsense. I only suggested it," he claimed with a sheepish grin. "Alana is a fantastic young lady. The same way you made me a better man—she has the ability to do the same for Ford."

My husband had the equivalent of selective eyesight. If he actually saw what was right in front of him, he'd realize Ford and Alana looked *nothing* like us. Mason was more concerned with his son fitting into his idea of a picture-perfect life. His point of view: *Just follow this roadmap I've set because I know what's best for you better than you do.*

But there was something I knew better than Mason. I knew exactly how a Pope Man loved. He loved with his *whole* heart.

I recalled the first and the last time I'd seen the *look of love* in my Ford's eyes, and it was all because of one person. And it wasn't the one he was with now.

If I were granted a single wish, it would be for my son to get that look back.

Ford

Monday morning, I hadn't stepped a single toe outside of my dad's office before a global communication had gone out.

I could almost hear him saying: *"Sherry, the second you see Ford's toe leave my office, hit the send button."* Knowing him, he'd had that email queued up and ready to go since last Friday, when he'd first offered me the job.

From: Mason & Eliza Pope
Subject: Personnel Announcement
To: All LRPI Employees

The office of the CEO is very pleased to announce that Bradford "Ford" Pope is the newly appointed Director of Propel the Future.

Propel the Future, also known as PTF, is a groundbreaking LRPI initiative that promises to impact the global marketplace in a major way within the next five years. With the entire industry relying on the wave of PTF, the LRPI leadership deemed it necessary to create a team that is fully committed to the program's success.

At the head of PTF will be Ford Pope. Ford is currently transitioning from his previous role as Executive Manager of Cosmetics. As a major contributor of the team for the past three years, Ford has been instrumental in acquiring three companies that are now thriving under the LRPI portfolio.

Ford graduated summa cum laude from Stanford University with a degree in Economics. He also has renowned published works in the Stanford Graduate School Business Journal. His first composition led to a spot in the prestigious active learning program for honors business students, allowing him an opportunity to intern for a semester at Zinfinite's corporate headquarters.

Please join us in congratulating our son, Ford, on his newest endeavor.

Best regards,
Mason C. Pope and Eliza C. Cooper-Pope
Co-CEOs, LRPI

Even though it had been two days since the announcement had gone out, I found myself re-reading it from time to time. It was so surreal.

I'd already begun assembling my all-star team. I was able to land an HR expert, a numbers guru, a marketing mastermind, a master strategist, and an essential jack-of-all-trades badass.

My brand-new team already rivaled any other group at Pope Tower. It would have been even better if I'd been able to score Knight and my sister. Then, Alana could slide in for the win. Perhaps after the smoke cleared, Dad would change his mind and allow me to have everyone I wanted.

On top of building a new group from scratch and getting pulled into a dozen new meetings, I had other commitments lingering in the background. One was my old job, though my father was swift to tell Natalie he didn't want me doing anything for cosmetics. Anyone else would have been expected to have a two-week transition period between jobs. I guess the rules didn't apply for the son of the CEOs.

But being that I'm more like my mother in the temperament department, I refused to leave Natalie high and dry. That woman had done too much for me and my career for me to abandon her like some loser.

I'd be logging over eighty hours that week, and that didn't include Saturday or the time I'd be working from my home office.

Another distraction that prevented me from being over one hundred percent focused on my new job wasn't work related. The diversion was blonde with blue eyes.

Technically, I wasn't supposed to be helping Harper. But I couldn't stop myself from obsessing over her crappy situation. I hadn't taken Gerts off the case, so he continued to keep me updated with his findings on the Cramers in Nevada.

I didn't give a shit what Harper said—a lawyer working pro bono wasn't going to turn over every rock and build the strongest case for her. The clowns going after her were millionaires. She was going to need my help to ensure she and her mother got to keep her kid.

Yeah, I know... Alana wasn't going to like it the slightest bit. My girlfriend couldn't care less that my ex was going through a traumatic ordeal. Any normal guy who'd had his heart smashed to smithereens by his first love would've rejoiced in her fiery downfall. But I couldn't bring myself to feel anything but guilt over Harper's misfortunes.

I'd known Aiden was no good, and I should've protected her from him.

I skipped lunch and settled in my temporary office on the north end of the twenty-ninth floor. I'd be working out of there until my permanent office, located on the south end, completed construction in two weeks.

The room was generic and empty, unlike my last office on the nineteenth floor. Possessions like my baseball memorabilia and a framed copy of my Stanford GBS Journal article were all boxed up in the corner. Decorating any office was the last thing on my mind.

My PTF starting lineup was in full force, but I needed an assistant coach. Some say the number two should be the support manager. For me, the executive assistant held the playbook. If it weren't for the support of Sherry and Lola, my parents would be lost. Those ladies were the unsung heroes.

I was preparing to interview the third candidate who'd come highly recommended by Lola, my mother's EA. I wasn't totally wowed by the first two, so hopefully, this woman was everything Lola claimed.

Moments later, my door sprung open, and I greeted the candidate.

Marisol Ramirez was attractive and in her mid-thirties. She stood about five-five and sported a black skirt suit with a ruffled cream blouse. Her hair was brown with highlights and pulled into a bun. When she extended her hand to shake mine, I caught a glimpse of a diamond ring and matching band glistening on her left hand, which gripped a thin leather binder.

"Thanks for coming, Mrs. Ramirez. I'm Ford Pope," I said in introduction.

"Call me Marisol. Thanks for the opportunity. By the way, this building is *insane*," she awed.

"First time here?"

"Yep," she smiled.

"Well, welcome. Have a seat." I motioned her over to the two white padded chairs nearby. Once we sat, she unzipped her binder and took out a sheet of paper.

"Do you have a copy of my resume on hand? If not, I have one here for you."

"That won't be necessary. I thought we'd have a more informal discussion. I'd like to get to know you outside of what's on that paper."

"Oh… okay, then." She returned the page back in her binder and put it aside.

"Tell me how you met Lola Gibson?" I started.

"Lola and I worked together as temps five years ago at an insurance company. She struck gold working for your mother, so I'm here to try my luck. Lola says fantastic things about you," Marisol beamed.

I smirked. "What did she say?"

"That you march to the beat of your own drum, and you earn your own keep."

Her words caused me to blink twice. I couldn't believe my mother's right hand said that about me.

"I worked for a family-owned car dealership not long before moving on to the insurance company," Marisol said. "I had to deal with the owner's kid on a daily basis. Frankly, he wasn't worth a damn."

I burst out laughing. I appreciated her frankness. We'd get along just fine.

"Seriously, everyone else who worked there referred to that kid and others like him as having a PHD, which stands for *Papa Has Dealership*. We all knew that his PHD wouldn't be worth a damn if he ever left the confines of his daddy's little kingdom. The kid was lazy and always expected his father to cover his tail every time he messed up."

It boggled my mind that people like that actually existed. I didn't have the patience for people who didn't hold their own. My sisters and I worked really hard despite who our parents were. Nothing was ever owed to us. It was earned.

"So, tell me a little bit about yourself," I prompted.

"Well—I'm married with three dogs."

"No children?"

"No. Our pups are our babies," she said proudly.

"I totally get that," I smiled back.

"You never have to worry about me going on maternity leave. However, I will be taking all of my required vacation since my husband, Manny, and I love to travel."

"Where do you like to travel?" I asked, intrigued.

"We have a Gulf Stream RV, so we load up the dogs and roam the country. We love to go hiking at some of the most wonderful places."

"That's amazing. I've always wanted to do that…travel the land in an RV," I said in admiration.

"Do it. There's nothing like driving through the mountains and by the streams. Then, there's the fall season in the Carolina Mountains. Words alone do it no justice. I can't wait for our next road trip," she wistfully mused.

"I bet," I replied, envious.

"You know, I believe in embracing the simple things in life. I don't aim for anything shiny or extravagant. I'm not attracted to what the world may deem as the *ideal life*—the life of a jet setter. I love my simple life with my simple husband," she giggled.

I really like this woman.

"Unlike many others, I'm not fooled by things that look good on the outside but hold absolutely no substance underneath. I'm always looking for something deeper than what's on the surface. That's the kind of life I lead. That's the type of person I am."

Her words pricked at something somewhere deep inside. What she says absolutely struck a nerve.

An hour later, Marisol Ramirez was officially my newest hire.

Twenty-Six

Ford

One month into the new job, and it was so far, so good.

My team was already making major headway, preaching the gospel of PTF. Just about every department in the organization had aligned their next year's goals with the initiative. I had the full support I needed to set all gears in motion.

It helped having a powerhouse office manager to keep me on my toes. When I'd first hired Marisol, she had the 'executive assistant' title. We'd since changed her title to 'office manager.' It was a fair consolation since HR wouldn't accept my proposal to name her 'Force Commander.'

There was absolutely nothing Marisol Ramirez wasn't on top of. She kept me honest and was a godsend when it came to brainstorming ideas. I knew right away she was more than just a secretary. She was my eyes and ears. I already trusted her judgment more than I trusted anyone else's on my team.

Being insanely busy kept me from getting into trouble. The downside was that my free time with Alana, friends, and family had suffered. I'd missed many Sunday dinners at my parents' place, much to my mother's chagrin. Since she'd be heading into surgery on Thursday and not returning to work until after the New Year, Mom guilted Alana and me into doing lunch with her and my dad. She'd given me an earful this morning in my office.

"Ford, I know you have a ton of responsibilities and a new team to boot, but it's a shame we work in the same building and hardly ever get to spend any time together. I can't even remember the last time you've been by the house. Topher really misses his big brother."

I dreaded sacrificing my Monday Man Lunches with my baby bro. I also hadn't seen my little sisters, the twins, in a while. I was too busy running the biggest initiative at the company, and it was a major time suck.

Before Mom left my office earlier in the morning, she'd made sure Marisol blocked my calendar for lunch so I wouldn't have an excuse to skip.

Yeah, yeah, yeah… I needed to be a better son.

I needed to be a better big brother.

I needed to be a better boyfriend.

Alana and I hadn't gone out on a Friday since I'd started the new gig. I tried making it up to her by staying in bed with her Sunday mornings, where I was forced to watch old episodes of *Gilmore Girls*. Full disclosure—I hadn't *really* been playing fair. I'd distracted Alana with sex and *Gilmore Girls* ended up watching *us*.

Ten minutes before I was scheduled to meet my dad for a quick PTF discussion, I heard a knock on my office door. I knew right away it was him, since my mom had already made an appearance. If it were anyone else, Marisol would normally introduce them over the speaker. Mason Pope needed no introduction.

"I was just on my way up to your office," I tell him.

"I'd just come from meeting Mick in his office and thought I'd swing by here since I was in the neighborhood," Dad said as he took a seat opposite my desk.

Not seeing him in the seat of power was odd. Mom had sat in the same chair he currently occupied more than once. This was the first time my dad had come here, and he looked out of place. To balance the universe, I stood from behind my desk and started to walk around it to join my father. He held up his hand, commanding me to freeze.

"This is fine where we are. Sit down." I obeyed. "Your mother informed me we're having lunch shortly with you and Alana," he said with a smirk.

"I couldn't get out of it this time," I exhaled, rubbing my forehead.

"Resistance is futile, son. Whatever your mother wants, she gets. That goes for all women. If you haven't already learned that by now, you will soon since you're living with Alana."

My lips tightened in a line. I wouldn't necessarily say that Alana had been getting everything she wanted out of me these days. I did appreciate her patience as I laid the groundwork for my new department. As often as I could, I reminded her that this wouldn't be the norm. This up-front grind was just a stepping-stone to a better future.

A better future… for us?

"Speaking of Alana," he started.

'When are you going to ask her to marry you, son?' I could already hear what he was going to say in my head.

"I'm impressed with the team you've assembled. However, I think you need another rock-solid data analyst. Your data manager can't do it alone. Alana would be perfect—"

"Dad…" I said, cutting him off, "…I already told you, that can't happen."

He looked at me as if I'd beamed down from another planet. "Don't be ridiculous. It's obvious even from my brief discussions with her that she wants to work on a high-profile project. There's nothing bigger than Propel the Future right now," he argued.

Wait… Alana's been meeting with my father? I quickly shoo away the thought and remain on topic.

"You're not hearing me," I tittered, masking my dire impatience.

"What am I not hearing?"

"I told you, I'm not putting Alana on my team until I can have Knight. And since that's out of the realm of possibility, I'm not going to backhand him by taking someone who works for him."

"Alana is your girlfriend—you live together. She has the advantage. You're not sleeping with Thibodeau," he frowned.

There's no reasoning with the man, I swear.

"No, but Eva is," I countered.

"Don't," Dad shuddered. "Please don't remind me."

He shut his eyes in horror, and I snorted at the ridiculousness of it all. He apparently didn't mind me living and sleeping with my girlfriend. Even after all of these years, he was still having a hard time imagining any daughter of his getting laid by their longtime boyfriend. I would never understand how my father's mind worked.

"You won't admit it, but I will. I see Alana joining our family in the very near future," Dad proclaimed.

And there it was, just like fucking clockwork.

"You need to help her get to where she needs to be. You're going to need her by your side since you'll be running this company long after your mother and I are gone."

Not this shit again.

"Dad, can we *please* discuss PTF?" I appealed, exasperated.

"Fine, but this conversation is far from over."

Oh, I knew it wasn't.

"Hey," I cooed from behind her back. Startled, Alana turned from number-crunching at her computer and looked up at me.

"I thought we were meeting downstairs in the lobby?" she asked, beaming.

"I had a quick chat with Knight. Since I was down here, I thought we'd head to the lobby together."

Promptly, she locked her computer screen and stood to meet me. We were practically nose-to-nose, but she would only rub my bicep. I really wanted her to kiss me—I knew she wanted it—but it wouldn't be the proper thing to do.

"I wish we were going home instead of lunch," I whispered silkily.

"Be honest, Pope, if your mom wasn't making you do this, you wouldn't be trying to take me home," she smirked.

I jutted my head back, affronted. "Why do you say that?"

"Ford, you've been knee-deep in PTF. I barely see you anymore," she reminded me as she grabbed her purse.

"I know," I acquiesced. "I promise, that won't be the case for long. I almost have a full team. My managers are interviewing to fill the spots underneath them. Once everything's in full swing, I'll start working semi-human hours again."

"I'll hold you to that. But it's funny... Not too long ago, I was the one working crazy hours. Now it's you." She looped her arm in mine, and I led the way toward the elevators.

"Blame it on PTF. It was first your headache, now it's mine," I quipped.

As we proceeded down the hall, I spied the empty desk that once belonged to my sister. While I'd been building my new team, Eva had been attending school and starting anew at Isla Cole. It was probably the longest I'd gone without seeing my sister, not counting my time at Stanford.

I really missed seeing her around.

Alana and I entered Club Sahara to meet my folks. They'd gone ahead of us, taking a separate car since they needed to run an errand on the way back.

"Ford!"

I flinched at my name being called. Standing before us was the blonde hostess who'd once flirted with my three-year-old little brother and me.

"Laura... hi," I greeted. I could feel Alana's eyes burning a hole into my face.

"Your mother and father just got here. They're at your usual table," Laura offered with all of her pearly whites on display. It hadn't occurred to me until then that she'd paid absolutely no mind to my girlfriend, who was holding my hand the entire time.

"Thanks, Laura, we'll head right over," I responded.

"Have a great lunch, Ford," she called out in the sweetest voice. I nodded, then led the way to our table.

"What was that all about?" Alana whisper yelled.

"What?"

"She obviously has the hots for you. I was invisible," she sparked with amusement. I scoffed in response, dismissing the notion, but I couldn't deny it. Laura had given me her number.

"Hey, perfect timing. We just ordered side salads for everyone," my mother said as we approached.

"Sounds good," Alana agreed.

The two of us hugged my parents before taking a seat opposite them.

"Your father was just telling me how well things were going with PTF," Mom started.

"It's going better than I imagined," I concurred.

"That's a leader's dream. No hiccups so far. Stay the course, and it will only get better," my father encouraged.

"The downside is that I don't get to see much of him," Alana tossed in as she leaned into me.

My father gave me a look that said everything. With his eyes alone, he told me I could rectify the situation by allowing my girlfriend to work for me. In response, I tightened my mouth, letting him know this wasn't the time or the place to rehash this.

"Ford, you don't need to work around the clock anymore. You have managers under you now," scolded my mother.

"I know, but they're busy setting up their teams. Once everyone's in place, I'll be able to spend more time at home," I said to her before turning to Alana. The glint in her eye told me she'd rather see it happen first than take my word for it. She then turned to my dad.

"Mr. Pope, I can't thank you enough for offering to mentor me."

I gaped at her, wondering if my father had approached her recently and offered to be her mentor. This was the first time I'd heard any of this.

"It's my pleasure," he answered.

I was beginning to lose my appetite at the thought of my father working behind the scenes to get his wish by way of mentoring my girlfriend. I knew he was going to start planting little bugs in her ear so she'd begin forcing the issue of joining my team. Fuck—I should've seen it coming.

I looked to my mother, who was just as taken aback as I was. "I guess I wasn't the only one who didn't know," I remarked.

My mother's frown turned sideways at my dad, but she shook it off. The man was going to get an earful in the car.

I turned to Alana, who played it coy. "I was going to tell you. It only just happened yesterday."

This was sounding worse and worse. She'd known about the mentorship for what… twenty-four hours? Why was I just hearing about it? This was kind of a big deal. The CEO of LRPI was going to be mentoring her. That same person was also my father. You'd think she'd warn me first, but *nah*.

"I haven't mentored a young professional in quite a while. It was long overdue," my father said matter-of-factly.

Motherfu—

"Would you two like anything else to drink besides water?" the waiter interrupted.

I took it as a cue to regain my composure. "No, thank you." I cleared my throat.

"Water is fine," Alana echoed. A server came around the waiter with our salads.

"I didn't know what type of dressing you wanted, so I ordered you what Ford likes," my mother said to Alana.

"Blue cheese is good," Alana beamed.

Aww, Mom remembered to order me my favorite dressing.

As I chomped away, I couldn't ignore the fact that my father was now mentoring my girlfriend. I needed to know who approached whom.

No, scratch that. I was pretty sure I knew how it happened. Alana saw my father in passing, they shot the shit for a few, and suddenly my father got this *great idea* after hearing how things have slowed for her since PTF was taken away from her team. I guess my dad figured he could kill two birds with one stone and urge Alana to speed things up in all directions, both business-wise and personally.

The whole thing made me more amused than pissed. Mason Pope was a master manipulator.

"Mr. Pope, I'm fascinated by how you and Mrs. Pope met. She had no idea you were the CEO."

My parents began reminiscing about their love story with Alana. They started with my Texan mother struggling in LA and literally taking out my father's trash, then ended at her ruling one of the largest global conglomerates by Dad's side.

My mother gazed lovingly at my dad, and his adoration mirrored hers.

"When we started working together, she'd been the only person who'd ever called me on my shit and ever lived to tell about it. I had to marry her," my father mused. Mom snorted right before he gave her lips a gentle peck.

If Eva were here, she'd cringe. But seeing my parents still madly in love after all these years warmed my heart. They stared at each other like they were the only ones in the room.

"I love what you two have," Alana gushed. "I hope I have a chance to work with Ford one of these days and be a team just like you."

Pin drop.

Both my parents turned from one another and focused on us. I honestly had no idea how to respond to that. I wanted to squirm in my chair. Mom homes in on Alana. Meanwhile, my father gave me that same look he gives each time I tell him I can't hire my girlfriend. I was beyond ready for a subject change.

"Ford's the hardest worker I know," Alana continued. "He obviously learned that from the two of you. When I look at you, I kind of see *us*—or what I hope we'll become, at least. You are such an inspiration."

Alana, Alana, Alana.... How in the world was I going to get a handle on her?

"I see Alana joining our family in the very near future."

My father's words from earlier circled back.

I glanced at her once more before turning to my mother. She was back to exchanging flirty glances with my dad, and a thought crossed my mind.

Liza Pope is everything a wife and mother should be.

I looked back at Alana, who was already staring at me. She smiled. I smiled.

She's so fucking gorgeous.

Was I staring my future in the face? Was I delaying the inevitable?

Hell... should I buy her a ring?

Liza

You've got to be kidding me.

I wasn't getting the warm-fuzzies from Alana. What she said had thrown me for a complete loop. If it weren't for Mason being so darn cute, my outrage over Alana's problematic monologue would've been more evident.

Mr. Pope would be getting an earful in the car for failing to tell me about his newfound personal mentorship program with our son's girlfriend. That had definitely come out of left field. Whose idea had it been anyway? I knew very well what was happening, and it was sickening how they were attempting to manipulate Ford.

My hope was for Ford to stand his ground. He valiantly refused to hire Alana on his team since she worked for Knight. And if he believed he wasn't ready to get married, then he shouldn't. Mason needed to leave those two alone and let them live. He was way too occupied with the idea of who'd take over after he and I left the company. We had plenty of time before any changing of the guard needed to happen.

Sure, the whole lot annoyed me—but as strange as it sounded, I was happy to be distracted with something other than the dread of my impending surgery. I could tell with each passing day that Mason was worried about it, too. It was why I did my best not to display my nervousness to those around me. I either kept my fears to myself, or I shared them with Jessie. My sister had been my rock, showering me with loads of positivity. But even she couldn't stop the erratic patter in my chest as each day brought me closer to my fate.

Three more days.

The night before surgery, I didn't sleep well at all.

Apparently, neither did Mason.

For what felt like two hours, I lay in bed with eyes wide open, staring into darkness. I was sure Mason thought I was peacefully sleeping when he carefully crept out of our bedroom to occupy himself.

Once I'd had enough of staring into nothingness, I freshened up and dressed in plain sweats, a t-shirt, and a hoodie. I was about to be cut open, so I didn't feel the need to break out my Isla Cole romper for the occasion. I found Mason in the kitchen with his coffee and iPad. It was a few hours still before the twins were set to get up for school.

"Good morning, baby," Mason hummed, kissing the crown of my head.

"Mornin'."

His coffee smelled divine. I would have died for just a sip.

"Did you eat?" I asked.

"I had toast."

"That's it? Want me to make you something? I know we're up sometime before Trisha—"

"Sweetheart, I'm fine. I'll have Russ grab me something while you're in surgery. I didn't want to eat much, knowing you had to fast."

I swooned. My dear, sweet husband wanted to be in the trenches with me. I wrapped my arms around him and pressed my head against his chest.

"Ninety minutes or less," I singsonged. My sister's mantra had been on repeat in my brain for the past three days. The second fear tried to creep in, I simply replayed those words.

"Ninety minutes or less," Mason echoed under his breath. He kissed my lips softly, and I could taste the Columbian dark roast on his lips. My eyelids clamped down in angst.

Fifteen minutes later, we were in the back seat of the sedan holding hands while Russ chauffeured us to the hospital. I could tell from the firmness of his grasp that my husband was becoming increasingly agitated the closer we get to our destination.

"You know, we've made this trip at least four other times," I said longingly.

A trace of a smirk appeared on his gorgeous, tired, and worried face. "Yeah, but this is different. This time, we won't be bringing home any babies."

"True, but the end result will hopefully be a more comfortable, less hormonal life for me," I quipped.

He pulled me into him and rubbed my arm before kissing my forehead. "Now, Mrs. Pope, there are certain hormones that I insist must remain after the surgery. You know… the good kind. The ones that make you insatiable."

I playfully slapped his lap. "It's way too early for such talk."

"It's never too early—or late, for that matter—for *such talk*. You should know that after nearly twenty-five years of being with me."

He was so right. Sex had never been off-limits with us. And even at the ages of fifty-six and forty-six, I didn't see things ever slowing down with us. My husband was as sexy as ever. Some said the sexual prime for a man was in his twenties. This wasn't the case with Mason. No matter what milestone he reached—thirties, forties, fifties—sex with him continued to reach another level.

I'd never be tired of getting laid with him.

That man worshipped and adored my body, cesarean section scars and all. He always went out of his way to make me feel beautiful, sexy, and loved. The aftermath of this hysterectomy would be no different. The only challenge we faced would be the required six-week wait post-surgery.

"We'll just have to be creative, baby."

He'd spoken those words to me in bed the night before. He'd even recited them after the births of each of our children. And yes, Mason and I had always been creative in pleasing one another until it was safe to have sex again.

When we got to the hospital, the inpatient process was long and tedious. There was all the paperwork, followed by the waiting. We were later taken to an area where I was assigned a small room. There, I changed into a thin, cheap hospital gown that would expose my entire rear if I wasn't careful. I then climbed up on the gurney and played the waiting game. Mason was at my side when the anesthesiologist made an appearance and explained what to expect during surgery. Then, a nurse began to work an IV into my right arm.

Ninety minutes or less.

I'll be home long before dinner.

Five minutes later, two towering men in scrubs arrived. Mason stood from his chair and squeezed my hand. I shut my eyes, fearing the nurse and the two men with her would have to fight my overzealous husband. But after two decades of being with him, I'd learned how to soothe the savage beast.

"Ninety minutes or less," I whispered to him. "I can't wait to get home. I'm going to have Trisha make me a big juicy steak."

"You can have whatever you want, baby. Just come back to me quickly and safely. I'll be here waiting," he said with urgency in his eyes.

"I highly doubt you'll get to eat that steak tonight," the nurse interjected. Mason ignored her and smiled at me, assuring me I'd damn well have whatever it is that I want. Honestly, I could've eaten a whole cow right then since I'd had to fast before going under anesthesia.

After we exchanged *I love yous,* I was wheeled away. I looked back and saw my sweet husband waving despairingly at me. But it was his loving smile that gave me so much hope and comfort.

Ninety minutes or less.

When I reached the almost blinding operating room, the two men carefully lifted and placed me on the operating table. Someone off to the side clipped a new bag to my IV, and the anesthesiologist instructed me to take several deep breaths.

After just two breaths, everything suddenly faded away.

Twenty-Seven

Ford

"Oh, God," I gasped.

All the air was sucked right out of me, and I'd forgotten how to breathe.

"She lost a lot of blood," he said, barely audible.

I'd never in my life heard my father sound so helpless.

It dawned on me that I was no longer sitting behind my desk. Instead, I stood there, numb. It was supposed to be a quick outpatient procedure. She was supposed to be on her way home.

What went wrong?

"Is she going to be okay?" I felt myself shaking as the words struggled out of me.

No… not Eliza Pope. Not *my* mother. This couldn't be real.

"No one knows." My father was succinct, but I knew he was going out of his ever-loving mind. He was a fixer, and this was something he couldn't fix.

I went to my laptop and began shutting it down. "I'm on my way now. Does Eva know?"

"Not yet. She's in class."

"I'll send her a text to call me as soon as she's done."

"Good. I'll call your grandparents and Jessie," he said soberly.

"Okay—I'll be there soon," I said, wrestling my laptop into my backpack.

"Drive carefully," Dad warned.

"I will."

I slung my bag over my shoulder and headed out the door. Immediately to my right, my office manager was typing away at her desk. "Marisol, I need to leave for an emergency. I doubt I'll be back today, so cancel all my meetings," I said in a hurry.

Her face fell. "Is everything okay?"

"I don't know yet, but I promise I'll call and fill you in."

"Let me know if you need absolutely anything at all."

"I will, thanks," I called back as I rushed into the open elevator.

I stopped on the tenth floor and took long strides until I reached Alana's cubicle. I was relieved she was there. "Hey..."

She swiftly turned to see me with my coat and backpack and was taken aback. "You're leaving?"

"It's my mom. I have to go to the hospital," I said quietly, careful not to break down at the sound of my own words.

Alana sprung to her feet. "My God—what happened?"

"I don't know... She lost a lot of blood. That's all my dad knows right now."

Quickly, Alana grabbed her purse and coat. "I'm going too."

"No... stay. I promise to fill you in the second I know anything."

"I'll be too out of my mind to focus here. I want to be there for you," she pleaded.

"I know you do, sweetheart," I said, grazing my hand over her soft cheek. "But my dad and grandparents will be there. We're just going to be sitting and waiting anyways. You'll be much more productive here instead of going crazy with us."

"I'll go crazy here. Don't argue, I'm coming with you. Let me just tell Knight first."

The surgeon exited the private waiting area, leaving my father, my sister, Grandpa Pope, Alana, and me behind to pick up all of the pieces he just threw at us.

"...severe blood loss and infection..."

His words continued to echo in my head over and over again like a Katy Perry song as Alana snaked her arms tightly around me.

"...severe blood loss and infection..."

"...unconscious..."

Grandma Pope didn't cut the surgeon any slack. When he'd left, she was right on his tail. She and our entire family had donated a shit ton of money to this hospital for decades. They were going to give her answers, or hell would be unleashed.

If everything had gone as planned, my mother would've been home and in bed hours ago. But it was approaching three o'clock, and she was still there with no chance of going home anytime soon. Donner was picking up the twins, who had no idea our mother wouldn't be home for dinner tonight. The very thought of that overwhelmed me.

The doctors couldn't even tell us when my mother was going to wake up. They didn't even know how bad the infection was. They didn't know what effects, current or long-term, that her blood loss during surgery would have on her.

We. Knew. Nothing.

I'd heard my father muttering something under his breath over and over again... something about *ninety minutes*. It was so unsettling.

Earlier, when the doctor had tried to segue into his 'prepare for the worst' spiel, my grandmother immediately stopped him. I'd almost sunk to the floor because I'd known he was telling us to anticipate my mother's death. My sentiments weren't far off because Eva was now bawling her eyes out in the corner of the lobby, and my father rushed over to help calm her down.

Alana buried her head in my chest, and Grandpa Pope placed his hand on my shoulder.

"No matter what, everything is going to be fine. We'll all see to it as a family," he said softly.

Suddenly, all those talks my father had given me over the years flooded into my consciousness—the *pull-yourself-up-by-the-bootstrap* lectures and the *the-family-is-counting-on-you* sermons. This was one of those moments he'd always warned would come.

I needed to suck up my pride, step up, and be there for my family. It wasn't just about me anymore. Dad shouldn't have to worry about LRPI while my mother's life hung in the balance. I looked at my crying sister with our crestfallen father, who was comforting her when he himself needed comforting. Then, I thought about my baby brother, and my heart fell into the pit of my gut.

I needed to stop focusing on leaving the covering of my family. It was no longer about my five-year plan. The *Ford Inc.* vision was no longer a priority. When my mother fell ill, it was no longer about me and my dreams.

I was a Pope.

The Pope name was the biggest name in this godforsaken town. We were one of the most influential families in the country. The world, even.

We. Were. One.

Now, the entire family was counting on me.

I'd been working my ass off over the past four days. Not only was I up to my neck with PTF stuff, but I'd been filling in for my parents at every facet of LRPI.

Fortunately, my mother was on the mend. She was now awake, and the infection appeared to be subsiding. Unfortunately, we still didn't know when she'd be able to leave the hospital. Dad refused to leave her side, so Grandma Pope stayed at the estate with Topher and the twins.

I felt so distant from everything going on at the hospital. I pretty much lived at Pope Tower so I could keep the multi-billion-dollar global operation running while my family remained in crisis. It was a strange position to be in.

As I sat behind my desk making corrections to my data guru's presentation, Marisol peaked her head through the door.

"Hey," I said.

"How's it going?" She entered my office and approached my desk.

"It's going," I chuckled ironically.

"How's your mother?"

"Better, so they tell me." I shrugged

She winced. "When was the last time you saw her?"

"Friday."

"Ford, that was the day she went in. You haven't been back to see her?" she asked, dumbfounded.

"My father wanted me to take care of things here."

"Which you have. But you still need to see your mom. Make sure you go and see her today, okay?" she pleaded with me.

Immediately, I started feeling guilty. My father and sisters had been calling with updates, so I figured I was fine picking up the slack at work.

But hell—I'd almost lost my mother. Marisol was right, I should've been there in person, telling Mom how much I was grateful that she hadn't left us.

"I will. I promise," I vowed, smiling weakly at my *force commander*.

"Good. By the way, Alana has been by to see you. Actually, she'd stopped by a few times this week while you were tied up in meetings. I'm not sure if she told you so."

I narrowed my gaze. "She hadn't said anything."

I saw my girlfriend late nights at home, and she hadn't mentioned needing me during the day. I'd respond whenever she called or texted, so it was puzzling that she hadn't brought up her random visits to my office.

"She is rather difficult to read," Marisol frowned, holding a bit of skepticism in her expression.

"I thought that was just all women," I smirked, but immediately turned it off when she didn't find it humorous. I hope I hadn't just crossed the line. I didn't need HR or Dad on my ass.

"I'm a good reader of people, and Miss Alana... I can't read her," she said.

I could tell that Marisol wanted to say more, but she stopped herself.

Did she not approve of my girlfriend?

I dismissed the thought.

It was just after seven-thirty when I arrived at the hospital. I'd told Alana I would pay my mother a quick visit before going home. Alana herself had stopped by here earlier to see Mom.

I almost walked past the small lobby on the way to my mom's room until I saw Eva sitting alone in a corner. She appeared to be doing homework.

"Hey," I called out, and my sister put her work aside to hug me.

"Hey," she exhaled, visibly relieved.

"How's she doing?" I asked.

"Better. They told us to step out of the room so they could check her vitals and all that stuff. Of course, Dad told them to go straight to hell. He's still in there," Eva smirked.

I laughed. "I am not surprised."

"Grandma Julia is flying back from Texas in the morning and staying with Mom until she recovers."

"That's good."

"Knight says you've been kicking ass all week at work," my sister said with a tinge of pride.

"I'm trying. I'm being pulled in so many directions right now," I sighed.

"I bet. Wish I was there to help."

"Me too," I grinned. I'd missed seeing her around at Pope Tower. She'd left a blank space when she began interning at Isla

Cole Fashion Headquarters, located a few miles away from the parent company.

"I'll be back after graduation," she revealed.

Her announcement took me by surprise. "Are things not going well at Isla?"

"It's going great there, actually. ICF is a well-oiled machine. I really miss the challenge of the workload at the home office. I miss randomly stopping by your office to chat. I miss seeing Mom and Dad. I *loved* working with Knight. We made a great team. I miss the Nutty Buddy's at the café. They don't have those where I work." I laughed as she continued. "I miss everything. Well... everything but that Germany fiasco."

"That was an anomaly. Between you and me, I'm still working on figuring out what went wrong. Personally, I don't think you and Thibodeau had anything to do with that," I told her in confidence.

"Hell, you and me both. Knight is still clueless about how that error even got there in the first place. I know I didn't mean to send that draft to Ingrid. I always sent her the standard weekly report."

"I know. We'll figure this out," I promised.

"But all of that other stuff seems so distant right now. Mom's been in the forefront of everyone's minds," she said soberly, and I couldn't have agreed more. "The twins have been a wreck, and Topher keeps asking if Mommy's going to be alright." Eva began choking back tears, and I pulled her in close.

"Sis—I honestly don't know how you do it... Working a challenging job while attending advanced classes, all while maintaining a healthy relationship with your live-in boyfriend. Now, add Mom's health on top of that—"

"Ford... I literally feel like I am going to fall apart," her voice cracked.

A lone tear broke free from one of her eyes, and I sank.

Me and my big mouth.

"Mom has to pull through *or...*" She paused to gather her words. "Or else I don't think I can do it anymore."

What on earth was she saying?

I gave her a squeeze. "Mom is going to be fine. She is progressively getting better instead of worse. If things get too overwhelming, you can always put work on hold for a while."

"If anything, I'd leave school. I need to keep working. It's been the best distraction for me."

I frowned. "Eva, don't be silly. Mom would lose her shit if she knew you were thinking about dropping out of college. You're almost there. Hang on."

My sister appeared to be weighing the pros and cons. I didn't care—she wasn't dropping out of school. Not if I had anything to do with it.

My mother's hospital room was unlike any other in the place. It looked more like an upscale hotel suite than a place for a patient. I guess it didn't hurt that our family was the biggest donor of the facility.

Something told me the hospital didn't provide everyone here with the same huge-ass sixty-four-inch television. And my mother's bed appeared to be a top-of-the-line king-sized Sleep Number bed. There was no doubt that all of this was courtesy of Mason Pope.

"Ford," Mom called to me, her familiar cheery voice showing signs of fatigue.

She was a sight for sore eyes, sitting up in bed with a book propped in her lap. She looked fucking fantastic. No one could tell she'd been knocking on death's door only a few days ago. It looked like Mom in bed, reading a book and being fabulous. I kneeled down and hugged her cautiously.

"Be careful." Dad startled me from behind. I hadn't noticed he was in the room.

"They just told me I can go home tomorrow," Mom grinned.

"That's… That's awesome," I sighed in relief.

"She is still heavily medicated," my father interjected, taking a seat beside her on the bed.

"How are you feeling?" I asked.

"Overly medicated," she chuckled, and I laughed.

"You look great," I raved.

"You're too kind, Ford," she waved me off.

"I'm serious," I insisted.

"He's right, you know," Dad interjected.

"Is Eva still here?" Mom inquired.

"She's in the lobby finishing up her homework," I answered.

Mom turned her attention to my father. "Mason, can you give me a moment with our son?"

I gaped at her. She was actually kicking him out. My father hesitated, not wanting to let her out of his sight, even for a minute.

"Please... just ten minutes. In the meantime, why don't you check on our daughter?"

"Fine. Ten minutes," Dad mumbled petulantly. He kissed her on the forehead then turned to me, wearing a sad excuse for a smile. I lowered my head to keep from laughing. Then finally, he left.

"Sit," Mom whispered, gesturing to the bed where Dad had sat. "So... what's been going on while I've been away?"

"Well, we finally got the first wave of PTF through stage one. Then, I sat in for you and Dad at the budget planning meetings—"

"I don't want to talk about work," she interrupted with a gentle grin. "I want to know about what's going on with *you*."

I had to think long and hard because all that I've been up to since she had been here was work, work, and work. Oh... and shitty thoughts about how awful my life would be if this woman beside me was no longer in it. I felt a pang in my chest and had to battle the feeling. I was losing.

"Ford?" Her gentle touch on my arm brought me back to reality. I sighed in relief.

"I'm just glad I still have you here," I whispered. A tear escaped my eye. It was the first time I allowed myself to cry.

"Honey. I'm not going anywhere," she said with promise.

"Dad?" I stepped all the way inside the lobby, and he looked up. My sister was no longer there. "Where did Eva go?"

"Home. She'll be at the house tomorrow when we bring your mother home. By the way, that was only eight minutes," he smirked.

"I know. She started yawning, so I told her to rest."

"Good."

"Alana and I will stop by this weekend."

"Your mother and I look forward to seeing you both," he grinned.

"I have a favor to ask," I spilled, all of a sudden.

I'd opened Pandora's Box and couldn't take it back. It was better I commit, or else my father would drag it out of me. His interest was now piqued, and he was all ears. I'd rehearsed the words in my mind first before speaking them out loud.

Dad, I need your help to propose to Alana.

Hell—I couldn't believe I was actually doing this. This meant I'd be sticking a knife in the part of me that had once longed for another. Just like she had changed, so had I. I was no longer the same Ford who'd worshiped the ground Harper Benton walked on.

That was the boy.

I'd become a man, and it was high time for me to *man up*. Unfortunately, it had taken my mother nearly dying before I realized what was most important.

Family.

Stay tuned for part 2 of The Family Business, *Mercy or Pain*!

Acknowledgments

To my family and friends. A special shout-out to my good friend S. Rivera for believing in me enough to keep reading my chicken scratch. ;)

To the pros who help make my books look beautiful: Shannon Passmore (cover design), Stacey Blake (formatting), Dawn Lucous (proofreading), and Christi Whitson (editing).

To my readers for devouring everything I put out there. I adore you!

I dedicate this duet to those who've read and loved this story once before. This was one of my favorites, and I'm so excited to share it with new readers.

Thanks, everyone, for your loving support.

Stay Sweet,
 TK

About the Author

You can take the girl out of Detroit, but you'll *never* take Detroit out of *this* girl.

For TK Cherry, it's pop—not soda, and Tim Hortons over everything else.

Born and raised in The Motor City, TK now enjoys little or no winters in the Carolinas. By day, she's a spreadsheet whiz and frequent flyer. By night, she lives for keeping her loyal readers on the edge of their seats with steamy tales of happily ever after. TK is also a single mom to a pretty cool young man.

Other Books by
TK CHERRY

The Hottie in Finance
Bernadette
California Love
On the Other Side
A Nocturnal Rendezvous (Nighttime Cravings Book 1)
A Young Moon (Nighttime Cravings Book 2)

Coming Up Next:
The Family Business: *Mercy or Pain* (Arcadia's Crest Book 2)
***An Insatiable Eventide* (Nighttime Cravings Book 3)**

Be the first to know about the next juicy adventure and sweet giveaway by signing up for the newsletter at tkcherry.com/cherrypicking.

You can also follow @tkcherryfiction on Facebook, Instagram, and Twitter.

CPSIA information can be obtained
at www.ICGtesting.com
Printed in the USA
LVHW031003090121
675852LV00002B/193